Praise for

A DECLARATION OF THE RIGHTS OF MAGICIANS

"A rich, sprawling epic full of history and magic, *Declaration* is *Jonathan Strange* with international politics and vampires. I loved it."

—Alix E. Harrow, author of *The Ten Thousand Doors of January*

"A witty, riveting historical fantasy.... Parry has a historian's eye for period detail and weaves real figures from history—including Robespierre and Toussaint Louverture—throughout her poetic tale of justice, liberation, and dark magic. This is a knockout."

—*Publishers Weekly* (starred review)

"I absolutely loved it. It held my attention from the beginning and throughout. It's a beautiful tapestry of words, a combination of carefully observed and researched history and a well thought-out and fascinating system of magic. An absolute delight to read; splendid and fluid, with beautiful and complex use of language."

—Genevieve Cogman, author of *The Invisible Library*

"Fans of *Jonathan Strange & Mr Norrell* will be enchanted by this sprawling epic of revolution and dark magic." —*Locus*

"Impeccably researched and epically written, this novel is a stellar start to what promises to be a grand new fantasy series."

—*Booklist* (starred review)

"It's no simple task to wrangle fifteen years of tumult in a few hundred pages, but Parry manages it with a deft hand. Her alternate history puts a human face on the titans of the past, while weaving in supernatural elements that add a whole new dimension. I stayed up well past my bedtime to find out what happens next."

—Marie Brennan, author of the Memoirs of Lady Trent series

"Impressively intricate; fans of the magic-and-history of *Jonathan Strange & Mr Norrell* will be delighted."

—Alexandra Rowland, author of *A Conspiracy of Truths*

"Full of rich character development, *A Declaration of the Rights of Magicians* is a book for readers who enjoy sprawling historical fantasy novels.... It's a complicated and historically rich novel." —*BuzzFeed*

"This magnificent and indulgent story balances a deep understanding of the historical trends and details of the age with a talent for twisting reality.... Enthralling from beginning to end. —*BookPage*

A Declaration of the Rights of Magicians

By H. G. Parry

The Unlikely Escape of Uriah Heep

The Shadow Histories

A Declaration of the Rights of Magicians

A Radical Act of Free Magic

A Declaration of The Rights of Magicians

The Shadow Histories: Book One

H. G. PARRY

This book is a work of fiction. Names, characters, places, and incidents are the product of the author's imagination or are used fictitiously. Any resemblance to actual events, locales, or persons, living or dead, is coincidental.

Cover design by Lisa Marie Pompilio
Cover illustrations by Shutterstock

Author photograph by Fairlie Atkinson

Redhook Books/Orbit
Hachette Book Group
1290 Avenue of the Americas
New York, NY 10104
hachettebookgroup.com

First Paperback Edition: January 2021
Originally published in hardcover and ebook by Redhook in June 2020

The Library of Congress has catalogued the hardcover as follows:
Names: Parry, H. G., author.
Title: A declaration of the rights of magicians / H.G. Parry.
Description: First Edition. | New York, NY : Redhook, 2020.
Identifiers: LCCN 2019032229 | ISBN 9780316459082 (hardcover) |
ISBN 9780316459105 (e-book)
Subjects: GSAFD: Fantasy fiction.
Classification: LCC PR9639.4.P376 D43 2020 | DDC 823/.92—dc23
LC record available at https://lccn.loc.gov/2019032229

ISBNs: 978-0-316-45907-5 (trade paperback), 978-0-316-45909-9 (ebook)

Printed in the United States of America

LSC-C

Printing 1, 2020

This one's for my parents, William John and Dorothy Lynette Parry.
Thank you for everything.

PART ONE

RISING

West Africa

They came the summer she was six. She and her brother were alone in the house when strangers broke in, armed with muskets and knives. Her brother yelled to her to run, but she stumbled on the ground outside, and a pair of hands seized her. They took her brother too. She never knew what happened to her parents.

When she saw the blanched white faces and pale eyes of the men to whom she was to be sold, her attempts at bravery broke, and she burst into tears. Her brother and his friends had told stories about the ghosts that came and took people away. The ghosts lived in a hollow world, they said, that roamed the sea and swallowed people up. The people brought to them were placed under evil magic, so that their minds fell asleep and their bodies belonged to the ghosts.

The man who sold her told her that it wasn't true. The ghosts were men, white men, and they were from a country over the sea. They didn't want to feed her to their hollow world—which was called a ship and was used for traveling oceans. They only wanted her to work for them in their own country. It was true about the magic, though. They would feed it to her on the first day. From then on, she would belong to them.

They took the men and older boys into the ship first. Her brother crying out to her as she was torn away from his arms wrenched her heart in two. It was the last time she would hear her name for a very long time.

It was dark in the belly of the ship, and the fetid stench was worse than anything she had ever imagined. She cried and fought not to go down, but one of the men cuffed her hard so she was dizzy, and before her head could recover she was lying in a tiny, filthy space with shackles about her wrists and ankles. The metal was cold, and sticky with someone else's blood.

When they gave her the food that would spellbind her, she swallowed it. She wanted to. In her village, when the children had talked about the ghosts that took people over the seas, they had said that your mind fell asleep under the spell. They said it was like dying, and she wanted to die.

She waited while the creeping numbness took her fingers and her toes and her heart. She waited until she felt her breathing become harsh and regular and her tears stop. At last she could not move even her eyes. She waited for her thoughts to still in the same way, as she might wait to fall asleep on a hot night; she longed for it, as an escape from the fear and the pain. But it never came. Her body was asleep. Her mind was still awake inside. When she realized this, she screamed and screamed, but her screams never made it farther than her own head.

All the way across the world, she was awake. She couldn't move unless they told her to, not even a finger, not even to make a sound. She breathed; she blinked; she retched when the motion of the ship became too much. Outside of this and other such involuntary spasms, she was helpless. But she felt everything. She felt the bite of iron at her wrists and the cramping of her muscles as her limbs lay rigid in the small space. She felt the grain of the wooden floor against her skin as the ship rocked, rubbing until her back and legs were raw and bleeding. She smelled the urine and blood and vomit, and she heard the strange, jarring language of the men tromping the decks overhead. Sometimes, right before they were fed and the last dose of the spell was beginning to wear off, she heard the others in the hold begin to groan or sob or speak. All day, she fought to make a sound herself, just enough to call out and see if any of her family were there to answer her. But then the men would come with their food again, and the hold would fall silent. If someone else had died, that was when they took the bodies away. Sometimes they took people away who were still alive, and did things to them. She didn't know what they did, but they came back more broken, and sometimes they didn't come back at all.

She didn't know where her family was, and everything hurt so much. She was a child. She had never hurt like that before.

After they sold her in the marketplace, they branded her. Part of this was to mark her, once and for all, as property. She belonged to a sugar plantation now, in Jamaica. In time, she would learn what that meant.

The other part was to test that the spellbinding really had taken effect entirely. One of the men in line in front of her let out a strangled noise when the iron seared his flesh, and he was taken away. She didn't know what happened to him.

She was perfectly bound now. The metal touched her skin and scorched it with heat that seemed to go clear through to the bone. In her head, she writhed and screamed. Her body never made a sound.

Her new owners named her Fina. From now on, she was to answer to that name, and that alone.

France

Camille Desmoulins was five years old, and he was playing with shadows.

It was midsummer's eve, and Guise was sleepy and sunbaked in the deepening twilight. Camille was outside the main town, down by the river, where the grass grew thick under the old stone bridge. He was too young to be away from home alone, but his father was at work, and his tutor, on such a languid evening, was content to believe that his pupil liked to study alone. Soon, he would enter the tiny makeshift schoolroom to check on his charge and realize, with irritation and alarm, that he had wandered away again, but that would come too late. In fact, Camille did like to study alone. Today, though, his magic had stirred in his blood and set his heart racing. He had come to the river to make the shadows dance.

The shadows with which he played weren't shadows of anything in particular, or they didn't seem to be. They lurked in cracks and crevices between the borders of this world and another, watching and waiting. Camille stirred them with a feather touch, as lightly as he could, and they responded at once. He swirled them in the air, the way one might swirl a leaf in the water, making patterns, watching the ripples. He paused once to scratch his wrist, where his bracelet was beginning to heat in response to his magic. The bracelet had been locked about his arm from infancy, as was the case for all Commoner magicians. Its smooth metallic band was meant to grow with him, but it always felt too tight. It felt particularly so today. The air was translucent with light and shade.

It was at this point that he usually stopped, before his bracelet could scald him further. This time, however, he did not. The evening bewitched him. It all seemed a lucid dream: the green-blue sky, the cool water, the warmth of the summer air. He reached out with his magic, and pulled.

The shadows began to converge. What had been faint wisps of darkness gathered in front of him in a tall plume like smoke. His bracelet burned at his wrist, hotter and hotter. He drew the shadows closer. They struggled; his heart beat in his chest like a kite tugging at the end of a rope in a high wind. The plume of smoke-darkness writhed, twisted—and then, at last, resolved itself into a single black shadow. Human-formed, trailing lighter fragments like whispers of fog. It turned to Camille and looked at him.

Something was screaming: a high, piercing note that penetrated the haze of magic and heat. Dimly, Camille recognized that it was coming from his wrist. His bracelet wailed a long note of warning, and still it burned, hotter than ever, so hot that reflexive tears spilled down his cheeks. But the pain was nothing compared to the wonder he felt. There was a living shadow in front of him, and it was real, and it was him but not him at once. It was tall and thin—a human shape, yes, but one that had been stretched like dough under a baker's hands.

The shadow regarded him for a long moment. Then, quite deliberately, it bowed. Camille bowed back, his burning wrist held clumsily apart from his body. It was as though his soul had opened its eyes for the first time.

"Get back!" Without further warning, a pistol shot cracked the air. There was a faint hiss as the shot passed through vapor, and then the shadow was gone. Nothing but a smoke trail was left to show it had ever been there.

Camille screamed. The bullet had not hit him, yet he felt it sear as though through his heart, and the nothingness that came to engulf him in its wake was worse. His cries joined the wail of the bracelet, as though both were being killed together. He screamed, over and over, as the crowd drawn from the village by his bracelet's alarm rushed forward. He was still screaming as Leroy the blacksmith grabbed him by the arms and held him roughly, careful to avoid the shrieking piece of hot metal at his wrist. He still screamed as the Knight Templar from the village came on the scene. He screamed right until the Templar, fumbling, touched his bracelet with the spell to silence the alarm, and then he stopped so abruptly that some of the onlookers thought he was dead. He wasn't. He was white and limp, but gasping, as Leroy caught him up in his arms and took him to the Temple Church.

He was in the underground cell for twelve hours. The Templar tried to offer him food, and even words of comfort. Camille was a tiny waif, with eyes too big for his face under a fringe of black curls, and the Templar was not a monster. The child remained curled up in the corner, unresponsive, shaking, and distraught.

It was perhaps the best thing he could have done, though he could not have known or cared. By the early hours of the morning, Jean Benoit Nicolas Desmoulins had come to bargain, quietly, for the freedom of his son. He was a well-connected man in the town, a lawyer and lieutenant general of the local bailliage; it was unlikely under any circumstances that Camille would be convicted of illegal magic and carted off to the Bastille like a common street urchin. But by the time Desmoulins arrived with his purse and his double meanings, the Templar was unnerved enough by the small, haunted figure in the bowels of the church that he was willing to surrender him without a fight. He had taken illegal magicians before—even underage ones, even in Guise. He was used to their fear and their guilt. Little Camille was incapacitated by neither. He could not imagine what was happening in the child's head, but it sent a shiver down his spine.

For a while, when they brought him home, there were fears that nothing would ever happen in Camille's head again. His father, still burning with shame and anger, pushed him into his mother's waiting arms. Camille had walked to and from the carriage under his own power, but he still had not spoken.

"Take him," Desmoulins said roughly. "Not that it'll do much good. My son and heir, no better than an idiot now. Those bastards. Someone needs to teach them a lesson."

He had underestimated the resilience of small children, or at least of this one. Late that morning, Camille came back downstairs, fed and washed and rested, and little the worse for his dark night. He spoke as brightly and intelligently as he ever had, a little too much so for some people's liking. But he had changed. His voice had been clear as a bell; now it had an unmistakable stammer that never went away, no matter how his father frowned and encouraged in turn. At times his eyes would stare, disconcertingly, at things that weren't there. He had been somewhere that nobody could quite understand. And every so often, at church, or in the street, the local Knight Templar would look up to see Camille watching him, and would know that he had not forgiven it.

London

Autumn 1779

On the night of 22 October 1779, John Terrell, London saddler and unbraceleted Commoner, was surprised in his bed by a would-be burglar brandishing a pistol. Strictly speaking, it was his wife who surprised him. Her cry upon awakening to a dark shape entering their bedroom woke Mr. Terrell in turn, and the burglar swiftly found himself lying on the floor, groaning from a blow to the head. The commotion woke the neighbors, who arrived on the scene to find Mr. Terrell holding the man down while Mrs. Terrell held the heavy poker that had struck him. The burglar was arrested.

The Bow Street Runners were not impolite enough to ask how the burglar came to be struck from behind, when the only two occupants of the house were both in front of him in bed. Unfortunately, the burglar was more than happy to tell them, as soon as he had recovered speech. The Terrells were soon wakened again, this time by a member of the Knights Templar knocking on the door. A week later, while the burglar in question still languished in Newgate Prison, John Terrell was standing in the dock at the Old Bailey, facing charges of unregistered magic and failure to report a magical Inheritance to the appropriate authorities.

It was a perfectly ordinary incident. It would not change the world. But it was as good a place to begin as any.

William Pitt was late to the parliamentary debates that night, not because the trial had run late—in fact, the judge had adjourned early to attend a dinner—but because he had held back to argue the case with the senior advocate.

"The point is," he said, as his older colleague gathered his notes, "Mr. Terrell would have been legally within his rights to use his Inheritance had he been registered. Even Commoners are allowed to use magic to defend themselves, if circumstances call for it. They clearly called for it in this case. His house was broken into, and the housebreaker was armed. Mr. Terrell used his weak telekinesis to pick up a fire poker and hit the assailant from behind. It's hardly vampirism, is it?"

"The problem is, he *wasn't* registered," his colleague said. "The Temple Church have no record of his magic. He had no bracelet." He said it patiently, in Pitt's opinion. John Drudge had been working these courts for twenty years—Pitt's entire lifetime. He would probably have quite liked to go to dinner himself, rather than be pressed about a routine case of unregistered magic by an inexperienced junior.

Given this, Pitt managed to be patient in turn, even though his thoughts were racing. "Yes, I know. And of course he cannot avoid punishment for that. But *had* he been registered, the incident itself would not have been illegal. His bracelet would have detected the use of magic, the Knights Templar would have been summoned, he may even have appeared before the courts, but he would have been cleared. If we can argue that, the judge might agree to drop the charge of unregistered magic. In that case, the only thing he's left with is failure to report an Inheritance. That's practically a misdemeanor."

"It's ten years in the Tower of London," his colleague reminded him, but he was paying attention now. "Hardly a misdemeanor. Besides, to my knowledge there has never been a case of failure to report an Inheritance without a charge of illegal magic. How could there be? An Inheritance couldn't be detected if it weren't used."

"It happened in Norwich last year," Pitt said. He'd gone to check during the brief recess earlier that afternoon, spurred by a faint memory of reading it in the papers. "Not under these circumstances, I admit: the man's relatives informed the Templars, and the Templars confirmed the Inheritance without any documented incident of his abilities being used. But it gives us some precedent. And ten years in the Tower is a good deal better than the thirty-five he'll receive with the illegal-magic charge added."

His colleague was wavering. "It's very clever, Mr. Pitt. You've forgotten one thing, though. The prosecution can still argue that the self-defense law doesn't apply, since he was defending his wife and not himself."

"That's true," Pitt conceded. It was their usual stumbling block. "But it's still a chance, which is more than he has now. If the prosecution are distracted enough by us pressing for failure to report only, it might just slip by them. They may well try to argue, as you just did, that you cannot have failure to report without an illegal-magic charge, and let the question of self-defense rest altogether. Which, by the way, is an interesting precedent to set for future cases, isn't it?"

His colleague hesitated a moment longer, then smiled reluctantly. "Oh, very well. We'll try it, at least. I'll speak to the judge at the club tonight about changing the plea."

Pitt kept a smile of triumph off his own face, but he suspected some of it came through in his voice. "Thank you."

"It won't make the Knights Templar very happy, mind you," the other advocate warned. "Unregistered magic has been climbing every generation—they want to come down hard on it these days."

"With all due respect to the Knights Templar," Pitt returned, "surely that's for the law and the government to decide."

Said law and government—or at least the House of Commoners, which Pitt considered the same thing, though intellectually he knew better—were assembling at five o'clock that evening. As fortune would have it, the debates had not quite begun as Pitt fought his way through the crowds. The public gallery was scarcely fifteen feet above the floor of the House of Commoners, and its pillars thrust down among the benches right into the midst of the debaters. Below, he could see Edmund Burke arriving, and the prime minister, Lord

North, with an entourage about him. Charles Fox was already seated and talking on the opposition benches; his bright yellow waistcoat was stretched across his round frame, and his bushy eyebrows were animated as he turned to a new arrival. Already the visitors' platform was a rowdy crush of people.

Pitt had been five when he had first been brought from the safe haven of their family home to watch his father speak. Their mother had been at home with little James, but his tutor had brought him along with his older brother and sisters. The five Pitt children were only a year or two apart in age, all educated at home and constantly in the company of their parents or each other. John, eight years old and destined for the army, leaned over the railings to wave at their father; Hester stood with her usual self-possession at his side. Harriot chatted to their tutor excitedly with half a protective eye on her younger brother. Even then, William Pitt had been tall, thin, and awkward for his age, quietly confident in adult company but shy in crowds. Coming after a frosty evening outside, the sudden enveloping warmth of bodies had overwhelmed him, as had the equal warmth of the shouts and protests while the debates raged below. He had felt that he was pitching on a storm-tossed raft above crashing waves, only the waves were people and ideas, and the storm around him was the same. It had taken his breath away.

"Do you hear the walls singing?" his tutor had said, bending down beside him. Pitt had listened attentively and thought he could. It was a faint pulse and hum, felt more than heard. His elder siblings paid it no attention: they had seen it all before. "The panels are made of laburnum laced with silver. They respond to the speeches. Particular combinations of language and ideas make them vibrate and chime. The great orators, like your father, can play them like a symphony."

"But Father's not allowed to use magic," Pitt had pointed out. It was before his father had been titled. "We're Commoner blood."

"Words have a magic of their own, William," his tutor had said. "Especially in here. It has nothing to do with blood."

Pitt had been working in the law courts for a year or so now, and on the whole he enjoyed it. His brain reveled in its mix of order and invention, and he enjoyed the company of his colleagues, most of whom were lively and quick-witted and so appreciated those qualities in him. He liked the occasional opportunity, as with his case right now, to make a difference. There was no doubt in his mind, however, that it was employment only to support himself until he was old enough to take a seat in the House of Commoners. He needed the work, and he was grateful to have it. But he needed politics like he needed the air he breathed, perhaps because it had always been part of the air in his home growing up, perhaps because it was indeed in his blood.

This, he had been told, was where change happened. Not in the courts, one Mr. Terrell at a time, but here, where words had power to make a building sing and alter the course of the country.

"Good evening," came a voice. The politely insistent tone implied that it wasn't the first time it had been said.

It took Pitt a few moments to locate the speaker. The voice that had addressed him had been pleasantly resonant, even melodious, yet its owner was tiny: almost a foot shorter than Pitt, and his slight figure was half-swallowed by the crowds. He was a young man, perhaps Pitt's own age. His features were not striking or remarkable, leaving only a vague impression of strong eyebrows, a delicate cleft chin, and a nose that turned up at the end. There was an air of lively curiosity and intelligence about his face and eyes, however, that drew Pitt's attention toward him out of the press of people.

Unfortunately, if he had ever seen either features or owner before, they had made no impression, and he couldn't now put a name to them. That wasn't uncommon for him, but it was very embarrassing.

"We've met once or twice at Cambridge," the man said, without a hint of reproach. Apparently, he had recognized the problem. "You would have no cause to remember. You were always doing something studious, and I was and am being constantly persuaded to do anything but; I'm also nobody of real consequence. As a result, I know that you're Mr. William Pitt, younger son of the famous Earl of Chatham, and you have no idea what peculiarly impertinent person is forcing himself upon your notice. I hope you'll forgive me."

The introduction, and the impish smile that accompanied it, was so without any trace of unease that Pitt felt his usual self-consciousness abate.

"I'll forgive you," he countered, "if you remedy my ignorance immediately."

"I'm William Wilberforce," the man said. His cheeks were flushed, either from the cold outside or the hot, rambunctious atmosphere of the platform, and his eyes were twinkling. "My father was a Commoner merchant from Hull, and I'm supposedly reading at Cambridge, although I fear I spend more time outside its walls than in lately. As I said, I'm being actively encouraged to do as little work as possible. If you desire proof, ask me what brought me into London."

"What brought you into London?"

"I'm glad you asked. I was told I might as well spend some time here and enjoy myself, since my inheritance—monetary, I mean, not magical—means I have no real need to pass the exams. My own tutor told me this. But in fairness, I've found London extremely diverting. I only came into the House last week because a group of us were walking between a dinner engagement and a ball and wanted to escape the snow, if I'm honest, but as you see, I've come back alone today when there's been but a light frost. I've shocked you."

"No, of course not," Pitt said, more stiffly than he intended. He had been brought up to regard a visit to the House of Commoners as a reward for being exceptionally well behaved, and therefore to hate the thought of idle spectators. He hadn't meant to hold that against his new acquaintance, though, and he certainly hadn't meant to make it obvious he was doing so.

"That is a very polite lie," Wilberforce said adamantly. "I was watching you, and your nose wrinkled a little in distaste. It was the look given to me by a gambling friend of mine when I mentioned that I quite like playing cards, and the look given to me by my religious aunt when I was very small and said I liked the parts of the Bible that had animals in them, so I know it well. Just tell me I'm committing heresy."

It was Pitt's turn to smile. "Very well," he said, matching Wilberforce's gravity. "Coming into the House of Commoners to escape the snow is heresy. Akin to using hundred-year-old wine to clean your toothbrush."

"Thank you so much for explaining." His tone became a little less playful. "In fact, I'm taking it more seriously than I made it sound. I don't, you see, happen to agree with my tutor that I have no need of anything except my inheritance. I want to have a career of some kind very soon, and I really did find the debate last week fascinating."

"Which one did you hear?"

"It was about the American War," Wilberforce said at once. This could have described any number of debates from last week, but from the way his face ignited, Pitt suspected he knew the one he meant. "Edmund Burke called for the government to make peace."

"Again." Pitt felt his own excitement ignite at the memory. "I heard it too."

"He was brilliant, wasn't he?"

"He was. At the end he was transcendent."

"The part that went—I can't quite remember the phrase, but it was something about how the struggle for liberty always manifests as a struggle for the right to magic—"

"'Abstract liberty, like other mere abstractions, is not to be found. Liberty inheres in some sensible object; and every nation has formed to itself some favorite point, which by way of eminence becomes the criterion of their happiness. It happened that the great contests for freedom in this country were from the earliest times chiefly upon the question of magic.'" Pitt smiled at Wilberforce's look, slightly embarrassed. "I tend to remember speeches. Did you agree with him?"

"Wholeheartedly, as far as making peace with America is concerned. I know your father did too. What he said about magic and liberty just made me think about the reverse, in this country."

That was unexpected, and interesting. "How so?"

"Well—it struck me that if struggles for liberty usually take the form of struggles for the right to practice magic, then the liberty of a given nation ought to be reflected in how freely magic is practiced in that nation. And our magical laws really are terribly out of date, aren't they? There's almost no leeway for Commoners to use their magic at all, even when it would be foolish for them not to do so."

"Dear God, yes." The courtroom was fresh in his mind. "There's but one legal exception allowing for magic in the case of self-defense. The accused has to be under direct attack, with clear and present risk to his life. There are a thousand other reasons why a Commoner might reasonably use magic: to push a child out of danger, to warm a freezing house in winter, to heal a dying man. The law needs to account for them."

"Do you not agree, then, that legislation of that kind can be abused?"

"All legislation can be abused; that's what courts are designed to prevent. We need to reexamine exactly why magic is illegal to Commoners and make sure the laws reflect that and nothing else. We also need to—"

The renewed commotion in the gallery told Pitt that the debate was beginning down in the House. For once he felt a flare of disappointment—not because he wouldn't have the opportunity to finish, but because he wouldn't hear the reply. He hadn't had such a promising start to a conversation in a while, and certainly not with somebody he hardly knew.

"Better give them a turn, I suppose," Wilberforce said, with such convincing magnanimity it made Pitt smile. "Tell me what you were thinking later, though?"

"If you're still here at the end of the debates," Pitt promised. He had work to do for the trial tomorrow, but that could wait. "Most won't stay."

"Oh, believe me," Wilberforce said, "you will find it nearly impossible to lose me."

The following day, John Terrell was sentenced to ten years in the Tower of London for failure to report an Inheritance, after a hard-fought trial that lasted well into the evening. The charge of unregistered magic was dropped without sentence. The courtroom was plunged into uproar as the sentence was passed, and Pitt, sitting in his place by the senior advocate, couldn't help but feel a quiet glow of triumph. It was an unprecedented victory: an admission that even an unregistered magician could use his or her abilities in an act of self-defense without prosecution for the act itself. It also, though most wouldn't have noticed, stretched the definition of "self-defense" by more than a little.

It wasn't, he was painfully aware, quite so much of a triumph for Mr. Terrell. The man stood as if dazed, the pallor of his face already that of a prisoner, and looked with anguished eyes at the tearful woman who was surely his wife. He would be parted from her for but ten years, Pitt reminded himself. However difficult that would be, it was still an astonishing improvement on thirty-five.

He told Wilberforce about it as they dined at White's that night: the two of them had met once again in the House of Commoners and once again found their conversation had spilled outside the debates. This had involved Wilberforce rearranging what seemed to Pitt a dizzying entangle of social engagements, but he assured Pitt that he was notoriously unreliable, and his friends would expect nothing less.

"It's just a piece of legal trickery, really," Pitt said. "But with any luck the issue will be raised in Parliament the next time somebody tries to implement fairer penalties for unregistered magic."

"Good," Wilberforce declared. "And if nobody has done so by the time you're old enough to run for Parliament, you can bring it up yourself."

"Or you can," Pitt returned.

"If I ever decide to run for office. I still don't know if I will."

"Oh, I'm fairly convinced you will. After all, you were there at the House again tonight, when there were only intermittent showers."

Wilberforce smiled, though something passed across his face. Not quite a cloud, but a shadow of a cloud. "The last time I tried to do something I thought was important, it was not received very well by my family. I was twelve, and I decided I wanted to retire from the world, join the church, and become a Methodist."

"Really?" Pitt glanced at his companion's very un-Methodist-like demeanor with what could charitably be called surprise, but confined himself to saying, "I don't think I've ever met a Methodist."

"My aunt and uncle are Methodists. I went to live with them for a time, after my father died. But don't worry, you still haven't met one. My mother and grandfather were horrified. They pulled me from that house at once and banished me to boarding school for a course of strict hedonism. I think no parents ever labored more to impress their child with sentiments of piety than they did to give me a taste of the world's diversion."

"Did it work?"

"Oh yes. I'd make a terrible Methodist now. I like society too much. But I don't think I ever quite recovered from the idea that there was something greater."

"Well," Pitt said, "perhaps you need to know the world in order to find it."

"Perhaps." His smile this time had its customary warmth. "It's a good beginning, at least."

"It is," Pitt agreed. Neither of them was quite sure what it was that was supposed to be beginning, but it didn't matter. They were twenty. Everything was beginning.

England/France

Summer 1783

Afterward, they were never sure who had decided they should spend the summer recess in France. It had seemed to happen naturally, as the days lengthened and the talks in the House of Commoners grew steadily more heated.

The world had shifted since Wilberforce and Pitt had met in the visitors' gallery. It had been three years since Wilberforce had crossed the floor of the House of Commoners as member for Hull, thrilling with nerves and a vague, unfocused sense of purpose. His nerves had lasted as long as it took him to realize that the language of the House of Commoners was not so different from the language of any social gathering: a matter of listening with great interest to what was being said, forming his own sentiments in response, and putting them to words. His sense of purpose had lasted longer, though the causes it latched onto remained erratic. He spoke up for odd bills that aimed to improve the lives of Commoner magicians, as he'd planned; he also lent his voice to tax reforms and education and reconciliation with America after the War of Independence. If he still occasionally felt a wistful sense of something further out of reach, he didn't let it trouble him. He was a popular and energetic MP, he was at the center of a high-spirited social circle of lively young politicians, and he was very happy.

Pitt, on the other hand, had shot across the House of Commoners like a meteorite, except, Wilberforce corrected himself, meteorites fell to earth, and his friend had shown no sign of doing so. Within the first few weeks, he had given his maiden speech, and the walls had resounded with a clarity that was still being talked about on slow nights in the club when there was little else to discuss. By the age of twenty-three, he was chancellor of the exchequer. Quite how this had come about, nobody was entirely sure. His parentage helped, of course: the House of Commoners, despite its occasional pretensions to radical democracy, loved tradition and lineage. It helped also that the government of Great Britain had been in a state of flux for years, a situation worsened by the aftermath of the war in America. But Wilberforce suspected that, even with a different background and in a different political climate, Pitt would still have made his mark. The world simply seemed to be sharper and clearer to him than it was to anybody else Wilberforce had ever known. To be fair, he also worked harder and longer than anyone Wilberforce had ever known and, irritatingly, thrived on it.

The government itself, though, was desperately unstable. Since the end of the American Revolutionary War had forced the collapse of Lord North's government, the House of Commoners had been in a state of upheaval as the king hunted for a prime minister whom he did not actively despise. Shortly before Parliament had disbanded for the summer, another shift had taken place, and the government had switched back to the old prime minister, North, in an alliance with Charles Fox. They had invited Pitt to stay on, despite the furious political battles that had raged among the three of them over the last year or so, but Pitt had declined on principle. Until things shifted again—and they looked to do so very soon—he was out of office.

Wilberforce had been concerned that Pitt would be disappointed to leave the administration without any promise that he would ever be in government again, but in fact Pitt had met him on the evening in question positively buoyant.

"I've just become a humble backbencher," he announced. "Supper?"

"Starving," Wilberforce replied, and the two of them had joined a general throng of their friends at their club and stayed up all night, talking and laughing until Wilberforce had almost fallen off his chair—although that might have been the quantity of wine he had consumed. Trying to match Pitt glass for glass, he had learned early in their friendship, was no light endeavor.

As they stepped out onto Pall Mall afterward, the day dawned bright and dazzling. Their friends had been talking vaguely of returning to their respective London lodgings to get to bed; at the sight of the perfect blue sky, white stone buildings, and crisp green trees lining the pavement, the two of them mutually agreed that it made far more sense to travel to Wilberforce's country house and go boating on the river. Their friend Edward Eliot was the only one who agreed with them about this. The young Commoner had been a third in most of their expeditions since before they had all taken seats in Parliament: he shared their love of wordplay, countryside, and politics, and his delicate, rather dreamy face, with its large dark eyes and pointed chin, belied a mischievous sense of humor. Everyone else thought what they were proposing was quite mad, which was true.

It was after this, as they lay on the grass, saturated with sun, river, and the languorous unreality of having been awake for thirty hours, that the decision to go to France was made. None of them had ever been across the Channel nor spoke any French, but in the fine, hot afternoon it had sounded like the easiest thing in the world.

"Do you want to stay near town to see what might happen, though?" Wilberforce asked Pitt. "There's still talk of a new government being formed."

"God no," Pitt replied. "I want to go on holiday, thank you." He rolled over and sat up, blinking in the glare. "In all seriousness, I shouldn't be needed in town once the House rises, and there's very little chance anything will be decided until the next session. The new government should be stable at least for the summer. I'm free to go away—for the first time in a year, I might add."

And, though none of them said it, for potentially the last time in years to come. Even with only the three of them, it was difficult to gauge what Pitt thought about the whispers currently being traded about Westminster.

Eliot, always sensitive to the feelings of others, was quick to change the subject. "Are we connected with anybody in France?"

"Surely we must be," Pitt said, a little drowsily. He'd settled back down on the grass and closed his eyes. "Wilberforce knows everybody in England between the ages of eighteen and sixty-five. Statistically speaking, one of them must know somebody in France."

Between then and jumping on the boat a few weeks later, Wilberforce suspected that conversation represented the longest sustained practical thought any of them had given to the issue, although somebody—opinion now differed greatly as to who—had furnished them with a letter of introduction to a gentleman named Monsieur Coustier of Rheims. That, they assumed, was all they needed to establish themselves in French society.

The morning after they arrived in Rheims, they got up far too late, dressed in their best clothes, and with some awe went to present their letter to the address they had been given. They almost missed it, because it was a smaller house than they had expected, and when they asked in a mixture of terrible French and half-understood English for Monsieur Coustier, they were pointed to a shabbily dressed Commoner standing behind a counter distributing figs and raisins.

Somehow, their only letter of recommendation was to a grocer, and not a very eminent one. They had no means of entering French society at all, and now no plan at all for their time on foreign soil. They knew nobody, and couldn't speak the language. And they had six weeks of their holiday remaining.

They bid a courteous farewell to Monsieur Coustier, left the building, and stood outside in mutual bewilderment. Then Wilberforce caught Pitt's eye, and suddenly the two of them were laughing so hard that people around them began to stare. Eliot managed to keep a straight face for longer, but not by much.

After that, they simply bought some wine, bread, cheese, and overpriced pastries they liked the look of, and went back to their hotel. More than a week later, they were still there.

It wasn't that Wilberforce objected to the situation, particularly. He was enjoying the company, which was excellent: Eliot kept them in a steady stream of lighthearted banter, and Pitt, away from Parliament, was at his most relaxed and high-spirited. He was enjoying France, which was giving them clear, beautiful days of sunshine and warm nights of starlight amid intricate buildings and winding streets. He was even enjoying the wine and food, which although not of the best quality was plentiful and delicious. But somebody had to make an objection; it was Pitt's job, really, but since he didn't seem minded to do it and Eliot wouldn't be concerned if Pitt wasn't, it fell to Wilberforce. He wasn't very good at it.

"We should do something, you know," he pressed. "While we *have* succeeded in becoming very familiar with the inside of this room and with cheap French wine, we're probably missing a good deal of the country. We also haven't made any progress on learning French, which is unsurprising since the only people we've really spoken to since arriving are each other."

"How can it be that none of us speak French?" Eliot asked rhetorically. "We're Cambridge graduates, for God's sake."

"We know some Latin," Wilberforce offered. "Pitt's fluent."

"Wonderful. All we need now is an ancient Roman with a place at court."

"That wouldn't help," Pitt said, apparently quite seriously. "We still wouldn't have a letter of introduction to give him."

Eliot shrugged. "We could catch him in a tiger trap and force him to introduce us."

"What would we use for bait?"

"Something not readily available in ancient Rome, presumably."

"Shoes," Wilberforce suggested, drawn in despite his best efforts. Inevitably, however seriously they started, conversations between the three of them eventually turned down the path of pure nonsense. "And hair powder."

"Fog."

"Functional emperors."

"Tiger traps."

"Ex-chancellors of the exchequer?" Wilberforce suggested, with a mischievous grin in Pitt's direction.

"Oh, they had plenty of those," Pitt returned. "Only they called them by their ancient name: lazy, unemployed pleasure-seekers."

"What did they call MPs for northern constituencies?"

"Friends of grocers!" Eliot put in, and his glee was enough to set them all laughing until they were struggling for breath and could barely remember what had been so funny.

"We really can't stay in these lodgings much longer," Wilberforce said, after they had subsided into giggles. He couldn't help but feel his argument became less and less convincing the more they did just that. "I know we've been trying to ignore it, but they do have fleas."

"I *was* trying to ignore it," said Pitt, stretching out in his chair with a sigh. "Thank you."

"And this is not very good wine. We've probably destroyed at least half our mental faculties already."

"I am attempting," Pitt said, "to prepare myself for my inevitable future position. Clearly, a prime minister should have only half the mental faculties of a chancellor of the exchequer."

Wilberforce snorted, yet he felt a touch of unease. He knew Pitt hadn't meant anything by the rejoinder, but it came too close to the political realities they had been avoiding.

Pitt evidently caught Wilberforce's discomfort, because he straightened and rose at once. "You're right, of course," he said, crossing the room to refill his glass yet again from the bottle on the mantelpiece. He suddenly looked a little more like the young man who could take down opponents three times his age in the House of Commoners without an eyeblink, and less like the one who had last night lost to Wilberforce in a pillow fight. "We should do something. We do, after all, know one person in town: Monsieur Coustier. And though we vastly overestimated the poor man's influence, he was very kind to us and is still a respectable tradesman."

"He supplies to the Knights Templar," Wilberforce said. "There's a Temple Church here, not so far away. If he were to effect an introduction to some member of the Order—"

"They might be able to introduce us to the right people," Eliot finished. He raised his glass in a toast. "I'll drink to that as a plan."

"I would too," Wilberforce said, "but someone's taken the wine from my glass and filled it with a colorless and tasteless substance. I think they call it air."

"What barbarian would do such a thing?" Pitt said dryly, offering the bottle. Wilberforce held out his glass, and the wine flowed. The stars were coming out.

Outside the haven of their hotel, the France they had come to was in the grip of social unrest. The American War of Independence had left the country heavily in debt, driving the monarchy to impose taxes that enraged Commoners and Aristocracy alike. Poor harvests had left the country on the brink of famine and created smoldering resentment of the well-fed Aristocracy and still-more-extravagant royal family.

To make matters worse, the king of France had been born that rare phenomenon: a member of a royal family without a trace of magic. His ancestor's powers had been of such strength that he had earned the moniker the Sun King—partly because those powers were the unusual combination of fire and weather magic, but partly because it was said that during his blazing reign the last of the illegal shadows still haunting Europe after the end of the Vampire Wars had dispersed. Louis XVI could give no such protection: he didn't need to, perhaps, but it was still not a good omen. Superstition stated that a king's magic was linked with his country's, and for a country to be without a mage-king left it vulnerable. The Knights Templar, in response to their monarch's weakness, had clamped down harder on Commoner magicians than in any era before. They thought they were doing the right thing.

And beneath the surface, something was moving. Something that spoke of change, and of revolution, and of blood.

* * *

By mutual agreement, the three English travelers went to bed comparatively early and comparatively sober: half past two in the morning, and with the floor tilting only slightly as they made their way to their respective beds. It was a still, balmy night, and Wilberforce was asleep seconds after his head touched the pillow.

It seemed barely half an hour before a voice woke him, and it was.

"Wilberforce? Are you awake?"

It was Pitt, Wilberforce realized as he forced his eyes open. The room was dark, but he could make out his friend's tall, thin silhouette in the faint moonlight coming through the shutters.

"Of course I'm not awake," he said sleepily.

"Shh," Pitt warned, with a glance at the bed nearest to the door. Eliot, stretched out beneath the blankets, stirred but didn't open his eyes. "Don't wake Eliot. It's not necessary, and I don't think he'd take it well."

"Take what well?" His mind was responding more to the seriousness of Pitt's tone than to his words, but he propped himself up on one elbow. "What's wrong?"

"Nothing, possibly." Pitt hesitated, which was unusual enough to catch Wilberforce's further attention. He seemed to come to a decision. "If I asked you to trust me on something that might be difficult for you to believe, could you do so without asking questions?"

"Of course."

"No, I mean truthfully. Wake up a little, and give it thought."

Wilberforce rubbed his eyes and tried to blink himself back into awareness. It was difficult when sleep and wine were still lying heavy on him, but he found the answer was very simple.

"Yes," he said, more firmly. "I would trust you on anything."

"Without asking questions?"

"Well, I can't promise not to ask, but I wouldn't object if you declined to answer." Wilberforce's mind was clearing, and with it a thrill was creeping down his spine. Whatever this was, it was clearly going to be important. "What is it?"

His bed creaked in the darkness as his friend sat down at its foot. "There's something stalking this street at night," Pitt said bluntly. "I think it's a shadow, and I think it's a rogue one. Whatever it is, this is the third time I've been woken by it going past the window, and I strongly suspect it's only the third time because it's only the third time I've been in bed at three in the morning."

Wilberforce felt the thrill turn cold.

Nobody could quite explain what shadows were—even the Knights Templar, after centuries of study, could only speculate. Perhaps they were manifestations of pure magic; perhaps they were beings from another plane of existence, pulled through by shadowmancy. Perhaps, as the Catholic Church had once contended and some of the more rigid religious sects still believed, they were demons. Shadowmancers only shrugged when they were questioned about it: to them, a shadowmancer friend had once told Wilberforce, it was like asking the nature of the sunlight or the wind. What mattered was that they could reach out and summon them forth. Some were frail and wispy; others, summoned with more power or skill, had human shape, and even the beginnings of human features. They had an understanding with their shadowmancers—for them, they could perform certain tasks before dispersing into the ether, or, by less ethical magicians, they could be bound to an object and kept as a curiosity. Wilberforce had been to a dinner only last month where the pride of the table had been the shadow-possessed teapot, bound more than a hundred years ago with an order to obey the bloodline and always keep the tea warm. It was considered rather ostentatious, but perfectly safe.

If a shadow escaped its bonds, however, it was loose in the world. Shadows couldn't hold a weapon, but the very strongest could kill with a touch. Their motives were inscrutable and unpredictable. And they could be very, very dangerous.

"Have you seen it?" Wilberforce asked. "I mean, how did—?"

"I haven't seen it. This is why I'm forced to ask you to trust me. I felt it pass in my sleep—rather like an eclipse, or a sudden plunge into icy water. The first two times it happened, I put it out of my mind. This time, it must have lingered longer. It's still a warm night, isn't it?"

"Yes," Wilberforce said, surprised. "A little too warm, if anything."

"Not to me. It's at more of a distance now, but I still feel as though there's a cold mist in the air. I've felt like that before, most strongly when I dined at Lord Harcourt's three years ago. His entire kitchen is shadow-animated."

"Very well," Wilberforce said slowly. This, as Pitt had warned, raised more questions than it answered; he had never heard of anybody—even a shadowmancer—being able to sense when a shadow was nearby. But he had been told he would receive no answers to his questions, so he tried instead to turn his thoughts to the matter at hand. It was difficult, because something about shadows made his heart shiver. They always had, even the lowest forms inhabiting trick teapots. Some of this might have come from the chapter of his childhood spent with his aunt and uncle, who had assured him such things were against God. Yet Wilberforce wasn't particularly religious now, and still the sensation lingered. It was a cold, irrational fear lying beneath his knowledge of their potential danger that had nothing to do with what they were or what they might do to him, and that he had never been able to explain to anyone. Certainly he wasn't going to tell Pitt, who was never afraid of anything.

"We mean to visit the Templars tomorrow anyway," he said. "If we could alert them—"

"So you do believe me?" Pitt interrupted.

"Do you mean do I think you to be lying, or mistaken?"

"Do you think me to be either?"

"No, of course not! I can't think of anybody less likely to imagine something like that, or pretend to. Of course I believe you."

"Thank you," Pitt said, with just a hint of a sigh. Any relief he betrayed was short-lived. "The Knights Templar won't, though. They'll be suspicious enough of our story as it is; they'll say, I imagine, that three respectable members of the English gentry do not find themselves lost without connections in a disreputable hotel."

"They don't know us, do they?" Wilberforce said. "So what do you want to do?"

"I want to follow it and at least get a glimpse of it, to see what we're actually dealing with," Pitt said. "And I'm afraid I have to ask you to come with me."

"Into the streets, at three o'clock in the morning, to follow a shadow?"

"That is what I'm asking, yes."

Wilberforce considered. The idea was terrifying, of course. But that was beside the point.

"Just us?" he checked. "Not Eliot?"

Pitt shook his head. "As I said, he wouldn't take this very well. He'd come, out of loyalty, but he would never quite forgive me." He hesitated. "There's also the fact that he's almost certainly going to marry my sister."

Pitt's eldest sister, Hester, had died in childbirth three years earlier, only a few months before Pitt's younger brother had been killed in the service of the navy, and Wilberforce had never met her. Harriot Pitt, though, was part of their circle often: a dark-haired, graceful young woman, pure Commoner, with her younger brother's cleverness and good nature but none of his shyness. Wilberforce liked her very much. Eliot had been besotted with her since their introduction.

"Well, yes," Wilberforce said. "I think everyone knows that except him. Is that a problem?"

"Not at all, in the way you mean. I'm sorry, I really can't explain. I can only ask you to accompany me."

It made no sense at all. But that, after all, was what he had been warned of. "And if I said I thought this would be unwise, to say the least?"

"I would agree, and wish you good night."

"And then go out alone."

"Of course."

"Let me get my coat."

By the time Wilberforce had dressed hurriedly in his breeches and flung his coat over top, Pitt had ducked out of their rooms and come back. This time, he held two pistols.

"Take one," he said. "In case we need it."

Wilberforce looked at the weapon with a feeling of recoil. "Where did you get them?"

"Under the counter downstairs. I thought an establishment such as this would keep at least one close to hand while greeting guests, and it turned out they had two."

"These lodgings are even more disreputable than I thought." Wilberforce hesitated, then imagined the insubstantial press of cold shadow fingers against his chest and forced himself to wrap his own fingers around one of the pistols. He'd been shooting before, but only with a rifle, and he hadn't exactly distinguished himself. His eyesight had always been poor.

Outside, the crooked street was silent, lit by only a few dim pools of lamplight. They had been out at night once or twice since they had arrived, and Wilberforce knew that if they took a shortcut down an alleyway and then turned a sharp left, they would find themselves in a far more populated area, where drinking and cards ran riot. Along the stretch of cobblestones where the hotel stood, and indeed down the others where Pitt led him, everybody seemed to be in bed. He wished fervently he was the same.

They walked for a long time, first one way and then another. There was no sign of the shadow. After a while, he began to hope . . . not that Pitt had been imagining things, because that would be like hoping Pitt could fly, but that he had been mistaken. Or, since he couldn't quite make that fit with his idea of Pitt either, that the shadow had gone for the night. If it had walked the streets every night since they had been here, surely it would do no harm tonight if they failed to find it?

And then movement flickered in the corner of his eye, and he caught his breath.

In the glow of the lamplight, it was there: a shadow without a body to cast it, an elongated human form of black smoke. He had seen sketches of higher shadows in the newspapers, and in school; once or twice he had glimpsed them in houses that had summoned them as servants. But this was real. Suddenly, he knew without being able to put it into words why he had been so afraid of them.

"There," Pitt whispered beside him. "I knew we were close."

"We need to get away from here," Wilberforce said. His voice sounded steadier than he felt. "Right now."

Pitt didn't answer, and Wilberforce glanced at him sharply. His friend's eyes were fixed on the shadow, and they had a look that made his heart sink. It was not unlike the look he gave a rival politician in the House of Commoners before he got to his feet to tear him to pieces.

"Whatever you're about to do," Wilberforce said as calmly as possible, "please don't even think about it."

"It's too late, I'm afraid. Don't worry: you can stay here. I'm going to cross to the other side of the road and attempt to get it within range of my pistol. If it moves, toward you or toward me, run. Fire if you get a clear shot, but if you miss, I do mean it, Wilberforce: run."

"And let it take you? Please, let's go."

"I don't intend for it to take me."

"Don't be ridiculous!" Wilberforce hissed, but Pitt was already gone.

Wilberforce made a strangled noise of frustration, then belatedly cocked his pistol and raised it.

The shadow stood across the road, directly in front of him. Out of the corner of his eye he saw Pitt, blurred by distance and the darkness outside the circle of lamplight. Pitt raised his pistol, and Wilberforce closed his eyes instinctively as the report of the gun resounded in the quiet of the night.

The bullet didn't miss. It also didn't hit. Instead, the shadow turned at the last moment; the shot hissed harmlessly through the dark vapor of its arm. Its gaze fell on Wilberforce. He had thought that was impossible, since shadows had no eyes, but he was wrong. It was looking at him. His muscles tensed to run, or to fight—but just not to fire his pistol. The instinct simply wasn't there.

Whatever he would have done was moot, for the shadow's look didn't stay on him for more than a single, horrible half second. Instead, it kept turning, head and body, to face Pitt.

Pitt had been reloading, quickly and expertly, but when the thing finished its slow revolution, he froze. His pistol lay half-loaded in his hand; then that hand dropped to his side. Wilberforce couldn't make out what was playing over his face, not with the dark and the distance, but he wasn't moving.

Strangely, for a second, the shadow seemed to return his stare. The two of them looked at each other in mutual stillness. Then, without warning, the shadow lunged forward.

Like most Commoners, Wilberforce had been instructed in how to defend himself from a rogue shadow. It had been at grammar school, back in Hull, and a class of ten-year-old boys had stood solemnly in a row while their schoolmaster had marched in front of them with a stake.

"If you have a pointed stick," the master had said gruffly, "stick them with it and run. It won't kill them unless you're very fortunate, but it will delay them. If you don't, just run. You might survive if you make for a crowded area."

"What if you want to do battle with it?" young Wilberforce had asked.

The master had stopped directly in front of Wilberforce and given his frail, undersized self a long, hard look. "Just run, William," he'd said.

Wilberforce thought about this advice as the shadow hurtled toward his friend, but only for a moment. He raised his pistol and fired.

The pistol sparked with an explosion of gunpowder, devastating in the quiet street. It was, unfortunately, far less devastating to the shadow. Pitt gave a startled cry, but the shadow only stopped stark still, then turned slowly toward Wilberforce. He fumbled for another pistol shot with shaking fingers. It was no use. The shadow, a deeper darkness over the gray light of streets that were no longer familiar, was focused entirely on him, and he realized he had never until that moment understood what evil was. It cut through to his marrow and left him hollow and formless.

"What on earth, Wilberforce?" Pitt's voice came, and even though it sounded annoyed and scared, it instantly put the ground back under his feet. He was in France, and he wasn't alone. "Where was that shot supposed to be aimed?"

"I left my eyeglass back in my room!" Wilberforce called back defensively.

"Oh, in the name of—!" Behind the shadow, Pitt raised his pistol and fired.

The shadow jolted, and Wilberforce at once felt the horrible pressure lift from his heart. For a second, the shadow remained still, and the world around them held its breath. Then, with a shriek that faded into a sudden rush of wind, it dispersed into vapor and blew away to nothing.

Wilberforce stood there. He wasn't sure yet what it was that he was feeling, but it was the most important moment of his life.

Dimly, he became aware of his friend running across the road toward him.

"Are you hurt?" To anybody else, he would have sounded remarkably self-possessed. Wilberforce had learned by now that Pitt sounded at his most self-possessed when he was badly shaken. "How close did it get?"

"I'm fine." His own voice came out faint, and he swallowed hard to clear it. Wilberforce, when he was badly shaken, simply sounded badly shaken. "It didn't touch me," he clarified, in something more like his usual tone. "You dispersed it in time. Are *you* all right?"

"Mm." He put his hand to the side of his head, pulled it away, and managed a wry smile. "Your bullet clipped my ear, though."

"Oh no," Wilberforce exclaimed with a surge of horror. "Badly?"

"Not at all. As far as I can tell, I've had worse shaving."

"I'm so sorry."

"No, please, don't be. I'm the one who should apologize: I shouldn't have missed that first shot. It's a good thing I didn't come on my own."

Wilberforce nodded. Now that it was over, he was shaking like a leaf in a high wind. "I need to sit down."

"So do I," Pitt confessed, and the two of them collapsed against the wall behind them and slid down to the ground. Wilberforce felt the stone snag his coat several times on the way but didn't care.

They sat there for a minute or so, as their sharp, ragged breaths gradually slowed and calmed.

"It wasn't marked," Wilberforce said.

"No," Pitt agreed. "It was either rogue or illegal. I hope it was rogue. I'd rather not have a dark magician coming after us."

"It was looking at you. When you shot it the first time, and perhaps even before. It didn't move forward at once; it stopped to look."

"Well. I was looking at it as well. It seems fair."

"Do you know why it would do that?"

"No," Pitt said. "At least—I've never had it happen before."

Wilberforce nodded and knew to let it drop.

"And what about killing a shadow in the dead of night?" he said instead, leaning his head back against the stone behind him. "Have you ever done anything like that before?"

"Of course not. If I had, I wouldn't have missed the first time."

"You seemed to know exactly what to do."

"I read about it at Cambridge. Apparently the trick is to hit the center. I always secretly wanted to try it."

Wilberforce shook his head. "You're an extraordinary man, Mr. Pitt."

"As are you, Mr. Wilberforce." They were silent for a moment, and then Pitt began to laugh softly.

"What?" Wilberforce demanded, feeling his own mouth start to curve in response.

"I'm sorry," Pitt said, shaking his head and making an effort to regain his composure. For once, it didn't work. "It's just... you really are a terrible shot."

Wilberforce gave him his coldest look for half a second, then couldn't hold back a laugh of his own. "That's not fair! I didn't read about how to banish shadows in Cambridge. I didn't know where to aim."

"So you were forced to decide between me and the lamppost."

"Decide?" Wilberforce said with a perfectly straight face. "I just couldn't tell which was which."

Pitt was clearly in the mentally ticklish state much more common with Wilberforce, and that was enough to push him over the edge into helpless giggles. Wilberforce joined him there. The shock and fear had drained away. In its wake was an elation not unlike that of his first electoral victory at Hull, but deeper and sweeter.

The sky was beginning to lighten; soon, the sounds of voices and bread ovens would be stirring faintly behind the doors that lined the streets. Wilberforce rose stiffly and stretched.

"Come on," he said, nudging his friend with his shoe. "We need to get these pistols back before the owners notice they're gone, and before Eliot wakes up and realizes we've vanished. And then we have an appointment with the Templars."

Pitt sighed. "Can we not just sit here until the sun rises, and then go back and sleep until late afternoon?"

"You *are* a lazy, unemployed pleasure-seeker when there's no politics to be had, aren't you?"

"Absolutely. That is why I just gave my night to vanquishing evil from the world." He got to his feet and stretched in turn. "I hope you're not too sorry that I dragged you into it."

"I'm very glad you did," Wilberforce said. "I couldn't feel its influence like you could, but when it went, it felt...right. As if something had lifted. I can see why the Knights Templar give their lives to the destruction of dark magic. Can't you?"

"Quite honestly, no. It wouldn't be my choice at all. But in this case, the streets are safer, and I feel much better on a purely personal level. It's no real matter, but it's nice to be warm again."

"It's going to be a beautiful day," Wilberforce said. "Do you think we should tell the Templar official about this when Coustier introduces us?"

"I think," Pitt said, "whoever the poor man is will have enough difficulty comprehending us as it is."

Some hundred miles away, in the provincial town of Arras, a young advocate was awake as well. He was a small, neat figure, not only in height and dress, but in manner, in movement, in person. All his life, he had taken up very little space in the world. He sat at a table by his bedroom window, where the last of the moonlight pooled with the light of his candle on the page, and the reflection caught the eyeglasses perched on his nose and turned them to milky discs. Behind them, his green eyes were narrowed in concentration. They were a cat's eyes; his face, too, had some of the lean, pointed quality of a cat's. Yet he lacked a cat's air of relaxed disdain. Instead, his limbs were hunched over the desk, and he was frowning. He did this often.

His name was Maximilien Robespierre. As yet, this meant nothing to anyone, not even to him.

In this instance, his frown was occasioned by the notes of a case in front of him, which he would be presenting in court in a few weeks. His client had been charged with illegal telekinesis in the act of stealing a loaf of bread; the theft had been minor and ineffectual, but the magic was enough to put the man in the Bastille, and the added criminal charge enough to transmute the sentence to death. His family had been starving, and so had he; the telekinesis had failed because the man was too weak to levitate anything farther than a few feet. Unfortunately, this was no defense in the eyes of the court, nor yet in the eyes of the law.

There was no way to win, and he knew it. His colleagues had told him that he was mad to demand the chance to fight it, at the cost of other more lucrative cases. He fought those lucrative cases too, of course, when he had to. In the last few years, he had repaid the family debts left by his disreputable father, gained a reputation as a bright and dedicated advocate, and fought to bring the Robespierre name back to respectability. He was quiet, fastidious, proud, and warmly regarded, though few except his brother and sister could claim to know him very well. But he wanted *this* case, and others like it. He had a vision in his head: of a different France, one whose Commoners could use their magic freely, not to steal to feed their children but for their own education and enlightenment. He could see it more clearly than he could the dirty cobblestones outside.

And so he kept writing, crossing out, and rewriting, trying to find the right words to bring his vision to life. Outside, the shadows deepened, almost swallowing the light of his candle. He pushed his glasses farther up his nose as the paper blurred. He yawned once. He was not aware of falling asleep, and he was never afterward certain if he had.

He was standing in his childhood garden. The house that had once belonged to his family, before their fall, stood tall and graceful across the lawn. It was a dark night, the coldest, darkest part of night, it seemed to him, right before the dawn. And yet a single light burned in the house, on the second floor. The rustle of the wind brought the oversweet scent of decaying roses, and the iron tang of blood.

In one sick moment, he realized where he was—or when. The light was on in his parents' room: they had been awakened by the housemaid. There had been a knock at the door; two men had arrived. And he stood where he had hidden almost twenty years ago, waiting for his life to end.

"No," he said, very quietly. He knew nobody would hear him; he didn't even know whom he was talking to. He said it anyway. "No, not here."

It was then that he saw the figure coming toward him out of the trees. He would never have seen it in the darkness normally, even with his spectacles. But this was not the physical world, and his mind's eye was clear.

"Maximilien Robespierre," the figure said. A male voice, soft and precise. Its owner stopped a few feet away—a tall, slender shadow among shadows in the grass. "This is interesting."

"What is?" Robespierre demanded—angrily, to cover real fear. His heart was racing. This was not a dream, though he'd been here in dreams before. This was magic. "Who are you?"

The figure dismissed the question with a wave of his hand. "We needed to talk. But I wasn't expecting it to be here. Unless...Of course. This was where it happened."

Against his will, Robespierre looked back at the house. Upstairs, the sound of a door bursting open; in the wake of the crash, outlines played against the lit window. His mother, slender and frail, leaping out of bed; two tall men that he knew without seeing bore the red cross of the Knights Templar across their chests. His father's voice was loud, slurred with sleep or drink.

"Who are you? What are you doing here?"

Robespierre wanted to run to them. The back door was unlocked; it led to the inner staircase; he could be in his parents' room in moments. He couldn't move. His limbs were rooted in place by childhood terror. If they came out into the garden...If they found him...

"Whoever you are," Robespierre said to the figure, as calmly as he could, "whatever you're doing, make it stop."

"This is your side of things, I'm afraid, not mine. As I said, I only wanted to talk. I came into your mind—or at least, the place where our minds could meet. I didn't expect it to be quite so vivid. This is your mother's arrest?"

Robespierre didn't answer. Against the lit window, in terrible shadow theater, his mother's arm was gripped by a large hand. She twisted against the table—the white table, at which she had sat only that evening making lace. He had watched, fascinated, as her deft fingers wove a thousand threads together, in and out, leaving something perfect in their wake. The table crashed to the floor.

"I read the records," his visitor said. "The Knights Templar came for her when the neighbors reported a dead bird flying on broken wings outside the grounds. Necromancy. One of the unforgivable magics. She was sentenced, taken to the Bastille, and put to death within weeks. Strange, wasn't it, that after hiding her abilities for so long, she would let a little thing like that destroy her. A dead bird."

"You have no right to talk about her." Robespierre had to speak tightly around the lump constricting his throat. "What do you want?"

The figure seemed not to hear him. "So you were out here, watching from the garden? A strange place to be at this time of night."

"I heard them coming, that was all." It sounded too defensive to his own ears. "I saw the sign on their carriage from my window. I slipped out the back door to hide."

"From a Templar carriage coming up your street in the middle of the night? How perceptive of you. Or paranoid. And you didn't think to wake your parents?"

"I never thought this would happen. It wasn't my fault. I was six years old. I thought— Oh God."

A scream shattered the night: a child's scream. Charlotte, his little sister, woken to their house torn apart. He should have been there with her—he should still go to her now, in whatever memory or dream this was. He couldn't move then, and he couldn't move now. Terror gripped him too tightly. It was his mother's voice that went to her.

"Don't cry, Charlotte." She was breathless, tearful, brave. He didn't need to see her face to know what it looked like. "It's all right. Tell Maximilien it's all right. For God's sake, won't you at least let me say goodbye to them?"

No reply came from her captors. In all the times he had seen this in his memories, he had never once heard the voices of the Knights Templar. They must have spoken. He just couldn't remember.

"Yes," the figure in the dark said. "I understand why you came here."

The front door slammed shut. Memory magnified the sound to the force of a gunshot. His stomach contracted, and he gripped the tree beside him. The garden now was quiet but for Charlotte's cries, and those were spiraling down into whimpering, bewildered misery.

He had gone to her, back then. It had been far too late, and he had been clammy and knotted with fear, but he had at least gone inside then. This was where his nightmares usually ended. Yet here he stood, still, with the strange figure beside him. For a long time, he couldn't speak.

"Who are you?" he repeated at last.

"In light of what I've just seen," the figure said, "I would say that I'm someone who can help you out of the bushes. But it doesn't do to get too metaphorical inside somebody's head. You really have no idea what I am?"

"None at all."

"Then I have you at a disadvantage. I know you very well. I know what happened to your mother. I know that your father abandoned you and your siblings soon after her death and left your family name in poverty and disrepute. I know about your years of schooling, your legal career, your friend Camille Desmoulins and his taste for the revolutionary. I know about your attempts to publish your pamphlets and essays; I've actually read them, unlike most. I know that you want to change France. I've come to make you a proposition."

"And what might that be?"

"I can make people listen to you."

Robespierre actually found a laugh at that. He had very little practice with laughter; it wasn't surprising it came out closer to a choke. "To me? Forgive me, but if you know me as well as you claim, you'll know that nobody listens to me. Nobody ever has."

"Camille Desmoulins did, at university."

"Yes, well." The mention of his old school friend calmed him a little. "Nobody listens to Camille either. The only difference is, it doesn't stop him talking. He wants a revolution."

"So do you. Let's not pretend, Robespierre. I told you, I know you."

"So do I, then. But I don't see how it can be brought about. Perhaps I lack Camille's vision."

"I've read his pamphlets as well. He writes better, but your vision is much further-reaching than his. And he lacks your particular magic."

Any desire to laugh dried up. "What magic? What are you talking about?"

"I told you I knew you, didn't I?" The figure paused, just a beat too long. "You have a strain of mesmerism in your blood. It's dormant at the moment; the Templars noted it at your christening."

"Oh." Robespierre suspected he paused a beat too long as well.

"Oh, that. Yes, it's true; it comes from my father's side, I presume. But—"

"It's dormant. Quite so. But if it were awakened, you could nudge and influence. You're not registered; nobody would suspect, if you were careful and clever, and you are both. You could save the illegal magicians you are so keen to represent, or at least have their sentences reduced to imprisonment rather than death."

"Some would say a life in the Bastille is worse than death."

"Not if France changes. They could be free in a few years. If things go according to plan, they could all be. That is my proposition: I can awaken your mesmerism and fire it to an extent that this country hasn't seen for years. I can give you the strength to free France from its Templars and its Aristocracy and its oppression. The strength to be more than a poor lawyer from Arras. The strength to embody a revolution."

A chill crept up his spine. It was both frightening and exhilarating, like stepping outside on a black, stormy night. "And what would you ask in return?"

"For the moment? Nothing at all."

"Nobody asks for nothing," Robespierre said flatly. "Not these days. If you know my life as well as you claim, you know that since my father left, nobody has ever given me anything except to make better use of me."

"True," the figure acknowledged. "And I do want to use you. But what if I wanted to use you for the good of France? What then?"

The garden was quiet now. Only the sound of Charlotte crying, and it was very faint. The light had gone off at the window.

As it happened, the Temple Church in Rheims had just as difficult a time comprehending the three English travelers as Pitt had predicted. In fact, the Templar in question took one look at them as Monsieur Coustier struggled to explain and decided they were sinister and possibly dangerous. Monsieur Coustier was either unwilling or unable to translate his words to them, but it didn't take them long to work out what *des intrigants* were.

"He thinks we're spies," said Wilberforce. He didn't know whether to laugh or be very worried. His natural inclination was to laugh, but not if he was actually about to be tried for espionage.

"Frankly, I'm insulted for England," Pitt said. "If he thinks our country doesn't have better spies than three hopelessly disorganized twenty-four-year-olds who have blundered into the Temple Church because the wine ran out..."

"It doesn't have better MPs," Eliot pointed out. He was looking distinctly uneasy.

"Is he going to lock us up in prison?" Wilberforce asked.

"It would probably be an improvement on our hotel," Pitt said.

They weren't quite put into cells, though they were held in the waiting room for some hours while the Templar went to report to his superior that he had three Englishmen of very suspicious character, who their grocer claimed were very important gentlemen but who were staying in wretched lodgings with no attendants and no papers. By this time, Eliot was convinced they were all going to be locked up, Wilberforce was inclined to agree, and Pitt was so adamant that they weren't that Wilberforce suspected he thought the same.

But they were young and privileged, and for them the world was still a kind one. As it happened, the Master Templar was a generous man who spoke excellent English. He listened to their explanation and, to their immense relief, accepted it. As a Master Templar, he explained, he was used to believing improbable things; besides, he had been twenty-four once himself. Within a matter of hours, they had moved from their disreputable lodgings to the Master's very comfortable house—a huge improvement for everybody but the fleas.

For the next week, the Master delighted in letting them explore while he provided huge meals, long conversations, and the best wine France could offer. This was, it transpired, somewhat better than what they had been drinking. They went to the theater every night, understood less than one word in three of the plays, and spun their own increasingly nonsensical versions of the plots as they walked back under the stars.

And then, at last, they were invited to Fontainebleau, in order to be introduced at court.

Marie Antoinette, queen of France, was a highly accomplished fire-mage. The marriage, it was rumored, had been made to bring magical blood back into the royal line when it became plain that Louis XVI had inherited none of his own. She was also exquisitely beautiful, or, at least, knew how to use her ornate gowns, elaborate hairstyles, and impish smile to seem so. Word had reached her of their adventures with grocers and Knights Templar before they were introduced, and she plainly found them hilarious.

"I'm afraid you'll find the company here far less exotic," she said, laughing, in heavily accented English. "Only royals and Aristocrats, none of them at all interesting."

This, of course, was not true. Royal courts throughout Europe were always riots of magic: the royal families were bred for the strongest Inheritances and the most magical bloodlines, and the favorites and hangers-on tended to be Aristocrats with at least a modicum of magical skill. George III in England was a very powerful shadowmancer, but he preferred to keep magic strictly regimented even among the royal family. His court was thick with unwoven spells. The court at Fontainebleau, by contrast, glittered with it. Both king and queen were fascinated by obscure bloodlines and magical practices, and it was not uncommon to see fireworks spark suddenly in the banquet hall or illusions clatter through the dining tables as though they were back at Cambridge amid a mess of rowdy Aristocratic undergraduates. Wilberforce had a fascinating conversation one night with a druid, the first he had ever met, and Eliot swore he had seen a unicorn in the surrounding forest. It led Wilberforce to assume that magic was far less restricted in France than in England as a whole, though Pitt disputed that as the three of them sat out on one of the balconies late one night.

"It's really only that the Aristocracy use their magic more freely here," he said. "Or at least, so I understand it. Their Commoners are still braceleted; the Temple Church operates by the same code; their Commoners caught using magic are locked in the Bastille as ours are in the Tower. I think the penalties are worse, actually. They give life sentences for unregistered magic here. And their bracelets burn hotter than ours when they detect magic stirring in the blood: it's a punitive measure, rather than a warning."

"It was very mundane in Rheims before we fell in with the Templars," Eliot agreed. "Mundane, and a little grim, did you notice? Being here is like being in another world entirely. Everyone seems to be an Aristocrat and a magician. I'm not entirely sure how it is that we're invited. I must admit, I feel rather like somebody's going to find me out."

"We all do, I think," Wilberforce agreed. "Well, perhaps not you, Pitt, since you're at least an Aristocrat."

"In name only," Pitt pointed out, almost defensively. "I was born a Commoner. My father wasn't titled until I was seven."

"Well, yes, Pitt," Eliot said. "But before that, he was prime minister."

It was actually something of a surprise to Wilberforce to realize how famous Pitt already was in France; partly, as Eliot said, for his parentage, but also for his skills, youth, and promise in office. There were moments when Wilberforce caught sight of him surrounded by the wealthy and the powerful and suddenly felt he couldn't possibly have just spent a week in a wretched hotel drinking cheap wine with him.

Eliot still did not know of the night of the shadow. Wilberforce was not quite sure why, now that the danger had passed; he knew only that it felt like Pitt's secret to keep or reveal, and as Pitt had said nothing about it, neither had he. He tried to dismiss it from his mind, and in their new surroundings it wasn't difficult. Already, it seemed like a dream. But every so often he thought about it, and wondered.

* * *

A few weeks later, Wilberforce hurried up the stairs to their rooms, hot and dusty after a long walk through the surrounding forest. Pitt had returned earlier that afternoon with most of the party, but Wilberforce and Eliot had stayed on with the rest to walk what they were told was a very short loop in the trail. It had been longer than expected, and now he was cheerfully worn-out and facing the possibility of being late for dinner. They were all running out of good clothes to change into after so long spent at court, and Eliot had cursed the two of them for being such vastly different sizes that there was no possibility of swapping coats and shirts around.

Pitt's door was ajar, so Wilberforce paused to rap his knuckles briskly on the wall panel alongside it.

"Come in," came the absent reply.

Wilberforce duly stuck his head through the door. "I just thought I'd tell you we were back," he said. "You missed the most incredible flowers—"

He paused, seeing that his friend wasn't listening. Pitt was standing by the window overlooking the forests, studying a letter that he held tight in his hand. His face was unreadable, as it had not been all summer.

Wilberforce remembered the clatter of hooves against the courtyard cobblestones as he'd come in. "Has that come from England?"

Pitt nodded slowly, without looking up. "It requests that I return immediately. They're forming a new government."

Wilberforce entered the room and closed the door behind him instinctively. "When?"

"Now. Immediately. Which will probably mean after a few months of pitched battle, but things are set in motion."

"And does it say...?" He trailed off, not sure how far he could go.

"Not in so many words," Pitt said. "But yes. It does."

For a second, Wilberforce wondered if he could have misunderstood what his friend had meant. He knew he hadn't.

"The king wants you to head the government."

"It's far from settled."

"But it's what he wants." His friend didn't answer, which was all the answer he needed. He shook his head in wonderment and tried to decide if he felt any trace of jealousy. A little, perhaps, though not for the reasons some might think. He had no desire for power, and certainly no desire to head the British government. But he knew that for Pitt, government wasn't about power, or not solely. Pitt believed in serving the country—deeply, truly, to an extent Wilberforce had never seen in anyone else. This, to him, wasn't an offer of a position, but a calling. If Wilberforce was jealous of anything, it was that he had never found that kind of calling himself.

"Are you going to accept?" he asked.

"I never said that I wanted it," Pitt said, a little defensively. "I said that—"

"I know, that you had no great desire to come into the government in the first place, and you have no great reluctance to go out whenever the public were disposed to dismiss you from their service. I was there. It was excellent. I took notes."

"I turned it down the first time the king suggested it to me."

"You were twenty-three. Far too young. You're a whole year older now."

"I truly did mean it."

"I never meant to imply you didn't," Wilberforce said, immediately dropping his light tone. He'd meant to make things less solemn, but that had been foolish. Of course they were solemn. "I believed you. I think everyone believed you. But you did want it to happen, at some point. In the back of your mind, you did go into politics hoping to head the government someday. Of course you did."

"I suppose." He shook his head. "Yes. Of course I did. I just didn't expect it to be now."

"I don't think anyone could have reasonably expected that," Wilberforce agreed. "But apparently it *is* now. Or it could be, if you accept. Are you going to accept?"

"Do you think I should?"

It wasn't spoken with any particular import, but Wilberforce realized at once that it was an important question, and unexpectedly, his answer would be very important in turn. This, after all, was what they had been avoiding as they'd explored and laughed and reveled in being young idiots submerged in a foreign country. All this time, it had been waiting for them on the other side of summer.

"It will be difficult," Wilberforce said, and knew he was stalling. Nevertheless, what he was saying was true. "Almost impossible. Even with the support of the king, you'll be fighting for the support of a hopelessly deadlocked House; nobody's been able to hold the office for more than a few months at a time recently. Fox and his people will try to destroy you—politically, mentally, even physically. Nobody your age has ever done anything like this."

"I know," Pitt said. "But I didn't ask if you thought I could. I want to know, honestly, if you think I should try."

Wilberforce considered his friend carefully. It was something he had done often in the early days of their acquaintance, when he had been trying to learn about the real person hiding beneath the proud, reserved surface Pitt was apt to present to the world. He didn't bother so often now: after years of friendship, laughter, politics, countryside holidays, evenings at the club, and long, serious conversations that stretched across entire nights, he thought he knew that person as well as anyone. Certainly the reverse was true. Yet right now, he was struck by the sense that he was seeing something that waited even further beneath the surface. He wasn't sure what it was, except that it was potentially extraordinary.

None of that, though, was something that could be put into easy words.

"I think you will do it," Wilberforce said finally, and simply. "And I think, from what I know of your abilities, your character, and your principles, that you will be very well suited to it."

He could have said more, but from the quick, self-conscious smile that flitted over his friend's face, he knew that, spoken honestly, was all he had hoped to hear.

"Thank you," Pitt said. He shook his head briskly and looked out the window at the forests of Fontainebleau as if surprised not to see the grimy pavements of London. "I need to get back to Westminster."

"We'll return with you, obviously," Wilberforce said. "I'll inform Eliot."

"That's very kind of you. I wish I could urge you to stay on and see out the end of the holiday, but the truth is, you'll probably be needed back in London too—by me, if not by the country at large." Pitt's eyes had already regained their good humor. "It's a shame they couldn't have waited until November. This was rapidly becoming the greatest summer in living memory."

"It still is, as far as I'm concerned. We'll have to do it again, but with better letters of introduction."

"Absolutely. Next time, we might be able to connect ourselves with a peddler, or a chimney sweep."

"Or an ancient Roman," Wilberforce said with a laugh, and left quickly to find Eliot. Both the corridor and the day outside were the same as they had been a moment ago, but he couldn't shake the feeling that from now on everything was going to change.

The following day, Wilberforce, Pitt, and Eliot began their journey back to England. On the same morning, on the second floor of the house he shared with his siblings in Arras, Robespierre prepared to save a life.

He rose at six, as usual. As usual, he worked for two hours as the sun rose, until the barber arrived to dress and powder his hair. He dressed quietly, meticulously, as usual; he ate a very light breakfast of bread, cheese, and coffee, as usual, then returned to his room to work for another hour or so until it was time to go to the courts. He was so deep in thought that he almost forgot to say good morning to Charlotte at breakfast, and then forgot he had done so by the time he came to leave for work, but this, too, was usual. She rolled her eyes and had no idea of the anticipation tightening his nerves.

"I don't suppose you have any idea what you want for dinner

tonight?" she asked at the door. In the years since the night their mother was taken, she had grown into a strong-minded, sharp-tongued young woman. Her dark eyes had a way of constantly measuring up his everyday self against her ideal of him; finding him wanting was, paradoxically, the way she expressed her utter faith in what he could be. He understood this, and when he remembered, he did what he could to make the gap between everyday and ideal as small as possible. But today this simply wouldn't work. It was a bright, clear morning, and he couldn't fathom anything as far away as dinner.

"I have no idea," he said. They both knew he would eat very little in any case. His stomach was always still in knots after the courthouse. Today it would be more so. "Honestly, Charlotte, whatever you want. I think I might be back late this evening, actually."

The courts at Arras were beginning to fill as Robespierre made his way across the cobbled courtyard. He managed to return the greetings of the other advocates with nods and tight-lipped smiles, and to breathe. To everyone else, this was a fairly usual case of a man caught in an act of illegal magic. Nobody was surprised to see Robespierre defend him—it was exactly the kind of case he was known for. Nobody had any reason to suspect anything was about to happen, and they would not notice when it did.

Still, right until the end, he wasn't sure he would be able to do it. It would be breaking the law—a corrupt law, but even so. He was still a child in a garden, hiding in the thorns while children screamed. He disgusted himself. Excuses and recriminations chased each other around his head until he heard the judge call his case, and then he stood and broke the law. There was really nothing else he could do.

He had practiced once or twice in the privacy of his own rooms, alone; this was the first time he had dared reach for the full force of his mesmerism in public. His own newly awakened magic flickered at his touch, gentle and pliable. A second later, his benefactor's magic joined his, and it caught fire. The intensity of it was beyond anything he had expected. It scorched in his veins and throbbed in his heart. His breath caught; he adjusted his spectacles, certain it must be visible in his eyes. When he spoke, his voice no longer seemed his own.

"Abel Perrault is here because he attempted to use illegal telekinesis to steal a loaf of bread for his family." He was speaking to the judge, but he felt mesmerism spill out across the entire room. "Given the evidence of illegal magic, I cannot ask you to acquit the prisoner. The law only allows for two possibilities: the Bastille, or the hangman's noose. Of those, I hope you will consider the former. But I hope you will also consider the *unfairness* of the case against the prisoner—if not as an official representative of this country, then as one of her citizens, who should care about her people. And, having considered this, although I cannot *ask* you to acquit the prisoner, I hope that you *will*."

It was nothing he wouldn't have said already. Nobody watching could have pinpointed any difference in him. He was polite, intelligent, painfully precise. He drew facts and arguments from his mind as a biologist might draw out specimens from a box, one at a time, to be flayed open with a scalpel. His voice was still too weak and too quiet. But the room listened. He could feel it listening as he never had before.

"Think of this," he said in the end. "Monsieur Perrault committed an act of illegal magic because he was starving. He is charged with this, and with theft. If current laws were not so unfair, the magic would not be a crime. But more to the point, if magic laws were not so unfair, there would have been no need for the theft. Monsieur Perrault's only son is a weather-mage. If he had been allowed to use his magic, the family crops would not have failed this spring through want of rain. They would have had food to sell at the market, and still more to feed themselves. They could have bought bread. Monsieur Perrault would not be facing the hangman's noose. And, what's more, Monsieur Perrault's youngest daughter, who starved to death in her crib last month, might still be alive."

He sat down to scattered applause. The mesmerism left a rush of cold in its wake; he was trembling from the chill as well as nervous tension. He felt sick, if he were honest, and not at all like a revolutionary. Yet when he heard the verdict come back, acquitting the prisoner of all charges, he knew that he was exactly what he needed to be. The world had shifted under his words. In that moment, like the parting of a veil, he could see the France around him resemble the one in his head: the one that was united, and equal, and free.

Jamaica

Summer 1783

There were bands of escaped slaves in the hills around Fina's plantation. When Fina had first heard the overseers grumble about them, a few months after her arrival, she had thought it was impossible. She and everyone she knew were forced to take the bitter gold alchemical compound twice a day, morning and evening; her days and nights were spent screaming in her own head and never being heard. Escape was not even a dream, much less a possibility. She believed the overseers had made the brigands up to give themselves another reason to hate the slaves.

But it was true, she came to learn in snatches. There were ways to escape, though none of them were for her. Many other plantations weren't quite as paranoid as hers: the slaves there were given the compound only in the morning, to save costs, so by night they were free to move and talk. Some slaves were left unbound altogether. Some were even freed on purpose by their owners as a reward for service, and of those some might choose the life of a brigand in the woods instead of a so-called respectable one among their former captors.

Many more, though, had been freed by the brigands themselves. They came and raided the plantations, at night or in the middle of the day, when the slaves were dispersed across the fields. They burned crops and buildings, disrupted the sugar production, and—most important of all—took away as many of the enslaved as they could. In the woods, the brigands held the rescued men and women down while their bodies fought to return to captivity, until the spell had passed from them and they were free. The chance of one of their raids was one of the great hopes of the slaves' lives.

Fina hoped for them too, but that hope scared her. When she had first been put to work as a child, she had spent her days struggling to move of her own volition. Any movement, anytime at all. It could have been an eyeblink, a twitch of a finger, and it would have been worth months of silent struggle. It never happened. After a year, it had broken her. She stopped fighting; or, rather, her fight turned inward. The energies that had once gone into trying to move were desperately channeled into trying not to think. Many of her early memories had already failed; she willed the rest away. She let her limbs move on command and tried to drift away inside her own head. She tried to become what they pretended to think her, not for their benefit but for hers. At seven, she thought she could cease to be. What hurt most of all was the fact that if she succeeded, nobody would ever be able to tell the difference.

She didn't succeed, of course. As she grew older, she stopped wanting to. In the darkest hours before dawn, when the alchemy was at its lowest ebb, many of the enslaved men and women around her were free enough to whisper to her in the dark, consoling her and urging her not to give in. She didn't know how they knew what was happening to her inside her head when she couldn't speak herself, and at first she refused to listen. But gradually her thoughts had opened to them, as though a wall had been chipped away one pebble at a time. Even though her resistance was never strong enough to whisper back, she learned to hold on to herself: to count the strokes of her machete; to try to remember the words to the songs the others sang at night; to focus on the changing seasons. She found a place that was neither her early hope nor her later despair, and she was too afraid of either to venture outside it. This was her life now. Whether from the spellbinding or from her own early efforts, she could barely remember the time before the ship had swallowed her up. She couldn't remember her old name, or her brother's. Wishing for freedom felt like wishing for childhood to return.

When she was twenty-seven, one of the bands attacked her plantation.

She was out in the fields on that day, laboring to cut the sugarcane that would be collected and taken to the processing plant. The sun was hot overhead, and she was sticky with sweat and throbbing with fatigue. The machete she held was heavy in her hands, and its handle rubbed the blisters between her thumb and forefinger. The overseers called out the commands as they walked their sections of the field. Their voices resonated in her ears when they were close enough, but always over the light mesmeric field that the spell in her blood picked up and obeyed.

"Swing, cut! Swing, cut! Swing, cut!"

A shout cut through the air then: not the overseers' orders, but a high, wild cry. Even through the spellbinding, it raised the hairs on the back of her neck. The overseers' commands cut off abruptly. She kept cutting—the orders didn't need to be continuous to need obeying—but she felt the hold on her lessen. The tang of smoke was in the air.

"Stop still!" her own overseer barked belatedly, and her muscles locked tight. Her gaze was fixed to the ground. Yet the cries were growing louder and multiplying; the ground reverberated with footsteps as the overseers from different sections rushed past.

"It's one of those bloody slave armies," she heard one of them tell another.

Fina's heart began to beat faster. Like the others, she stayed as she had halted, with her machete poised for the next swing, and yet the overseer was gone. The heat of the sun was on her back. Rifle fire and shouts drifted across the field; there must be a battle raging in the distance. For the first time in a long while, her nerves ached with the longing to straighten, just to see what was happening. Who was winning? Were the overseers chasing off the bandits, or was there some chance that one of them might make it to her? She was small, light, and easy to carry. If they saw her there, they might snatch her, even though she'd be less use as a fighter than some of the others. If she could just—

And then she stood up. It happened almost before she was aware of it: suddenly, inexplicably, she was no longer looking at the tight-packed earth and vegetation at her feet, but out across the sugarcane field that she and her fellow slaves were harvesting. The field seemed to go on forever, rows of towering yellow-green plants under a pale, cloudless sky, and human figures were dotted about it like milestones.

Part of it, close to the edges, was on fire. The smoke thickened the air; she tasted the grit of it on her tongue, although it was not close enough to catch in her throat. It was no ordinary flame: it roared and danced unnaturally, rushing in furrows toward the overseers while leaving great swaths of sugarcane untouched. Fire magic.

The overseers were running toward the smoke, pointing their pistols and muskets and stopping every now and then to fire. Other men, black men who looked strong and fierce, fired back. One of the overseers—Harry, who always cracked the whip too hard—fell clutching his arm, and Fina's blood thrilled.

Not all of the band were returning fire. Others ran back for the hills while the gunfire covered their retreat; they ran in pairs, and each pair carried a slave between them. She could tell they were slaves by the way the bodies hung, rigid, between them: one bandit held the shoulders, arms looped under the armpits, and one took up the feet. The escape was swift, practiced, perfect. She imagined them rehearsing the hold in the evenings, in the camps beneath the trees. They would be clustered around the light of a fire, maybe, bold and cheerful, laughing as one stumbled or dropped another. She felt a sudden longing for that life. In that moment, she felt no fear at all.

Take me with you, she pleaded in her head, although there was no way they could reach her, even if they had been able to hear her. All the hope and defiance she'd ever suppressed rose to the surface. *Please. I'm right here; I can see you. See me standing, and come back for me.*

But they were already going, the last of the fighters retreating behind the carriers into the trees. Slaves ran to smother the fire; obviously, the overseers were giving orders once more. The last of the band disappeared. She nearly sobbed with frustration.

She heard the crack of a whip and remembered suddenly where she was. At once, she lowered her head and bent back over her work. The ground at her feet once more filled her entire vision. No more sky, no more flames, no more fighting. It was over.

"Swing, cut," came the call, layered with mesmerism, and without her will her aching muscles took up the machete and swung at the sugarcane.

"Bastards," she heard a rough voice say, sounding out of breath, and realized that two of the overseers were very close. "There are more of them every year, you know. We need more soldiers here. Follow them back to their hideout and finish them off."

"They'd never get them in those hills," the other scoffed. "They know them like the back of their ugly hands. Plus more than half of them are magicians."

One of the great benefits of spellbinding to the plantation owners was that it dulled a slave's magic to nothing. One of the great dangers of escaped slaves was that their magic returned with the use of their limbs, and when it did, they tended to use it.

"That fire there—that was a fire-mage's doing," the first overseer said. "And they say the leader's a mesmer."

"They'll never amount to anything. A few slaves and some crops—the master won't be happy, but it's not worth a war."

She still listened to them, but without much interest. Now that the crush of disappointment was settling, something else was sinking in.

She'd straightened on her own. For the first time in three years, her limbs had moved and drawn themselves up of her own accord, obeying some impulse of her will that she had sent them without ever thinking it could be received. She tried again, but the spell once more held her tightly; her body continued its work swinging its machete back and forth. Whatever had happened, it had already passed. It had only been for a moment.

It had only been for a moment. But for that moment, she'd been free.

London

December 1785

It was one o'clock in the morning, and Pitt was speaking in the House of Commoners. This was far from an unfamiliar sight, despite the best efforts of the opposition to make it one. It was a special occasion only to Pitt, because the bill that he was introducing happened to be one that he and Wilberforce had been thinking over for a very long time—since, in fact, he had defended John Terrell on charges of illegal magic and found the case complicated by the issue of self-defense. Commoner magicians were allowed to use magic to defend themselves, the law determined, but not to defend others. As a lawyer, he had managed to circumnavigate the issue. Now, as prime minister, he was determined to knock it down.

"This country decided a long time ago that we could not expect anyone, Commoner or Aristocrat, to find themselves under threat and not act to save their own lives, even if that necessitates illegal magic." He raised his voice effortlessly over the shouts from the other side of the House. "If we cannot expect magicians to refrain from using magic in the defense of their own lives, how can we possibly expect them to refrain from doing so in the defense of those they love?"

"Mr. Speaker, if we start accepting excuses for illegal magic, as the honorable gentleman suggests," someone called back from the opposition benches, "might that not see a relaxation of other laws surrounding Commoner magic? Might bracelets not become a mere formality, and explosions of magic on the streets a common sight?"

"I really couldn't speak to that," Pitt said dryly, "without indulging in illegal divination." He carried on over the titters from his own cabinet. "If the honorable gentleman means to ask whether such outcomes would be *inevitable* given the passing of this motion, then my answer is no, of course not: the relaxation of any one law does not lead to the relaxation of others unless this House deems it necessary and appropriate. That is how law and government work. We thankfully have yet to see regular explosions of any kind on the streets. What we could stand to see, now and always, is more compassion for Commoner magicians who try to obey the law, and less of the courts' time wasted in pointless trials that result at best in undue distress and wasted resources, and at worst in families torn apart and livelihoods ruined."

He sat down at last, on a crest of exhilaration. The walls were striking a low, achingly clear vibrato; it was one of those moments, which came so frequently in the House and so rarely anywhere else, when he felt completely and utterly himself. His speech had worked. He knew it had, even before the final votes were announced and the bill was found to have passed by a very respectable margin. The words had been right, the room had resonated, and the law had changed.

"Well, that went extremely well," Henry Dundas said to Pitt as the House collapsed around them into a rumble of footsteps and shuffle of papers. The wily middle-aged Scotsman had been one of the masterminds behind Pitt's appointment. Pitt had been wary of him the first time they had met, but as it happened they were perfectly suited both politically and conversationally, and they had fallen into the habit of staying up late into the night planning the next day's maneuvers and drinking what were staggering amounts of wine even by Pitt's standards. Dundas had learned drinking, arguing, and strategizing at the Scottish law courts and was a force to be reckoned with at all three. "We'll have a strong majority this year, if I'm not mistaken."

"I wouldn't be too sanguine about that," Pitt said. He was trying to be calm and collected in the still-public gaze of the House, as he felt a prime minister should be; as he had been practicing this since he was an excruciatingly awkward fourteen-year-old at Cambridge, he was very good at it. Inside, though, he was exultant. "This was a humanitarian issue. Fox had no objections. After Christmas, we'll have him to contend with."

"And he'll have you to contend with," Dundas returned. "I'm looking forward to it."

Pitt let himself smile, just for a moment. "So am I."

In the year and a half since the king had appointed Pitt head of the new government, relations between Charles Fox and himself had gone from guarded courtesy to outright war. The older politician was easily Pitt's equal in rhetoric, and almost comically his opposite in person: plump, vehement, expansive, legendary for his excesses in gambling, wine, and womanizing. The two of them had grown up, ten years apart, in the shadow of the famous political rivalry between their fathers. Now, history was set to repeat itself with a vengeance. More than once in the early days, it had seemed as though Fox would force him from office before the election even took place.

Pitt had refused to back down then, as he had refused to back down through one of the most cutthroat elections in the history of English politics, and he had won. His reward was that since then, he had debated, planned, argued, budgeted, considered, calculated, and attended meeting after sitting after meeting almost without a day's respite, sometimes it seemed without an hour's. His head was a constant storm of ideas, and they tumbled over each other to be put into the world.

When he had been proclaimed head of the new government in the House of Commoners, the opposition had burst into laughter. They weren't laughing now.

Eliot caught up with him as he left the House and stepped out into the crisp night air. The stars overhead had the crystalline brightness of shards of ice.

"Are you still joining Harriot and me for breakfast tomorrow?" Eliot asked. "I know you said that if you had time—"

"I don't think I do, unfortunately," Pitt said, with genuine regret. He felt the last of his public reserve fall from him as he turned to face his friend—now, as of a few months ago, his brother-in-law. Eliot had, after months of dithering, finally done what everyone had predicted and married Pitt's elder sister, Lady Harriot. It was an excellent match, in every way that mattered: Harriot was, as Pitt had told Eliot, really far too clever and beautiful for her new husband but didn't seem to realize it, and the two of them were hopelessly in love. The only one not happy had been Eliot's father, who had wanted his son to marry into a wealthy family with a title more than a generation old. Fortunately, the fact that Eliot's new position in Pitt's government brought with it a title of its own and a decent salary had quieted his protests.

"It's because you won't wake up in time for breakfast tomorrow, isn't it?" Eliot answered him knowingly.

"In practice, that's very possible. In theory, it's because I'm still hoping to actually see the country house I bought during the recess before Christmas. The plan is to wrap up all my London business tomorrow and then try to go out to Kent the day after. I'm already being optimistic with that plan, given how many things I have left to do. If I actually try to eat as well..."

He was only half-joking at the last, but Eliot laughed. "Oh well, never mind. It's in my best interest, since we're planning to come spend Christmas out at your house too, and we can't in good conscience if you're not there."

"I don't see why not. I used to go out to Wilberforce's country house all the time when he wasn't there. He thought I was quite mad, but plenty of people think that now for far stupider reasons."

Eliot smiled, then hesitated. "Wilberforce wasn't here this evening."

"No. He's been unusually reclusive lately, hasn't he? I sent him a note to remind him this was up for a vote tonight, but he must have missed it." He belatedly caught Eliot's tone. "Why? Is something wrong?"

"Not exactly wrong," Eliot said, which deepened Pitt's apprehension to actual concern. "It's only that a few of us have received similar letters from him: Smith and Arden yesterday, and I myself this morning. We were sure he would have written to you too."

"He may have, actually. I haven't had the chance to read the post this evening—yesterday evening now, rather. What do the letters say?"

"I think I'd better let him tell you himself," Eliot said.

The library at Lauriston House was a little small for Wilberforce's liking, and in summer it missed a good deal of afternoon sun thanks to an inconveniently placed oak tree. In winter, however, the crackling fire warmed it beautifully, and the worn armchairs were like open arms offering refuge from the cold outside. Since Wilberforce had entered Parliament it had seen its share of joyous, idiotic parties, when a host of unruly young MPs had filled it with games and pranks and too much wine; it had seen quieter evenings, too, when he and Pitt and Eliot had read by the fire or spun threads of nonsense as the skies lightened into dawn. Lately, when Wilberforce had been alone in the room, it had seemed filled with the ghosts of those evenings; he had seen them as a succession of steadily older versions of himself and his friends, bursting through the door and throwing themselves on the window seat. It had been comforting in a way; in another, like everything else, it had twisted his stomach with guilt at time misused.

Pitt followed Wilberforce into the room somewhat more sedately this time than he had in those days, but that was out of respect for the conversation ahead rather than any innate maturing: his friend had changed very little since he had taken power, despite the added pressures and cares. From the frown that had crossed Pitt's face as they'd greeted each other, Wilberforce suspected he himself was not looking quite so young and vital. He had lost a good deal of weight in the last few weeks, and though he didn't think his health had suffered, he was starting to feel the difference as winter sank in its claws.

"Sit down and warm up," Wilberforce invited, pulling out a chair unnecessarily. "I've been hiding in here all morning. It must have been icy getting here."

"Both roads and carriage," Pitt confirmed. He sighed a little as the warmth of the fire reached him. "Much better."

"Tea?"

"Better still." His eyes took in the room with obvious pleasure. "I've missed this place. How long has it been since I visited?"

"Here? Weeks, I think. Months. You used to be out here almost every day. How long do you have now?"

"All morning, if we need it. I'd already arranged to go out to Holwood this week; I've rearranged to stop here on the way."

Wilberforce felt a stab of guilt, not so much at disrupting the smooth running of the country as at the realization of the concern he was causing. "It was very kind of you."

"It was very important."

"Still. I know you've been impossibly busy lately."

"Not *impossibly*; I'd say improbably, if that. I still haven't pushed through a fraction of what I meant to. It's a good thing I started young; it's going to take the rest of my life. We *did* manage to pass the bill allowing for defense of others in the case of unregistered magic, by the way."

He said it without reproach, but Wilberforce caught his breath in horror. "I completely forgot! That went through on Friday, wasn't it? I'm so sorry. I had so much to say about it too."

"There was no need. It was a comfortable victory; your vote wasn't required. Thank you, Richard," he added to the footman as he was handed a cup of tea.

"I'm sorry," Wilberforce repeated. "I just—I haven't been myself lately."

And there it was. By silent agreement, they sat without speaking as Richard retreated. Despite the easiness between them, Wilberforce couldn't quell his anxiety, and he was sure Pitt felt the same. There was too great a chance that everything could change once again.

"So," Pitt said, settling back in the chair. "Reading between the lines of your letter, I couldn't help but form the idea that you've been having a rather more difficult time than any of us realized."

Wilberforce, who had been preparing himself for ideological confrontation, was thrown off guard by a rush of gratitude. He should have known his friend better.

"I didn't want any of you to realize," he said. "You all have problems of your own—especially you. And it seemed too personal a thing to discuss with anybody. Or perhaps I didn't know clearly enough what I was feeling to let myself discuss it." He shook his head. "It's still difficult to explain. I told you about my brush with Methodism when I was twelve, didn't I? I think not long after we met."

"I remember. Your mother sent you on a course of strict hedonism. I thought you said it worked."

Despite everything, he smiled. "You say that exactly as if it were a childhood disease I'd managed to get rid of."

"I don't mean it to," Pitt said, with a wry smile of his own. "I apologize. But this is a little outside my usual vocabulary."

"I understand. You're quite right, really; it did work, for a while. I still don't think I'd have been a good Methodist—I do believe, as you said when I told you, that you need to know the world to do any good in it. But it stopped working a long time ago. Parliament kept working a little longer, particularly helping you. It still isn't enough."

"Enough for what?"

He had asked himself the same question many times, yet still couldn't put his answer into the right words. Perhaps it didn't matter. "For me. For the world. For God, especially. My thoughts and studies led me to believe that I had misused my entire life until this point, and that I needed to be reconciled with God in ways that seemed continually to elude me."

"I cannot imagine any thoughts or studies that would tell *you*, of all people, that you had been doing something wrong. The rest of us would have some excuse. I drink too much, never answer letters, and make sarcastic remarks about the opposition. Eliot panics and falls in love with unsuitable women, sometimes simultaneously. You never so much as cheat at cards."

"Everyone does things that are wrong, but that wasn't really the point. It was that I wasn't doing anything *right*. What I read told me, quite simply, that living for my own enjoyment and my own public career was not enough, that if the religion of the Church of England was indeed true, then it was the most important thing there was, and it required all of me. I tried not to believe this, and it was impossible, and so I believed it, and that was harder still. I hope the worst is over now—I think it is, if I can get on the right path."

"I'm sorry I didn't know," Pitt said. He looked troubled, and Wilberforce wondered if he had glimpsed something of the hours of anguished introspection that had made up his recent days and nights. He didn't think so—such things were completely outside Pitt's character—but he had learned not to underestimate his friend. "I can't flatter myself that I would have been of any assistance whatsoever, but you needn't have gone through that alone."

"I did need to," Wilberforce assured him. "It helped. That's why I want to remove myself as much as possible from company and politics for a while, at least until I can face them with a quieter conscience and a soul better ready for God."

"I won't insist that you have nothing in your soul that anyone could possibly find fault with," Pitt said carefully, "because you clearly feel otherwise, and I can't claim superior knowledge of God. I'd like to ask, though, what exactly you intend to do. You've said you still intend to be part of the world, which I must admit is a relief to me, but your letter mentioned leading a very different life, commencing with a period of retirement. It didn't explain the degree or the duration of this retirement; it didn't explain how the future of your life is to be directed, when you think the same privacy no longer necessary; and it didn't explain what idea you've formed of the duties which you are from this time to practice. I'm sure you understand my concern."

Wilberforce's smile was genuine this time. "You do like things to be outlined and quantified, don't you?"

"I've found that sooner or later they have to be."

"I'm sure you're right. But those are all questions I'm to some degree struggling to answer for myself." He paused. "Are you concerned for my political support?"

The question came out with an edge he hadn't intended, but Pitt didn't take offense. To him, perhaps, it was reasonable and obvious. "Primarily, I'm concerned for your happiness. But I can't deny that I'd miss you in the House of Commoners if you left altogether—I'd miss your company in every other respect too, if you honestly mean to retire from society, and I think you're far too well loved in general to be allowed that luxury. There would be riots at half the clubs in London. If you're referring to any public conduct to which your opinions may lead you..." He thought for a moment, then sighed. "Obviously, few things could go nearer my heart than to find myself differing from you on any great principle. I trust and believe that it is a circumstance which can hardly occur."

"But if it *should* occur?"

"If it ever should," Pitt said firmly, "it's impossible that it should shake the sentiments of affection and friendship which I bear toward you. They are sentiments engraved on my heart and will never be effaced or weakened."

Wilberforce smiled again at that. "I hope you believe that I feel the same, and that it comes as a great relief to me to hear you say so. I have no wish to lose my friends."

"But you *do* have a wish to isolate yourself from them, by your own account."

"You think me foolish."

"I would be the last person in England to think you that, and I certainly don't mean to imply it. I do, however, worry that you are deluding yourself into principles which have the tendency to render your virtues and your talents useless both to yourself and mankind."

"You mean by no longer speaking in the House of Commoners."

"That, certainly. You're a very good speaker; you have the greatest natural eloquence I've ever heard. But even more, by withdrawing from society. Society is where you thrive. I don't mean that in the fashionable sense. You have a gift for seeing people at their best, and for bringing out the best and most joyful in them. I've never seen anybody who can forge friendships as quickly and as deeply as you. That's a far rarer talent than good public speaking. To be honest, I've always envied you for it."

Wilberforce was not quite sure what to say to that. He had never thought of himself in quite those terms before. He had never realized that Pitt had.

"Thank you," he said. "I really do think, though, that I can be of more use elsewhere. Somewhere where I can do God's work, not only my own."

"And you have some idea where that might be?"

"I think I may be beginning to," he conceded. "That time in France...These past few months, I've been thinking back to the moment when the shadow dispersed and everything seemed to be right again. I felt very close to something meaningful on that night. I feel it's something that would be worth my life."

Pitt nodded slowly. "You mean to become a Templar."

"Perhaps." He tried not to flush with embarrassment. "In time. If I can ever make myself worthy. I suppose...I want to vanquish evil. I don't think, even now, I quite understand what evil is, but I know what it felt like when it passed."

"You are aware that your eyesight is terrible, aren't you? When we were in Rheims, you almost shot me."

"I know," Wilberforce said ruefully. "But if God intends such a life for me, he will guide my hand."

"I don't doubt it."

"As, I can only imagine, he must have guided my hand from quite destroying Britain's political future the last time I held a pistol."

Pitt didn't smile at that, as Wilberforce had intended he should. Instead, he seemed deep in thought. Wilberforce, knowing by experience that something important was forthcoming, sat back in his seat patiently and took another sip from his teacup. It was pleasant in the warmth of the fire, and more pleasant still to be finally speaking aloud what had been oppressing his mind for so many months. Something heavy and constricting had been cut from him, and he was surprised by how much physically lighter his limbs felt. Whatever happened now, he was at least being open again.

It was longer than he had anticipated before his friend looked up with sudden purpose.

"Wilberforce," Pitt said. "I'm going to tell you something that I've never before told anyone. I will not ask you to swear not to divulge it, because you may feel you have to, and I trust your judgment implicitly."

"Of course anything with which you choose to entrust me will be my honor to protect," Wilberforce said immediately. "Anything right, I mean."

"I don't know if you will think this wrong. I hope not. You are, of course, familiar with my family bloodlines to an extent."

"Yes, of course. The Grenville line is pure Commoner, with no manifestations of magic as far back as the records show. The Pitt line is—that is, apart from—"

"It's ordinary Commoner blood also," Pitt supplied as Wilberforce stumbled, "apart from a strain of magic that goes back several hundred years."

"Blood magic," Wilberforce said. "I've heard the rumor."

"And I doubt you heard it by that term. It's far too polite a euphemism for political gossip. You would have heard it called vampirism. And you would have heard that it emerged to a slight extent with my father."

"He had mesmeric abilities, didn't he?" Wilberforce said. Neither of them had talked about their deceased fathers very often, to his memory, but of course he knew about the career of the Earl of Chatham. "He was braceleted until he was awarded his title. But that's nothing unusual, and certainly nothing dangerous. For a person to be deemed an illegal vampire, they would have to meet... certain other requirements."

"I know," Pitt agreed. "I happen to meet them."

Wilberforce didn't say anything at all. Somewhere, he knew, he was feeling great shock, but on the surface of his mind was nothing but cold, numb disbelief.

Blood magic had been illegal throughout Europe for more than two centuries—since, in fact, the end of the Vampire Wars, when rival families of blood magicians had come to power simultaneously in England and France and almost torn Europe apart in their battle over territories. Wilberforce had learned about the wars in boarding school as a period of blood and darkness that had lasted a hundred years: wars where vampire kings drank the blood of their own people and their enemies to increase their powers, where necromancers worked with them to raise armies of the dead with dark arts long since lost, where magic reigned on the battlefields. Finally, the Knights Templar had stepped in. They had not only overthrown the vampire kings, but also eradicated all traces of blood magic from Europe (and it seemed, at least so far, to be a uniquely European strain of magic). It was the start of their absolute authority over policing and regulating uses of magic—an authority that was still respected even after England broke with the rest of the Catholic Church. More important, it was the end of vampirism. Part of the reason that even Aristocrats were required to be tested for magic at birth was so that if an infant showed even the slightest sign of blood magic manifesting, the child could be instantly put to death. It was not something Wilberforce had ever expected to encounter in his lifetime, much less in his house.

"Do you want me to go on?" Pitt asked.

"Please," Wilberforce managed.

Pitt nodded and looked down at the table briefly before speaking again. His voice was as steady as ever, but Wilberforce could see unaccustomed nervousness behind his eyes.

"I was classified ungifted Commoner at birth," he said. "And for most of my childhood, I was. When I was fourteen, as you know, I was sent to study at Cambridge. I was young, but it was thought that I would be able to cope with the work. Within three weeks, I was dangerously ill. It must have been developing for a while, but I was so busy that I didn't notice, or ignored it. I woke up one morning burning with fever that nothing could ease, not even magic, and after a short time my stomach began rejecting anything they tried to feed me. It was generally thought that I would die, and I was removed home in order to do so. The university claimed to have no idea what was wrong, and perhaps they were telling the truth. Perhaps they were trying to protect me. I've obviously never been able to ask."

"I've known people whose abilities didn't manifest until they were quite old," Wilberforce said automatically. "Not violently like that, though. They just developed over time."

"Late manifestations of magic happen more than the Templars will admit—and the tests at birth are useless if the magic hasn't awakened. It's of no consequence with Aristocrats, but the Temple Church doesn't like it when Commoners escape braceleting. In my case, of course, being an Aristocrat wouldn't have saved me. If I'd been born with my particular magic, I would have been killed upon inspection. As it was, I nearly spared them the trouble by dying myself. Blood magic isn't like the kind that your friends manifested. My body remade itself on the way to adulthood, very slowly and very uncomfortably. But in any case, I intended to die. I never had any intention of taking what I needed to survive."

"Which was human blood."

"More or less. I don't know how much you know about blood magic—I only knew a little myself when I was fourteen, and we had it in our family history."

"Very little," Wilberforce said. "I know the vampire kings could control entire countries with their minds. And they never aged once they reached adulthood, and they never died."

"As far as I know, that's true. The drawback is that it requires blood sacrifice. For the magic to work, the magician needs to kill, and take into themselves the lifeblood of others. And it isn't just for magic. The magician—vampire—needs the life of others to live at all. My father's doctor knew this, of course, even if the doctors at Cambridge didn't. He should have had me killed as soon as I arrived home. He didn't."

Pitt paused, waiting for Wilberforce to ask a question, but Wilberforce found he couldn't. He simply looked at him.

After a moment, Pitt went on. "Toward the end of the Vampire Wars, alchemists were experimenting with an elixir that allowed vampires to eat ordinary food instead. It never worked more than partially; afterward, it was made illegal, for fear it would allow the last of the vampires to escape detection without curbing their need for blood. But because I had only a weak strain of blood magic, and because he'd been my doctor from a very young age and he was fond of me, Dr. Addington decided to try it. At first I couldn't keep that down either, and I deteriorated further. I don't remember very much of that, but my parents told me they came very close to forcing him to stop and let me die in peace. But he kept adjusting it, and finally, without warning, it began to work, and it's worked ever since. I still take it, every evening. I've never taken human blood."

Wilberforce took a deep, shuddering breath and let it out again. "Then surely you don't—"

"Fit the classification? Believe me, I do. If the elixir stopped working and I wanted to stay alive, I would need somebody else's life. As I said, that's how blood magic works. It's supposed to make those with my particular Inheritance essentially immortal, which is inconvenient for those who would rather have a normal lifetime without facing the choice between murder and painful death."

"That's why you knew the shadow was there in France," Wilberforce said slowly. "Was that why it was looking at you? Remember, I asked you—?"

"I remember," Pitt said. "It surprised me too. Shadows don't usually notice me in particular. I'm not a shadowmancer, as true vampires are. I do notice them, though, yes. And I notice bloodlines."

"But that's all you have? All the abilities, I mean."

"That and strong mesmerism. I've never used that—well, not since I learned how to repress it."

Wilberforce brushed that off. "But that's a legal ability, for an Aristocrat, which you are. Your father had it too. And you don't need to murder to survive, and of course you wouldn't, even if you did. Surely the Templars wouldn't classify you as illegal? It's not as though you're dangerous."

"I am," Pitt said. "Believe me, even with the alchemy, I am."

"Why?" Wilberforce said. "I know I have no right to ask—"

"You have every right to ask," Pitt corrected him, too calmly. It occurred to Wilberforce too late that Pitt was trying very hard to answer all his questions, and that it must be almost physically painful for him to do so. Pitt didn't like talking about private matters at the best of times; this was very private. It was life and death. "The way it was explained to me, when I was fourteen, was this: vampiric abilities are designed for the domination of others. Sensitivity to bloodlines for their value as energy. Mesmerism to kill more easily, obviously, but more importantly for control, because pure vampires don't only crave blood; they crave power. If I were to use those abilities, I would be trying to turn to my purposes something intended for destruction, and eventually they would destroy me."

"Good God," Wilberforce said. "You must have been terrified."

Pitt looked at him for a second and then laughed. Wilberforce hadn't meant to dissolve the uneasiness between them, but he noticed it dissolve, and smiled himself.

"Well, at the time I assumed I was going to die, so it was a purely hypothetical terror. But yes, in retrospect, there probably isn't a reassuring way to tell someone that if they use the magic they need to survive, they'll become a monster."

"They shouldn't have told you that. You were a *child*. And it isn't true—at least, not more true for you than it is for anyone else. To some extent, we all have the capacity to become monsters."

"To *some* extent," Pitt agreed cautiously. "The capacity is rather greater in an unregistered magician, and certainly in an illegal."

"Why should it be?" Wilberforce said. "They're human beings—you, certainly, are a human being."

"You *are* aware that the Tower of London is full of human beings who have been put there solely for having magical Inheritances that they failed to report?"

"Perhaps that's unfair too," Wilberforce said, and realized that he'd said something important. He was beginning to understand that he'd never, for all the talk he and Pitt had had about magical legislation, really thought about magical Commoners as he should. Nobody in his family had ever inherited magic; those of his Commoner friends who did kept their bracelets hidden and never spoke of them. He didn't know any unregistered magicians.

Except he did, of course. He was sitting right opposite one.

"I don't think the Knights Templar would agree with you," Pitt was answering him. "The cells are almost at capacity at the moment, I believe."

"But they would kill you if they knew about you," Wilberforce said. "They wouldn't lock you up; they would kill you."

"Yes." His voice was quiet. "Yes, they would. And that *did* terrify me at the time, of course. I understand their reasons; I can even agree with them, on principle. But when I was fourteen, I very much did not want to die like that."

"You would still prefer not to, I assume," Wilberforce pointed out. He remembered suddenly why they were having this conversation and felt a sudden and unexpected flash of anger. "Did you tell me this to prevent me becoming one of them? Because you think that if I do, I'll now be forced to kill you?"

"Not at all," Pitt said, slightly surprised. Wilberforce believed him. He'd known his anger was unjustified, but things he'd felt secure in had been greatly shaken, yet again. "I never thought of that. I have every confidence that you would no more support the Knights Templar in something you believe to be wrong than you would support me. If I ever were to meet my death at your hands, I would undoubtedly deserve it."

"Now you're making fun of me."

"Only a little," Pitt said, with a much-needed smile. "In truth, I'm not sure why I told you—except to explain any personal biases I may have against one of my closest friends becoming a Templar, and because I feel you deserve to have the information. Perhaps I shouldn't have. As you point out, it does put you in a difficult position."

"I'm glad you did," Wilberforce said, as sincerely as he could. He wondered briefly why it was so often more difficult to sound sincere when you truly were. The shock was beginning to wear off now, the faint horror was beginning to seem shameful, and what remained was the realization that he had just been honored with a great show of trust. "Eliot doesn't know, I take it?"

"No—not unless Harriot's told him, but I asked her not to. You understand why I couldn't let him know—not when he was about to propose to her and not now that they're married. It's a question of family bloodlines. I couldn't jeopardize her happiness by making him reluctant to marry into our family, or to have her bear his children."

"Eliot would have married your sister anyway," Wilberforce said firmly. "I understand that you want to protect her, but he wouldn't have cared one bit. Nor do I, by the way. Whatever path I decide to follow, of course I won't divulge your secret. God will understand perfectly."

"Will he?"

"Of course," Wilberforce said, surprised. "My dear Pitt, do you really think that anyone, much less a demi-vampire, could retain their reason and their goodness and become first minister of this country before the age of twenty-five had God not intended it? You're meant to be exactly where you are."

"Are you going to talk like this all the time now?"

"Absolutely," Wilberforce said with a straight face. "From now on, I will never speak of anything less serious than Providence and one's immortal soul, and never smile even under the utmost duress. That is what we religious people are like."

"Don't jest. It's exactly what I'm afraid of."

"That is rather ironic coming from you. The last time I dined with you, you wouldn't be silent on the subject of national debt. National debt. At the dinner table."

"At least I came to the dinner table. You sound as though you mean to withdraw from such frivolities entirely."

"Not withdraw entirely. I just want—" Wilberforce sighed. "I don't know what I want. I don't know anything; that was really what I realized all those weeks ago, and what I'm still realizing, every time I have the delusion that I have any answers whatsoever. I don't even have the questions, most of the time. There are flashes of light, that's all, and I'm trying to relearn everything I thought I knew by them. It's hard."

"I've made it harder. I'm sorry for that, for the sake of your immediate well-being, but I can't say that I'm sorry in the long term if it prevents you from making a too-easy decision."

"I won't be argued out of my principles," he warned.

"Of course not. But surely the principles of Christianity are simple, and lead not to meditation only but to action. I suppose if I was trying to tell you anything about the Templars, it's that their thoughts and practices haven't changed greatly in the last three hundred years—longer, probably—without change being forced upon them. They work to ideas of good and evil that are perhaps fundamentally the same as yours, but they rarely challenge their application. You, on the other hand, just said it was unfair that so many unregistered magical Commoners were in the Tower of London. We've been talking for years about magical reform. You can't tell me you wouldn't miss those opportunities to change the world. Isn't that why we entered the House of Commoners?"

"The Templars do act as well," Wilberforce pointed out. "They act against dark magic. And against—" He broke off, catching himself.

"They do," Pitt agreed. "And a lot of what they do is very admirable and necessary. I do wonder, though, if you've ever been to the Tower of London?"

"No," Wilberforce said. "No, I have not."

"You may want to pay it a visit."

The first thing that hit him was the smell. With his eyes effectively blind, it seemed a living thing rushing out at him from the darkness:

a sour tang of sweat and vomit, a more pungent undertone of excrement. Wilberforce coughed involuntarily and felt bile rise in his throat.

"What is that?" he asked.

"The Tower of London," the Templar answered him. "Or rather, the prison wing."

There was always at least one Templar stationed at the Tower of London; it was usually a fairly strong magician, in case of emergencies. It was an unpleasant job, Wilberforce knew, so the position was shared and rotated as often as possible. Fortunately, the man on duty this month was a friend of Wilberforce's from Cambridge. Frederick Holt had been a year above him, an Aristocrat reading magical theory and science, and had taken orders shortly after his graduation. He had grown more serious in the years since, but he was still the good-tempered, soft-faced young man who loved cats and had eaten enormous quantities of the Yorkshire pie Wilberforce had always had sent from home. When Wilberforce had written to him requesting a visit to the Tower, even if it wasn't strictly aboveboard, Holt had been easy to persuade.

"Is it always like this?" Wilberforce asked as he struggled not to breathe too deeply.

"Once a week they throw some water on the floor to keep it from being too bad," Templar Holt said. "That was this morning, actually. Be careful you don't slip in the dark. Oh, and do watch the doors. They're charmed to give a pretty nasty jolt if you touch them without a key, and you don't have one."

The inner walls of the corridor were dimly lit by torches burning in brackets, as well as by the lantern Holt carried. Wilberforce could make out the cell doors on the other wall, albeit hazily; more important, though, he could hear the calls and jeers coming from within the cells as the lantern threw shadows on the bars.

They wouldn't all be Commoners, Wilberforce knew. The Tower of London was generally reserved for magical criminals, like the far more notorious Bastille in France. There were magical crimes that could be perpetrated by Aristocrats: dark magic, illegal summonings, death curses. Those were what he had primarily been imagining when he had turned his thoughts to the Templars, remembering the night in France. He hadn't realized, then, how common conviction for unregistered magic was; as all children were tested at birth, it should have been nearly impossible to commit. In fact, as he had found out in the weeks since Pitt's visit, unregistered magic was the second-most-common reason for Templar arrests, after illegal magic from braceleted Commoners. Either something was very wrong with the tests or, as Pitt had suggested, late manifestations were far more common than anyone admitted. The prisoners he was passing weren't all Commoners, but most of them were.

"This is the one you were asking after," Holt said as he stopped at one door. "Low-level telekinetic, failure to report. You say Pitt knew him?"

"I'm not sure he ever met him, as such," Wilberforce conceded. "Their paths crossed, a long time ago. May I go in?"

"He's not dangerous," Holt said. "But stay near the door. I'll unlock it."

The cell, when Wilberforce entered, was gray with light that came from a slat near the ceiling, from which a faint draft could be felt. Apart from this draft, the space was airless, and the musty smells hung like a fog in the air. John Terrell was a large man, Wilberforce thought, but he seemed withered by the space around him. His hair and beard were unkempt, and his shirt was filthy and threadbare: prisoners, Wilberforce knew, were provided with nothing that they did not pay for themselves, and plainly Mr. Terrell could not afford very much. There was a lump of bedding in one corner, as well as an empty plate and mug, but nothing else.

"Mr. Terrell?" Wilberforce said. "I came to see you. I'm a friend of... well, one of your advocates. From your trial."

He wondered if Mr. Terrell knew that the junior advocate for his defense had since become prime minister of Great Britain. The man stared at him uncomprehendingly, squinting through his matted fringe of hair.

"You were an unregistered magician," Wilberforce went on after a pause. "My friend told me about you: how you were sentenced on failure to report alone. It was quite a landmark case. I wanted to talk to you about... what that was like. Not the case, I mean, but—before you were caught. I want to understand. Would you mind talking to me?"

John Terrell kept looking at him. "Do you know about my wife?" he asked finally. His voice sounded husky with disuse. "Amelia. Is she safe?"

"I don't know," Wilberforce was compelled to admit. "I should have found out, I'm sorry..."

He should have too. He cursed himself for being so thoughtless as Mr. Terrell turned away from him to face the wall. Of course he should have asked about Mrs. Amelia Terrell. His only excuse was that he'd had no idea that Mr. Terrell wouldn't know.

Ten years, Pitt had managed to get the sentence down to. Ten, from thirty-five, on an unprecedented technicality. John Terrell had been in prison for six years—four more to go. Wilberforce had thought this practically no punishment at all. The terrible thing was, compared to what others were receiving, it was.

"I'll find out," Wilberforce promised, but it wouldn't do any good. It was very unlikely that the Templars would let him visit John Terrell again.

The following day, Wilberforce returned to the House of Commoners. By chance, he arrived just as Pitt was getting out of his carriage; when Wilberforce hurried to catch up to him, his friend was too preoccupied to notice him until he called his name twice.

"You were right," Wilberforce announced without further preamble.

"Probably," Pitt said. "About what was I right this time?"

Wilberforce made a face at him but didn't let himself be distracted from his mood. A cold wind was blowing. The politicians bustling past them toward the House of Commoners seemed chased in like leaves. "Those people in the Tower of London don't deserve to be there—at least, too many of them don't."

"I don't think I ever exactly said that," Pitt reminded him. He had made the transition to full seriousness now. "I said, or implied, that I didn't think you would be comfortable as the one locking them up without question."

"Because it isn't fair. It isn't fair that Aristocrats should use their abilities without consequences while Commoners are put in places like that for lifting a box with their minds—or live in hiding, too afraid to use the abilities in their blood or even to admit to them."

"It isn't fair," Pitt conceded. "But you'll never stop an Aristocrat using their magic, and they don't want Commoners using theirs. It's been that way for a very long time."

"Here and in Europe. In Africa and parts of the Middle East, they have no restrictions on magic at all."

"They have a great many things in Africa and the Middle East that we don't have here. We're probably the poorer for it much of the time. I'm not sure untrammeled magic is one of those times."

"Why not?"

"Because magic is dangerous. Believe me, I know." He couldn't say more in public, but Wilberforce took his meaning. "It's unpredictable, it's difficult to police, and it's nearly impossible to regulate in a family that hasn't been monitoring its bloodlines since the dawn of time. Not that the last has much meaning anymore, I'll admit: half of the noble families in England were created Aristocracy only in the last century, and wealthy Commoners have been recording their family bloodlines for generations. The distinction between Aristocrat and Commoner is entirely arbitrary in terms of magic by now, if it was ever anything else. But that's the theory behind the current laws."

"You can't possibly be content with that, any more than I am."

"Of course I'm not. I have reservations about the idea of unrestricted magic. But of course I agree that Commoner magicians are sent to the

Tower far too readily, for far too long: that's why we broadened the concept of self-defense. I agree that there must be a better way of managing things. What I outlined was simply the way things are."

"And since when have you not been ready to challenge the way things are?"

"I *am* ready," Pitt said. "I'm only wondering if you're talking to me about this as someone about to embark on a political crusade or on a religious retreat."

Wilberforce laughed reluctantly. "You don't give up, do you?"

"It's not usually considered a desirable tactic for the head of the British government, no."

"Then, for your information, I suppose I am back in politics," Wilberforce informed him. "But not the way I was before. I still want to follow God, if I can. But I suppose—I'm looking for something important to do, and change. I do think you're right, that I couldn't do that from within the church, even as a Templar—perhaps especially as a Templar. I think I want to see if I can do so from here."

Pitt smiled a little. "Which brings us back to the start of the conversation."

"Which was?"

"I was in fact right."

"Oh, do shut up." He turned to go in, then turned back as a thought struck him. "Are all prisons as bad as the Tower of London?"

"The Tower has a certain reputation," Pitt said cautiously. "But from the little I know—and that is probably far too little—all prisons are fairly squalid, yes. I think Newgate is supposed to be even worse. Why?"

"I was just thinking," Wilberforce said, "that we should really do something about that too, shouldn't we?"

England

1787

For Wilberforce, the next few months were like awakening from a fevered delirium. The world seemed glittering, new, and wonderful, and at the same time, to suddenly make *sense.* Every blade of grass was a revelation.

He had thrown away so much of his life. He was determined to make it up.

The next summer recess, he devoted nine or ten hours a day to reading everything he had neglected to read during his dissipated university career, and then some: the Bible, obviously, but also Locke, Pope, Rousseau, Dr. Johnson, Voltaire, Cowper, Shakespeare. He studied magical theory, political thought, religious doctrine, poetry, and history. He filled his brain with words by day and felt their essence seep into his soul overnight.

"It's all very well for you," he told Pitt when the latter came to complain that half his books were in Wilberforce's house and he never answered letters anymore. "I have to catch up, and I'm so far behind. I spent my university days going to parties. You did all this reading when you were still a boy."

"I certainly did not. I've never read Cowper in my life."

"You should. He's wonderful. And I never did answer letters—that's something else I should improve about myself. I'm almost as bad as you in that regard."

"As bad as that?" Pitt said dryly. "Are you even eating at the moment?"

"Of course. I had dinner with you only last week. Just not very much. What do you recommend I read next?"

Pitt sighed and cast a critical eye over the stacks of books. "Milton, Paley, and Thucydides," he said. "But I won't answer for the consequences."

There *were* consequences, of course. His eyesight, already weak, clouded even further; his already thin frame whittled down to nothing. His mother, though she refrained from the horror that had accompanied his twelve-year-old conversion, was uneasy. Some of his friends were the same. Nor was the period of intense mental anguish over: every day, he would begin brimming over with hope and end berating himself for the expectations he had failed to live up to. But it didn't last long enough to hurt him. His family and friends relaxed once they had talked to him and not noticed any marginal difference in his manner. It was a period of transformation and rebirth; he emerged, in the cooling autumn rather than the spring, and unfurled his wings.

In November, with Pitt's support, he proposed a bill that would ban the commonly abused practice of Aristocrats using mesmerism and alchemy to limit their servants' freedom. The process, called alchemy-service, required the servants to drink a mixture each morning that would render them more susceptible to strong mesmerism, and thus more pliable during hours of work. It led, Wilberforce convincingly argued, to abuse of vulnerable housemaids, countless acts of exploitation, and degradation for all involved. The ban passed the House of Commoners easily and then, with more difficulty, the Aristocrats.

In the New Year, he set his sights even higher. During the dark days of January, he wrote down the myriad of problems that were poisoning Britain from the inside out: not only magical oppression, but debauchery, child prostitution, squalid prisons and workhouses, exploitation of the poor, drinking, drug trafficking, pornography.

Not all of these could be dealt with immediately; most, unfortunately, would be possible to curb among the Commoners but not the Aristocrats, who were the worst offenders. And yet he determined he would try. What he intended was nothing less than a complete moral reformation of society.

This, he supposed, could justly be considered his life's work; at any rate, it was very likely to take an entire lifetime. And yet he still didn't feel quite satisfied. Something told him that there was, if not something more important, then something missing. If he was to be in politics, then he felt certain he was to be so for a reason—something less abstract, and more pressing. Perhaps even something more dangerous. Something that compared to the vanquishing of a shadow on a French street one summer night.

In the spring, he found it.

Parliament had run until two that morning, later than had been planned, and Pitt's cousin Grenville had elected to return to his London accommodations rather than join them at Holwood House. Wilberforce and Pitt, however, still firing on adrenaline and verbal swordplay and their own cleverness, had mutually decided they wouldn't have gone to bed until sunrise anyway, so they might as well spend as little time in the city as possible and stop for a very belated dinner on the way. By the time the carriage wheeled through the gardens of the modest country house, the stars were fading, and Wilberforce was yawning so frequently he was having difficulty keeping up the thread of the conversation.

"I think I may be too old for this," he said gravely as he climbed out of the carriage and into the crisp predawn air.

"Don't say that," Pitt complained. He still looked remarkably alert, although Wilberforce knew from experience that his friend would sleep later and more soundly than himself once he actually got to bed. "You're but twenty-seven; I reach twenty-eight in a week or so. I'm not ready to be consigned to regular hours and potential senility quite yet."

"You're a schoolboy. I read it in the papers. I am merely an aging backbencher."

"I suppose racing you up the stairs is quite out of the question, then?"

"Absolutely not."

Wilberforce had lost that race; his shorter legs were at a disadvantage, and his bedroom door was farther down the corridor anyway. Now, some hours later and after a good sleep, he put on a burst of speed as his friend came up behind him, and with a leap forward felt the sunlight give way to shade and his hand make solid contact with the bark of the oak.

"Victory!" he gasped, coming to a halt against the tree. "I claim the Wilberforce oak!"

"You started running before me," the prime minister complained, putting his own hand on the tree to check his momentum. "If you hadn't, it would have been my victory."

"I know," Wilberforce said cheerfully. "That's why I did it."

"I thought you were intent on following the path of God."

"God probably wants you to have to make good on your promise to me. Wilberforce oak?"

"Wilberforce oak," Pitt conceded, "but I reserve the right to a rematch."

"It's your garden," Wilberforce said. He collapsed in the damp grass, his lungs straining for air and his legs beginning to tremble. For a moment, he felt as though he were back at his own home, three or four years ago, when his friend had been only chancellor of the exchequer and politics had seemed to go hand in hand with boating all day in the sun and talking all night. There had been times, during his darkest nights of doubt and self-recrimination, when he had thought he might never feel so happy again. In fact, his joys and friendships felt stronger now. Like the tree they were under, their roots ran deeper, and the branches reached higher. "It's a fine garden. You should be very proud of it."

"It's a much-needed break from financial reform," Pitt said, throwing himself down next to Wilberforce. His cheeks were flushed with the cool spring air, and his reddish-brown hair was escaping from its queue as he fought for breath.

"It's a fine much-needed break from financial reform. You should be very proud of it."

"Thank you. What about the financial reform?"

"Excellent. But with fewer begonias."

"I knew I'd left something out."

Wilberforce struggled to form a reply but was forced to use his remaining air for laughing instead.

It was early afternoon. Around them, the gardens were enveloped in a beautiful spring day, and the wind in the branches and the drone of a solitary bumblebee seemed to fill all the world.

"Pitt?" he asked after they had sat in silence for a while.

"Mm?"

"When we first turned our attention to magical reform, you said that we would never prevent Aristocrats from using their Inheritances."

"I remember."

"Did you mean that? Do you really think that Aristocratic magic cannot be curtailed?"

"I said you'd never prevent Aristocrats from using their Inheritances altogether," Pitt corrected, turning to face Wilberforce. "That's not quite the same as curtailing it. Obviously, they can and are prevented from using *dark* magic all the time. We've made a few moves in that direction already."

"And who decides what constitutes dark magic?"

Pitt sighed. "This is leading to something particular, isn't it?"

"How did you guess?"

He smiled a little. "I recognize the symptoms. So what is it?"

"I was approached recently by a Mr. Thomas Clarkson," Wilberforce admitted. "An unbraceleted Commoner, from Cambridge, about our age. He's a passionate campaigner against—"

"Slavery," Pitt finished. He looked characteristically thoughtful. "I know of him, actually. He wrote an essay against the practice when he was at university, and found his own argument so convincing he devoted his life to abolition."

"That almost sounded a little sarcastic."

"Did it? I'm sorry. I didn't mean it to be, not even almost a little. I thoroughly approve of his aims, if that's what you mean to ask. He approached you to help him?"

"And his friends," Wilberforce said. "They're all ardent moral reformers—mostly Quakers and evangelicals. I've corresponded with some of them about these magic reforms, and about easing conditions in prisons. It must have been one of them who gave my name to Clarkson. In any case, he left the essay of which you spoke at my house, and asked to call on me, which of course I arranged as soon as possible."

"What did Clarkson say to you?"

"Well, rather a lot, actually," Wilberforce admitted, with a slight smile. "I don't think I could have stopped him had I wanted to." He thought about the tall, impressively built Commoner who had sat next to him in his drawing room that day. The teacup Wilberforce had given him had sat abandoned on the table as he dived repeatedly into his enormous travel bag, and his dark, heavily lidded eyes burned brighter and brighter as he warmed to his subject.

"He showed me some of his research, for a beginning. I'd read about it somewhat myself, of course, but Clarkson has been all over the country gathering information. How much do you know about the practice?"

"I know that natives of Africa are captured and sold to work in the sugar plantations out in the colonies," Pitt said. "I know they are subjected to a peculiar combination of alchemy and strong mesmerism designed to control their every action. I know it's a filthy trade and a disgrace to our nation."

"It's worse than that. It's an abomination." He paused, trying to collect his thoughts and rein in his feelings. "The Africans are packed into our ships by the hundreds. On the first day, they're force-fed an alchemical mixture. They call it spellbinding. In its grip, it becomes almost impossible for them to move or speak except to obey the commands of their new masters."

"Essentially," Pitt said, "the intention is to reduce them to property."

"Exactly," Wilberforce said. "Those who hold out too long are thrown overboard on the third day. Many more die on the journey from illness or injury, or sometimes they just die. If they survive, they're sold to the plantations, to spend the rest of their lives laboring in horrifying conditions. Its wickedness seems to me so enormous, so dreadful..." He trailed off, finding himself for once lost for words. "Clarkson came to me because we had just passed the ban on alchemy-service: that was a far milder version of spellbinding, of course, but the principle was not dissimilar. Clarkson wanted to know if I would be willing to follow that with a motion to ban the practice of spellbinding the human beings taken as slaves. It's tantamount to torture."

"And of course, most of those plantations belong to Aristocrats," Pitt said. "More of them are dependent on slavery for their livelihoods than would care to admit it. Hence your original question."

"That entire trade is built on the back of dark magic," Wilberforce said. "Far worse than anything unregistered magicians could ever do—far worse than the occasional stray curse or rogue summoning that may put even an Aristocrat behind bars. It involves the bewitchment of hundreds of thousands of innocent people. If the Knights Templar wanted to fight against evil in the world, and evil magic in particular, this is where it is."

"Or rather, if *you* want to fight against evil in the world," Pitt corrected. "And, of course, you do. So what did you say to Clarkson and his friends?"

"I told them that I had no objection to bringing forward the measure in Parliament, when I was better prepared for it, and if no person more proper could be found," Wilberforce said. "And I've been helping them collect evidence for the preparation of such a measure, when time permits. But..."

"You clearly don't doubt the practice should be abolished," Pitt said when the silence had lingered a little too long. "So why are you hesitating?"

"Answer me this first. Do you think it would be possible to pass a bill to abolish spellbinding?"

"I think it would be extremely difficult," Pitt said, which was as close as he ever came to saying something couldn't be done.

"Why?"

"For one thing, spellbinding works to suppress magic. Without it, it would be more difficult for slavers to control any of their captives, but it would be impossible to control those who were powerful magicians. Testing and braceleting every slave would be impractical and expensive, especially when the Knights Templar have so small a presence in the colonies; besides, magic can be performed through bracelets if the wearer is determined. Africa practices magic freely; one of the major reasons we and other countries have been able to colonize there regardless is because our alchemy in particular is more advanced and we can employ amulets and spellbinding. Without spellbinding, many of those taken or born into slavery would rise up and take themselves back."

"Exactly." It was the same conclusion he'd come to. "And they'd be *right* to do so—which is the most important point. They have a right to their own magic; they have a right to their own freedom."

"So therefore," Pitt concluded, "there's little point in abolishing spellbinding. You really need to abolish slavery outright."

"That, after all, is what Clarkson and his people are working toward. And I think, really, it's what he's hoping that I'll agree to fight for."

Pitt nodded slowly. "And?"

"And that's... well, it's such an undertaking." It was what he meant, but he meant more than what Pitt's practical mind would understand him to mean. "Far more so than the steps toward freedom of magic we've taken for Commoners here. It will take years, probably, rather than months, if we can ever do it at all. And the forces aligned against us are enormous and powerful. As you say, there are a good many powerful Aristocrats dependent on slavery—and an even greater mass of Commoner merchants, traders, plantation owners..."

"Opposition has never stopped you before."

"No," Wilberforce agreed. "And I really think we could do it. I certainly think we *should* do it. But—"

"Then do it," Pitt said immediately.

"Do you really think it will be so easy?"

"Of course not. Slavery is a huge source of revenue—not only for slave traders and plantation owners, but for anyone who deals with them. Abolishing it would go a great deal against what some see as the public interest. And the idea of the end of slavery itself—that is going to terrify people for more than one reason. As you said, many of those currently spellbound are powerful magicians, from a society that doesn't regulate its magic. Their freedom poses a threat to everything our economic and social power is built upon. But their captivity, and everything it entails, is disgusting. People know that—or they can be made to. And then they simply need to be persuaded to vote according to their morals rather than their interests, or at least convinced that their interests are not so threatened as they fear."

Wilberforce nodded slowly. "And do you think I could do that?"

"Honestly," Pitt said, the careful neutrality fading from his voice, "I think you were born to do that. It's clearly uniquely suited to your character and talents."

Wilberforce nodded again. He felt as though he were standing on the brink of a vast drop, wondering what was waiting to receive him at the base of it. Pitt, unexpectedly, had put that feeling into words. He was born to do it. This, perhaps even more than anything else he had achieved so far, was what all those weeks of anguish and self-reflection had been pushing him toward. It made the whole thing seem so much larger and more awe-inspiring than it already was, and that scared him.

"Which is why," Pitt added, with a touch of embarrassment, "I gave your name to Clarkson when he wrote to me six months ago asking me to recommend someone who might be sympathetic to his cause."

Wilberforce stared at him. "*You* gave him my name?"

"I mentioned it. I knew you already had an interest in the matter of magical legislation—ow!"

Wilberforce had pulled out a handful of grass from around the base of the tree and thrown it hard enough to impact his friend's shoulder. There might have been a dirt clod still attached.

"Is this how it's going to be from now on?" Wilberforce demanded with mostly feigned indignation. "I do something only to find my career has once again been masterminded by the shadowy machinations of my prime minister?"

"While I'd love to claim Machiavellian cunning, I honestly just forgot to mention it to you. I had no idea he'd actually call on your house."

"You forgot to mention it to me?"

Pitt shrugged defensively. "It was while I was being brilliant with finances; I was busy, then I was tired. Stop throwing grass at your prime minister."

"Not until you apologize."

"For what? Helping you toward what may well be the great objective of your life? The way I read it, you should thank me."

"I'll thank you," Wilberforce said, ripping out another handful and throwing it in the same way, "when you apologize."

Pitt dodged the missile, but a few wisps of grass and leaves settled in his hair. "Well, then," he said, scooping up his own handful. His aim was somewhat better and got Wilberforce on the side of the head. "I apologize."

"Apology accepted," Wilberforce said. He rubbed the back of his neck, where some of the damp grass had escaped down his shirt collar, and made a face. "And thank you."

"Thank-you accepted."

"So I have your support in this matter?"

"Unconditionally," Pitt said immediately, and with more seriousness. "I'll do whatever I can."

"I don't like to take advantage of your position. But in this case—"

"Don't worry about that. Please let me know, with complete frankness, if I can do anything for you, and I'll tell you with equal frankness if it's too much. And in this case, as you say . . . I read that essay as well. Do you want to acquaint me with the particulars?"

"I thought we were going to help dig the pond. You were very insistent about it."

"We can do both. Particularly as it means you really do have to help, since I'll be able to keep a close watch on you while we talk."

"And I thought I needed to campaign for the rights of slaves *abroad*." His sense of trepidation was fading now. If God had indeed sent him a task, at least he had sent him plenty of help as well. "That sounds like an excellent plan."

As the cool weather began to set in that year, Louis XVI declared his desire to tighten the restrictions on Commoner magic. He was acting on the advice of the Temple Church leadership, who warned him of growing unrest in the streets. They proposed that any magic connected to revolutionary action be treated as dark magic, subject to execution by breaking on the wheel. They proposed, more dangerously, that this law would apply not only to illegal Commoner magicians, but to Aristocrats as well.

They had reckoned without the *parlements*. Even those who cared very little about the rights of Commoner magicians were horrified at the threat to their own. The *parlements* were regional courts; they had no power to make or change laws, but they had the power to obstruct the king. The Parlement of Paris took the opportunity to point out that in fact, with winter approaching, the *lifting* of certain restrictions would save lives: last winter, Commoner fire-mages had frozen to death when their own magic could have saved them and their families. They called for something akin to the self-defense clause in English law, to be enforced not by the Templars, but by common men: a clause that would allow Commoners to use their magic if it was clearly for their own good and that of their families. Until it was granted, they refused to agree to any further restrictions, even on the darkest of black magic.

In Arras, late at night, Charlotte Robespierre paused on the landing in front of her brother's door.

"Are you still awake?" Her surprise would have been more convincing had it not been the third time she had asked. "It's three in the morning."

At the desk by the window, the candle had burned low. Brount, their little dog, lay under the desk amid stray rejected papers, thumping his tail peacefully. Robespierre sat writing, hunched over the pen as it scratched the page. There was no frenzy about his movements: he radiated perfect calm. It was only that his calm seemed, even to him, to have a touch of mania about it. Three in the morning often does.

"I'm not tired," he said, without looking up.

"You can't still be working on your trial. You always have that prepared in advance."

"Of course I do." The hard wooden seat was stiffening his back; he wriggled his shoulders once, spasmodically, to loosen it. Now his attention had been drawn back to the physical world, he wished he could put his pen down and stretch, but he didn't want to give Charlotte the impression he was open to conversation. "This is a pamphlet. I need to persuade the people here to fight for the new magic laws. The courtroom isn't the place for that, but I don't have a voice anywhere else. I'm not an Aristocrat. I need to write it down."

Charlotte yawned. "So an abstract principle of magic is keeping you from your bed."

"It isn't just about abstract principles. It isn't even about magic. The kind of clause the Parlement of Paris wants will save lives."

"So write that and go to bed."

"I *am* writing that. That is precisely what I'm writing."

"I'll bet you aren't," Charlotte said astutely. "You've probably put in all sorts of flourishes and rhetoric and gone on forever. Nobody wants to read it, you know."

He bit back his retort and forced himself to swallow it down. She was right. He thought, rightly or wrongly, that what he had written was very fine. Certainly he thought it was true. But there was no stolen mesmerism in pen and ink, as he had in the courtroom, and without it his words were just words: well-reasoned, articulate, and no different from anybody else's. Nobody would publish them; he could do so at his own expense, of course, and would, but nobody would care.

Realizing no argument was forthcoming, Charlotte patted him on the shoulder with more sympathy. "Don't take it so much to heart," she said. "You're a bundle of nerves lately. It isn't good for you. Anyway, you have a magic trial in the morning, don't you? Someone accused of something—?"

"Unregistered weather magic," Robespierre said. "Yes. I think we can have him acquitted."

"There you go, then. That's something."

"It isn't enough," Robespierre said in the garden of his sleep.

"No," his benefactor said. There might almost have been a trace of satisfaction in his voice. "It isn't enough. Not yet."

In Paris, William Eden, ambassador for Great Britain, broached the subject of slavery at the negotiating tables. He was a shrewd, experienced Aristocrat whose career had encompassed everything from lord of trade to spymaster in the American War. His estate in England bordered Pitt's, and they were friends as well as colleagues; he was also very fond of Wilberforce. In this case, however, he felt he had been rather put upon by the two of them. He was only meant to be negotiating a new trade arrangement.

"I've had a letter from England that, as soon as Parliament opens again, there will be a move to abolish the slave trade," he told the men seated around the table. "It's very likely to pass; Mr. Wilberforce has been known to get similar bills through before. The prime minister supports it entirely and feels that, as one of the greatest obstacles to any restrictions on the slave trade is the argument that France will merely profit by England's restraint, it would be very much appreciated if France would agree to prohibit the practice simultaneously with England. Your king has the power to do it with the stroke of a pen."

(Something moved among the men at the French side of the table. It stirred across their thoughts like a breeze across the surface of a pond.)

"It would only be a prohibition against the slave trade, you understand," Eden said. "Not the practice of spellbinding, and certainly not slavery itself."

"Not yet," one of the Frenchmen said. "But I cannot think that such restrictions are intended to end there. We have abolitionists and social reformers in our country as well, you know. They're a troublesome species."

"Well, this might even help placate them," Eden suggested. "As well as those who object to the magic laws your king wants to bring in. They believe in the rights of the common man, after all. This concession might be seen as very hopeful."

"A little too hopeful, perhaps, sir," the man replied dryly. "I notice you were careful to mention that this wouldn't impact spellbinding or slavery. But those are the touchstones of the revolution around here, you know: free magic, and liberty."

(It listened.)

Eden laughed uneasily. "Revolution. An overstatement, surely?"

"It's always an overstatement," the man said. "Until the rioting starts."

Arras

October 1788

Maximilien Robespierre arrived home far later than usual. He was uncharacteristically flushed, and his green eyes were alight.

"It's happened," he said to Charlotte before she had even finished opening the door for him. Brount flung himself ecstatically at Robespierre in a flurry of black-and-white fur; Robespierre ducked to ruffle his ears affectionately. "It isn't a rumor. A royal proclamation came from Versailles only this afternoon. A meeting of the Estates General has been called."

"I know. A letter from Augustin came about the same time." Their younger brother had taken up Robespierre's old scholarship at the College Louis-le-Grand, learning to follow him into law. "From Paris. He says the streets are in chaos."

"So they should be. This is the beginning of something. I know it is."

The Estates General was composed of three parties: the First Estate, the Knights Templar; the Second Estate, the Aristocracy; and the Third and largest, the Commoners. The three groups had not assembled in more than two hundred years. The king was ordering them to do so now only because, after a year of hopeless deadlock, he had still not managed to pass any new restrictions on Aristocratic or Commoner magicians. The Parlement of Paris was proving particularly obstinate; most thought cynically that their main objective was to exercise their power to annoy the king. Yet the outrage over the proposed magic laws was genuine, and it was not going away.

The king, then, was relying on the combined forces of the Knights Templar and the Aristocracy to support his wishes at the Estates General, and to subdue any rebellious Commoners who might be elected to the Third Estate. In this, he had miscalculated greatly. The Knights Templar's numbers had declined in recent years, and their powers likewise. The Aristocracy were divided among themselves over whether their allegiance lay with their monarch or their fellow human beings starving on the streets. And the Commoners would not be subdued.

"The meeting is set for early next year," Robespierre said. "I need to be there."

Charlotte frowned. "In Paris?"

"At Versailles. At the meeting. I need to be elected to represent the Third Estate."

His sister must have known what he had meant from the first, but her face still registered doubt. "You're a provincial lawyer, Maximilien. You have no experience in politics."

"Until now, I've had no opportunity. Things are changing. Or they will, if we can make them. I need to make sure of that as well."

There was clearly more she could have said; the look she gave him implied that she was doing him a great favor by not doing so. Perhaps she was startled out of her usual sarcasm by his excitement. He was usually a creature of such quiet, unalterable habit.

"Well, you need to eat first," she contented herself with saying. "I've put dinner on the table."

"I've no time, I'm afraid." He embraced her quickly as he moved past her, to lessen the sting, but he nonetheless moved past. Brount followed him, wagging his tail. This, at least, was habitual. "There's a meeting in the town hall tomorrow to discuss the elections. I need to prepare. I'll be up in my study."

"It's called a bedroom."

He ignored this. He didn't see why a room with both a bed and a desk couldn't be a study as well as a bedroom. Certainly he worked more than he slept.

"Oh, did we hear from Camille as well?" he asked, turning on the stairs. "I think he's in Paris at the moment."

She rolled her eyes, on firmer ground. "You and that Camille."

"You've never even met Camille." He managed to keep his patience. "We haven't seen each other since school."

"I don't have to meet him to know he's unstable. The way he writes about this meeting is downright dangerous. I don't understand what he wants half the time. I don't think he does, except that it involves fire and blood and people shouting in the streets."

"So we did hear from him." He had long since given up trying to stop Charlotte from reading his letters.

"Of course we did. He intends to stand for deputy as well, back in Guise— There! I saw that face."

"I didn't make a face."

"You did," she countered, triumphant. "You know very well he has no chance of being elected. They have no regard for him in his hometown. Why should they? He's only there when he runs out of money and has to return to his parents, and when he is, he offends everyone. And God knows what he gets up to in Paris."

"No worse than most get up to in Paris," Robespierre said, although for all he knew it was perhaps a little worse. Camille knew better than to tell him. "Well. If he isn't elected, I'm sure he'll find a way to be in the city."

"No doubt. He wants to throw what's left of his legal career aside for one as a pamphleteer, from what I can tell. I'm not sure how he plans to pay for it—or who he thinks will publish him. Frankly, what he writes, nobody would dare."

"He's very clever. And very excited."

"So he probably hasn't considered either question."

He had to concede that she was probably right, on all counts. Camille Desmoulins at university had been all light and shadows, fire and joy, dancing from thought to thought like a dragonfly over surface water. Robespierre, whose ideas ran deeper and more serious, had found it difficult to keep up; though he was barely two years older, he often felt like a parent struggling after a precocious child. Yet he knew Camille could see his vision for France, and share it: the country of free magic and free ideas and free people. And though Camille's temper tended to burn hot and fast while Robespierre's, once lit, never went out, their anger smoldered very well together.

"He'll be in Versailles if it kills him," he told Charlotte. "As will I."

When Robespierre finally fell asleep that night, he woke once more in the garden.

He was accustomed to this by now. Many times over the last five years, he had found himself in the darkness, surrounded by swishing grass and the scent of dying roses. The house had been quiet since the first time, though sometimes a light burned at the window. Each time, his benefactor had been standing on the path, waiting. And each time, he had stood before a court the following day and felt his eyes blaze with secret mesmerism. Under his influence, prisoners had been acquitted of illegal magic, received lesser sentences for theft, and escaped death by the gibbet. It was exhausting, but it was exhilarating, feeling others' minds open to him, reaching out and pushing them to his will, seeing justice done and things set right.

This time was different. His benefactor was not standing; a latticed table and set of chairs were on the lawn, and he was seated there. The night sky was clouded, and the breeze in the air had the sting of a building storm.

"Maximilien Robespierre," his benefactor said, as he did every time. Robespierre had long suspected it was not a greeting, but a necessary component of the magic that brought them together. What that magic was, he had never been able to discover. There was little access to magical theory in Arras, and he was forced to be careful not to arouse suspicion. He was practicing illegal magic himself now. He couldn't save France from within the Bastille, and certainly not from beyond the grave.

"I thought I might see you tonight," Robespierre said.

"I read in the papers that Mademoiselle Dubois was acquitted of illegal magic."

"She was," Robespierre said. That had been two weeks ago; in the recent excitement, he had nearly forgotten. Elle Dubois was a maid in the house of a local Aristocrat; she had, at thirteen, unexpectedly manifested strong telekinesis. The Aristocrat in question had responded by locking her in a cellar and calling the Knights Templar; when her father remonstrated, he was arrested for assault. "Thank you for your assistance. She was braceleted and released without charge. But her father could not be saved. He had already been sent to prison by *lettre de cachet*. I condemned that entire rotten practice, I felt your power in my words, and yet—"

"Exactly. The condemnation was the important thing. People heard it, and they felt the injustice of a father imprisoned on the whim of an Aristocrat for trying to protect his little daughter. I know you find it gratifying to free the weak, and that certainly has its place, but a revolution needs blood—the blood of martyrs as well as the blood of kings." He waved a hand at the empty chair. "Sit down, Maximilien. There's something we need to discuss."

Robespierre sat, cautiously. It was the closest he had ever been to his benefactor. In the faint light through the clouds, he could see lean, sculpted features and eyes that seemed unnaturally large and dark.

"I need your help tomorrow," he said before his benefactor could speak. "There's—"

"I know what there is. And yes. You certainly do need my help, tomorrow and in the coming months. But first, I need something from you. Tonight."

"Tonight?" Robespierre frowned. "I don't understand. I'm still only a lawyer. If I were to be elected to the Estates General..."

His benefactor smiled, a visible shifting of shadows on his face. "What kind of help do you imagine I require?"

"I assumed...I thought the aim of this exercise was to put me in a position to change things. Laws, working conditions, and so forth.

You're clearly an illegal magician. I imagined, at some point, you would want a specific law changed for you. I thought you wanted a society where magic was free."

"I see. Very logical, based on what you know of the world. And quite true, of course. But not tonight. Tonight, I only need your magic."

"You want me to mesmerize somebody?"

"No." He paused. "Have you never wondered why I approached you in the first place? I mean why I approached you, specifically. There are hundreds of unregistered magicians in the country, or people with latent powers who could become magicians with my help. If I had needed a mesmer, there are many I could have chosen. Why would I come to you?"

"I never thought about it."

"Not true. You thought about it. You almost asked, at the time. But you were too afraid of the answer."

"Very well." Robespierre tilted his head and tried to squash the swirl of fear in his stomach. "Give me the answer. Why me? What do you need from me, if not mesmerism?"

"Necromancy," his benefactor said.

The garden was silent. A single light kindled in the top window of the house. By the faint illumination, Robespierre stared at his benefactor. As always in their dreamworld, the face in front of him was sharp and well defined, but he knew now that his mind's eye had never been clear at all.

He swallowed hard before he managed to speak. "I'm not—"

"Don't lie." For the first time, the cultured voice was laced with the scorn Robespierre recognized from childhood tormentors. Yet still, it was not unkind. It was almost affectionate. "You can't lie very effectively here, haven't you noticed that? And in any case, I know the truth. You're a necromancer. You're the only living necromancer in France, perhaps in all of Europe."

"I'm not." He could hardly breathe. His rapidly beating heart needed more air than the garden held. "I can't— How do you know?"

"I've always known, in the same way I knew about your mesmerism. I can feel it in your blood. I felt it from very far away. It glitters in the darkness, like a strain of black jade in weathered rock. I felt it kindle all those years ago. It was here in the garden, wasn't it? It was the reason your mother died."

Robespierre said nothing. In the lit room of the house, footsteps echoed, and shadows moved against the window.

"You were six years old. You found a dead bird. You were sad it was dead; you grieved for it. The magic flowed from you, animating limbs and cartilage and frail wings. A late manifestation, though not so late as some. The bird flew away on that first burst of your power and fell dead outside the garden walls."

"I didn't *find* the bird." The words were torn from him in short bursts like gasps. Mesmerism, it had to be, the lightest, most skillful touch he had ever heard of. But if his benefactor was already a mesmer himself, then... "It was mine. I raised it. My sisters—Charlotte and Henriette, before Henriette died—they begged me to let them look after it. They killed it. They left it out in a storm, and it died of terror. It wasn't their fault. They were too young. I should never have let them. It was so beautiful. I couldn't bear... How do you *know* this?"

(Inside the house, he heard his mother's voice. "It's me you want." She sounded so calm. How could she be? How could she have been so brave, when he was always so frightened? "There's no need to shout. I'll come with you.")

"She had the gift as well, of course," his benefactor said. He was looking up at the window. "It was from her you had inherited it. They never looked once they had found her; they should have retested you all, of course, but tests are so expensive. She exposed herself to hide you, and died for you. She stepped up to them and let them put a hangman's noose around her neck, all to protect you. And you have never been able to forgive them, or yourself."

(His sister was screaming. "It's all right," his mother said. "Tell Maximilien it's all right.")

"What are you?" Robespierre whispered.

"You know what I am. You've always known what I am." His benefactor stood. "This is no time for forgiveness, Maximilien, not after all these years. This is a time of blood and fire and revolution."

For just a moment, Robespierre forgot his horror. "The revolution is really coming, then?"

"It's almost upon us. And we need to be ready for it."

There was no choice. Not now. He wondered now if there had ever been. "What do you need of me?"

"All of you," his benefactor said. "Eventually. But for this occasion, I need you only to do exactly what I say."

Early that morning, Charlotte Robespierre opened the back door to find her brother shivering on the step. A coat was thrown roughly over his shirt and breeches, and his face was streaked with dirt. He flinched at her touch before he appeared to recognize her.

"Maxime!" She lowered her voice as he motioned her to be quiet. "God. What happened?"

"Nothing," he said hoarsely. He staggered to his feet, brushing aside her help. "Don't touch me. Don't ask me any questions. Please. I need to clean up. They'll be meeting in the town hall this morning..."

"*Something* clearly happened! You're not the sort of person who—"

"*Please.*" His face was enough to silence her. However annoyed she was by her elder brother's rigid pride, she could never bear the rare moments when it collapsed. What lay beneath it was so terrifyingly vulnerable.

"All right." She wanted, unexpectedly, to reach out to him, but he had told her not to touch him. "I'll get you some clean clothes. But you can't possibly go to the meeting. Look at you. You're freezing."

"I'll warm up." He managed a shadow of a smile for her. "It's been a long night—a horrible night—but I'm quite well. I don't want to talk about it. I need to be at the meeting."

A few hours later, Maximilien Robespierre joined the thronging crowd at the town hall. There were so many people that they spilled out into the courtyard, where they listened encircled by winter trees and graceful white buildings. Some who saw young Robespierre get up to speak noted that he looked rather pale, even by his standards. Yet those who heard him agreed that he had never sounded so convincing.

London

November 1788

I refused to eat the food they gave me. I knew not what it was, nor what it would do. I knew only that I wanted to die, and that food would force me to live. They came to me on the second day and held red-hot coals to my lips, and told me that if I didn't swallow my dinner, I would be made to swallow those. I spoke no English then, but I understood their meaning. By then, the people around me were already lost."

Clarkson's voice, often dry and even bitter, was surprisingly soft as he read the words by candlelight. Around him, the Society for Effecting the Abolition of the Slave Trade listened. They were silent, without even a gasp or a shudder, but their silence was heavy with revulsion.

They were an intelligent, passionate collection of people, and Wilberforce had come to know them very well over the last year. The oldest, Granville Sharp, was a Commoner lawyer who had been fighting for the individual rights and liberties of freed slaves on British soil for as long as Wilberforce had been alive; the youngest, Zachary Macaulay, was barely twenty, freshly returned from working at a slave plantation in Jamaica and still in the first grip of disgust at what he had seen there. Olaudah Equiano and Ottobah Cugoano had come to the meeting from the Sons of Africa, the group of twelve ex-slaves working to end slavery and aid London's poor black community. Hannah More, the brilliant playwright and scholar, sat by the fire, her face grave as she made notes in a tiny book. Outside Wilberforce's house in Old Palace Yard, just across the courtyard from Parliament, the late autumn night was dark and rain-scattered; inside, discussion burned hot and bright.

"That was from a freed woman now living in London," Clarkson said, lowering the paper. "But I have a good deal more from sailors who have worked or still work on the vessels. I spoke to over a hundred of them this summer."

"They're willing to speak out against their own trade?" Macaulay asked.

Clarkson's mouth twitched. "With a few drinks in them."

"They suffer too," Wilberforce explained. "Not just in their conscience: overcrowding and disease kill a good many of the crew. Many of them just won't speak openly because of the power of the merchants. Can we distribute that testimony to the public as soon as possible, Clarkson? The sailors', too, preferably. They'd complement each other."

"It's being done," Clarkson said. "And Miss More's poem on slavery is still causing a stir."

"I read it in Windermere." He turned to the dark-eyed older woman next to him and found a smile in the wake of the lingering pain of Clarkson's report. "It was magnificent. Truly. I read it to everyone I could find in my house—which was quite a number of people, considering. Some of them I'd forgotten were staying with us at all."

"Did they all share your opinion?" Hannah More asked with a raised eyebrow.

"I wouldn't have had them in my house if they didn't."

"That's very gratifying, thank you." She meant it, too, though her intelligent face was serious once more. "Sadly, it doesn't in itself free slaves. My sister and I want to publish a pamphlet too, about our findings on the detrimental effects of spellbinding, but I doubt it will be well received. Most aren't interested in our kind of scholarship."

The More sisters were part of a growing group of braceleted Commoners who had taken to studying magic on a purely academic level. Many of them were women or members of religious sects unwilling to bind themselves to the Knights Templar—Miss More, a Quaker, was both. The Templars didn't like it, of course, but as long as the Commoners never acted upon their studies, there was nothing they could do about it.

"I think we can make them interested," Wilberforce said. "We have to try, at least."

"Am I to take it, then, that you want us all to continue to stir the public while you approach Parliament?"

"More than ever." It was something he'd given a great deal of thought when he was lying awake in bed. "We have truth and right on our side. It's a political advantage like any other. We'd be foolish not to use it. Right now, the public support slavery because they haven't looked at it; I want us to show it to them. If we lay it wide open wherever they turn, then they will no longer be able to keep from seeing it for what it is. I doubt it will sway the most hardened of the slave trade's supporters, but it may help with those who want to follow their conscience but fear the reproof of their voters."

Equiano nodded from across the table. "We were of a similar opinion. You know, I daresay, that Cugoano published his own thoughts on the slave trade last year. With his help, and Clarkson's here, I want to publish a book of my own in the New Year. It would be a complete account of my life, much like that which Clarkson just read tonight. I've never been put to work on a plantation, and I was spellbound only for the passage from Africa to Barbados. But I know what it is to be kidnapped and sold, and I know what it is to be a slave."

"That would be wonderful," Wilberforce said. It was an understatement; the hairs stood up on the back of his neck. Equiano had spoken to him about his past before, in glimpses: he knew about his childhood in Africa, and his account of the Middle Passage. The thought of men and women across the country reading those words made him think, not quite for the first time, that they might actually achieve what they meant to do. "It will do more good than a thousand speeches in Parliament."

Clarkson nodded. "And how are things set to deliver the first of our thousand speeches in Parliament?"

"We're set to move against the slave trade as soon as Parliament opens," Wilberforce confirmed. "We're still awaiting word from France, but Pitt is confident we can convince them to abolish the trade simultaneously with us. That will do away with the inevitable arguments that France will move in to profit if the bill passes."

"They say that Parliament might not open next week after all," Hannah More said shrewdly. "And when it does, it might be otherwise occupied. The rumors are that the king has gone mad."

"Those are rumors, as far as I know," Wilberforce said. "I haven't heard anything more than you. Certainly the king has been unwell, but I doubt it poses a great deal of threat to the government—and certainly not to the bill. I have every hope we can get it passed this year. Then we can look at our move against slavery itself."

Miss More didn't seem convinced, but she said nothing further.

"I still think we should move against slavery itself," Granville Sharp said. "We may as well start as we mean to go on."

"I wish we could." It was already an old discussion. "I would love to be completely open about what we mean to do. Unfortunately, my experience of Parliament is that we need to move very cautiously. They'll be terrified enough at the prospect of losing the trade; the more they suspect the full scope of our plans, the less likely they'll be to allow us any ground at all. And it would be far more difficult to persuade the French monarchy to abolish slavery outright. They'll want to cling to spellbinding too, I'm afraid. They're very paranoid about magical uprisings over there at the moment."

"They should be." Granville Sharp snorted. "The Knights Templar have been bearing down on their magical Commoners like wolves since young Louis came to power."

"I met His Majesty Louis XVI," Wilberforce said absently; he had fished a diagram from the biscuit crumbs on the table. "He was very kind."

"He may be," Sharp said. "But he's weak, and the Templars are frightened. Once you've been in this game a little longer, Wilberforce, you'll realize that fear is the most dangerous obstacle to reform that there is."

Wilberforce only half heard him. He was still looking at the diagram. It showed a ship, in broad mathematical outline, and the ship was packed with small black human figures. Several different cross sections showed, with notes and equations, how 482 such figures could be crammed into every available space in compartments the size of coffins. It looked like an illustration of a tin full of the toy soldiers a rich parent might buy a child. It was precise, and perfectly worked out, and monstrous.

"The trouble with that one," Clarkson said, following his gaze, "is that it only shows how many each ship is *supposed* to fit. They pack them with six hundred or so. Too many Africans die on the journey. They need to make a profit."

Wilberforce let the paper fall back to the table. His fingers felt tainted. "This won't take long." He really believed it. "Once people see things like this, they won't let it go on."

It was almost three o'clock in the morning when the last of the society left with their allotted work to do and promises to meet again in a very few days. Wilberforce went to see them off at the door. The air from the nearby Thames was biting, and light rain cast a veil over Westminster; the buildings looked pale and ghostly behind it. In the grip of winter, there seemed to be no other soul about for miles.

He was very surprised, then, when he stepped back inside only to be informed by his butler that Pitt was waiting for him in the library. Evidently, he had called half an hour ago and told the servants not to alert Wilberforce until after his guests had dispersed.

"Do you actually sleep at night?" Wilberforce said as he entered the library.

"Because I evidently roused you from your bed with my arrival," Pitt said wryly. He stood and put aside the book he had been reading. Neither of them could leave an unattended bookshelf alone for long.

"But I do apologize for calling so late. I just returned from Windsor, and I needed to speak to you."

"Not at all—I'm delighted to see you at last." Pitt had meant to finally visit Wilberforce at the Lake District over the summer, but business had meant that once again he had been kept close to London. "How was the king?"

Pitt sighed. "It's difficult to say. It might just be a fever—it's the right time of year for it. But certainly when I spoke to him, his mind and his magic were very disordered."

Wilberforce had meant it when he had told Hannah More that he doubted King George was in any true danger; he blinked now with surprise. "His magic? But that shouldn't be affected by any illness of the body. That would mean—"

"His magic is turning on itself, yes." It was rare for magic to turn on itself: it happened in very, very strong bloodlines, lines that mingled unlikely inheritances and incongruous strains. Unfortunately, royal families in any European country intermarried to propagate exactly those kinds of bloodlines. Highborn Aristocrats had been known to die or be rendered permanently insane from their magic before, and it was often explosive and dangerous. But it had never, as far as Wilberforce knew, happened to a king of England.

"It's too soon to tell yet," Pitt added. "He was delirious. It might have only been that."

"I hope so, of course. But still—"

"But still," Pitt echoed. "Yes." He shook his head. "I didn't actually come in the middle of the night to bring you news of the king. There was something else."

Wilberforce pulled his thoughts back to the present. "It's not another rogue shadow, is it?" He was not at all serious—it was only that something about the lateness of the hour and the mysteriousness of the visit had taken him back to the tiny Rheims hotel—and so he was startled to see Pitt's expression become very serious indeed. "Oh dear God..."

"Believe me, I was as surprised as you are—and I probably looked about as thrilled at the prospect. I noticed it three days ago. I told myself it was probably perfectly legitimate, and that there have been more and more high-level shadows in London as displays of magic are beginning to become so fashionable. But any high-level shadow kept out in the world for more than a day needs to be registered with the Temple Church. I've made some discreet inquiries, and according to them there should not be one in Westminster. Particularly not in the abbey, and that's where this one is."

"Westminster Abbey?" Wilberforce glanced instinctively out the window: beneath the fine speckling of rain, the walls of the abbey were clearly visible across the courtyard. "Are you certain?"

"Quite, I'm afraid. If I wasn't before, I became so on my way here tonight. The cold from that church would freeze the Thames, if it were physical rather than supernatural."

"I don't see how you can tell the difference, in this weather. It feels cold enough to me, and I can't feel shadows. Do you think it has anything to do with the king's illness?"

"I don't see how it can. There's no way it could have made contact with him without being seen. Besides, shadows don't make one ill. Dead, perhaps, on occasion." He went on before Wilberforce could comment. "But even so, I'd very much like to take care of it before Parliament meets. Preferably tonight, if you would be willing and that would be convenient for you."

"You want to go after it," Wilberforce said slowly, "and you want me to go after it with you." He had known that, really, but he wanted it put into words. They made him feel sick with dread.

"I hate to ask, especially after Rheims," Pitt said with a sigh. He clearly understood Wilberforce's feelings perfectly; he may even have shared them. Wilberforce didn't think Pitt was afraid of any shadow, but he certainly didn't look happy. "And I really have tried to think of an alternative. I don't necessarily want to dispatch it ourselves this time—if we see it, and it looks beyond us, we can at least tell the

Knights Templar we've seen it. I just don't feel I can report it to the Knights Templar yet, as I felt I couldn't in France—you now have some idea of why, I think."

"I could report it to the Templars myself," Wilberforce offered. "Westminster Abbey is actually closer to my house than to yours, so it would seem reasonable. I could say I had seen it. They wouldn't need to know you were involved at all."

"That's very kind of you, but you haven't seen it. Neither have I. It hasn't allowed itself to be seen. I'm not sure how well your story would hold up under the questioning of the Templar shadow hunters. Besides..." He hesitated for such an unusually long time that Wilberforce's attention was caught. "This is going to have to be another leap of faith on your part, I'm afraid, because I can't put it into words that make logical sense. But this shadow feels connected with the one in France. I don't see how it could be the same one—we dealt with that one pretty thoroughly—but its presence has the same quality. And that makes me think it's not a coincidence that this one has appeared in Westminster."

"That *does* make sense," Wilberforce said. He understood now why Pitt was having difficulty with it. "It doesn't have to be logical. We're discussing shadows and blood magic—there are different kinds of sense involved. But I don't like this. This isn't a side street in France, and we're not twenty-four anymore. This is the heart of London, and you're the head of the British government. It's dangerous. It was dangerous then—we were just too young and arrogant to understand."

"You mean I was. And I agree, I was—I took it far too lightly—but I'm not now. I honestly do think we can deal with this before Parliament convenes. And I, at least, would prefer to do so without involving the Knights Templar. I do understand if you feel you can't accompany me this time. In that case, would you be so kind as to remain here? I will almost certainly return by daybreak. If I haven't, however, it would be helpful to have someone notify the Templars that something quite serious has probably transpired."

"You're entirely in earnest about that, aren't you?"

"Of course I am."

Wilberforce sighed. "Let me get my coat."

From the beginning, it felt more dangerous than France.

Wilberforce had been in Westminster Abbey before many times, during services and ceremonies, and once or twice just to enjoy the hushed quiet of old stone steeped in centuries of prayer. He had never been there in the dead of night, and if he had, he suspected it wouldn't have usually been like this. It was infected. He was aware, as he hadn't been in Rheims until they had practically walked into their quarry, of something tangible in the air. It may, of course, have been only his memory of the last shadow, and probably was, but that didn't prevent him from shuddering at the touch of every slight draft. The high vaulted ceilings, usually so breathtaking, seemed to drip with it. The monuments to dead men through which they were walking stared down at them as if stricken in silent horror. Inexplicably, it made him think of the accounts from the captured slaves Clarkson had been reading them that night.

It was terrible. And yet, through his growing fear, Wilberforce felt suddenly, fiercely glad that Pitt had asked him to come. Whatever its reasons for coming here, the shadow had no right.

They had entered through the north transept—where, Wilberforce remembered, Pitt's father was buried, though it did not seem a tactful moment to mention it—but Pitt beckoned him forward.

"Do you know where the shadow is?" Wilberforce asked.

"I think so." Pitt seemed a little surprised and, for the first time, uncertain. "I think it's in the nave, not far from the west entrance. But I could be mistaken—I never usually know anything that specific."

"I wish you had in France," Wilberforce said. "It would have spared us two hours sleepless in the dark streets."

Pitt smiled, but distractedly. "Well, it may yet be two hours here. As I said, I could be mistaken."

Looking at his face, however, Wilberforce knew it wouldn't be. He was not at all surprised when, almost immediately after they turned the corner toward the long, high row of Gothic columns, Pitt said quietly, "There it is."

It took Wilberforce some time to see it, and not only because of his eyes and the dark. The hundred-foot ceiling and vast chamber seemed to swallow up mere human-sized figures, even on the brightest of Sunday mornings when the nave was filled with worshippers. But then, with a jolt, it came into focus opposite them. It was black against a pillar—and yet not the solid black of a shadow.

"But that's..." He shook his head. "That's not a shadow. That's a human being."

"It's a shadow," Pitt said. There was something like wonder in his voice. "It's a shadow wearing a human body. It's an undead."

There was nothing about the figure from this distance to mark it as anything other than human. It was solid; it had all four limbs intact; it was clothed in the rough garb of a tradesman, albeit a ragged one. Yet it never occurred to Wilberforce to doubt. It wasn't human. His heart felt as though somebody had laid a finger on it and turned it to ice.

"How?" he managed, in a whisper. "Is that even possible?"

"I don't know. Nobody should know. There hasn't been an undead in the world for hundreds of years. Not since the Vampire Wars."

"Can it still be destroyed?"

Pitt took a moment to respond. "Oh—yes. Yes, it can. But it takes a very precise shot: it's through the heart, or not at all. I don't know if I can be so precise. We should probably withdraw. You were right; we shouldn't have come."

That was the most sensible course, obviously. Wilberforce had not brought a pistol at all: his eyesight was worse now than it had been in France, and he had no wish to put an accidental bullet through the west window or the prime minister of Great Britain. But he did have a stake, the standard sort available for self-protection, and his hand tightened around it.

"Can we draw it outside?" he heard himself ask.

"Why outside?"

"I scarcely know myself," Wilberforce confessed. "Perhaps because it's a church. Perhaps because it wants to be inside. It just— I don't like it being in here. I don't want to leave it, even if we can."

Pitt nodded slowly. He thought for a moment, and his eyes flickered quickly to the stake in Wilberforce's hand and back to the tall, thin figure.

Wilberforce decided to spare him the trouble of saying the obvious. "If I run for the door," he said, "and it comes after me, do you think you can shoot it as it passes?"

"It would be extremely dangerous for you."

"Well, I hardly feel very safe standing here waiting for it to move." The shape was beginning to turn its head. "And your pistol is more likely to hit a moving target than my stake is, so it will have to be me that draws it off. Quickly, please, because it's already moving."

"Run," Pitt said, and Wilberforce ran.

The nave of Westminster Abbey was 170 feet long. As he dashed across it with his back to the darkness, it seemed ten miles at least. For a terrible moment, almost the worst in his life, his fingers fumbled on the bolt that was drawn across the inside of the door, and he was certain he would never get it open. At once, it yielded, and the hinges creaked as he drove his shoulder into the door. He burst out into the cold, wet air, and he kept running.

From Westminster Abbey, a shot sounded.

Wilberforce checked his pace halfway across the cobbled courtyard and spun back to look. He was breathing fast and heavily, partly through exertion and partly through fear, and the rain stung his face.

A second later, he heard the splash and thud of footsteps, and then saw Pitt running toward him.

"Did you hit it?" Wilberforce asked as his friend stopped a short distance from him.

"No." Pitt was already reloading his pistol. "It's a shadow amongst shadows in there. I think I might have shot Richard II."

"Oh, wonderful. That repair will be coming out of taxpayers' pockets."

"I'll increase the rate of taxation on hats or something. Nobody will notice."

"I was going to buy a new hat next week."

Pitt cocked his pistol and pointed it at the entrance to Westminster Abbey. "Very well, I'll increase the rate of taxation on mistresses. We'll let Fox pay for it."

Wilberforce laughed, even as he tightened his grip on his silver-tipped stake. Fortunately, there was a moon shining through the gaps in the clouds, and the courtyard was palely illuminated. Above him, the western facade of the abbey loomed tall and white.

"Was it following us out?"

"Oh yes," Pitt said. His gaze was fixed on the abbey. "It was following."

Despite himself, Wilberforce shivered.

Then, out of the corner of his eye, he saw a flash of movement and whipped his head around to see the figure emerging not from the west entrance, but from the north. For just a second, the familiar and unbearable sense of evil settled over his heart and took his breath and his voice away.

In that second, the figure started across the courtyard, directly for the prime minister.

He barely had a chance to call "Pitt!" and see his friend turn sharply first to him and then almost instantly in the direction he was looking, before with a sudden rush the thing was headed his way instead. He heard the click of Pitt's finger on the trigger but no corresponding explosion as the gun misfired, and then the thing he had feared all his life was upon him.

It was so dark he couldn't move, and so cold he couldn't think. Something impacted him hard in the left side, and he slipped and fell to the wet ground. Just for a moment, the undead loomed over him: a rough, bearded face, waxen and decayed. Under bristling red eyebrows, where human eyes would be, the dark of a shadow leered out and swallowed him up. With sheer desperation he lunged upward with the point of the stake just as a gunshot cut through the night.

Then, all at once, it was over. Wilberforce lay doubled over on the ground, wet and numb and shaken clear through, but the world around him was right once more.

"Wilberforce!" Pitt's voice sounded as though it wasn't the first time he'd called his name. "Are you hurt?"

"I'm fine," he said, or tried to. He was, too, except that for some reason his legs wouldn't work and neither would his voice, and the fog around him was thicker than usual and very cold.

Then, in a rush, pain engulfed him, as though a match had been placed to his left side and ignited, and his flesh and bones and organs were suddenly ablaze. He glanced down, gasping, and saw that they were not, but that a good deal of the rain soaking him through was not rain at all.

"Good God," he heard Pitt's voice say. "Wilberforce? Can you hear me?"

"Yes—yes," he managed. He tried to focus on his friend's face, which had to be there, but his eyes were too misted. "What's happened?"

"It's gone," Pitt said. He didn't quite sound like himself. "It didn't touch you in the way a shadow would. But it had a knife. Of course it would. Why would you create an undead and not arm it? I should have—"

Wilberforce tried to move and barely held back a cry. His vision dimmed, and when it lit again, the world was even more ghostly, and he felt faint and sick.

"Steady," Pitt was saying. "Just a moment..." Something rough and spongy was being applied to his side; despite himself, he writhed away from the pressure, but a hand held his shoulder firmly.

"Steady. Can you hold that cloth there?"

"Of course," Wilberforce said faintly, without moving. "Did you kill it?"

"The undead? No," Pitt said. "No, you did. Your stake went through it the same time as its knife went through you. I was completely useless. I'm going to get you out of here now, understood?"

Wilberforce nodded, and then he felt an arm slip around his shoulders and lift him. The quick movement was like being stabbed again; it cut through the haze in agony more exquisite than he'd thought possible. He cried out, a noise something between a scream and a sob, and the motion stopped at once.

He gasped with relief, even though the fire at his side wasn't much better. "I'm sorry," he heard himself say. "I'm so sorry. It hurts."

"I know." Pitt's voice had regained its usual tone: it was as kind and as cheerful as if they were sitting in the Lauriston House library or under the oak at Holwood. If there was a trace of panic, it was buried very deep. "It's perfectly all right."

But it wasn't. They were right outside Westminster Abbey; people would be passing. He couldn't remember why that was important, but it was.

"Wilberforce." The voice seemed to be coming from a very long way away. "Can you still hear me?"

"Um..."

"Listen to me. Your house is only around the corner. I only need to get you there, and you'll be all right. But I need you to stay awake, and stay quiet. Can you do that?"

"I..." He tried to answer, but he couldn't remember the question anymore. The rain was falling still, and he thought it was mingling with tears on his face. "Why is it so cold?"

"It's England." There was a pause; then the voice became suddenly brisk. "Wilberforce, what's Psalm twenty-seven?"

"What?"

"Psalm twenty-seven."

He blinked slowly and tried to stir himself. "Which one's that?"

"I haven't the slightest idea. Tell me."

"I don't remember."

"Yes, you do. Of course you do. Just—"

"Yes, I do," he said suddenly. Something of hope and strength flared briefly within him, reviving his wits long enough to grasp at the memory. "Um . . . 'The Lord is my light and my salvation; whom shall I fear? The Lord is the strength of my life; of whom shall I be afraid?' "

"Good. Keep going."

" 'When—when the wicked, even mine enemies and my foes, came upon me to eat up my flesh, they stumbled and fell. Though an host should—' " He broke off, both crying out and stifling the cry at the same time; he had been lifted off the ground in one swift motion that wasn't quite swift enough to spare him. Something inside him twisted, and the world dimmed again.

Please, God, don't let me die, flashed across his mind. *I'm not ready to die.*

"You're doing very well," Pitt's voice said. "Just keep going."

" 'Though an host should encamp against me, my heart shall not fear,' " he said, or thought he said. He was so cold. " 'Though war should rise against me, in this will I be . . . will I be . . .' "

The rain was falling harder. In minutes it would wash the cobbles clean and leave only a long-dead body, lying on the ground with a stake through the heart.

Jamaica

Autumn 1788

She was free of the spell almost all the time now.

That moment on the field had been the last time she had moved on her own for many months; as the seasons changed and crop season began and the days and nights of backbreaking work went on relentlessly, she had started to doubt her own memory of it. But then, one day, her sore knee had twinged as she set down a load on a cart—the knee she had twisted years ago and never been allowed to rest—and she had shifted to a more comfortable position without thinking. After that, it happened more and more. She closed her eyes when the sun was bright; she shifted the heavy machete in her hands to ease her blisters; she could straighten to ease her back when the overseers weren't looking. The mesmeric commands in her head faded to a whisper; after a year or so, she actually had to force her body to follow the verbal commands given. That was hard, when she was so sore and exhausted that it was all she could do to stay on her feet at times. But she had to move with the others, as fluidly and mechanically as her aching limbs could manage, and not allow even a noise of protest to betray her.

The dark early-morning hours during the planting season were the best times. They always had been, even when the spell had still held her. In the crop season, they worked through to the morning, with a few hours to rest grudgingly allowed in shifts. Slaves at the processing plant would collapse and tumble into the fires or lose their limbs in the grinding machinery when exhaustion slowed them. But during the planting season, night was when they were left alone together in the barracks built to house the slaves, and after a few hours without commands the evening's dose began to wear off. All but the weakest could wriggle their shoulders or shift position, and that was a victory in itself. The ones who could speak whispered to each other and told stories. Augustus had told the best stories before he died, legends like those she could dimly remember from her childhood, but sometimes he'd work in the names of the people they knew and make everyone laugh. As the darkness lightened around them, they would talk more seriously: about the bands of escaped slaves, about the possibility of resistance at a crucial moment, about escape. It was worth sacrificing a few precious hours of sleep for that.

Best of all was when they sang. Jacob would start, his hand beating a rhythm on the floor, and those who could would take up the words and the beat. When she had been younger, she had lain there, her limbs thrilling with the vibrations of the floor beneath her; now she could sing, too, and sit up and laugh or cry with the words. Sometimes, when the music was angry, a reckless defiance would take her, and she would get to her feet and dance, to scattered cheers and a renewal of the music. To move completely freely, answering to no one, was so great a joy in those moments that she didn't care if the overseer came in and saw her. That was worth more than sleep; at her most joyful, she felt it would be worth dying.

During the day was dangerous, though, as well as difficult. They beat her more now than they had before. Part of the reason might be that she could hardly hear the commands anymore, and trying to follow what everyone else was doing made her slow. But they beat her when she wasn't slow too. The whip would catch her back unexpectedly, and it took all her strength not to cry out. She wondered if at some level they were trying to surprise a cry from her, or something even more damning. In some way, perhaps, they knew that she did not belong to them. There was nothing to outwardly betray her: her eyes still had the flecks of green that showed the presence of the spell in her blood; she kept her face expressionless; she made no trouble.

But they still seemed to suspect her. If they knew for certain, they would kill her.

"You have to go," Molly said to her as they lay in the sleeping quarters. Molly was one of the ones who could speak, in the long hours just before dawn. She couldn't move, except sometimes to turn her head. "You need to get away from this plantation."

"I can't," she said. The rest of the slaves were asleep, she thought, but not many could have listened even if they were awake. They were from different parts of Africa, and when they spoke to each other, it was in a creole version of English. She and Molly were speaking their own language—Molly had grown up only a few miles from where Fina had been taken. When she had met Molly, she hadn't remembered the words. Molly had kept talking to her, and she'd remembered. "If they catch me, they'll kill me."

"They'll kill you anyway. You can't hide what you are forever. I've been to three different plantations in my life, little one, and I've talked to many of us there. I've never heard of anyone breaking entirely free of the spellbinding, as you have."

"Perhaps they wouldn't mind. Even here some of the slaves are unbound: the ones they use as overseers, and the house slaves. Some plantations don't bind their slaves at all. If I told them I didn't want to hurt them—"

"But you do. I know you do. You want to hurt them badly. You may be frightened, but you're angry—I'm not sure even you understand how much. And your anger is so much more dangerous than Augustus's was, because you know how to keep it inside you until the time is right. It's more dangerous, too, because you're a magician."

"I'm not."

"You are. Nobody could resist the spell entirely without powerful magic of some kind. Perhaps you haven't found it yet, but it's inside you, and it's making itself known. The unbound slaves you talk about never have magic in their veins—the plantation owners would never be so foolish. If they want to leave a slave unbound, for any reason, they pay to have them tested for magic first so they can make sure they'll be safe. You're not safe."

Fina didn't answer that. She didn't know how to say that she wanted to be safe.

"I don't remember being free," she said instead. "Not really. Even if I did manage to escape, I wouldn't know how."

"Yes, you do," Molly said. Her voice was uncompromising. "Everyone knows that."

"I'm not brave like you. I'm not like the ones who fight to take themselves back. I couldn't turn and hit the overseer, like Augustus did last year. I'd be too scared."

They had killed Augustus. They had force-fed him enough of the spell to lock him rigid, and they had ordered him to stand still while they set him on fire. The white overseer had ordered the other slaves to watch him burn, and Fina had stood and watched.

"You *are* brave," Molly said. "You've lived like this since you were six years old, and you haven't let them break you. I watched you come back from despair when you had nothing but our voices and your own thoughts to hold on to. I watch you suffer every day and not show a glimpse of it on your face. That's bravery. You'd be braver still once you left. Having more to lose makes you brave."

"I don't want to leave you," she burst out. That was what she really meant. "You and Jacob and the others. I don't want to—I *can't* just leave you here to get beaten and worked to death without me. You're my family. I love you."

"And we love you," Molly said. She spoke softly now. "Of course we do. But that's why we don't want you to stay here." She paused. "Maybe you could join one of the bands in the hills. Then you could come break us out, like that band a few years back."

It might be like that, she knew. But she couldn't believe it, or see herself doing it. She also knew, and maybe so did Molly, that if she escaped, they might kill Molly to deter the other slaves from escaping as well. It had happened once before, when Sam had run away. They claimed that they thought the slaves could forge no relationships. But they always seemed to know which one of them to hurt to punish another.

"Would you go?" she asked. "If you could? Would you leave me?"

Molly was silent for a time. "No," she said. "No, little one, I wouldn't. But you need to, all the same. If they find out how powerful you are, they'll kill you."

Fina knew that. It was why she hadn't told Molly about the flashes that had cut across her vision, twice over the last few months and more intense each time. Once she had seen the inside of the processing plant as she had lain down to take her rest, in a flash of heat and flame. Another time, in the burning sun, she had seen the cool white parlor of the owner's house, somehow familiar although she had never worked there. She didn't know what it meant, or what the magic awakening in her could achieve. But she knew that once she admitted it was real, and hers, she really would have to leave. And she had nowhere to go.

London

November 1788

It would, Pitt decided, be easier to break into the Bank of England via a secret tunnel from Kew that did not exist than it was to gain access to William Wilberforce when a host of friends and doctors had anything to say about it. It was a comfort, in a way, that his friend had so many people concerned about his well-being. He knew Wilberforce was genuinely, seriously hurt, and still drifting in and out of real danger. But it was frustrating.

"I'm the prime minister," he told the healer. "Directly after this, I have permission to see the king."

"And I will not prevent you from seeing Mr. Wilberforce, sir," the doctor said. He was a moderate empath, but a Commoner—another who would have been able to do his job far better without the restrictions of a bracelet. "But you must understand that he's still very weak, and the laudanum he's been given to dull the pain is going to make him very drowsy. Please try not to tax his strength. His injuries are very serious."

The doctor had no idea that Pitt knew very well how serious his injuries were, since nobody knew that he had been there when Wilberforce had sustained them. Only a few, in fact, knew that Wilberforce had been injured at all. Most knew only that he was dangerously unwell and unable to leave his bed, a decline seen as very sudden and surprising for an undersized but previously healthy twenty-eight-year-old. Fortunately, Wilberforce was so generally well liked that the papers and the other MPs had responded with concern rather than suspicion; even Fox had stopped Pitt yesterday to inquire if Wilberforce was improving. Most politicians would have been judged deserving of such an illness, if they weren't suspected of conveniently inventing it. The Nightingale of the House of Commoners was not one of them.

"I promise to be extremely careful," Pitt assured the healer. "Could you please let him know I'm here?"

It had been a long time since Pitt had remembered to think of Wilberforce as diminutive, but the man lying in bed seemed impossibly tiny. His face was white and drawn, his tangle of brown not-quite-curls lay unbrushed and unpowdered over the pillows, and his eyes were dulled. He managed a shadow of his usual smile at the sound of his friend's steps, however.

"They tell me I'm no longer ill enough to refuse the trouble of your visit, Mr. Pitt," he said. "Although God knows I'm not a man to enjoy the company of those he esteems and values."

"Hurtful as that is, I'm relieved to hear you say it," Pitt returned, trying to keep his own voice light as the door quietly closed behind them. "When I was told last week that you were actually turning visitors away, I believed you were either dying or dead."

Wilberforce laughed a little, and winced. "I really do apologize for having to turn you away. I believed I was either dying or dead also, which made it even harder. I'm much better now. How is the king? I thought I heard you say you were on your way to see him after this—which, I may say, was beautifully haughty of you."

"Thank you very much. The reports of the king from his physician are troubling, I'm afraid. Despite what I said, I did hope that the shadow was connected in some way, but if it is, destroying it hasn't made any difference. The report I received yesterday used the phrase 'perfectly maniacal.' I'm visiting him with Dr. Addington—partly, I have to admit, to see if he can offer a more optimistic diagnosis."

"That's Henry Addington's father, isn't it? The one who..."

"My father's doctor, exactly. The one who saved my life. And before you ask: yes, the fact that I've contacted him does indeed mean that I'm concerned the king's magic is turning in on itself. I trust him to be able to tell me, which is more than I can say for the court physician—who is very likely in the pay of the Prince of Wales." He forced himself to go on before Wilberforce could reply. "I wanted to tell you how sorry I am for what happened. I should never have asked you to help me go after an unmarked shadow—much less what it turned out to be. You were quite right: I was far too confident, and it was far too dangerous."

"No, you were right," Wilberforce said instantly. "I knew that as soon as we saw it, though like you I can't quite explain it. It was our evil to stand against."

As usual, Wilberforce had managed to articulate in a few words something Pitt was struggling to frame into thoughts. The trouble was, as usual, it made no sense.

"What *was* it?" Wilberforce added. His eyes kindled with some of their customary light. "Where did it come from?"

Pitt hesitated. "I can't be certain."

"If you can make an uncertain guess, it's a good deal more than I can do. It was an undead. The first to be seen for hundreds of years. Only a necromancer can create an undead, is that right?"

"Half-right." Pitt glanced at the door instinctively, to make sure it was closed. It was, but he sat down on the bed so that they could talk more quietly just in case. "Apparently it takes a necromancer and a shadowmancer working together to create an undead. A necromancer can animate a body for a short time after death, but that's only an echo. The personality of the dead man or woman returns, along with their magic and their memories, for a very short time. To create a bona fide undead, he or she needs a shadow. That's all an undead is: a corpse used as a vessel for a shadow. A necromancer anchors the shadow to the body, and it serves the shadowmancer who summoned it as a shadow always does."

"So it would require two magicians."

"Exactly. The problem is, it's highly delicate, highly specialized magic. It's not something either party does by instinct. The knowledge has been deliberately lost since the Vampire Wars—I had to read through half my library to find even what I've just told you. And there *are* no necromancers anymore, at least according to popular belief. The Knights Templar see to that."

"Well," Wilberforce pointed out, "there are no vampires anymore either, according to popular belief. Yet you do fairly well for yourself."

"True. In which case we would be looking for a necromancer whose magic, like mine, manifested late and wasn't caught. That wouldn't be at all surprising, now that I think about it. Necromancy is only magic like any other. As long as they refrained from using it, nobody would ever know."

"And yet they used it. They didn't only use it; they used it to perform an act of magic that hasn't been seen for more than three hundred years. In my experience, most illegal magicians only want to hide. What does this one want?"

Pitt didn't answer directly. "I spoke to the Templars about the body. It's fallen to their jurisdiction. They have no way of knowing that it was walking around after its soul left the premises, of course, but they still find it peculiar."

Wilberforce managed a very faint smile. "Two causes of death, I would imagine."

"Its throat was cut and it was drained of blood some time ago. The stake through the heart, of course, was recent."

The smile faded. "The poor man."

"Judging by his clothing and the contents of his pockets, they think he either came from France or visited there very recently."

"And so you think there's a necromancer in France."

"I would swear that there wasn't one in London. I would know. And we know there's a magician in France with the habit of calling rogue shadows."

"Dear God." He shook his head. "What's happening over there?"

The question hung in the air, unanswered.

"I'll write to the Templars in France," Pitt said at last. "Magic runs in families. If we have a list of magicians who were executed for necromancy, even at birth, it might give us a place to start."

"I doubt you'll find one. I can tell you from experience investigating magical crime, the Templars don't like to share."

"Let me worry about that," Pitt said, and knew it was unhelpful. "At least for now. According to the healer guarding your bedroom door, you're going to be convalescent for months yet." If he was going to recover at all, was what the healer in question had actually said, but that wasn't something Pitt intended to repeat even to himself.

Even without the addendum, it was the wrong thing to say. "I can't be," Wilberforce said. "I know the doctor means well, but he doesn't understand: I really can't be. We're presenting the slave bill soon, and there's still so much to do before then—"

"Quiet," Pitt said, with a warning glance at the door: if the healer thought that his patient was being distressed, he would be through the door in a shot, and he hadn't looked like a man who would hesitate to throw out the prime minister. "Don't worry about the slave bill. I already meant to reassure you that I'd take responsibility for it myself. I'll make sure it doesn't disappear while you're recovering."

"You have enough to do," Wilberforce argued, but weakly. His frown had eased.

"Not remotely. It's been hours since I've had a worthy political crisis. I was already bored." He let his voice become more serious before Wilberforce could respond. "I promise to do everything that you would do yourself, were you able. I'll even present it to the House for you, if you really want, though I do think that had better wait until you're healed. It's more suited to your talents and contacts than mine."

"I think you're right," Wilberforce agreed. "But if you could see the way ready as we planned, that would be more than I have any right to ask. Thank you." He sighed. His face was whiter than before, and the dark circles under his eyes were more pronounced. "Bother. I don't mean to sound ungrateful, I'm very grateful, but... There's no way to keep this from delaying things, is there?"

"Just one," Pitt said. "Stop worrying about it, and get well quickly."

That did, at least, raise a more characteristic smile.

Before he left, with a promise to go straight to call on Clarkson, Pitt turned back to regard his friend.

"This may be a strange question," he said, "but would it be possible for you to leave town for a few months?"

"I'd planned on doing so," Wilberforce said slowly. "My cousin Thornton wants me to come stay with him out at Clapham while I still need looking after. Why?"

"Thornton." The name was vaguely familiar: he associated it with a gentle, strong-jawed face and a steady voice. "He's one of the MPs for Southwark, is he not? He was a banker before that."

"Yes. He joined the Abolition Society recently. We were excellent friends growing up."

"Good. Then if I were you, I would accept his offer."

"I will, of course. But...you can't possibly think I'm in any danger. The undead is gone. And surely I was only attacked in the first place because I wandered into Westminster Abbey with a stake."

"In which case you spend the next month or so in the countryside instead of in London to no purpose, which sounds enviable. I don't think you're in any further danger; at least, I don't understand why you would be. There are still a thousand things about that night I want to understand. But for now, I'd appreciate it if you'd humor me."

Normally, Wilberforce would not have let that pass; fortunately, at the moment, he was too exhausted to push the matter. "Of course. I'm sorry; I don't think I ever thanked you for getting me to safety."

"You know you don't have to," Pitt said seriously. He very rarely slept badly—he was faintly notorious for it. Wilberforce could be kept up until dawn by even minor worries; Pitt, whenever he finally managed to get to bed, went out like a candle and, like a candle, tended to stay out. The night after Wilberforce had been hurt, he had woken no fewer than seven times, each time more reluctant to close his eyes again. The image of the shadowy form dissipating to reveal his friend lying contorted with pain on the ground had been vivid in his mind.

He hoped that was all that had shaped his suspicions. The night in Westminster Abbey had been very dark, and his senses had been heightened in ways he could not quite understand. He didn't trust his own thoughts, much less his own feelings. But a shadow seemed to be hanging over London, and over France, and he couldn't deny that he would be relieved to have Wilberforce out from under it.

The royal residence at Kew was really more of a house than a palace. Everything about it was intimate and gentle: the redbrick front that welcomed visitors, the white-shuttered windows, the vast expanse of green around it, even the winding nine-mile road from Westminster that led to its gates. It was a domestic haven for the royal family, rather than a center of pomp and grandeur. Pitt had called on the king there a few times. Dr. Anthony Addington, beside him in the carriage, had never been. His eyes behind their spectacles surveyed the building with eager criticism as the carriage pulled up.

"It's not a bad mansion," he allowed. "Still, you'd expect more from His Majesty. Your father's house isn't much smaller."

"He *has* more," Pitt pointed out. "This is the most private, and it's close to London."

"It's also heavily shielded." Addington had been an experienced practitioner in magical ailments when he had saved Pitt's life at fourteen. The doctor was in his midseventies now but missed nothing. "Did you see that, coming in the gate? Those crests were silver and ash. Designed to ward away shadows. The king is a shadowmancer, I believe?"

"He is." Somewhere, deep where he usually kept it hidden, Pitt's own magic was beginning to stir. The carriage was colder, suddenly, than it had been. He pushed it aside, as he would a headache or an unwanted thought. "All the palaces are bespelled against magic—to the extent that those spells ever work."

"The question is," Addington said, "in this case, are they keeping something out, or something in?"

He felt it the moment he stepped from the coach. As he had once told Wilberforce, Pitt was used to sensing the bloodlines of those around him. They flickered somewhere between his mind and his blood and his magic: dark strands of unmanifested abilities, glowing shards of weather magic or shadowmancy or fire magic. Usually they were a whisper on the edge of his awareness, like a faint breeze or a blur of conversations at a club he had no interest in eavesdropping upon. This was a scream.

"What is it?" Dr. Addington asked. He was looking at Pitt very shrewdly. He, out of everyone in England, probably knew exactly what it was.

"Nothing," Pitt said firmly. He drew himself together; magic roared dizzyingly in his ears. "Nothing at all."

But of course it was.

His Majesty King George III was in a darkened bedchamber on the ground floor. Alone among the plain, homely rooms of the rest of the house, the walls gleamed with gilded designs, ornate and beautiful. The sight could have been one of grandeur, had Pitt not known that the designs were, like those on the gate, symbols wrought from silver and ash bespelled to contain powerful magic. Besides, the king was in no way dressed for court. A dirty smock hung from his emaciated frame; the leather straps that bound him to his chair cut into thin wrists and bony ankles. George's eyes were wide as if in horror or surprise, while his mouth moved in a soundless monologue. The two doctors—one in black, the other in a Templar's robes—stood well back.

The room was alive with shadows. They spiraled out from the king's chair, some light gray and formless, others darker and almost with the appearance of men. They writhed in the corners of the ceiling and wreathed the walls like smoke. The air had the filthy, frigid haze of a London winter.

Pitt stood very still. He didn't, at that moment, trust himself to speak.

"I don't believe," Dr. Addington said, "my diagnosis is going to be needed."

England

The Regency Crisis

The madness of a powerful mage-king isn't the same as the madness of an ordinary person. The madness of a mage-king means the entire country convulses.

The royal families in Europe were deliberately bred from strong magicians, and while, as Louis had proved, that was no guarantee of strong magic manifesting, in George the lines of shadowmancy had run very pure indeed. Even Bethlem Hospital, with its shielded rooms for containing the more dangerous magicians whose powers were outside their control, couldn't have kept London safe from him. In any case, no member of the royal family would ever be subjected to the privations of a common asylum. Instead, the king was confined to the palace at Kew, and everyone but his doctors and their helpers were sent a safe distance away. Thrill-seeking crowds came to the gates to see what they could spy. There were occasional bursts of fire or lightning in the vicinity—George's latent bloodlines awakening at odd times. For the most part, though, the palace walls swarmed with a veil of light-gray shadows.

In theory, none of these shadows were quite powerful enough to kill on contact. In theory, they were contained by the alchemy, and by the king. In practice, only the most loyal would chance it.

The shadows weren't the only things that swarmed. So did the king's enemies.

George was clearly in no state to rule the kingdom, much less protect it from theoretical magical threats. He was a danger to it and those around him. His eldest son, the Prince of Wales, was all too eager to step in as regent until—he said—his father was fit to return. He was a strong magician in his own right: a weather-mage, from his mother's side of the bloodline, with weaker strands of shadowmancy. He was also a rake, a spendthrift, and the despair of his quiet, pious father, not to mention the close friend and drinking partner of Charles Fox and the Whig opposition. Fox rushed home from Italy, where he had been closeted with his mistress Mrs. Armistead. Parliament opened later in the year than usual, but to a storm of excitement.

"What will happen if there's a regency?" Pitt's sister Harriot asked him at the breakfast table. The Eliots, as usual, were staying in Downing Street while Parliament was in session. They had given up the pretense of looking for a house of their own by now, when the prime minister's residence was large enough for several of them.

"Then the Prince of Wales takes the throne," Pitt replied. "If he has his way with the agreement, it will be very, very difficult for the king to take it back again. He'll certainly replace the government—his supporters have already claimed the roles between them. Fox will be prime minister, apparently."

Harriot knew this, of course. She had grown up as steeped in politics as he had. "I meant what will happen to you? Will they ask you to be part of the new government?"

"I wouldn't give them the opportunity. I have no desire to serve under Fox—and frankly, I don't see the point of it. I wouldn't be able to do much good there."

"So you'd go into opposition?"

"Maybe." The idea wasn't particularly appealing. "Or I'd leave politics entirely. I'm still qualified to practice law, after all."

She burst out laughing. "You'd never do it."

"I would."

"Oh, you would for a while, to prove a point to yourself. But you wouldn't be able to stay away from the House of Commoners. It's all you have."

"It isn't *all* I have."

"What else do you have? Friends don't count. You have some very good friends, but they're all in politics. Our entire family is in politics, frankly, since you made John lord of the admiralty."

"I have . . . oh, I don't know. Books. Riding. Landscape gardening."

"Those are distractions from politics. You'd get bored with them very quickly if you had nothing else."

"Well, then," Pitt said. "I'd better make sure I don't lose all I have."

There was no need to hurry into a regency so quickly, Pitt maintained that night, to a swell of support on one side of the House of Commoners and derision on the other. At present, the king's illness looked to be only temporary. There was no reason whatsoever to think he wouldn't recover. In the meantime, a committee was appointed to examine the records of the last time a similar regency occurred, just in case, to determine the proper form such a regency might take.

The last case was more than four hundred years earlier, before the Vampire Wars. It was a delaying tactic, but it was also just the way Pitt thought.

The gossip and speculation and fears weren't confined to Parliament, or even London. They spilled across the quiet common at Clapham where Wilberforce was recovering with his cousin Thornton, and crept into every nook and cranny of the house.

"The opposition are claiming that without a mage-king on the throne, the country is open to attack," Hannah More said when she came to visit. "Which if they knew anything about magic, they'd know was superstition. There's no spell that links a king and the country—the idea that the king needs powerful magic is merely tradition stemming back from the days before the Concord, when a king used to ride into battle at the head of an army of magicians. At least Fox is being honest. He just wants the Prince of Wales on the throne."

"There's still hope the king might recover," Wilberforce said, from where he sat curled up on the couch with the newspaper. He was allowed out of bed now, though barely, and he had been following the situation in London with concern. "Pitt just needs to keep Fox at bay long enough to give him the opportunity."

"It's already been six weeks," Thornton said. "He has the doctors on committees now, arguing about whether or not the king is getting better. That could go on indefinitely, but Fox won't let it. Neither will the Knights Templar. They prefer George to his son, but they want a magician on the throne. And to be fair to them, if one of those shadows escapes the king's control—or if the king, in his madness, unleashes them—"

"There's one thing I'll bet good money that the Knights Templar haven't told the government," Miss More said. "The king isn't the only strong magician to have lost control of his magic this winter."

"Really?" Wilberforce looked up. "Who else?"

"Nobody of any name, and none so dramatic. Just minor hiccups, almost all shadowmancers. The Commoners have mostly been arrested, poor souls, and the Aristocrats are being treated at their estates. One or two are at Bedlam, which is how I heard about it. A few of us went out there to report on conditions—which are disgraceful."

"Excuse me," Thornton said, half-amused. "I believe he's supposed to be resting."

"No, really, I'm quite all right," Wilberforce said. His knife wound throbbed sickeningly, but he sat forward. "Tell me about Bedlam."

Wilberforce wrote to Pitt about the incidents Miss More had spoken of, careful to highlight that they had occurred around the same time as the undead had come to Westminster. He received no reply, but he was used to that. He knew the letter had been read.

The king was no better after Christmas. The doctors sent daily reports: by carrier at first, and then, as the urgency increased, the Downing Street daemon-stone took its place on Pitt's desk for the first time. Daemon-stones on one level were simply very powerful shadows that had been summoned forth and, rather than allowed to take shape, had been bound to a black stone from which they could never escape. Once bound, they could communicate with each other across any distance of land and a short distance of water, which allowed messages to pass between those who used them in the blink of an eye. They were highly useful, and highly sought. Yet they were rare, not just because summoning and binding such powerful shadows was near impossible, but because most shadowmancers strong enough to do so refused. Higher shadows didn't exist to be enslaved, they said. It was a friendship, a communion, a sharing of trust. It was a terrible thing to bind one. They would serve you because they had to, but they would never forgive you. Fortunately, Pitt wasn't superstitious about shadows, and he didn't share Wilberforce's dread of them—even after the visit from the undead. The magic in his blood chilled him every time he picked one up, but he was running on youth and nervous energy, and this was easy to disregard.

The reports themselves were harder to dismiss. Harder still were the visits to the king in person.

Pitt had known the king for a very long time: his father had served as his prime minister before him. George was both stubborn and frustratingly manipulative; like most monarchs, he was an obstacle to the workings of government more often than he was an aid, particularly when it came to anything at all revolutionary. But he was also a kind man, and a clever one in his own way. He would have been devastated to know of the danger and fear his shadows had wrought—perhaps he did know it, and that was why he looked gripped by such horror. George had grown ragged and filthy over the months of his confinement; his wrists were open sores, and his face was gaunt. In some respects, the madness—or, rather, the illness—of a powerful mage-king was exactly the same as that of an ordinary person.

Harriot was writing a letter to their mother when Pitt came home from Kew Palace one night before Christmas. She took one look at his face and winced. "Is it that terrible?"

"Exactly that terrible, I would say, rounding up or down to the nearest decimal point." Usually the hour's drive was enough for the cold from the king's shadows to wear off. Either the shadows were growing thicker or prolonged use of the daemon-stone and lack of sleep were taking a toll, because he was still shivering, and his head had been aching all day. He really needed to write a letter of his own before the House sat tonight, but instead he gave in to temptation and sank down onto the couch by the fire. The warmth from the flames danced on his skin without quite touching the chill in his blood, but it was a little better than nothing. "I need to present the Prince of Wales with the constitution tomorrow. I don't think I'll be able to convince the House of the king's good health for much longer. He doesn't even recognize me anymore."

Harriot abandoned her letter and dropped down on the sofa next to him. "Is it like being with Father?" she asked. "When he was ill?"

"A little." It couldn't have been admitted to anyone outside the family—not even Wilberforce or Eliot. The times when their father's mesmeric strain had turned on him, and his brilliant mind had been momentarily submerged, were deeply private. But Harriot understood. "More than I'd like. But there's something else. I feel, with the king, that he's trying to tell me something important."

"Like what?"

"I don't know." He thought of the letter Wilberforce had sent him. "I'm not certain he knows, consciously. And I don't know how to help him."

"He might be able to tell you under mesmeric influence."

"It's possible. But I'd need a mesmer powerful enough to extract the information from the tangle of his thoughts without snapping them—and they'd need to be someone who could be trusted with that information once they had it. There are a few powerful mesmers in the country, but none who fit both criteria."

"It's a pity Father is no longer with us," Harriot said. "Or Hester—she could have given you all the mesmerism you wanted."

Pitt smiled at that. Their sister had inherited a strong dose of the family mesmerism without any of the complicating blood magic. Her eldest daughter, little Hester Stanhope, had inherited it from her—fortunately, the Earl of Stanhope was an Aristocrat, so there would be no restrictions on her magic.

"You could do it yourself, you know," Harriot said.

His smile faded. "No, I couldn't."

"Why not? If it's important—"

"A lot of things are important. If I use mesmerism for one, I'll use it for all of them."

"As do many legal Aristocrats, within limits that I'm sure you wouldn't violate. Nobody would know."

"That isn't the point."

She sighed. "As far as I can tell, blood magic without blood is only magic. It makes no difference what you call it. I've never understood why you need to be so afraid of yourself. Father was one stroke of magic away from being a vampire, and he used mesmerism without a qualm."

Pitt would have willingly died rather than admit that their father—their dazzling, eccentric, loving father, whom he had reverenced more than anyone else on earth—was rather too careless about his magic. But it was what he sometimes thought.

"The strain wasn't quite so strong with him," he said instead. "He was still legal. It was a risk he chose to take."

"I suppose you think him marrying and having children was a risk too. And yet we wouldn't be here without it."

He was startled into looking up. "Why do you say that?"

"Hester used to think it was why you never seemed interested in being married when the rest of us did. I hoped not. But it just struck me, in light of what we were saying when all this started. You do need more in your life."

"You sound like Wilberforce, except that he's usually talking about God. He isn't married either, by the way."

"Oh, that's different. He will, without any doubt, when he gets around to it. We're not sure you will."

He wasn't sure he would either. It wasn't only his magic, although that was part of it. He just never felt the need. His life was whole; there simply weren't any gaps in his day or his self where he could imagine anyone else fitting in. Certainly there weren't at the moment.

"If it was what you were thinking," Harriot said, "I wanted to let you know you were wrong. Our family magic shouldn't make the least bit of difference."

"And yet you've never told Eliot what I am."

He didn't say it with reproof, but she fell silent.

"That isn't fair," she said at last. "You asked me not to tell him."

"Would you have told him if I hadn't?" He didn't torture her by waiting for a response. "Of course not. Hester never told her husband either. I don't know if John has told his wife, but I doubt it. Because you want children with them, and there's every possibility that they won't agree when our family magic manifested so recently. Don't think this is a reproach: I agree completely. But please don't tell me that the kind of magic makes no difference."

"Very well." Her voice was uncharacteristically quiet. "I won't. But don't tell me what I wouldn't tell Edward and why. If I don't share your secret, it's to protect you. There may be other reasons—I truly don't know—but that will always be the most important. And I'm not in the least bit afraid of what our blood will do to my children and Eliot's. I'm sure they'll be perfect."

"I know—all of that. I'm sorry. In any case, this doesn't help the king, and I can't delay the debates any longer."

"You'll just have to win them."

"Not really possible, in the long run. Fox is completely correct: if the king's magic is awry, he's far too dangerous to have on the throne. I can only draw things out and give him a chance to recover."

"Only that?"

He smiled a little, despite the pounding in his temples. "Well," he acknowledged, "not quite *only* that."

The constitution the government presented was insulting. The Prince of Wales barely read it before throwing it to the ground and taking up his pen in disgust. The storm cloud swarming over his rooms at Hampton Court could be seen a mile away.

"You really are pushing things too far," Fox told Pitt bluntly on the way into the House of Commoners. "At this rate the prince is going to forgo having you thrown out of government in favor of having you executed."

"I'm very sorry to hear that," Pitt said. "We could have a regency tomorrow if His Royal Highness would agree to the terms."

"By the terms you propose," Fox returned, "it would be no regency at all. You've curtailed the prince's rights to nothing. I'm fairly sure Charles I had more power in the dungeon before they cut off his head. And you know that very well."

"I see your point," Pitt said. "We'll be happy to negotiate further, of course."

It was now February. The king had been out of his magic for four months.

And then, as quickly as it had began, it was over. The very day before the constitution was due to be signed, the king woke up and asked quite reasonably for his breakfast. The odd wisp of shadow darted about the curtains, but the air was otherwise clear. By the following morning, it was as though nothing had ever happened. George III was sane again. His magic was completely under control.

Wilberforce arrived back in town with the first rush of spring. The House of Commoners was thronged with MPs trying to convey their pleasure over the king's return—with a few exceptions. Fox was gracious in defeat, but he was also honest.

Pitt was perfectly composed in the House that evening; afterward, at Downing Street, he was the precise buoyant mix of high spirits and exhaustion that Wilberforce remembered from when he first took power. It made him smile.

"So the king really is sane?" he asked.

"I saw him again this morning," Pitt said, "and there was no trace of stray magic. His bloodlines have settled too, which the Templars have no means of knowing. He's entirely recovered. I hope the same can be said of you, by the way?"

"Not as much as I'd like." Wilberforce never saw the point in being less than candid when people asked him how he was. They must, after all, really want to know. "I'm rather relying on divine grace and laudanum to keep me upright. But I'm very glad to be back. Do we know what caused the king's magic to turn like that?"

"The Templars don't, though they won't admit it in so many words. From your letter, I assume you agree with me that it must have something to do with the dark magic on the Continent."

"I do," he said. "I'm not surprised the shadowmancers in Bedlam reacted to the creation of an undead; it was a significant act of shadowmancy as well as necromancy. But moreover, I think the king was reacting to the undead as an attack upon England. The royal family's magic is connected to England, whatever scholars think. In ways we can't explain, perhaps, but it is. Whatever happened that night, it was more than just a solitary act of dark magic—which would be alarming in itself."

"I think that's very plausible," Pitt said. "Tomorrow I'll be very curious about it. Tonight, in all honesty, I'm only curious about what a full night's sleep feels like. I've entirely forgotten."

"Is that you telling me to leave?"

"Absolutely. Get out. Before you do, though, how is the abolition bill? Is there anything I can do for it?"

"Not if you want a full night's sleep. The last batch of evidence Clarkson brought is nightmarish. Thank you for pushing through the motion to regulate conditions on ships, by the way. I know it was more difficult than we expected."

"I truly was surprised about that," Pitt said, more seriously. It was one of the few movements that had been made toward abolition since the king's illness. That, and Wilberforce's own removal from the House, had between them all but stopped the campaign in its tracks. "I was surprised, too, that France refused to ban the trade after all. I know we were prepared for opposition, and I still believe you can do it, but I'm afraid it's going to be a battle."

"We'd better take the battle to them, then. The king's back on the throne, and I'm back in the House. It's been long enough."

He said it as confidently as he could. Inwardly, though, he couldn't help but feel uneasy, about more than abolition. The king's madness had been an unexpected shadow. It had lifted now, but it had left its marks, and he couldn't help but feel that those marks would still be there when the shadow fell again.

London

May 1789

After his enforced absence, Wilberforce had forgotten how bustling the House of Commoners was before a major debate. The benches were filling rapidly as he crossed the floor, his cousin Henry Thornton at his side guiding him protectively through the crush of people. The House knew, of course, that he intended to introduce the long-delayed bill to abolish the slave trade today. Many stopped to promise their support; Charles Fox, having recovered from the disappointment of the king's return, jumped down from his seat particularly to shake his hand.

"Welcome back, Nightingale," he said. "I hope you'll leave room for me to speak tonight. I have a few choice words for those butchers in that vile trade."

"I'll try," Wilberforce said, smiling. "But please remember that you and Pitt are on the same side tonight, won't you? I don't want you to oppose each other out of habit."

"I won't if he won't," Fox said. He clapped Wilberforce on the shoulder with all the force of his stout frame, which hurt a lot more than he probably intended. "Don't worry. With both of us, the other side have no hope at all."

"Thank you," Wilberforce said. He meant it too. He just hoped it would be enough.

Outside the House, word was beginning to spread about the ill treatment of the slaves, and there had been a swell of popular support.

Olaudah Equiano's narrative of his life as a slave, published earlier that year, had set the country ablaze with indignation. Clarkson traveled up and down the country giving talks and demonstrations and left outrage against the trade in his wake. And yet the slave merchants still dominated the House itself, and—as Pitt had discovered for them—they seemed opposed to the most basic acts of human decency. Fleets of slave ships still traversed the Atlantic every day, crammed with their human cargo. Wilberforce had dreamed of them as he lay at Thornton's house, feverish and racked with pain. It had hurt far worse than any knife.

"Clarkson's up in the gallery, I see," Thornton remarked. Wilberforce tried to follow his gaze but couldn't make him out.

"He's been here every time anything related to the slave trade has been brought up, he told me," he said. "So has Sharp."

"They'll see something worth seeing today, hopefully."

"They will," Wilberforce said. He believed it, but he also wouldn't let himself think any different. They had to.

Wilberforce had been speaking in the House of Commoners since he was twenty-one, and he had long since ceased to feel any more nerves than he suffered speaking to friends in his own house. He knew the men there. He knew his own abilities, which he had confidence would not simply desert him when he had something to say. And until his recent enforced absence, he knew, he was faintly notorious for having something to say. Half the time, he would cheerfully jump to his feet with not even his scribbled notes to guide him, and to his surprise what he said could often sway individual votes. He never thought overmuch about making the walls sing: he simply listened; then he spoke, as he did in conversation. They were, after all was said and done, in conversation.

This time, though, as he got to his feet, his heart raced. The eyes of the men watching with, variously, encouragement, hostility, and curiosity seemed to pick apart everything he could say before it was ever said. And yet it wasn't their eyes that worried him. It was the imagined eyes of thousands of men, women, and children across the world, unable to watch him because their freedom and their magic and their voices had been relentlessly denied. The thought of those weighed on him far more greatly than either hostility or hope, and overwhelmed him with his own inadequacy in the face of the task God had set him.

He started with that.

"When I consider the magnitude of the subject which I am to bring before the House—a subject in which the interests, not of this country, nor of Europe alone, but of the whole world and of posterity are involved," he began, "it is impossible for me not to feel both terrified and concerned at my own inadequacies for such a task. I mean not to accuse anyone, but to take the shame upon myself, in common, indeed, with the whole Parliament of Great Britain, for having suffered this horrid trade to be carried on. We are all guilty—we ought all to plead guilty, and not to exculpate ourselves by throwing the blame on others."

He and the other abolitionists had planned their tactics very carefully. They had determined from the start to appeal not to the emotions of his listeners, but to cool, hard reason. All the meticulous evidence they had spent the last two years compiling was on display. Still, passion fired his own voice as he outlined the misery and desperation of the Middle Passage, and he used it to bring the House into his outrage.

"This, I confess, in my own opinion, is the most wretched part of the whole subject. So much misery, condensed in so little room, is more than the human imagination ever before conceived. I will not accuse the merchants—I will believe them to be men of humanity. I verily believe, therefore, that if the wretchedness of any one of the many hundred people stowed in each ship could be brought before their view, there is no one whose heart could bear it."

Colonel Banastre Tarleton shot out of his seat, as they'd expected. Not only was he the MP for Liverpool, the hub of the slave trade, but as a soldier he had fought with ruthless efficiency in the American

War. His opposition to any kind of magical reform, whether on the battlefield or in the House of Commoners, was without mercy.

"Perhaps the honorable gentleman would like to tell the House how he proposes slavery could continue at all," he said scathingly, "without shipments of new slaves brought in to replace those that die at their work?"

"To begin with," Wilberforce said before he could stop himself, "it might be a good incentive for plantation owners to ensure fewer poor souls die at their work."

He forced himself to calm down. This question, after all, was the most delicate part of this proposal, and one that they needed to tread around very lightly.

"There are many plantations now that spellbind their slaves only once a day," he said more reasonably. "By night, these men and women can move and speak; more trusted workers, at least those without magic, are not spellbound at all. Many of these men and women are permitted to have families, and children who grow up enslaved. If more were to adopt this practice, the population could easily be self-sustaining."

"So this can also be read as a call for an abolition of spellbinding?"

It was, of course—at heart, beneath the careful facade of practicality. It was a call for a great many things. But they couldn't afford to be suspected of that yet. They were pushing the door open and fighting for the slimmest of wedges; they couldn't afford for that wedge to be kicked out at once.

"Not at all." He was careful not to look at the gallery, where Clarkson and the others sat. "That would still be entirely dependent on the will of the plantation owners. But consider this: the alchemy used to spellbind is expensive to manufacture, it shortens the lives of the slaves, and it impedes their ability to perform their tasks. Plantations that limit its use are measurably more productive. I see no evil in its use being reduced by those that choose to do so. And if the abolition of the trade does provide incentive to improve the lives of the slaves in this way, I can see it only as an added blessing."

"And how does the honorable gentleman see the instant annihilation of a trade which annually employs upward of fifty-five hundred sailors and one hundred sixty ships, and which entails a large portion of our exports? Is such a loss to the country to be seen as an added blessing too?"

"It's interesting you should mention this." Once again, he fought to keep his voice calm—this time, against a flash of triumph. "I have in my hand a pamphlet which states, in very dreadful colors, what thousands and tens of thousands will be ruined, how our wealth will be impaired, one-third of our commerce cut off forever, while France, our natural enemy and rival, will strengthen herself by our weakness."

He raised his voice over the assenting calls from the House and the gallery.

"It might interest you to know, then, that this pamphlet was written fifteen years ago, when the American colonies rose up against us, and this House voted to grant them independence. Those colonies are free now: its men and women regulate their own magic and make their own laws, free from our control. I would therefore ask you, gentlemen, if this prophecy came to pass? Is our wealth decayed? Is France raised upon our ruins? On the contrary, do we not see, by the instance of this pamphlet, how men in a desponding moment will picture to themselves the most gloomy consequences from causes by no means to be apprehended?"

At the sound of his own voice, fluent and confident above the mutterings of the House, Wilberforce felt confidence rally within to match it. For three and a half hours, as the night wore on outside the candlelight of the House, he described the filthy conditions, the cruel treatment at the hands of the traders, the unimaginable torture of being reduced to property in theory while remaining in truth a feeling, intelligent human being. His throat was dry before he was near done, but his voice never faltered, and he ignored the growing pain of his knife wound to stand as straight and tall as his tiny frame would permit.

Finally, he took a deep breath and concluded. "There is a principle above everything which is political, and when I reflect on the command which says, 'Thou shalt do no murder,' believing the authority to be divine, how can I dare set up any reasonings of my own against it? The nature and the circumstances of this trade are now laid open to us; we can no longer plead ignorance; we cannot evade it. It is now an object placed before us; we cannot pass it; we may spurn it, we may kick it out of our way, but we cannot turn aside so as to avoid seeing it. This House must decide, and must justify to all the world and to their own consciences, the principles of their decision."

The walls were chiming, the high, clear nightingale note that was his and his alone. As he sat down in his place to a burst of applause that seemed to come from all corners of the House of Commoners, he knew that despite everything, he had managed to give the best speech of his life.

Two hours later, Parliament was dispersing around him, and he was as low as he had ever felt at the end of a session.

"They haven't defeated it utterly," Thornton reminded him comfortingly from beside him. "They've only called for the vote to be postponed until next year for more evidence to be heard and collected. That's a step in the right direction."

"Of course it is," Wilberforce agreed, marshaling his voice to sound optimistic. The wave he had been riding while speaking from the dispatch box had been so high that the fall was painful. The wound in his side was throbbing sickeningly, which probably meant his last dose of laudanum had worn off. "And we have over a year's head start on them in terms of gathering information. It's perhaps all we could ever expect. Are you going back to Old Palace Yard?"

"I think I will, if I can't find Sharp or Clarkson outside." Thornton had been lodging with him while Parliament was in session, which seemed only fair given that Wilberforce had been lodging with him in Clapham for such a large portion of the rest of the year. The two of them had always been on good terms, but their shared ideals and the time Wilberforce had spent recuperating at Thornton's house had drawn them even closer together. "I should probably get some rest—so should you."

"I will, very soon, I promise. But I want to try and catch Pitt first, to see if he has any ideas I can bring to the meeting this afternoon."

It didn't quite work like that, of course. He had to first run the gauntlet of people's compliments and commiserations, including those of a very annoyed Charles Fox; then, as soon as he cleared the debating chamber itself, the other members of the Abolition Society were upon him, filled with their own reassurances and disappointments.

"I knew this would happen," Clarkson said furiously. The abolitionist was bristling with indignation; beneath it, though, Wilberforce could see real heartbreak. If anybody had given their whole life to this cause, it was Clarkson. "I knew it couldn't be simply a matter of a few speakers being brilliant and honest; if it was, the country would be in a very different state altogether."

"This is a reasonable beginning," Wilberforce said, and knew he sounded unconvincing. "We'll keep gathering evidence, and then when Parliament opens next year—"

"Nothing is going to be accomplished through politics," Clarkson said, then caught himself. "Forgive me, I didn't mean that as a criticism of you. You did wonderfully; so did Fox and Pitt. But this is not the place where any real change is going to happen."

"It is," Wilberforce said. "I know how you feel, but I promise, on the right day, it is."

Pitt was waiting for him in the entranceway. The darkness outside had the crisp, quiet taste of after midnight.

"I underestimated you," Pitt said as Wilberforce approached. "I only thought you'd do brilliantly."

"It didn't quite have the effect I hoped for," Wilberforce said.

Pitt made a face. "I know. Unfortunately, it was so convincing a speech that the opposition couldn't risk putting it to a vote. I've still rarely encountered its equal."

Coming from somebody who had studied the great orators of

history and Parliament since he could read, that was a true honor, and Wilberforce felt his cheeks color with embarrassed pleasure. Fortunately, he was too tired and dispirited for pride to take a proper hold.

"I have to confess, I'm not at all sure I did the right thing in agreeing to the hearing of more evidence," he said. "The trade will go as usual all summer until Parliament reconvenes, and then the hearings will drag for months. It's a delaying tactic."

"You had no choice," Pitt said. "If you'd forced a vote, we might have carried it, but it would still have to pass the House of Aristocrats, and they'd use the lack of evidence to overturn it at once. It has to be done properly."

"*Will* it be done, though, is the question."

Pitt considered the question carefully, as usual. "The evidence is in our favor. We just need to fight for it to be heard—and Clarkson and your friends are very good at being heard. You'll have some long, difficult hours ahead next year, which I'm sorry for. The slave trade will do all they can to make sure their own voices drown yours out. But after how things went today... Unless the climate shifts radically over the summer, and I can't foresee why it would, I still think you can do it."

It was what he felt too, more or less what he had told Clarkson. But it was comforting to hear. It might not have been the end they all wanted, but it was a promising start.

"I have plans to go to Paris over the summer, in fact," Wilberforce told him, and felt a little brighter. "I'm still holding on to the idea of mutual abolition. Even though the king of France doesn't feel able to ban the slave trade with a royal decree, there are still strong hopes that it can be effected there by other means. The king's ministers were right when they said that free magic and liberty were touchstones among reformers over there. There's potential for real change to be made at the Estates General, aimed at freedom of magic for Commoner magicians, mostly, but I can't imagine anyone who feels indignant at the braceleting of their countrymen could be complacent about the spellbinding of their fellow man. It's possible that the reformers might be willing to incorporate the slave trade into the list of abuses to be done away with, if we approach them in the right way."

"It's possible," Pitt agreed, but more cautiously than Wilberforce had expected. "I agree it ought to be attempted. As your friend, though, I'd far rather someone else undertook the journey. Paris has been growing dangerously restive lately, and you're still not in the best of health."

"Clarkson will almost certainly volunteer to accompany me—and I'm very close to being well again."

"The undead came from France," Pitt said. "It seems a risk to follow it back there."

"We don't know for certain that it *did* come from France. The Templars in France had no record of any necromancy for the last hundred years, you said."

"And that troubles me in itself. Britain has certainly had an act or two of necromancy in the last century. For France to have no record of any at all in their own country, I strongly suspect somebody gained entrance to the Bastille and destroyed any mention of them. They must have known that the first thing anyone looking for a necromancer would do is to search for incidents of dark magic and then follow the bloodlines."

"Even if they did, France is a very big country. And why would it be a risk for *me* to go there, as opposed to anybody else?" A memory struck him, and stopped him in his tracks. "This has something to do with why you asked me to leave town last year, hasn't it? You never did explain that."

"There was never anything very much to explain. Only suspicions, and faint ones at that." Wilberforce looked at him steadily, and Pitt sighed. "Consider this, then. The shadow was waiting in Westminster Abbey. From there, it was in close proximity to many buildings of possible interest: Buckingham House, the Houses of Parliament, Downing Street, Whitehall. But it was in far closer proximity to your house at Old Palace Yard. And when we moved on it, and it was faced with the two of us, it chose to attack you rather than me."

"But that was pure chance, surely? It might not have recognized either of us. Perhaps I seemed an easier victim."

"Perhaps. I only know that no undead has appeared in London since. That means one of two things: whoever was responsible for the first was prevented from sending another, for reasons we can't fathom...or the one they sent had already accomplished its mission. You were about to move to abolish the slave trade. They knew that in France: William Eden saw to that, as did the abolitionists over there. You were almost killed. Since then, there's been no real movement toward abolition. And even among the reformers over there, abolition is not a popular idea."

"All the more reason for us to go now, surely," Wilberforce said. He resolutely ignored the chill around his heart. "You may be right, or not—really, I don't know. But I know I would hate to jeopardize a chance of negotiation because of one incident of dark magic."

"Still," Pitt said, but didn't complete his thought.

Paris

July 1789

Thomas Clarkson left England early in the morning, amid warnings of a storm and hurried arrangements for transporting his box of African artifacts and countless reassurances to Wilberforce that, yes, he really was quite content to make the journey to Paris in his place.

"Wilberforce, in the last few years, I've traveled some twenty-five thousand miles around England to gather evidence and lecture on the evils of the slave trade," Clarkson said finally. "This is the sole object of my life. It's immaterial to me where I go for it. And our friends are right that things could be very dangerous over there for somebody as close to the government as yourself, given the state of things; besides, a few months ago I was still hearing reports that you were going to die."

"I'm not going to die," Wilberforce said, but in the cold wind from the sea he looked very small and tired. It concerned Clarkson, who had seen him the previous year when everybody was convinced they were about to lose him. "I'm just not going to be very lively for a while. Again. Apparently I've overdone things."

"And by 'things,' you mean helping me abolish the slave trade," Clarkson said dryly.

"And by 'overdone,' I mean if you feel I can help you further, please send me word and I'll come straight to Paris," Wilberforce said, with a far more characteristic twinkle. It made Clarkson smile in response. "Thank you, as always. Do write to us when you can, won't you?"

It was just as well Wilberforce hadn't gone. The crossing was a rough one, and the bustle at the port in Calais not much better. As Clarkson journeyed by swift post chaise through the French countryside, the towns in which he stopped only seemed more restless. The people looked starving and ill. Incidents of robbery and violence were becoming more prevalent, and acts of unregistered magic were on the rise. A storm was brewing.

On the morning Clarkson arrived in Paris, Robespierre was having breakfast at the Café de Foy in the Palais-Royal gardens with Camille Desmoulins. The café, elegant in its shroud of tree-lined walks, had become an unlikely hive of revolutionary activity. On a fine day, it was crowded with diners and walkers, and the air felt rarefied and crisp with ideas. A few pedestrians pointed and whispered as they passed Robespierre's table.

They might have been pointing at Camille, who had gained a reputation for pamphlets too radical to print, but Robespierre heard his own name mentioned more than once. It had become one of the more renowned of the Third Estate. He had come from nowhere, small, pale, and unassuming, yet he had come fighting, and he called for reform on a scale that was dangerous and thrilling. His quiet voice spoke of a country built on Enlightenment principles, whose people were virtuous, where magic was a free resource to be used for the betterment of all, where food was well distributed and plentiful, where courts were in the hands of the people and not the talons of the Aristocracy, where the poorest Commoner was free to vote and grow and be educated. Plenty laughed at his opinions as being overly idealistic, even naive. Yet when he spoke, people listened. This was partly due to the illegal magic throbbing in his chest and permeating his words; he knew this, and he had no scruples about it. What he was saying needed to be heard, by whatever means. His vision for France was so clear now he could almost touch it.

It was work that had brought him to Paris from Versailles, but his meeting with Camille was more social than business. Until the meeting of the Estates General, Robespierre hadn't seen Camille since they had both been students at Louis-le-Grand. His school friend was little changed: dark-eyed and fragile, boyish and quick-witted. He had grown his black curls long and loose, as was becoming the fashion among the young radicals; as he spoke, he would push them back from his face in a manner that suggested he was not quite used to having them there. Robespierre, with his perfectly powdered wig and neat black uniform of the Estates General, felt ruefully like an accountant dining with a poet.

"The National Assembly of Magicians," Camille was saying from the other side of the table. "It's all everyone can talk about, you know."

"It's only a name, as yet," Robespierre said, in his usual role as cautious, indulgent elder student. He couldn't really muster much conviction. On this day, when the sky was high overhead and he sat in the midst of revolutionary fervor, he couldn't help but believe that anything was possible. "The king won't acknowledge us as a new form of government."

"The king doesn't have to. Nor do the Aristocrats." Robespierre had become more familiar with his friend's scrawled handwriting over the years than his voice; he had forgotten how pronounced his stammer could be, or it had become more so. When he was excited, his thoughts leaped too fast for his tongue to catch up. He was excited now. "They only have to fail to stop us. And they will. As they failed to keep you out of the Estates General."

Robespierre struggled to hold back a smile at that. Only three weeks ago, the king had reacted to the Commoners' demands that the Bastille be dismantled by closing the doors to the Third Estate. It had seemed to be the end of negotiations and of their dreams. He and his fellow delegates had, unanimously, refused to accept it. Assembling instead in a nearby tennis court, they had renamed themselves the National Assembly of Magicians and vowed never to disband until the rights of Commoners, both magical and mundane, were served by the powers that governed the country. The court had been hot and close, packed with the bodies of 577 Commoners; sun streamed through the windows overhead, and the air was thick with shouts. It had been the sweetest moment of his life.

"We had numbers on our side that day," he said. "They couldn't stop us."

"We'll always have numbers on our side. That's what the other Commoner magicians need to understand. They can't take us all. There are only a few thousand Templars of note in Paris; the number of Commoner magicians, braceleted or rogue, is in the tens of thousands, perhaps the hundred thousands. The Aristocracy know this. That's why they're so invested in the myth that Commoner magicians are rare; that's why they keep us ashamed of the bracelets, so that the true numbers are never revealed. One act of illegal magic, the bracelet sings, and the Templars are on them like dogs on a fox. But tens of thousands of bracelets, singing out at once... *They could never stop that.*"

He broke off with a sharp intake of breath; his knife fell to the side of his plate as his right fist clenched tightly.

Robespierre winced. "Camille..."

"It's all right." Camille shook out his hand impatiently, as one did to ease a bee sting, and picked up his knife again. His bracelet peeked from behind his cuff, glowing molten gold. Magic was coursing strongly in his veins; it always had when conversations became too heated. The burning metal must have been excruciating, yet beyond a flush of color to his cheeks and a brightness to his eyes, he didn't show it.

"I know how you feel. I do. But please try to calm down."

"This is no time for calm. This is the time for action."

"We *are* acting. You should have been there, that day when the king closed the doors. The tide is rising. The waters are churning. But it's hard to know when it will overflow."

Camille laughed. "That's your problem, Maxime. It's not a tide waiting to rise. It's a powder keg, and it's waiting for a spark."

Robespierre always thought it strange, afterward, that it should have been at that moment that the news came. But perhaps it wasn't.

The Revolution was all anyone really talked about these days. If it hadn't been that moment, it would have been another equally fitting.

"Camille!" The voice belonged to a man about their own age, plump and well dressed. He pushed his way through the tables, receiving annoyed looks from diners as their wine sloshed. "Have you heard?"

Robespierre didn't recognize the man, but clearly Camille did. He knew all sorts of people, most of them less than reputable. "What? What's happened?"

"The king has given the Templars discretionary power to arrest and hold any Commoner suspected of illegal use of magic, without trial," the man said. "The official decree came down only minutes ago."

"The Assembly asked for leniency for illegal magic!"

"They don't care what the Assembly wants," the man said. He was pink with indignation. "The king won't listen to us. It's a message to that effect."

"It's more than that," Robespierre started to say, but the man had already moved to the next table. He was brimming over with his own news and had no room for more.

"What more is it?" Camille asked.

Robespierre turned to him instead. "Without a trial, they don't have to prove use of magic at all. They can—"

"—arrest anyone, for any reason," Camille finished. His eyes had widened. "Dear God."

"It's because of the riots." Robespierre heard himself sounding very calm; inside, he was burning. They would suffer for this. He would see to it. "They want to be able to use illegal-magic charges to dispose of the worst of the dissenters. It's as if every Templar in the Order has been given a *lettre de cachet*—a countless number of them. They're afraid."

"They *should* be afraid!" Camille looked more furious than Robespierre had ever seen him, even when they were children. "They don't realize yet just how afraid they should be."

Before Robespierre could react, Camille leaped onto the table: his shoe narrowly missed Robespierre's plate, and the cutlery rattled. Not that it mattered. Breakfast was over. Neither of them had touched a bite.

"My friends!" he called to the café and to the streets.

"Get down from there!" Robespierre whispered, but without real conviction. A thrill raised the hairs on the back of his neck.

Camille, of course, ignored him. "The National Assembly of Magicians has asked for the Bastille to be dismantled. Word has just come that the king has awarded the Knights Templar powers to arrest and hold any Commoner magician without trial, as they see fit. Could our wishes be more insolently flouted? Could they show any more clearly their desire to see us dead before they see us free?"

It took Robespierre a moment to realize why his friend's voice sounded unfamiliar. For the first time in all the years he had known him, his stammer was gone; he had, somehow, outpaced it, or been carried above it. Without it, his voice was clear as the ringing of a bell.

"And what do you propose we do?" someone called from a table.

Camille's head turned toward him. "March on the Bastille! It's only stone and magic, after all. Tear it down, before they have a chance to use it against us ever again. Free those who have languished inside it for too long."

Most in the café were turning to look at him; a few from the path outside were stopping in their tracks. It wasn't enough: only Camille Desmoulins on a table, saying things they had heard before. Some were even beginning to look away. Robespierre saw Camille take a deep breath and square his shoulders. Then he let his magic loose.

Robespierre had often seen Camille scorched by the magic in his blood, but he had never seen the magic itself. He knew his friend could call shadows—that had been the incident that had nearly seen him in the Bastille as a child. He hadn't realized Camille was a fire-mage as well, and he hadn't realized that he was quite so powerful. The shadows around him swirled, gathered, not quite manifesting but casting the Palais-Royal into shades of soft gray. Sparks crackled from his fingertips, bouncing from the tables in glints of red and gold. The bracelet at his wrist glowed and then chimed, the endless, ear-piercing scream designed to bring Templars running. The braceleted magician was meant to be immobilized with pain by that point. Camille stood straight and tall.

Commoner magic, in broad daylight, on the streets of Paris. Robespierre, unexpectedly, felt tears spring to his eyes. They blurred Camille's face and transformed the tendrils of flame about him to flickers of light.

My God, he thought. *It's beautiful.*

"This is our birthright!" Camille said. Everyone was looking at him now; the patrons of the café, for the first time in Robespierre's memory, had fallen into utter silence. The only sound was the high, shrill wail of Camille's bracelet. "This was what was given to us by blood. If they want to take it from us, then I say we give them blood in return."

Quietly, without giving himself away, Robespierre let his own mesmerism flow, intertwining it with Camille's words and sending it through the crowds. It burned in him as usual, hot and fierce, but this time he sensed it was not needed. Some other, darker influence was already at work. For a moment, he could feel it like a touch on his shoulder.

"If you're wearing a bracelet," Camille said, "let it scream."

Robespierre never quite believed it was going to happen until other bracelets started to chime in conjunction with Camille's. The shrieking notes were eerie. They mingled with the voices of the crowd and the stamping of feet. They were the sound of stifled torment finally being heard.

But it was more than that. The sound was only a reaction to what was really taking place: scores of Commoners, all releasing magic that most had never used in their lives. Fire-mages, weather-mages, mesmers, metalmancers—the air hummed and throbbed with power. Fire, wind, and storm clouds raged under the bright July skies.

In that moment, Robespierre wished more than anything that he had been caught and braceleted as an infant—not for his necromancy, for which they would have killed him, but for his then-latent mesmerism. He would not have been able to use it in secret then; he would have had little chance of saving France. But he longed to be a part of that crowd.

Camille stood above them, the lights from his magic dancing on his face. "Come. Let's go free our people."

They moved through the streets in a giant wave, and as they did so, more rose and followed.

The first Clarkson knew of it was when he emerged from his hotel in the early afternoon, having arrived midmorning and retired to his room to breakfast late and refresh himself from the long, hot journey. The streets were seething with people, all crying out in either fear or excitement—possibly both. The city had been in a state of high alert when Clarkson had arrived, and riots had been breaking out among the Commoners for weeks, so at first Clarkson assumed it was another such outburst. As he listened, though, picking up a few scattered words from the babble of French dialect, he began to realize it was something more serious. A tiny thrill shot down his back before he was quite sure why.

"Excuse me," he said to a man plucked at random from the crowd: he seemed a little calmer than some, and had an open, honest face. Fortunately Clarkson's French was good. "What's the reason for this commotion?"

"You haven't heard?" the man said, in what Clarkson thought was surprise rather than scorn. "They're taking the Bastille."

"Who?" Clarkson knew about the Bastille, of course, the Parisian version of the Tower of London, which housed magical criminals in even more infamous conditions than its English counterpart. But news had been intermittent on the road, and he had not heard of any threat to it. "Who's taking the Bastille?"

"The army of the Assembly of Magicians," the man replied, and he certainly wasn't calm now. His voice rang with triumph and with pride. "A thousand Commoner magicians have surrounded the place. They're going to release the prisoners and seize the armory. They've just moved into the courtyard. Didn't you hear the bracelets screaming earlier? And the gunfire?"

Clarkson hadn't. The Bastille was some distance from his hotel, and he hadn't known to listen for it. Now, though, he thought he could discern the distant crack and boom of artillery, amid the shouts and cheers. When he looked in the direction the people seemed to be moving, he saw with a start that in the clear summer sky a mass of gray storm clouds was swirling over one specific spot. Weather magic. He felt the tiny thrill spark and catch fire. This was it. The Commoner magicians were indeed rising up.

The Bastille was an old fourteenth-century fortress, made impenetrable by ancient charms and good stonework, and it stood darkly in the heart of Paris. It was a formidable sight, more so than its English counterpart. The Tower of London, with its four elegant spires and white stone, had an ornamental look about it, as though one might easily call there for tea. France's prison for magicians was a great gray behemoth: eight solid towers linked by curtain walls, topped with crenellated battlements, and surrounded by fortified gates. It represented the stranglehold of the king and the favored Aristocracy over Commoners and unpopular Aristocracy alike, and for a long time there had been a growing sense that, sooner or later, it had to break.

It was breaking now—or at least, from where Robespierre was standing, it was being broken. The riot from the café had swept through the streets like a river after a storm. He had been pushed to the back in the chaos: Camille, in front, had been lost to him. They had come by a long, meandering path, halted every now and again by an onslaught of soldiers or Knights Templar, stopping to gather arms and supporters. But they had reached the prison.

They were no longer a riot. They were an army.

Around Robespierre, the army of the Assembly of Magicians—the Commoners of Paris—flooded the undefended courtyard and laid siege to the castle. Many simply opened fire with rifles or flung themselves at the closed drawbridge with axes and truncheons, but still more battered it with magic. The Bastille was reinforced with magic as well as stone: on the ramparts, there were Templar magicians working their own abilities to the breaking point in defense of the fortress. Fireballs flew freely; lightning from the swirling clouds above struck the battlements; the iron of the gates flexed and creaked under the touch of competing metalmancers. Gunfire blazed from above; some rioters cried out and fell as they tore at the walls. A young woman fell to the ground in front of Robespierre, her head a bloody wound; his necromancy stirred, and he knew he was in the presence of death. But the mob was growing louder. Their anger was a pulsing mass about him. It filled his senses, overwhelming them, so that his own sense of identity felt very fragile in its midst.

Robespierre had a pistol, but he didn't use it. He was not a man of great physical courage, and he knew this about himself. If it were not for the magic in his blood, he would not have been near the riot at all. But his benefactor's power blazed from him in hot, luxurious waves, aching to be used. Mesmerism was of little use in battle, really, but he did what he could. He pushed with it, sometimes to halt a soldier about to fire from the Bastille, equally often to push their own people through fear to fury. He had never used so much magic before, so indiscriminately. His head swam.

The sun was low in the sky when the attackers had a brief moment of triumph. One of the Commoners, a metalmancer, finally fought his way close enough to the main door to manipulate the great labyrinth of locks and chains keeping it closed. It was a momentary breach: the door was open for only seconds in total. In that time, one of the Knights Templar on the battlements flung his telekinesis, and the door swung shut once more. The metalmancer fell with a bullet to the neck. All in all, twenty-seven Commoners managed to slip inside the fort.

Almost by chance, Robespierre was one of the twenty-seven.

* * *

He had been near the prison wall when it happened, fighting to steer clear of the swinging weaponry around him. He had felt the rush of wind from the open door; on pure reflex, he surged forward with the others around him and found himself on the opposite side of the door right before it swung violently shut at his back. And then he was inside. Trapped, perhaps, but he could not feel it that way. In that moment, all he could feel was sudden awe.

This was the Bastille. This was where they had brought his mother, twenty years ago, to wait out the last days of her life. The imposing hall was lit by lamps, but after the sunlight outside, everything seemed a blur of shadows. He wondered if it had been sunny on the day his mother had come. Perhaps her first look at the prison had been clouded, as his was, by her second-to-last look at the sky.

This passed through his head in a fraction of a second. Soldiers were already coming down the corridor toward them; shots resounded in the dark. One of the Commoners in front of Robespierre cried out and fell. Robespierre cocked his own pistol and raised it. His heart was pounding. He was right at the back of the group now. There was almost no chance such a small group could get farther than they already had. But if they could...

Downstairs, his benefactor said.

It was the first time he had ever heard the voice in his waking thoughts. Perhaps it was because he was so faint and dizzy; perhaps the moment was so important that dreams and reality were beginning to merge.

He shook his head. "What?"

Go downstairs. There's a door to your left. Quickly.

There was indeed a door to his left, bolted but not locked. He ducked back from the crowd and opened it: in a glance he made out a curving row of steps that did, indeed, lead down. That quick glimpse was all he had. The soldiers were upon them. For an agonized beat, he saw his fellow revolutionaries raising their pistols and clubs, and he knew he should be with them. Then, in one swift movement, he slipped through the crack and pulled the door shut behind him.

It was utterly dark, and so the smell that hit him was like a physical blow: the same fetid fog of sweat, straw, and urine that had permeated the corridor, but stronger, and laced with undertones of decomposition. Unexpectedly, his necromancy uncoiled like a serpent inside him. Bile rose in his throat; the sudden quiet after long hours of battle made him stumble against the walls. He felt incapable of supporting himself without a swell of bodies and noise. On the other side of the door, he could hear the sound of gunshots, and of screams.

So many gunshots over the course of the day. And so many screams, as so many had fallen, and all from his side. Not enough to stop them yet. But enough.

Downstairs, the voice repeated.

"In a moment," Robespierre managed. "I just—"

This is the moment. You haven't much time. Downstairs.

The commotion outside the door was quieter now. Almost certainly, the people who had entered the prison in front of him lay dead on the ground. Firmly, he swallowed, fumbled in his pocket for a match, and struck it on the prison wall.

Good, his benefactor said.

At the bottom of the stairs was a row of cells, like others in the prison. All were empty but one, in which a woman, pale and emaciated, lay in a wooden cage. Robespierre picked his way down, careful of the slime underfoot.

Her clothes were tattered rags, and her hair, gray streaked and brittle, hung over her face. The cage, like the cell itself, was not locked. That told Robespierre all he needed to know, without needing to turn her face to the light and feel for the beat of a heart. He did both anyway.

"I came too late," he said aloud. "You were right. This woman—she's dead."

She is dead, his benefactor said. *And you are a necromancer.*

That was all that was said: his benefactor didn't tell him who the woman was, or why he should wake her from her final sleep. But his magic was raging, reaching out its tendrils of grief, and he needed no further prompt to let it go.

He had never used his necromancy on a human being before. That night months ago didn't count, that night that he tried never to think of. What he had poured into that man had not been his power, but something else. This time, it was pure, and it was right. He felt his magic stream through his hands into the frail body he held in his arms, and he felt the body start and gasp. The woman opened her eyes. They were blue.

He didn't expect her to be able to speak. When she did, his heart almost stopped, but with awe, not with fear.

"Who are you?" Her voice was soft, with a country lilt. "Where am I?"

"You died," he said. There was no other way to say it. "I'm so sorry. It must have happened recently, before they had time to take your body away. You're still dead, really. This isn't you. This is—I think the books describe it as the last burning ember in a pile of ash. I've stirred it to flame again. But the fire's gone out. What's your name?"

"I don't remember." She said it with wonder. "How can I not remember?"

"I'm sorry," he said again. "Madame—" (The term might not have been correct, but he wanted to call her something.) "Madame, my friends and I are trying to bring down the prison."

Her blue eyes drifted upward, where the sounds of battle bled through the ceiling. "The prison…"

"Can you help us? Our spells can't penetrate the walls. We're so close. I don't know what you can do. But if you can—"

He stopped. Her eyes had fallen back to look at him, a flicker of purpose in their depths. Without knowing why, he felt a shiver down his spine.

"Help me to the wall," she said.

Robespierre bent down beside her and slipped his shoulder under her raised arm. He barely noticed her weight as he stood, and her bones seemed as frail and insubstantial as those of a baby bird. She was very cold, and her body was stiffening with rigor mortis. Yet she walked.

The woman pressed her free hand to the wall; then, as Robespierre moved away at her nod, her other hand as well. She melted against the dank gray stone, and her thin ribs expanded and contracted as she drew a sigh.

"You should go now," she said. "Thank you."

It took Robespierre a moment to put the pieces together—the cage and the stone and the sigh. It took him a moment longer to realize what was about to happen now. This wasn't a lifeless husk, like the thing he and his benefactor had made. This woman was alive again, if only for a short while, with her sense of self intact. Her magic was intact too. The magic that had led her to be imprisoned not merely in the Bastille, but in wood, away from the touch of the walls. He nodded.

"Good luck, Citizen," he said quietly.

By the time he had closed the doors behind him, the walls had already begun to tremble.

Less than a minute later, there was a surge of green light and a groan like thunder. And then the top of the southernmost tower exploded.

To the crowd outside, it seemed loud enough to rock the world. Screams split the air; Clarkson ducked instinctively from what he expected to be falling rock. But his fears were groundless. There was no falling rock. The top of the Bastille shattered instantly into a fine, dry powder that clouded over the sky but left no debris larger than a pebble. The prison itself shuddered, and some of the walls crumbled and fell.

Stone magic. It was rare; Clarkson had never seen it before, although he'd read about it at Cambridge. There had been no true explosion; the masonry itself had been agitated until the stones had split apart into dust. None of the Bastille guards would have done that, and surely if so powerful a magician were among the hordes storming the castle, they would have acted before this. Which could only mean...

"My God," somebody said next to Clarkson. "The prisoners are free."

Clarkson looked at the fortress split open, the dust in the air falling like snow to settle amid the rubble. As he watched, he saw a flag rise from the shattered battlements, waving its three colors triumphantly through the smoke.

Clarkson had spent the last few weeks in a fog of hopelessness. The verdict at the House of Commoners seemed to make clear that nothing would ever change. Now hope burst through. It hurt, after so long, but the pain was sweeter than any pleasure he had ever felt.

Robespierre found Camille by what was left of the walls, as the attackers flooded the city. He was deathly pale, and there were tears on his face; he looked, like Robespierre, dazed and exultant and exhausted in one stroke.

"Oh... oh good," he said vaguely when he caught sight of Robespierre. His stammer was back, worse than usual. "You came. I—I wasn't sure..."

"You did it," Robespierre said. Part of him was just a little jealous that it was Camille, and not him, who had led the crowds. But only a small part. It didn't matter.

"I should have done it years ago. But it's done. It's finally done." Camille sat down very suddenly on the rubble.

"Are you all right?"

"Yes. No. One of the two. Ow!"

Robespierre had gently taken Camille's wrist. Under his bracelet, the skin was scorched raw; charred black flesh peeked out from beneath the metal, and blisters bubbled at the edges. "Dear God. Camille..."

Camille curled his arm to his chest protectively. "Don't," he said. "It's all right."

"It's not all right. You need to get it seen to," Robespierre said, as though they were back at school and Camille had scraped a knee. Through his weariness, he felt a surge of guilt that his own ability was so unfettered. "Discreetly, I suppose, so the Templars don't arrest you, but you won't be the only one. Honestly, I don't know how so many of you stood it. The magic that was flying—"

"It was their fault. The Templars. They keep the bracelets too sensitive, so they burn us all the time. It's meant to be a warning. The truth is, we've all got used to it. This wasn't really too much worse. The burning stopped after a while too. So did the screaming. I didn't know they ever stopped."

Robespierre hadn't noticed, until that moment, that the bracelets were indeed silent. "Perhaps someone stopped them. The Templars all have the power to silence the spell once an arrest has been made—perhaps one of the Templars wanted to prevent the dissenters being identified. They're not all on the side of the Aristocracy." He frowned as a shape against the sky caught his eye. "What's that?"

Camille gave it a fleeting glance. "It's a head on a pike. One of the guards'. There are more being waved about. Did you miss it?"

"I must have." He looked at the ghastly thing; from this distance, he couldn't see a face, only a hard, round globe on the end of a spike trailing ragged hair. He should have been horrified, he thought, but he felt nothing. It was too divorced from a human body; his senses were too flooded. Perhaps later he'd have nightmares, and not even remember what had caused them. "Did you tell them to do that?"

"Possibly." Camille laughed a little, breathlessly. "Or someone told me to. I need to sit down."

"You *are* sitting down."

"That's convenient." He brushed his hair out of his eyes with a shaking hand. "God. What a day."

Robespierre looked at the Bastille, lying in dust on the streets as the mob swarmed the courtyard. The early evening light gave it the distant gloss of a landscape painting. His green eyes glinted.

"The first of many," he said.

It was nearly dawn before Clarkson retired to bed. Already, the deep black of the sky was cooling to blue, and the horizon bore the first signs of the long summer morning. His body was protesting its exhaustion at the strain and excitement of the day, and the mattress at his back felt blissfully soft.

His mind, though, was still whirling, and he knew that he would not be able to settle properly to sleep for some time. Instead, he left the candle by his bed burning, and pulled out some of the documents from his traveling box. Rubbing the heaviness from his eyes, he began to read.

He didn't know how he came to be walking the streets of Paris. He woke to it so gradually that it was a while before he even thought to wonder: the cobbled street outside his hotel, the cool night air, the shapes of buildings in the darkness. It was a far darker night than the one in which he must have fallen asleep, and the sky hung cloudy and starless overhead. It was deserted, too, and a thick mist shrouded the pavement in front of him. A cold wind was blowing, and with it came the sounds of steel striking and voices crying out and the faint iron scent of blood. Logically, Clarkson supposed he was dreaming, but he had never felt more wide-awake in his life. Besides, the textures and sensations were too real for that. He was beginning to feel chilled, and the uneven ground bit the soles of his feet.

"Thomas Clarkson," a voice came.

"Yes?" Clarkson replied with a frown. He squinted into the mist but could see nobody. "You have me at a disadvantage. Who are you?"

A laugh came. "I hope you shall not be disadvantaged for long. In fact, I think we can help each other. You came to consult with the abolitionists over here, and you've wandered into a full-fledged revolution."

"Yes," Clarkson replied. "It's more than we could have hoped for."

"You think so?"

"Of course. This is only the start. There are people coming into power here who might be able to do something—really do something. They won't have to wade through parliamentary sludge for years in vain like us. They don't even have to wait any longer for their king to grow a spine. They're bringing about change as we speak; they can bring about this change as well."

"They can," the voice agreed. "They won't."

"You don't know that." Clarkson shook his head, anger flaring momentarily in his breast. "I don't even know who you are, for God's sake. How can you know that?"

"I know that the new order here will be sympathetic to your aims, but that they won't dare destabilize their economy and anger their merchants and sailors for some wretched souls tucked away thousands of miles out of their sight—any more than their king would. I know that of the six men you've arranged to speak with, two are paid spies for the French slave merchants. I know you've already begun to receive death threats from many less subtle."

"Begun?" Clarkson said with a snort. "It's not a recent development, you know. I've been receiving death threats for the last three years; they're just not usually in French. Two years ago I was nearly beaten to death at the docks in Liverpool."

"And eight months ago William Wilberforce was stabbed outside Westminster Abbey, around the corner from his town house."

That stopped Clarkson short. "Wilberforce? Do you mean that he was attacked? To prevent the bill from reaching Parliament?"

"Exactly so," the voice replied. "Did you not suspect it?"

Clarkson shook his head, not entirely in denial. "I suspected something more than he told us. He was too ill too quickly. But…"

"He probably doesn't know the motive for the attack," the voice said. "Not for certain. But I do. It was to prevent him speaking out against the slave trade in the House of Commoners."

"Well, they failed on that count," Clarkson retorted. "But for all the good it did, they may as well have left poor Wilberforce alone. We all may as well have. The House won't listen. They never will. The people will; that must be our hope."

"But they won't be able to do anything." Clarkson thought he could almost see the figure the voice was attached to now, through the darkness and the mist. It was a tall figure, about his height, but lightly built. "Even if they want to. They won't do anything here either. They'll listen, and they'll nod, and they'll agree that what you say is good and just and principled. They'll say what a shame it is. Some will even say it very loudly and angrily. But they won't act. People are dying, and suffering worse than death—hundreds of thousands of people. I know they weigh on your soul. Words won't save them. Somebody, somewhere, must actually do something, and it must be you."

"Oh, must it?" He said it sarcastically, but it was reflexive sarcasm. Inside, the tide of despair that he had struggled to keep at bay since the House of Commoners had made their ruling was breaking through. It poisoned his blood. "Why must it be?"

"You know it must be," the voice said. "You've known it ever since that day when you stopped halfway between Cambridge and London, your essay in your pack, and realized that if what you had written was true, it was time some person should see these calamities to their end. You knew that it must be you."

And he had. The moment came to him, as it often did in times of despair, and as always, he clutched at it. It had been only four years ago, but already it was beginning to seem so very far away. His essay on the question of human slavery had just won the Latin Prize at Cambridge, and he had been returning to London, as the voice had said. He had begun the essay as an academic exercise; he had expected to enjoy writing it. He had not expected to be overtaken with grief and horror at what his research was telling him, nor to spend his increasingly sleepless nights racked with nightmares. As he had ridden that day, despite the blue of the sky overhead and the summer's heat rising from the fields around him, he had been unable to settle. At times he had stopped his horse and dismounted to walk off his uneasiness. Over and over, he had tried to tell himself that what he had written could not be true: the trade could not possibly be so evil as that. By the time he had reached Wades Mill, where he meant to stop, he felt half-desperate.

And then, as the voice had said, it had come to him. Somebody had to do something. It was as though clouds had parted and a difficult and dangerous road had been revealed to him that was nonetheless indisputably going in the right direction. It had been the most important moment of his life.

"What are you?" Clarkson asked. "What do you want from me?"

The figure stepped out of the mist and introduced himself.

PART TWO

REVOLUTIONS

Paris

June 1791

Maximilien Robespierre, in his cramped lodgings at the unfashionable end of Paris, was dreaming uneasy dreams.

They started at the Louis-le-Grand. He was seventeen, dwarfed by the magnificence about him. He had been at the school for six years; he would be there another six yet, reading intently, studying fiercely, earning the law degree on the scholarship for which he had already worked so hard. On this day, he stood at the head of five hundred boys at the school gate, speaking aloud the oration that he, of all of them, had been chosen to deliver to the honored visitors. It was raining: a summer rain, hard and vicious and unrelenting. His borrowed clothes were soaked through, and he was chilled to the bone. He spoke on, conquering his chattering teeth and aching back, trying to keep his head and shoulders set proudly. The students had been waiting for hours.

The newly crowned king of France and his wife, Marie Antoinette, sat in their carriage as he welcomed them. They did not get out; he could not tell, through the veil of rain, if they looked at him at all. When he had finished, the carriage rolled away. Robespierre watched, and wondered, with a mixture of annoyance and anticlimax, what he had expected. He had the beginnings of a sore throat, either from the speech or from the weather.

Little Camille—fifteen, precocious, impossible—ran to catch up to him as they filed back inside. His voice, with its familiar stutter, had an underlying sympathy. "Strange behavior from visiting royals." He flicked his wet fringe out of his eyes. "It's almost as if the king thought *you* were there to see *him*, rather than the other way around."

His teachers told him that he had done very well. It was just how royalty was.

The stone courtyard around him rippled, changed; the battery of rain became a blast of heat.

He was on an island, standing on white shores surrounded by high, leafy plants. The hills were dotted with white colonial houses, incongruous European additions to the landscape. The sun scorched overhead and glared off the perfect water. That might have accounted for the heat, but there was in fact another cause. The island was on fire.

The houses were burning; in the far hills, the green of the trees was licked with orange flame and black smoke. Ash blew down to the beach in gusts; the taste caught in his throat and made him cough. He could hear shouts, some in French and some in languages he could not understand.

And there was more. Beneath the sand and the trees and the fire, hotter than any of them, was a throbbing pulse of hatred. It was too strong for mere emotion. It was tangible, physical, intense; the pressure of it made Robespierre wince involuntarily. He had felt it somewhere before.

He was in the garden. His benefactor was a darker shape amid dark trees.

"At last," his benefactor said. "Wake up. The royal family have fled the palace. This is it."

The city was in tumult at the news of the king's flight. Robespierre had to fight his way through crowds on the rue Saint-Honoré to make it to the National Assembly of Magicians. His usually meticulous wig was knocked askew, which left him flustered and off-balance; if it had been at all possible, he would have taken the time to go back and set himself to rights, but the news was too urgent.

The royal family had been all but under house arrest for months as the Assembly negotiated the terms of the new government. It had taken far longer than anyone had hoped. Nobody in the Assembly, much less the king, had been able to agree on what that government should be. It had seemed so simple after the fall of the Bastille. The National Assembly of Magicians had risen up, exactly as Robespierre had hoped. They had issued a proclamation declaring it the right of all citizens to be free to practice their own magic: a Declaration of the Rights of Magicians. Within a day, the Temple Church in Paris had been stormed, and the spell that held the alchemy in the bracelets active had been broken. The Knights Templar had tried to intervene, but it had been a long time since they were knights in anything but name. Like the monarchy, their power was symbolic when it came down to it. Symbols had power only as long as people gave it to them. It seemed that the time of the people had come.

And yet few other than Camille were truly ready to break with the king and the Temple Church and forge a French Republic of Magicians in cold blood; even Camille, whose revolutionary pamphlets were now flying off the shelves faster than he could stock them, was not quite prepared to suggest stringing up the king from a lamppost, as he was wont to recommend for other Aristocrats. As long as the king was safe and compliant, then most agreed France should become a constitutional monarchy, with the Temple Church still enforcing magical restrictions in a limited capacity. The only questions were how much power the king would have and how restricted magic would be, and these were discussed every day by the National Assembly at the Tuileries. They met in the old riding school, the only building large enough to accommodate them: it was hot in summer and drafty in winter, and every day Robespierre went home tired, hoarse, and discouraged. For too long since the Bastille, Paris had been basking in a theoretical revolution only, with demands for reform and uprisings more fashionable commonplaces than matters of liberty or death.

If the king had escaped with the help of royalists, and was prepared to come back and fight with an army from Austria, then everything was in jeopardy. For the first time in two years, there was a real threat of counterrevolution on the streets of Paris. And yet—if there *was* no king...if the monarchy had disappeared like a thief in the night... that, of course, would be an entirely different matter.

In fact, as Robespierre learned when he slipped into his seat, the royal family had already been caught again. They had made it to within thirty miles of the border before the National Guard apprehended them: the face of the king was too well-known to pass by incognito, and his attempts to impersonate a valet were not very convincing. Another king, in another time, would never have allowed himself to be taken by Commoner forces. But Louis had no magic, and though the Commoners of France still wore bracelets and in theory were not permitted to use magic, it had been more than a year since those bracelets had been cursed with their old spells. Marie Antoinette, it was true, sent a burst of fire in the direction of the first guards to approach the carriage, but they had been prepared for that. A water-mage intercepted her magic with a quick fountain, and Louis put a gentle hand on her shoulder.

"Stop, my dear," he said. He was kind and gracious in defeat, as he was at all times, but not very bright. "It was worth a try, at least."

"This doesn't alter our negotiations," Bailly, the mayor of Paris, insisted at the Assembly that day. "We present this to the people as a kidnapping. We get the king back in place as soon as we can. That must be an end to it. We can still be a constitutional monarchy within weeks."

"That's ridiculous," Robespierre protested. "The king abandoned his duties. He tried to betray France to its enemies. Can't you see *this is it?*"

Nobody heard him in the chaos that had followed Bailly's words; if they had, his words would have been dismissed anyway.

Camille was waiting for him on the street when the Assembly finally broke open and spilled into the evening. With last night's dreams still fresh in his mind, Robespierre was momentarily startled to see that his friend was no longer a skinny fifteen-year-old. In fact, the fall of the

Bastille had pushed him into the public gaze. He had no trouble selling even his most startling political writings now, and his dark-eyed, tousle-haired figure was a familiar fixture in revolutionary salons across the city. He had been married recently: Robespierre had been one of the chief witnesses at the wedding. And yet in every important sense, he really did often seem as though he had not changed since school.

"God," Camille said before Robespierre could even speak. "Royalists and hypocrites and fools." He made it sound like a song title. "At this rate, we'll be back where we started in no time, with a king on the throne and the knights in their temples."

Robespierre wasn't in the temper to calm his friend down this time. The frustrations of the last few hours were boiling in his veins. "They're bringing the king home. He'll be at the palace again by the end of the week. The negotiations for the constitution will carry on as before."

"The French Constitutional Monarchy of Magicians," Camille snorted. "It hardly has that ring of freedom to it, does it? I mean, it's hard to fit into a poem."

"It's ridiculous. This isn't just a matter of abstract principle anymore. The king betrayed us. I told them. He's *dangerous*."

"Fools always are." Camille glanced at Robespierre. "You're uncharacteristically ruffled, by your standards."

He knew he was—physically, for that matter, as well as mentally. It didn't improve his mood. Camille, of course, looked as though he'd tumbled out of bed five minutes ago, but that was intentional, and possibly even accurate. Robespierre liked to be more controlled, however unfashionable that was these days. But...

"I told them the king was dangerous," Robespierre repeated. "I told them we can trust neither the monarchy nor the Temple Church. They wouldn't listen to me."

It was something working with the National Assembly had taught him and that was particularly aggravating now: too often, even with mesmerism, even with status, people still didn't listen to you. He was getting better at employing magic now, better at speaking, better at articulating his visions. They knew he was right, and they heard him. They simply resisted both magic and ideas because what he said wasn't what they wanted to hear. With stronger mesmerism, perhaps, they wouldn't be able to resist. But he couldn't keep the entire Assembly mesmerized forever, and as soon as it wore off, they would start to wonder what they had agreed to, and why. Magic was free now, in practice if not by law, but laws and practices changed all the time.

"They'll listen to you in the Jacobins," Camille said. He sounded suddenly serious. It distracted Robespierre briefly out of his anger.

"They might listen more to you, if you'll speak."

Camille laughed. "Me? I'm a celebrity in that room—they tolerate me, even love me, because of what I am. But what I am is the spark that lit a revolution. You don't listen to a spark—you just catch fire. That's why I'm best on paper. It burns so quickly."

"You're best on paper because outside of it you trip over your own tongue."

"And you don't. I don't think you've ever let anything trip you over in your life."

"Tell that to the Assembly." His dark mood was back.

"Don't bother with the Assembly," Camille said. "Tell that to the Jacobins. They'll listen to you. They hear you. I'm not sure you're aware of the following you've been gathering lately. If you set yourself against the Assembly, the Jacobins will set themselves with you."

Robespierre turned that over in his head for a moment. "Would *you* set yourself with me?"

"I already have. Didn't you read the last issue of the *Revolutions*? Or are you asking if I'd support you now, tonight, this hour?"

"Yes."

"Which?" Camille relented before Robespierre had to answer. "Yes, I'll support you against the Assembly. Why wouldn't I? You're right. Of course you're right. The constitution is dead. The king killed it himself when he turned for protection to the enemies of France."

"It will be dangerous. There are plenty who would kill us for saying so."

"Not if we kill them first." Camille, as far as Robespierre knew, had never killed anyone in his life, not even during the fall of the Bastille. Yet somehow, nobody ever had questioned that he meant what he was talking about. "I keep telling you, Maximilien. As long as there are too many of us, they can't stop us."

"But who are we?" It was what was beginning to trouble him. "When you said that before, we were the Assembly and the people against the king and the Temple Church and the worst of the Aristocracy. Now we're all revolutionaries, in name at least. How can we tell our allies from the rest?"

"Stand up and denounce the Assembly," Camille said unconcernedly, "and you'll know."

The Jacobin Club was one of the many radical clubs that had sprung up around Paris in the wake of the fall of the Bastille, and it was by far the most powerful. It met in the library of the old monastery on the rue Saint-Honoré—a strange place for the birth of a new order, amid old books and religious dust, but it was convenient. More than that, it felt appropriate. The arched ceilings and high windows invested their discussions with order and seriousness, while the old riding school where the Assembly met always made procedures slightly absurd. Their membership had been increasing rapidly lately, with affiliated clubs springing up all over the country, so Robespierre expected it to be busy when he and Camille arrived. After today's events, everyone would be in attendance. What he was not expecting was upward of eight hundred people crammed into the room. The sheer number of eyes stopped him short in astonishment.

"There are your listeners," Camille said.

And they were. He had known, of course, that he had authority in the Jacobins; he had carefully cultivated it. In the two years since the Bastille, he had shone brighter and brighter, and here at least they respected his hard stance in favor of Commoner magic. But standing in front of eight hundred people, his voice going out to them in the flickering candlelight, he felt for the first time just what he had gained. It was more than respect. They believed in him.

"This should have been the greatest day of the Revolution," Robespierre told them, amid an angry rumble of agreement. "It might yet be. But we need to take action. The Assembly, despite my protests, is trying to tell you that the royal family were kidnapped against their will; you know that isn't true. The king has abandoned his post and his country. We need to put him on trial, as we would any other citizen."

"He was fleeing to the borders," someone said. "He wants to mount a foreign invasion to take back France."

"I'm not afraid of the enemy outside our country," Robespierre said. "We're a country of free magicians and patriots; they would be no match for us. The threat is from within, from those in the Assembly who are secretly conspiring to see a return to monarchy and repression. What scares me is the same thing that seems to reassure everybody else: it's that since this morning, all of our enemies speak the same language as us. Everyone is united; everyone has the same face. And yet the king would not have fled had he not known that he would find support in the capital. A king who still had a most secure crown on his head could not have renounced so many advantages without being sure of recovering them. Look around you, and share my fear."

He didn't need mesmerism this time. His pale, quiet face was fired with purpose. It spilled over and animated his audience like necromancy.

"I know that in thus accusing almost all the members of the Assembly of being counterrevolutionary, I raise up against me all the prideful; I sharpen a thousand daggers; I offer myself to all the hatred. So be it. I am ready to sacrifice my life for truth, liberty, and France. I have just put the nation on trial. I dare it to do the same to me."

Camille, caught up in the excitement, leaped to his feet and cried, "We would all give our lives to save yours!"

And, by the flickering candlelight in the old stone chamber, eight hundred Jacobins all swore an oath to protect Robespierre's life at the cost of their own. Over the next few days, letters trickled in from other branches across the country, declaring that they, too, would rally to save him. A group of the more powerful magicians offered to serve as an armed guard at all times. It was all rather hysterical. It was terrifying. It was wonderful.

"Now the king has aimed at the Nation," Camille wrote in his paper, the *Revolutions of France*. "It is true that he has missed fire, but it is the Nation's turn now."

It didn't happen that way. Instead, things spiraled dramatically out of control, then, as Robespierre felt he should have anticipated when Camille was involved, caught fire. Overnight, radical pamphlets were flying off the presses, followed quickly by petitions and calls to arms. They called for the removal of the king outright, and with him an end to France's Temple Church and all distinction between Aristocratic and Commoner magic. It was Camille's writing—that bewitching cocktail of sincerity, classical allusion, and playful cruelty—that spilled out into the crowds, but Robespierre suspected there were other forces at work behind it. Camille had a good many friends among the revolutionaries, all of whom had agendas of their own. Robespierre firmly believed that his school friend was loyal to him, but he was also under no illusions that he was loyal to him alone. Camille's neighbor Georges-Jacques Danton had been growing in influence of late, and his taste for uprising was far more in line with Camille's natural tendencies than Robespierre's caution.

Perhaps it could still work. But Robespierre couldn't help but be alarmed at how quickly the protests became violent and how ugly they were. Part of him had wanted the people of Paris to rise against the Assembly, though he would have preferred them to do it more quietly; had Camille's words set the entire city on fire, they might have been well and good. As it was, though, they lit up only a small faction of the population: the most radical and powerful Commoner magicians. And they blazed far too brightly.

"You have to tell them to stop," Robespierre told Camille as his friend sat writing at his desk. "This is going too far, too fast."

"For whom? For you?"

This was closer to the truth than he cared to admit, so he did not admit it. "For the majority of the country. We need to reassess the Assembly, put the king on trial, refine the laws. This is frightening people."

"You told us we should be frightened."

"Of the king's supporters. Of the counterrevolution. The last thing we need is for people to fear Commoner magicians again, or us. And people will, if you have them on the street calling for the removal of the king by force. What's more, you're attributing to me things I never said—and would never say in public. I never said that the royal family were a millstone around our necks."

"You did to me, in conversation—or near enough. I might have made it sound better. You certainly thought it. Do you mean to be one of those people who say one thing in public and one in private? Your friend Rousseau would have something to say about that."

Robespierre gritted his teeth. He hated it when Camille flung the words of his favorite philosopher back at him in an argument, and Camille knew that only too well.

"What on earth is going on in here?" Lucile Desmoulins put her head through the doorway of Camille's office. If Robespierre had been listening, he would have noticed earlier that the lilt of the piano she had been practicing had faded from the parlor; he hadn't, so it startled him. "Are you two fighting amongst yourselves now? I did say that was how it would end."

Robespierre liked Lucile very much—everybody did. She was a bright, vivacious, romantic twenty-one-year-old, far too good in every way for Camille except that she had decided to appoint him the love of her life. With her pointed face, dark eyes, and fashionable tumble of curls, she looked like a Renaissance angel—an illusion instantly dispelled as soon as something displeased her. Like her husband, she was a powerful fire-mage under her silver bracelet; her emotions raged fast and turbulent, and always near the surface.

"Lucile," Robespierre said, "would you please tell your husband that I'm trying to keep you both safe?"

"Lucile," Camille countered, "would you please tell Maxime how boring I am when I'm safe? Truly, I'm indescribably dull. You know this is true. You knew me before all this started, and all I used to do was drink, fail at my profession, and turn up at your father's house when I ran out of money to beg for his charity."

"Oh, is that what you were there for?" she asked dryly. "The rumor was that you were having an affair with my mother."

"Well, I couldn't have an affair with you. You were still a girl at the time, and you only cared about poetry and music and reading about Mary, Queen of Scots. I was a boring grown-up."

She grinned. "You were never boring. But I can certainly verify that you never seemed likely to amount to anything before all this started. My father wouldn't have let you within an inch of proposing to me before the fall of the Bastille made you a celebrity."

"The Revolution doesn't exist to make you interesting, Camille," Robespierre said, a little too loudly. Something twinged inside him when Camille and Lucile talked to each other like that, as though nobody else existed. He was jealous of something he couldn't quite understand. "Nor a celebrity. And this isn't the fall of the Bastille. It's the formation of a government. We need to act within the law."

"It's too late." Camille kissed Lucile's hand and took up his pen again. "The people won't listen to me, not if I told them that. I don't have the power to make people stop. All I've ever done is told them to go as far and fast as they can, and not to look back."

Robespierre watched as his friend's pen flickered over the page, leaving tiny, barely formed letters in its wake. Often it would jump backward to score through a sentence, or upward to dip into the lists of subjects and adjectives Camille kept pinned about his desk like ingredients; it would light on a period for a moment, then take off once more. The movement was as natural and graceful as the flight of a sparrow.

They had both written poetry at school, Robespierre remembered. Camille had been no better at it than him, perhaps worse. He was right about one thing: the Revolution had made him, as a person, a husband, and a writer. It had given him his language. The trouble was, it was a language far more permanent than Camille's own convictions. He believed what he wrote at the time, fully and absolutely, but then moved on, leaving the afterimage of his words. And behind him, those words took on a life of their own.

"Please," Robespierre heard himself say.

It wasn't very eloquent, but it made Camille stop writing and turn to face him. His bracelet clinked audibly as he put his hand to the back of the chair. All bracelets were inactive now; Camille had been flicking around fireballs and playing with shadows for months. But they were still tight about the wrist of every Commoner magician in France. It would be too expensive to bracelet the entire population for a second time; once they were removed, they were removed for good, with no chance of reinstating the spell. And they had not been removed.

Camille caught Robespierre's glance and followed it down to his wrist. His mouth quirked in a bitter smile. "I'm sorry," he said. "I'd do almost anything for you, you know that. I'll print a retraction on whatever I attributed to you that offended you, if it will make you happier. But I won't tell them to give up."

It ended, quite suddenly, in blood.

The day after the National Assembly voted to proceed with a constitutional monarchy, a crowd assembled in the sprawling gardens of the Champ de Mars with a petition calling for the removal of the king. It was a clear, warm Sunday, and the square had the excited atmosphere of a carnival. Families walked hand in hand, smaller children swinging between their parents so as not to get lost. Vendors sold hot food on the corners. Magic was being flung freely, and wondrously: sparks against a perfect blue sky, drops of water catching the sun in a cascade of light. Laughter was in the air. Only a close observer would notice, with a start, that two of the festive shapes hanging from a lantern were human corpses. The two unfortunate men had been caught earlier that day hiding beneath a seat and had been hung unceremoniously as spies.

By evening, six thousand men and women had signed the petition. It was then that the soldiers came.

The National Guard were led by General Lafayette. They had come accompanied by the mayor of Paris, Jean Bailly, and they had come to suppress the demonstration. Revolutionary fervor was running high, and most of the crowd laughed at the orderly rows of men with their buttons glinting in the sun.

"You can't send us away." The man who spoke up held his wife's hand in his own, and the two of them wore the red caps that had become the self-chosen uniform of Commoner magicians. "We're the true army of the Assembly of Magicians. We'll defend it even from itself."

"You're not an army," Bailly retorted, unwisely. "This isn't the Bastille. You're interfering with the lawful government of France."

The man's wife spat on the ground. "The law and the government is what the people says it is. We didn't pull down the Bastille to listen to men like you."

"The law and government is us!" Bailly had to raise his voice over the rumble of the crowd, which no longer sounded so amused. "You said it was, two years ago. Magic doesn't make a government."

Clouds were beginning to gather—weather magic, turned angry. All at once, a fireball burst out of the crowd. Lafayette, reacting with typical speed, pulled Bailly forward out of the way, so that the fireball fell in an exhalation of sparks where his horse had been only moments before.

One fireball, from one magician. Nobody knew who it was. It didn't matter. Before the smoke had cleared, the National Guard opened fire.

What had moments earlier been a peaceful demonstration was now a battlefield. The air was rent with the crack of rifles, and then the shriller sound of screams. The occasional spark flew from the crowds at the guard in retaliation; one soldier's hat ignited into a plume of flame. For the most part, however, the protestors ran, hands raised to shield themselves uselessly but instinctively from shots. People fell on the stairs, gasping and choking as their lungs filled with blood. One or two were trampled in the crush. As the paths cleared, bodies were left behind. Some were dragged to safety. Many lay where they fell, like flotsam after the turn of the tide.

Above the Assembly's headquarters at the Hôtel de Ville, the red flag of martial law was raised. It fluttered in the same faint breeze that stirred the blood-soaked dust across the ground of the Champ de Mars. Nobody had bothered to remove the corpses of the spies hung that morning; the breeze caught them too.

The Jacobins was almost empty that night. Of the hundreds who had packed it on the evening of the king's flight, most had withdrawn in fear to form a more moderate club across the street. They were cowards, but Robespierre could understand their fear. Even as he furiously denounced the massacre to the dark room, he was waiting for the National Guard to burst through the door. They had already been once, searching for those under arrest—Camille Desmoulins and Georges-Jacques Danton among them. They hadn't found them, and Robespierre had no idea what had become of them. He had heard reports that Camille had been taken at the Champ de Mars and beaten almost to death, but after a sickening hour of worry the victim had turned out to be quite another journalist who had the misfortune of looking a little like him. Nobody had accused Robespierre of direct complicity in the petition, but that didn't mean he was safe. The clash of arms and hate outside on the street struck a new, different chord from the savage joy of the riots around the Bastille. He feared it was only a matter of time before someone came to arrest him too.

In fact, the men who came for the Jacobins were off duty. They were also furious, drunk, and out for blood. Their pounding on the doors shattered Robespierre's speech. The Jacobins could see them in the courtyard, dark silhouettes amid flickering lights. Perhaps thirty—not a great number, but armed.

"Dear God," someone whispered; Robespierre couldn't tell who. "They're going to kill us."

"Stay calm," Robespierre advised, although his own heart was racing. "We've broken no law. Besides, they won't get in. Those doors have withstood more than a few soldiers in their days."

He doubted whether this was true, and he was right to doubt. As if to prove him wrong, the door burst open like a dam, and the room was flooded with soldiers. They were flushed with drink or with anger, probably a dangerous cocktail of both. The club rose at once to their feet; Robespierre, who was already standing, was grabbed by those nearest to him and shoved to the back.

"Stay down," the closest told him. "We won't let them touch you."

At present, at least, the intruders didn't seem about to touch anyone, or perhaps they were held at bay by the number of Jacobins pointing pistols of their own. It was common practice to go armed now. The air filled with angry catcalls.

"Traitors!"

"Revolutionaries!"

"Commoner magicians!"

The last was a typical enough slur these days, but in fact, many of those left in the Jacobins *were* Commoner magicians. Whether because those with magic in their blood really were more volatile, or simply because they were more fed up with being oppressed, they seemed to make up most of the more radical sects. And for some reason more mysterious yet, they seemed drawn to Robespierre. He was one of the more outspoken advocates of their rights, of course, but he wondered sometimes if they could somehow feel what he was.

If the guards felt what he was, they would kill him. They would kill him anyway, for being *who* he was.

"Do you think we *wanted* that massacre to happen?" someone retorted. "Robespierre told them to stop."

"They didn't, though, did they?"

"We should have killed them *all*—"

"They're calling us murderers now! They're saying we opened fire on women and children."

"You *are* murderers!" one of the Jacobins called back hotly. "And your king is the greatest murderer of all!"

One of the guards raised his rifle; at once, it was whisked from his hand in a blaze of silver metalmancy and flung against the wall. A single shot reverberated from the barrel as it hit. The chamber surged; suddenly, half the members blazed with fire magic, rippled with water, buzzed with lightning. The other half, terrified, cowered at the far side of the table. Robespierre was crushed amid the crowd; his foot caught a chair, and he heard it fall to the ground as he stumbled.

This was going to be a second massacre. Robespierre gritted his teeth and pushed to the front. It was more of an effort than he foresaw: the crowd around him were so determined to protect him that they had become an impenetrable barrier.

"Stop it!" he demanded.

The soldiers knew who he was. There was a hiss at his approach. Robespierre felt the heat of their hostility on his face like a blast from an oven. He met it and tried to keep his gaze steady. "We are not your enemies. We didn't start that protest. We didn't sanction that protest. None of us were anywhere near the Champ de Mars."

"You started all of this!" a soldier shouted, and the cry was taken up by the catcalls of his fellow men-at-arms. Still, they didn't move forward. "You want to bring this entire country down!"

"I want to save it!" Robespierre paused before his voice could rise too much; he forced his tone back to low, calm, hypnotic. He had not used his secret magic in the Jacobins for a while—he hadn't needed to, and it had seemed dishonest among fellow revolutionaries. These were not fellow revolutionaries. He let mesmerism spill into his words. "We all want to save the country. We are not your enemies."

"What was that petition about, then? Why were you calling for the removal of the king?"

I am going to kill *Camille*, Robespierre thought. He didn't mean it: he knew all this was hardly the fault of one petition or one revolutionary, and he was at this moment as terrified for his friend's safety as for his own. But still. Really.

"You don't want to murder me," he said, and hoped with all his heart his mesmerism was holding. Without it, he suspected, they would very much want to murder him. "You're soldiers. You obey orders. Nobody has ordered our deaths. Nobody will. Go home. If you kill us here, in our own club, you will start something that none of us want."

The silence that followed was fraught with the tensions gripping the entire country. Royalist and Republican, Commoner and Aristocrat, Templar and magician, the monarchy and the people, the old order and the Revolution. Robespierre focused his magic on thirty armed soldiers who had that morning fired into a celebration, and they looked back at a slight, bespectacled revolutionary who had called for the trial of the king.

Then, dazed, one of the soldiers lowered his rifle. As though a signal had been given, the others followed suit. One or two of them hesitated, resisting, and Robespierre quickly washed them with all the mesmerism he could muster; at that moment, he didn't care who noticed it. It took perhaps a minute, but at last, one by one, the soldiers filed out. Two of the Jacobin magicians at the front dashed past Robespierre, their hands still smoking, and flung the door shut behind them.

The chamber dissolved into relief. Robespierre, letting his mesmerism fade, felt suddenly as though he was in another world. The air that had been thick with conflict was now thick with cheers, all saying how magnificent he'd been. How clever and how brave.

He wasn't brave at all, and never had been. He knew that, in that moment. Camille was brave. Even at school, he had said what had come into his head, followed the quick, eager impulses of his heart, and never cared what anyone thought or what might befall him. Robespierre was scared all the time. Fear was a vein of ice at his core, and it never melted. He had faced the guards only because he was terrified of what they might do. Now that it was over, he wanted nothing more than to curl up in a ball and hide.

"Thank you," he said, instead. He had to clear his throat to be heard over the chaos, but he was used to that. "I think it's time we adjourned, don't you?"

Mesmerism didn't last very long. It probably wouldn't take the mob long to reconsider their retreat. And if they didn't come back, someone else would.

He didn't curl up into a ball as the room emptied, but he did sink down into an abandoned chair and rest his head in his hands, just until his heart could calm down. He'd been playing at being in danger of assassination when he'd stood up and denounced the Assembly upon the king's flight. But it was real. Those soldiers would have killed him. And, somehow, he had a long, dark walk through streets spilling over with rioters if he wanted to reach his lodgings tonight. He didn't even think he had any food or firewood left at the other end.

Cries of "Vive Robespierre!" were coming from the street. He probably wouldn't get far without being set upon one way or another, then.

I can't do this, he said silently. He had no idea if his benefactor could hear him. *You told me this would all be right. It's not right. I'm not brave enough.*

He had just got to his feet when a voice came from behind him. "Excuse me."

The speaker was perhaps in his fifties, with a kind, wizened face. He had the voice and bearing of a gentleman, yet also the brown skin of a man used to outdoor work.

"Monsieur Duplay, isn't it?" Robespierre asked, as the name fortunately came to him. He was a carpenter who had been attending the club for some months now. They had spoken only a few times, but it had always been pleasant. He rallied himself. "Can I help you?"

"I was hoping I might be able to help you," Duplay said, which was not something anyone had said to him for a long time. "I wondered if I could offer you refuge for the night. My house is just around the corner—not very spacious, I'm afraid, and I have a large family with which to fill it. I could only provide you with a small room. But it will be comfortable, and my wife will have supper waiting. You shouldn't risk traveling far tonight, not being who you are. And we'd be honored to have you, of course."

"Thank you," Robespierre said, and tried to say it normally. In fact, he could almost have cried. In that moment, the offer felt like the nicest thing anyone had ever done for him. "I'd like that very much."

Maurice Duplay lived in a two-story house on rue Saint-Honoré, with his wife, three grown daughters, young son, and nephew. It was, as he had forewarned, a large number of people for the cramped, crooked rooms, yet when Duplay arrived with a young revolutionary leader in tow, the family showed no sign of finding it an imposition. They greeted Robespierre with pleasure and concern, as though he were an old friend unexpectedly in need of their protection and with every right to claim it. The eldest daughter, Éléonore, took his coat; she was a dark-haired, serious-looking young woman, with brown eyes that lingered warmly on his face. Something in his heart tightened briefly, a very different grip than fear.

"We're so glad you could come," she said, as though welcoming him for tea. "Father talks about you all the time."

Duplay must have praised him highly: the younger ones were staring at Robespierre with something like awe. He managed a smile for them, and their faces lit in return.

"This man just talked down a garrison of soldiers come to murder us," Duplay told his family with some pride. "It was the bravest thing I ever saw. He's going to save the country someday very soon. We need to look after him."

"Are the soldiers going to come here?" asked the youngest daughter, Babette. She looked perhaps eighteen and seemed to regard the prospect with more excitement than fear. "Do we need to give our lives for him, like it said in the *Revolutions*?"

"Don't crowd him," Madame Duplay scolded, shooing them away. Her daughters had clearly inherited their round faces and dark hair from her, though she had grown plump and motherly in middle age. "He won't know what to do with this influx of family. The poor man's used to living alone."

But he wasn't. He was solitary by nature, but in Arras he had always lived with at least one of his siblings, and away at school he had lived in a swarm of other boys. The two years he'd been in Paris were the most alone he'd ever been, and he wasn't used to it at all. He didn't say so, but perhaps something in his face did, for Madame Duplay gave him a thoughtful look.

If he'd been in his own rooms, he would have sat up all night, listening for the sound of boots outside, racked with worry about Camille, starting at every knock at the door. As it was, food, comfort, and solicitude so soon after the terrifying events of the night hit him like a physical reaction. By the end of the supper Madame Duplay urged him to eat, he was struggling to keep his eyes open. Madame Duplay noticed, of course.

"Go upstairs," she said kindly. "Maurice will show you; the bed's already made up. You're safe here, you know, and there's no need to be polite. You must be exhausted."

His protest was swallowed by a yawn. "I'm sorry," he said. "I've had a very long day."

He had, in fact. But he didn't want to tell them it was also the first time he had felt safe since he had arrived in Paris.

Robespierre fell asleep that night in a small room overlooking the courtyard. He never went back to his old lodgings. The house, as it turned out, was to be his home until the end of his life.

★ ★ ★

The story was that there were fifty dead at Champ de Mars. It might have been less, in truth. It was enough. The tide, so sensitive to every pull of events these days, turned yet again, and it turned violently. There would be no republic. The National Assembly and the National Guard held the city in the tight rein of martial law. The most dangerous agitators were under arrest or in hiding. If anybody wanted them back, nobody would say. The constitution, so long in the making, looked about to be settled at once. Despite Robespierre's protests, it would not involve the removal of Commoner bracelets.

Camille was at the Jacobins the next day. A warrant had been put out for his arrest, but he had, with his usual brazen cheek, decided to sneak back to Paris and address the club while on the run from the National Guard. Robespierre's exasperation with his friend lasted as long as it took to see him and notice how tired and wan he looked.

"I wasn't even *at* the Champ de Mars," he told Robespierre in private. "It wasn't my riot. I may have flung a spark or two, metaphorically speaking, but I didn't fan the flames."

"Didn't you?" Robespierre asked, but wryly. In that moment, Camille was very dear to him. "You certainly didn't try to put it out, as I recall."

"Why should I? It might have worked. It *should* have worked. They've destroyed my journal too. I'll never get it published again. How do the royalists still have that power? I thought we were past this."

"It's a step backward," Robespierre acknowledged. "But don't give up hope yet."

"What about Commoner magic? Is there any chance of that being made legal?"

They'd discussed this at the Assembly just this morning. "Still illegal for now, but nobody's reinstating the spells on the bracelets. The new government will rule on that in a few months. I meant what I said: don't give up. We may have to settle for less than we want for a while. It doesn't mean we'll do so forever. Just—"

"I know, I know: calm down. God, if you had your way, this would be the calmest revolution in history."

"There is absolutely no chance of me having my way. I was going to say, make yourself scarce until things settle. Is Lucile safe?"

"Yes. Yes, she's gone to her parents. I'll send for her when I have plans. Danton's leaving the country."

"It's a good idea. You should do so as well."

"I won't leave the country. But you're right—I can make myself scarce. Just until—" He rubbed his brow. "I don't know when. It's not all over, is it? I don't think I want to live if it's over."

"I don't think it's over," Robespierre said.

"It isn't over," his benefactor said that night. "This is all according to plan."

"How can it be?" Robespierre said. Even in his sleep, he was restless and frustrated. "You can't tell me that massacre was part of any plan."

" 'Massacre.' A good word, isn't it? It sounds much worse than a few deaths. People don't forgive a massacre."

Robespierre struggled to master his disgust. There was surely no way his benefactor could have actually caused the incident at the Champ de Mars—whoever had thrown the fireball had done that, and his benefactor was no fire-mage. But it wasn't the first time Robespierre had felt his benefactor entirely too willing to play games with people's lives. He himself hated subterfuge; his mesmerism he saw as a necessary evil, the necessity of which would disappear once they brought about a new France. His benefactor, he suspected, thrived on it. "Surely that petition was our plan."

"Trust me. That petition was never going to succeed, not once the Assembly had ruled against it. Even if it had, it would have resulted in something too moderate and too temporary. As long as the king is part of the government, he is the true ruler of France."

"Perhaps. But things are worse now. The people are too frightened to challenge the constitution."

"Fear is a short-lived emotion. Resentment toward the monarchy will be stronger than ever now. When we're ready to make a move, it will be made swiftly. And we will be ready. I told you, didn't I? This is it."

"What can I do?" Robespierre's irritation evaporated. It didn't matter what his benefactor said. Camille's face was vivid in his mind. "I'll do anything at all."

"Kill the king of France," his benefactor said.

Saint-Domingue/Jamaica

August 1791

The French colony of Saint-Domingue was home to forty thousand white colonists, mostly wealthy Commoner businessmen and their employees. Fifty thousand more were freed slaves or mixed race, born largely of liaisons between white slave owners and their spellbound slave mistresses, and growing up in an uneasy liminal space between the two. More than four hundred and fifty thousand more were slaves. Many had been brought from Africa, in enormous ships like those that Wilberforce was working to abolish from the other side of a vast ocean. Many more had been born into slavery, on plantations where spellbinding was less rigid and family groups were grudgingly permitted. Some of these children were spellbound themselves from their first bite of solid food.

The colony exported millions of pounds of sugar, coffee, spices, cocoa, and snuff: more sugar and coffee than all the colonies of the British West Indies combined. Across the island, the plantations stretched for countless miles, baked by a blistering sun and surrounded by dazzling blue water. It accounted for nearly a third of the business of the Atlantic slave trade. It was one of the richest colonies in the world.

In August 1791, something reached across the oceans and set its slaves free.

As it happened, the first man to be killed in the slave uprising was Enrique Malet, younger son of a wealthy plantation owner. He was a natural mesmer, which made him ideally suited to overseeing and managing the two hundred or so slaves who formed his father's work-force. Technically, he was a Commoner, but in the colonies exceptions were made for those of a mesmeric bent on a plantation. His natural laziness and taste for easy authority made him more suited still. It was very little real work. In the mornings, he saw to the feeding of the slaves and pushed them out to their work with a vocal command overlaid with mesmerism. Throughout the day, the overseers would roam and command the slaves verbally should any specific adjustment to their work be required: he was only needed to reinforce the commands with mesmerism if a slave seemed to be struggling free of the overseers' orders, and to give the general commands to stop for water once at midmorning and once at midafternoon. Unless one of the slaves broke free of the spell entirely—which had not happened for some time—there was very little need for him to come to the fields. He could usually doze in the heat of the day and while away the remaining hours up at the big house with his slave mistress Henriette. In the evenings, he sent out the command for the slaves to return to their sleeping quarters. It always sent a small thrill through him, to reach out to all the hundreds of enchanted minds, push only a little, and see the vast hordes stop, straighten, turn, and come back across the fields in a great wave. His Inheritance was only moderate; with a free individual, he would have to strain for anything beyond faint mental control. The slaves, by comparison, were an extension of his own body. There was pleasure in exercising his control over them, as there would be in stretching or mild physical exertion.

The evening of the uprising was no different. The slaves came in, and Malet oversaw their evening feeding. They sat motionless on their sleeping pallets as the food was ladled into bowls. Their spell-green eyes gleamed in the dim light.

"Eat," Malet said, his voice overlaid with mesmerism, and as one they ate. It took twelve slow, rhythmic spoonfuls to devour the gruel. As it happened, Malet's plantation had recently become one of the few that laced the evening as well as the morning meal with the alchemical compound. The alchemy had to be shipped in from France, and it was very expensive; that, and the fact that it killed the slaves twice as quickly, meant that most masters thought it a waste of money as long as the slaves weren't required to work through the night. But Malet's father was troubled by reports of increased uprisings on other colonies, and he thought it worth the cost. This, more than anything else, contributed to Malet's early death. They couldn't have known.

On his last evening alive, Malet waited patiently as the slaves ate. He watched Henriette put her bowl down with the others and debated taking her inside with him. He decided against it. If he had decided otherwise, he might have died somewhat earlier, but not much.

"Sleep," he commanded, and as one the two hundred bespelled souls lay back and slept. The room was close with rhythmic breathing, and he went back to his house.

A storm was brewing outside: the sky had darkened with grumbling clouds, and the air was sticky with heat. Malet stripped to his shirt and breeches and settled in for a quiet night, reading the papers that so troubled his father while sipping claret from a decanter beside him. The news that France had become a constitutional monarchy had not yet reached the West Indies. The colonies usually held no daemon-stones: apart from the rarity of the stones, the spirits in them were limited in how far they could communicate over running water, and the vast stretches of ocean between Europe and the West Indies confounded them entirely. As such, reports could take months to travel between the colonies and France. There *was* a report about something called the Declaration of the Rights of Magicians, which from what Malet could tell meant that the Assembly thought everyone should be equal, but it had no power to make them so. All very confusing, but the claret was very good.

At eleven o'clock he was woken from a languorous doze by a sound from outside. He would have settled back down again had not the mastiff asleep on the rug looked up sharply and growled. It was unusual for the dog to react to outside noises: she barely reacted to the sound of her own name. Moreover, when he listened, the noise appeared to be ongoing, and coming from the direction of the slave quarters.

Before they had started spellbinding in the evening, it had not been unusual for the slaves to talk at night. Even during the day, he suspected that much of their seeming compliance came from the whips and watchful eyes of the overseers rather than the grip of the spell as the official story went. At night, if the alchemy was allowed to lapse, many of them were able to fight free of the spell to some degree: enough to whisper, to plan, to tell stories, to comfort each other, sometimes even enough to sing. He had heard them when he woke in the dark hours before dawn, and it always reminded him uneasily that what the slave owners told each other about the slaves was not always to be relied upon. But the slaves had only just been spellbound for the second time in twenty-four hours: they should not be capable of sound now. And he had never, even in the old days, heard anything as loud as this.

Malet stood, caught up his rifle and a lantern, and went to investigate. Had he not done so, he might have lived somewhat longer, but not much.

The rain had begun outside. The air seemed liquid, and thunder rumbled in the hills.

When Malet opened the door to the slave quarters, the long room was darker than the track from the house. Even with his lantern spilling light into the building, it took a while for his eyes to adjust and see what had been making the noise. The slaves were awake. Some were getting to their feet; some were already standing; some were moving about the room and stretching their cramped muscles. This movement accounted for some of the noise: feet on the dirt floor, a few connecting with the wall as they found their balance. But most of it was their voices. They were talking to each other.

Fear shot through him, but what it meant did not quite sink in. If it had, he would have closed the door. It did occur to him, though, that his dog was no longer at his side, and he had no idea where she had run.

"What are you doing?" he shouted. "Stop, all of you!"

They turned to look at him.

In the light from his lantern, their eyes no longer glinted green with the effects of spellbinding, but were as dark as his own.

They came toward him.

Malet felt blind panic now, and he glanced behind him for the door. But those who slept nearest had already closed off that retreat. He raised his rifle.

"Stop!" he ordered. "All of you, stop!" Had he been fixing his mesmeric strength on one of the former slaves, he might have made one falter—that was all he had ever been able to manage with free human beings. But he was trying to throw his power out over two hundred, and so they did not stop. They converged on him. A tall, thickset man yanked the rifle from his hands and struck him with it. Malet fell, his head ringing with the force of the blow, and together those nearest him beat him until he stopped moving.

That was the first death. After that, the former slaves broke out of the sleeping quarters, and they did not stop.

Within an hour, the big house was ablaze and its occupants killed. This was happening to other plantations also, across the island. The smoke rose into the sky, along with gunshots and battle cries and the screams of dying men, women, and children. And still they did not stop.

On another island, a few hundred miles across the ocean, Fina's eyes shot open. For once, she drew herself upright without thought or caution. Had she been seen by unfriendly eyes, there would have been consequences, even fatal ones. She didn't think about it.

"Did you hear that?" she whispered.

Only a handful of them could answer, so early in the night. But those who did whispered back, or at least shook their heads. No. They hadn't.

"What is it?" Molly asked. It was more rare for her to speak these days. That winter, an overseer had beaten her severely for working too slowly; the scars were slow to heal and left her with less strength to fight the spell than she once had.

Fina closed her eyes again, trying to hear better. Rain pounded on the roof; now that the last wisps of sleep were fading, it drowned out any trace of what had woken her. Whatever she had heard it with, it wasn't her ears.

"It's a call," she said. "A call to rise up and take revenge. A call to burn, and pillage, and destroy."

They believed her. Her ability to resist the spell, as slow to develop as it had been, marked her as special in their eyes: a great magician, in the parlance of the whites; a great woman, in terms of their own language, which drew no distinctions between magic and other strengths. They respected and envied her accordingly. The fact that they also protected her as the shy, timid sister they had known as a child was neither here nor there.

"Who is it?" Jacob asked. After her, he was usually the most free of the spell. "Is it a god?"

"Perhaps." Her mother had taught her about one god, but she had learned since then that there could be many others. "A god, or a spirit."

"Is it for us?" Jacob's voice: excited, hopeful. "Is the god calling us?"

Fina shook her head. "No. It's calling the slaves across the water. The French slaves, in Saint-Domingue."

The name caused a stir.

"Clemency?" Molly whispered. "Can you hear it?"

"I—can't—hear anything," Clemency's voice came, struggling through the spell. The young woman, barely sixteen, had been sold to the plantation from Saint-Domingue the year before: her Jamaican creole, though fluent now, still had the lilt of the French colony when her tongue was free enough to talk. It grew stronger as she rolled over to face Fina and Molly. "But there was an uprising near my old plantation just before I left. A free black man tried to convince France to give them equal rights to the whites, after their revolution; when he failed, he came back and led an army of free men against the planters.

They caught him and tortured him to death. That was the free blacks and mulattoes, though. Not us."

"This is the slaves," Fina said. "I know it is. The spellbinding over there has been broken. They're rising against their masters."

Clemency was known, even among the overseers, for her youthful quickness; Fina, who at Clemency's age had known only misery and fear, usually watched her capacity for joy with wonder and a little awe. Now, though, she was silent, and her expressive face was dark.

"If that's true," she said at last, "then I hope they kill them all."

Nobody spoke again for a long time.

"If they do overthrow the masters over there," Jacob said slowly, "the whites here will send help across to subdue the revolt. If we could get on those ships..."

"But how could we?" Molly asked. "The spell would never let us move that far."

"But if we could," Jacob said. Just for a moment, his eyes rested on Fina.

She turned away in the dark. Inside, her heart was thundering. She could get away—she was almost certain she could. The others knew it too, though they'd never speak of it if she didn't first. She thought of standing under an open sky, utterly at liberty, even the faint pull of the alchemy at her limbs dissolved. No whips, no pain, no anger. The thought was like jumping from a cliff with her eyes closed, not knowing if the sensation of the wind was falling or flying.

"Go," Molly whispered to her, as the others started up a song. "This is your chance."

"I won't leave you," she said.

"You will," Molly said. "You'll have to."

London/Paris

September 1791

Pitt never liked going into the Temple Church. This had nothing to do with the church itself, which was as small and exquisite as a miniature jewelry box. On a fine day such as this one, the sunlight warmed the light sand-colored walls and streamed through the stained glass until it felt like a tangible thing in the air. He actually liked the atmosphere of hushed whispers and concentrated thought as the Knights Templar, in their white robes with a red cross stitched on the chest, went about their research and investigations; it reminded him of the libraries at Cambridge. Many of the Cambridge scholars he had studied under had, in fact, been Knights Templar, specializing in Latin and mathematical theory. The Order contained some of the finest scholars in the world—in magic, of course, but also in some surprisingly obscure fields. It was why he was here, after all.

Why Pitt would have preferred to consult with the Knights Templar elsewhere had nothing to do with the Temple Church or its inhabitants and everything to do with the memories both invoked. This, after all, was where he had been brought for examination at the age of three weeks, like every other child whose parents found the London headquarters the most convenient. It was where his blood had been taken from a tiny pinprick in his finger and subjected to a series of spells by a knight of the Order while his family held him and waited. It was where he had been pronounced pure Commoner, no manifest Inheritance, and allowed to leave without a bracelet around his tiny wrist. He didn't remember this, of course. But he remembered being fourteen, miles from home in his first month at Cambridge, feeling his new abilities blossoming inside him and tearing him apart. He had been in so much pain, and the unfamiliar tangle of bloodlines about him was so overwhelming, that when he was awake, he had been unable to think of very much at all. Yet when he'd managed to drift into feverish sleep, he had very often dreamed of this place. If anybody suspected what was killing him in slow, agonizing degrees, it was here he would be sent and killed instead in one swift stroke of a knife. He wouldn't have blamed the Temple Church for it. It was the law. In some ways it would have been merciful. Certainly it would have been quicker and less painful than starving to death as the abilities settled; it would have been far less dangerous than trusting him to let himself die. But he had been fourteen, and he hadn't wanted to die—not at all, but especially not like that. He hadn't wanted his siblings' prospects to be blighted by public knowledge of what their bloodline contained, and he hadn't wanted the last thing he saw to be a strange room and a strange man bringing a blade toward his bare throat. He had woken from those dreams shivering convulsively, and it had taken all his self-control not to let his fear show.

Pitt was thirty-two now, and it had been a long time since he had been afraid of a dream. Still, he couldn't step into the building without his heart beginning to pound, his blood to rush, and his instincts to scream that he was someplace where he was very, very unwelcome. And he was. Fortunately, none of the Knights Templar knew it.

The senior Templar who was brought to him after a remarkably short wait certainly didn't seem to suspect anything amiss: he had the distracted look of someone pulled away from hard work and only half-conscious of the person in front of him. Pitt knew the look well because he felt it on his own face frequently.

"Master Forester," the man introduced himself. He was only slightly older than Pitt himself, despite his rank, and his fair curls and blue eyes lent a boyish air to his intelligent face. Strong alchemist, weaker strains of weather magic and metalmancy, unmanifested empathy, Pitt noted without being able to help it: his own magic was painfully sharp in these surroundings. Forester was braceleted, but that didn't mean he wasn't using his Inheritance within the church walls. There were special exemptions for Master Templars. "I'm one of the senior research magicians in the Order. I was told you were coming to discuss the slave revolt at Saint-Domingue?"

"I am," Pitt said. "Thank you for taking the time to meet me."

"Not at all," Forester said. His voice betrayed nothing but politeness. It was hard to know how he felt about being asked to brief the prime minister about something that he probably felt was no business of the government. "Thank you for coming. Shall we step into my office?"

Apart from the telltale squares of stained glass at the window, Forester's office could have been in any building in London: small, light, well-appointed, walled with bookshelves on which a combination of old leather tomes and more modern pamphlets were arrayed. Pitt could see studies of magic and theology, with the odd volume of astronomy or biography. The atmosphere of business and scholarship was reassuring; he would have quite liked to examine the titles in more detail.

"Your ministers would have told you the situation in Saint-Domingue as far as we know it," Forester said as he gestured for Pitt to take a seat at the other side of the desk. He folded himself and his white robes into the wooden chair opposite. "In fact, it's very likely you have information we don't."

"We received word yesterday that there had been a slave uprising in one of the French colonies last month," Pitt said. He knew he had to be very diplomatic: that was one reason he had come in person, and come to the church directly rather than gone to Cambridge or any other institute where magical research was done. The Templars' power was technically subordinate to Parliament and the Crown, but in areas of magic, it was always necessary to treat them with respect. He *did* respect them, on the whole. But they could be difficult, and dealing with difficult people wasn't always his strongest skill. "I assume your order did as well. It will be in the papers by now. Obviously, I hope we can work with you to ascertain the facts, as we do with all other areas of magical crime, but I don't believe either of us has any more information than the other at this point. The reason I've come is to see if your order can explain how, in their opinion, the enchantment failed so utterly at Saint-Domingue that the spellbound slaves there were able to stage a full-scale uprising."

Forester nodded. He didn't seem surprised—the Knights Templar had obviously been expecting it, given that they had assigned a research magician to talk to him.

"I don't know how much you know about spellbinding?" Forester said, his voice rising at the end to imply a question.

As he'd carried the abolition cause through Parliament on Wilberforce's behalf for many long months, and listened to Wilberforce carry it for several more, Pitt thought he knew rather a lot, but didn't say so. The Templar presumably knew of his part in the debates, and Pitt knew from experience that experts in any field didn't consider "rather a lot" to be very much at all.

"I know that it's part alchemical and part mesmeric," he said instead. "The slaves' food is mixed with a compound that is said to render them mindless and unaware. It's been firmly established, I think, that this is not actually what happens. The slaves are awake throughout the process and fight it constantly. But in this state, they find it very difficult to move without command, and very difficult to disobey a command given to them. In particular, they become extremely susceptible to mesmerism: quite a weak mesmer can easily command a spellbound slave, and a strong mesmer can move entire armies of them with a thought. Having said that, I believe they respond to voice commands as well."

"They do," the Templar confirmed. "But the hold of a mesmer is far stronger. If a strong mesmer were to take control of a group of slaves—"

"Their orders would supersede any verbal commands," Pitt finished. "Such as, for example, someone begging a slave not to kill them.

Is that what happened at Saint-Domingue? Somebody took control of them?"

Forester shook his head. "We're looking into that possibility, and it's still a possibility. But we're almost certain that the insurgents are acting alone, not by any orders. No mesmerism was involved. They are free people now. This was the alchemy."

"Someone removed the alchemical compound from the food?"

"Someone sabotaged it," the Templar said firmly. "If those slaves were being fed plain food, the magic would have passed from their system slowly. They would have woken slowly, over a day or so. The overseers would have noticed. No, they were given something that broke the spell completely, and all at once."

"How?"

"A new shipment of the compound arrived from France in early August. It traveled north, where supplies were scarce. That was where it all started: one tainted shipment. Apparently a few of the larger plantations had opened it within days—that was when the first of the fighting broke out. By sunrise, the affected slaves had stormed their masters' houses. Before word could spread about the tainted compound, more plantations followed—within days, it was widespread across the island. Once the freed slaves took a plantation, they could free the slaves within it simply by withholding the spellbinding compound from them. The last we heard, there were some hundred thousand slaves in revolt, and four thousand slave owners dead."

Pitt nodded. "So it was an alchemist."

Alchemy was a strange magic, at times as much science as supernatural. Very basic alchemy could be undertaken by people with no alchemical Inheritance at all—though some insisted that kind of work should more properly be called chemistry. True alchemists felt the elements in their blood and could combine or transmute them with a touch. This was usually on a small scale: some turned solids into gases or worked with small amounts of particular metals. With slow, patient study, others could stretch their abilities into more ambitious forms. Many medicines were made by alchemists, as were other chemical spells. The compound that spellbound was one of the most powerful and most complex of its kind to date, and only the very strongest were able to produce it.

"It was a very strong alchemist," Forester confirmed, or corrected. "And one with a good deal of talent. That spell is difficult enough to achieve in the first place; it's supposed to be impossible to break, or even to alter. I couldn't do it myself, and I've studied it for years. And the scale of it—this was no small sample in a mortar and pestle they altered. It was an entire shipment. This needed a true touch."

"Where did the shipment of the compound come from?" Pitt asked. "The alchemy isn't carried out in the West Indies, as I understand?"

Forester shook his head. "The ingredients are too delicate. The compound for the French colonies comes direct from Paris, as ours does from Liverpool. And, because I can see where your mind is going, yes, this very likely has something to do with the powerful magicians released from the Bastille two years ago."

"From memory, there were twenty-three strong alchemists in that prison," Pitt said. "That's not, of course, including those from other prisons or those who have emerged from hiding since."

"We're corresponding with the Order in Paris over the daemon-stones," Forester said. "But really, there's very little they can do. The new regime in France is not sympathetic to the Knights Templar."

"The Assembly hasn't broken with the Temple Church yet, to my knowledge."

"Not officially—not yet. But you must know, even though most of the Knights won't talk to the government about it so openly, that we've all but been forced out of Paris. Most of the Order have been forced to flee the cities for the provinces or even the borders; those who remain have no recognized power and hold their position solely through the tolerance of the mob. That tolerance won't last very long."

Pitt had known that, from the reports they had coming in from France. But it was startling to hear it from a Templar. "You're right. Most of your order wouldn't have told me that so openly."

"You knew." It wasn't a question. "The Templars in Rome are afraid of letting the governments of the world realize how weak we've become. But everyone knows. Three hundred years ago, we had the power to force the vampire kings off two thrones and bring order to Europe. Now we're scholars and clergymen, wholly reliant on the support of the countries we're meant to protect. And times are growing dangerous."

"In the meantime, our investigation is being confounded by others' revolutions on two fronts," Pitt said with a wry smile. "France and the West Indies."

"The revolution will reach here soon enough," Forester said grimly. "If we're not careful."

"Careful, how?"

Forester shook his head. "Nothing."

"No, really. Go on."

"France's alchemical compound is the same as ours," Forester said. It was as though a dam had been broken through. "If somebody can free French slaves, they or somebody else can free British slaves as well. And that isn't all. I can hear the sentiments forming on the streets here. Many are afraid of what's happened in France, but many others are inspired by it. We need to tighten our grip on unregistered magic under these circumstances."

"I'll take that into consideration." He understood the sentiment, but the fervor with which it was delivered chilled him. "But I'm not sure that won't cause more trouble, especially since the colony sabotaged wasn't even one of ours. Don't forget, it was by holding too tight a grip that the French Aristocrats brought about the Revolution."

"Well, that's the decision of the government, of course." There was a touch of irony in Forester's voice. "Our order exists to regulate magic and fight dark magic, not decide national policy—not anymore, in any case. But I would be very careful, Mr. Pitt, if I were you."

"Thank you." Pitt's own voice may not have been entirely free from irony either. "I do try to be that, as a general guide."

The news had reached Wilberforce only half an hour before. He had spent the morning in a dusty room with barely a handful of MPs, all but two of them out to prove that the evidence he and his friends had spent years collecting was nothing but lies. The hearings of evidence against the slave trade had dragged on for so long in the House and been so frequently postponed that Wilberforce had finally moved to have them passed over to a committee that would include himself and anyone with a mind to attend. It had worked—the process was moving faster—but it was hard, soul-grinding work. The meetings could stretch up to nine hours in a day, and it was painfully obvious that the minds who did attend were there to delay, not expedite, the process.

When he and Thornton had finally emerged, wincing in the bright sunlight, he was startled to see his friend Hannah More waiting for him. She had arrived in town only the previous afternoon; he had written to her and promised to see her at the Abolition Society that night, but not before.

"You need to talk to Pitt," she said bluntly. She all but took him by his thin shoulders and pushed him toward his waiting carriage. "I'd come with you, but I need to call on Clarkson. There's been a slave uprising in the West Indies."

By the time Pitt returned to Downing Street, Wilberforce was already there and waiting. He knew Pitt's office almost as well as his own—it resembled his own more than most people would think, with its Sisyphean mounds of unanswered correspondence—but this time he couldn't settle in it. He paced the floor, his stomach a cold knot of fear. Harriot had been able to fill him in on a few more particulars about the scale and violence of the rebellion, and his imagination supplied more still. The daemon-stone gleamed in the center of the desk, half-shielded by paper. It might have brought the news that morning, not from Saint-Domingue, of course—the messages couldn't traverse that expanse of ocean—but perhaps from Paris. It set his nerves on edge; the scar along his side throbbed. He wondered if the shadows bound to daemon-stones bore any resemblance at all to the one that had been bound to the undead.

"Well," Pitt said, by way of greeting. "Forgive my saying so, but you look rather worse than the French ambassador I spoke to this morning."

"You're forgiven," Wilberforce said. As usual in the face of Pitt's calm, his anxiety ebbed just a little. "And you look disgustingly self-possessed in the face of a crisis. How were the Templars?"

"Selectively helpful, intermittently alarming, thank you for asking. How are *you*?"

"Exhausted," he said frankly. Pitt sat down at his desk; he slipped into the chair opposite. "I've just endured four hours listening to a merchant explain that the Africans really *enjoy* being enslaved, they have a comfortable passage across the sea, and dances on deck. I told him they were spellbound and whipped, the only dancing they have is forced upon them when the captains decide that exercise would help them get a better price, and I almost told him that if that was his idea of enjoyment, he would probably benefit from it far more than the poor emaciated children in the holds of his ships, but Thornton kicked me under the table. Hannah More told me about Saint-Domingue," he added. "We all hoped you could tell us what's true and what isn't."

"Always a fraught proposition," Pitt said. He had laughed at Wilberforce's account of the merchant, but his face was grave again now. "What would you like to know?"

"How many slaves are free?"

"Nearly a quarter of the population, as far we know, but that information is weeks old. More will have followed: I doubt any shipments of the compound will even make it to the island now. The rebellion seems to have armed itself very efficiently. I would assume, too, though we've heard nothing of it, that many of the ex-slaves will be magicians in their own right."

Wilberforce shook his head. "Obviously, I can't claim to be upset that they've succeeded. But it sounds horrific."

"It does. And the reprisals from the French have doubtless been more horrific still. Either that revolt will be brutally suppressed, or the island will be plunged into civil war for the foreseeable future.

Regardless, the death toll is going to escalate. Here's something true that I didn't tell the Knights Templar: the white planters have offered to accept British sovereignty if we come and take back the colony for them."

"Really? The richest colony in the Caribbean? Are you going to—"

"No. It's not a situation we want to be involved in; under the circumstances, I doubt we could take it if we wanted to, or hold it if we did. For all we know, it's torn itself apart by now. I'm afraid the abolition bill might have to wait until next year."

Wilberforce had been expecting this, of course, but he shook his head firmly. He'd had the drive across town to think over the situation. "It can't. We've already lost two years to these ridiculous hearings and delays. We need to push ahead. You said the last time we presented that we had every chance of pushing the bill through once all the evidence had been heard."

"Provided nothing happened to change things. I didn't foresee the French Commoners overthrowing the Aristocracy. And I certainly didn't foresee this. The ongoing bloody massacre of thousands of slave owners is not going to endear people to the plight of the slaves."

"I understand that," Wilberforce conceded. "But can't they see that it's an argument *against* slavery? The slaves wouldn't revolt if they weren't desperately unhappy. And, from a pragmatic point of view, if the spellbinding can be broken, it's dangerous to keep accumulating a larger and larger army of tortured individuals—many of them magicians—ready to rise up and slaughter their oppressors."

"You don't need to tell me—I'm perfectly convinced. But any form of revolution, particularly magical revolution, is a sore point at the moment—or perhaps I should say a frightening point. Saint-Domingue isn't the only impending war I've had news of this week. Austria has issued an official warning to France that if they harm Louis or Marie Antoinette, the Austrian army won't hesitate to respond. And, more worryingly, France hasn't taken it well."

"But surely the Assembly won't harm the king. It wants to work with him."

"Factions of it do. But other factions don't. Some of those factions who want to work with the king also want war with Austria, because they believe their new Declaration of the Rights of Magicians should spread to other countries. And if they push for a war, then other countries are going to have to step in to stop them. Potentially even us."

It wasn't all new information, but it sounded far worse put together. "I had no idea the situation was so volatile."

"In fairness, neither did we. A lot of this came yesterday from the daemon-stone with our ambassador in Paris, and he didn't get it all from official channels. What troubles me more is that France's new constitution still hasn't agreed on the new laws regarding Commoner magic, and until then their bracelets are inactive. From what the Templar I spoke to today told me, they've all but broken with the Temple Church. It strongly suggests that if they do go into battle, they may break the Concord."

The Concord had been made between the major powers in Europe after the Vampire Wars in the fifteenth century. It was, essentially, a promise that no country's army would employ magic on a battlefield. As long as it held, and it had always held, there was no possibility of another plunge into dark magic like the kind that had nearly destroyed the world. Even America, when it had rebelled against British sovereignty a few decades ago, had accepted and held to the Concord; once they had become independent, they had taken the oath themselves. The alternative was too terrible to contemplate.

"They couldn't, surely?" Wilberforce protested. "It would raise all of Europe against them!"

"I don't know if they care. We *are* sending them an offer, in private, that England will be willing to recognize the Assembly as a legitimate government as long as they cease their aggression on other countries. It might work."

"It might work better if you made it public," Wilberforce said. "I'm sure it would produce an immediate effect in France."

"It wouldn't."

"It's such a monstrous idea that two great kingdoms are using all the talents which God gave for the promotion of general happiness for their mutual misery and destruction."

"Wilberforce, for God's sake, we are doing all we possibly can," Pitt sighed. It was such an uncharacteristic lapse that Wilberforce felt a pang of guilt. He had forgotten that his friend looked his most self-possessed when his calm was running out.

"Of course you are. I'm sorry, I didn't mean to imply otherwise."

"You didn't," Pitt said, having caught himself. "I'm the one who should apologize. It's just been a rather difficult morning. And I didn't mean to imply the abolition bill was entirely hopeless. I do think, though, that you might do better to wait until this blows over."

"And if it doesn't? If things only get worse, and we do head for war?" He shook his head. "This isn't only about political strategy, you know—there are human lives at stake. One year means thousands more captured and subdued against their will. It isn't my battle; it's theirs. Any chance of progress at all...I have to do what I can."

Pitt nodded slowly. "I understand. And if you present it, then of course I'll support it."

"Thank you." Wilberforce sighed himself. "I do appreciate what you're saying. I'm hopeful about Saint-Domingue, I really am. Perhaps they can come through war and find a solution. But in terms of our cause, this couldn't have been worse timed if it had been brought about on purpose."

"I wonder."

"What?"

"Nothing, possibly. It just occurs to me that this is not the first act of inexplicable magic connected with abolition recently. What we know, and the Knights Templar don't, is that someone summoned an undead a little over three years ago—*before* the storming of the Bastille, so not someone from within its walls. And the shadow in question almost killed the greatest political advocate of the abolition movement."

"You think the shadow in Westminster and the Saint-Domingue uprising are connected? But one, if we're correct, is aimed against abolition; the other freed thousands of slaves. Directly opposing aims, surely?"

"Unless the purpose behind the Saint-Domingue rebellion wasn't really their freedom. As you so correctly pointed out, if one wants to destroy faith in abolition, terrifying people with accounts of freed slaves raping, burning, and murdering is a very good way to do it."

"It seems a very elaborate ploy," Wilberforce said, but he couldn't quite dismiss the idea. "All the same, I'd be very interested to know if any of the anti-abolitionists in France are alchemists."

"I'll make some discreet inquiries," Pitt said. "It's a good deal easier than looking for a necromancer. And since the Knights Templar have very little power in Paris, I see no reason why we shouldn't investigate ourselves. God knows we have enough French eyes and ears in our pay these days."

It was the first time Pitt had spoken of the frantic building of intelligence networks rumored to be taking place on both sides of the Channel. Wilberforce glanced at the daemon-stone on the desk, and his stomach tightened.

The news about Saint-Domingue reached France at the same time. The National Assembly of Magicians agreed that the insurgents had every right to rebel, and even to demand their freedom. It was, after all, what they had been promised under the Declaration of the Rights of Magicians; it was what the Commoner magicians had risen to demand on the streets of Paris. They sympathized entirely. Unfortunately, they couldn't afford to grant freedom to them now. Not now that Austria had threatened them with war, and the colonies' imports were so badly needed. Not when it would be so inconvenient.

The trouble was, as Britain had learned, there were factions in the Assembly who wanted to go to war. It was as simple and as frustrating as that. The group that had formed around the powerful orator Jacques-Pierre Brissot, sometimes called the Girondins for the region many of them came from, was one of them. They had been friends with Robespierre and Camille in the early days, but their interests were beginning to diverge. They were nearly all unmagical Commoners, for one thing, and so they were cautious about magical rights in practice. They were more willing to work with the king. And, above all, they wanted to go to war. They weren't content to bring harmony to France, to build a republic. They wanted to spread the Revolution abroad, to increase France's holdings. They wanted an empire. And that, for better or worse, required the colonies.

Robespierre argued against the decision furiously in the Jacobins.

"How can we fail to grant freedom to the slaves of Saint-Domingue?" he demanded. "Their freedom shouldn't even be ours to grant! According to the principles of the Revolution, we are all equal, and all free."

"In principle, you're right," came a dissenting voice. "But in practice, without the slaves, the colony will perish."

"Then let the colony perish, rather than a principle!" Robespierre retorted. He reached for the flare of mesmerism; it came, but only the weak, reluctant mesmerism that belonged to him. His benefactor had not strengthened it himself for some time. Not since the night he had asked him to kill the king of France.

That, he knew, was the real problem—the reason the Girondins had been able to push the country as close to war as they had, against all Robespierre's wishes. It had been three months, and the command still echoed in Robespierre's head. When he would drift into exhausted sleep, he would hear it in the voice of his benefactor, with increasing anger. And still he had not killed the king. He had no intention of ever doing so. His benefactor was displeased with him, and so the full heat of mesmerism was being withheld from him. He was fighting for the new world with a blunt knife.

This was made all the harder by the fact that he was, by his own choice, no longer a member of the National Assembly. There was a new set of people on the Assembly now, many of them magicians. Robespierre had proposed, successfully, that none of the Assembly that had brought in the constitution be eligible to take office under it, in order to prevent corruption. It caused his reputation to soar even higher among the Commoners. They called him the Incorruptible, and the name stuck. He felt he'd done the right thing—even the strategic thing. True power, these days, belonged to those with popular support and not a title. Still, at times like this, he could find it in his heart to wish he had been less principled, less strategic, and more direct.

"The National Assembly are only concerned about the colonies and their wealth because they want to go to war," he told the Jacobins. "A war that France is not prepared for, and that will taint our revolution by turning it into an exercise in empire building. If we don't stop, we'll find ourselves in a republic no better than the ancien régime."

Many of the Jacobins listened to him, mesmerism or not. The Assembly didn't; or, at least, it found the pressure of the slave owners and anti-abolitionists too powerful to wholly resist. A delegation was sent to Saint-Domingue, granting equal citizenship to the middle class of free black and mixed-race people. It was an unprecedented advancement, it was true, but slavery remained the official policy of France. To Robespierre's surprise, his benefactor was unconcerned, even content. Even pleased.

"Leave it, Robespierre," he said in Robespierre's dreams that night. "You're wasting your time on battles that make no difference at all."

"How can you say they make no difference?" Robespierre demanded. "It's a question of liberty. What is this revolution about, if not that?"

"You need to trust me."

"I don't trust anyone." He paused. "You withheld your mesmerism from me again tonight. I need it. Now I've come this far, and defied so many enemies, it could soon become dangerous for me not to have it."

"You have no right to demand anything of me." His benefactor's voice was suddenly sharp. "I told you what needs to be done. I told you to kill the king of France."

"I told you," Robespierre said—firmly, without plea for understanding. "I can't do that."

"Can't, or won't?"

"Both. He's the king, for God's sake. Even if I wanted to walk in there and shoot him through the heart, he'd be too well protected. But I don't want to. I don't kill people, not even kings, and he's little more than a harmless prisoner now."

"A prisoner in a gilded palace, with a government at his back and a slew of countries at our borders that could go to war at any time to reinstate him. Hardly harmless."

"I'm not an assassin."

"Not an assassin, not a member of the Assembly. You're nothing at all, as far as I can tell."

"I'm not nothing," Robespierre said. His own anger rose in response. "Don't ever say that. I'm not."

"Then what are you? I didn't raise you up not to do what was necessary."

"You raised me up because you thought I could save France. I can."

"Not by making speeches in an old monastery you can't. If you want my help, you need to do what I tell you, and trust that I'm telling you for the good of what you care about. I've seen the France in your head, Robespierre. This isn't it."

It wasn't. It was better than the France before the Bastille, it was true. They were a constitutional monarchy. They had a National Assembly and the room to make new laws. Camille and the other petitioners had even been allowed to return home, with a full pardon, though their voices had been all but stifled lately. But it wasn't the France in his head. There was no freedom of magic, and very little freedom of any other kind either.

And yet surely the France in his head wouldn't come into being with blood sacrifice. Surely he had soiled his conscience enough already, that one night on the eve of the elections to the Estates General. His benefactor was right: he had been nothing then. Now his reputation was rising every day. It wasn't enough for him to be a revolutionary, as Camille was. He wanted to be a lawgiver: fair, just, principled, resistant to the tide of human passions. The people now called him the Incorruptible. He wanted it to be true.

"I don't believe in capital punishment," he said. "I certainly don't believe in murder."

"If you believe in France," his benefactor said, "you may find you'll have to start believing in other things as well."

Jamaica

Autumn 1791

Molly died in autumn. She had been fading for weeks, her breathing becoming harsher and slower, her resistance to the spell weakening until she was locked entirely within her own head. The overseers had given her medicine at first, then stopped. Since she wasn't better, the reason was obvious. They had decided she was past healing and determined instead to save money and get as much work as they could from her before her heart wore out. Fina sat by her side every night and held her hand in the dark until, finally, one night just before the dawn, she could no longer hear her breathe at all. She was free of the spell to cry now, but she didn't. Instead, she felt hot fury burn in her chest.

"Is she gone?" Jacob's voice came. It had none of its usual confidence; it sounded very quiet, and very tired. "Fina? Little one?"

"She's gone," she said.

The next night, she left the plantation and the island forever.

It wasn't too difficult to escape from the sleeping quarters at night. Even with all the trouble in Saint-Domingue, the masters didn't expect the slaves to be able to move. Half the time, they didn't bother to lock them in; when she tried the door, it slipped open at a push. The hardest thing was facing her friends for the last time.

"Don't go," one of them said as she passed, in the strangled whisper that was all she could manage. She was a small, pretty woman, little more than the child Fina had been when she arrived. In the two years she had been with them, she had rarely been able to get free enough of the spell for Fina to get to know her. Too many of those with whom she lived and died were blanks in her knowledge. "They'll hurt us if you go. They'll hurt us to punish you."

"You shut up," Clemency said to her. Her voice was fierce, but Fina suspected it was to hide tears. "Of course she's got to go. You'd go, in her place."

Still, the whisper made her hesitate, anguished. She was scared enough for herself. She was, deep down, still looking for an excuse to stay. She couldn't bear the thought of anyone hating her for leaving, the thought of them being hurt or killed, and cursing her name.

"Fina," Jacob said. He fought to sit, and fell back; it was too early in the night for that yet. "Look between the floorboards, by my hand here."

She dropped down beside him and felt for his hand in the dark. They had never touched before. His skin was warm; she felt a shock go through her body before she moved her own hand to the floor. She quickly found the gap he meant.

"There's a paring knife there," he said. Her fingernails caught on it as he spoke. "I stole it last winter, from the overseer. He looked up and down for it; it never came to him that one of us could have taken it. I thought I might use it on one of them, if I ever got free for a moment the way Augustus did. But I'll never get free enough to use it. Take it. You might need it."

She took the knife and folded her fingers around it gently. Something of courage returned to her. She took Jacob's hand again, wordlessly, and kissed it. He squeezed it with what must have been all his willpower; she felt the faint pressure, like the brush of a leaf.

"Go," he said.

"I'll come back." She raised her voice so that everyone could hear. It was her excuse—not to stay, this time, but to leave them. "I'm going so that we can all be free. I'm going to find the voice on Saint-Domingue, the voice that broke the spellbinding. When I find him, he can free us as well. We can rise up and reclaim ourselves. I'll come back."

They all knew it was more of a story than a promise that could be kept. But she was a great magician: she had heard the voice on Saint-Domingue, and she could walk free when none of them could. So they believed her, in the way that stories are believed. Their whispered blessings followed her to the door and helped her turn back once to wave them goodbye, even though she thought her heart would break.

Getting on board the ship was another matter. She knew there were many in port bound for Saint-Domingue: Jacob had been right about the governor promising support to the white planters. No militiamen were going—Britain, far away across the ocean, had not been prepared to offer its armies—but the British planters in Jamaica were more sympathetic, and many were sending arms and supplies to the ports under siege at their own expense. Clemency, who sometimes helped out in the gardens of the big house, had heard that at least one ship was planning to set sail at first light, enough time for Fina to walk from her plantation to the docks and get on board. She hadn't anticipated, though, how many people would be awake on each ship at this time of night, walking about its decks and checking the sails. Clearly, a ship being ready to leave port wasn't something that happened by itself.

For a long time, she crouched behind a stack of worn crates, watching the nearest ship's gangplank. Once she was on board, she was confident she could reach the hold and hide out of sight for as long as she needed. It was that dash across the narrow strip of wood that connected the ship to the dock that worried her. She only needed to be glimpsed, and it would all be over. She ran the distance in her head, across the docks and over the plank and into the open hatchway that led to the hold, over and over again, but she couldn't move. Fear was as strong as spellbinding.

As much by instinct as by conscious thought, she closed her eyes and reached for her magic.

It was there in her blood: she'd felt it work away at the spellbinding over the years, and touch her mind with odd glimpses of the sugar-processing plant and the white mansion. She took hold of it this time and threw it out at the burly sailor on the deck of the ship.

The feeling was very like slipping into sleep. At once, her awareness of her surroundings muffled and faded, and in front of her eyes was a new view: close to that from her own eyes, but fifty yards distant, so that the sea was black and close and the horizon filled her vision. The ship rocked beneath booted feet, and she felt muscles not her own shift to keep balance. She was inside the sailor's head, looking out through his eyes—eyes that were stinging in the salt spray and squinting in the early-morning dark. And, most important, not looking in her direction.

She had no time for wonder, or fear. She pulled away, blinking back to her own head. The view in front of her was her own: the gangplank was there, a short dash across the docks. And then, at last, she took a deep breath, gathered her courage, and ran it in reality. Her bare feet padded on the ground and made the plank bounce and rattle, but there was no cry of alarm. With her heart raging in her ears, she disappeared into the hold.

It was her second time in a ship. At first, the memory of her passage to Jamaica rushed back. She had thought she had forgotten it, but it reared up in her head like a snake. The hold in which she hid was a storeroom, not a dungeon: it was packed with weaponry, ship's biscuits, salted meat, and rope, not hundreds of people lying in their own filth. And yet she could hear the tortured breathing and rattle of chains; she could smell the nauseous waves of fear and death. It took possession of her body in ways she had not expected. For the first few hours, as the ship plowed through the warm Caribbean Sea, she shivered, retched, and sobbed in spasms, all the while trying to keep as silent as she could. She was wedged tightly behind a crate, and her muscles remembered their old captivity and flooded her body with panic. In that moment, she knew that Molly was wrong. She would never be free.

Gradually, though, her fear quieted. She soon lost track of whether it was night or day. Bells rang to mark the hours as she dozed. Above her head, she heard the drumming of footsteps, the call of voices, the crash of waves over the deck. Ropes creaked; the boxes around her groaned and shifted. Sometimes she would hear footsteps, and then she would lock her muscles and try to breathe as little as possible until they passed again. But nobody disturbed her. By what might have been the second day, she began to feel a curious pleasure in that. The trip itself was worse than some of the tortures that her masters devised for their slaves, but the muscle cramps and thirst and seasickness were inflicted by nobody but herself. She had escaped. Whatever happened to her now, even if she were found and resold, her old masters would never touch her again.

Her magic, now that it had been used once, was awake in her veins. She practiced with it, tentatively, afraid all the time that the sailors would feel her behind their eyes but unable to resist. From the tiny dark hole in which she had sequestered herself, she could reach out and open her eyes—or rather another's eyes—to bright sun and dazzling sea. The thoughts and feelings of those she looked through were a mystery to her, and the view was oddly silent: no splash of waves or roar of wind. But she could feel the salt on their skin, and the heat of the cloudless sky. She savored it, and the feeling of power it brought with it.

It brought other things as well, though—things she didn't understand. Once, on the edge of sleep, she saw a garden: dark, leafy, like nowhere she had ever seen in the West Indies or in her memories of Africa. There were two white men there: one small and pale, the other tall and cloaked in shadow. Her instinct was that this was her magic too, not a dream of her own. As far as she knew, her magic could only place her inside the heads of others. What she was seeing, therefore, must be inside somebody's head. But whose head, and where, and how, remained a mystery.

There was sound in this vision, as there was not when she saw the world outside. Leaves rustled overhead, and wind hummed through the grass.

"War is coming," the small man was saying. He spoke in a language she didn't understand, but the meaning came to her intact. "It's imminent. You need to help me stop it."

"It's imminent," the other agreed, in a voice that was oddly familiar. "And I've told you what you need to do."

The small man shook his head. His arms were folded tightly across his chest, as though he were cold, and his white face looked naked in the moonlight. His fine ginger hair bore traces of powder. "I don't believe you really want to stop the war at all."

"I never said I did," the other said.

Fina knew his voice then. It was the voice that had called the slaves to rebellion, the voice she had come to find. The garden looked a very long way away, and yet in some way he was very close.

She was asleep when the ship arrived at Saint-Domingue. The sound of shouting woke her: shouting, and running footsteps. It was not the cheerful bustle of sailors sighting land and readying the ship for docking. The cries had notes of horror and wonder; the steps were the erratic staccato of panic. Without thinking, heart beating, she reached out with her magic and looked.

The blaze of light that greeted her was not the sun this time. The skies were pale gold with twilight, and the sea was white and silver. Not far from the ship, the coast of Saint-Domingue peeked over the horizon. It was on fire.

Through the eyes of the sailor, Fina saw a wide, circular bay surrounded by high mountains and dark green trees; beyond the docks were what had once been graceful streets and white houses. Now those same houses were blazing; many more, farther from the ports, were black and gutted. The streets were caked with soot and debris. The sharp reports of rifle fire sounded in the distance, as did the occasional scream on the wind. It was the view, though Fina did not know it, that Robespierre had seen in a dream six months ago and an ocean away. It had been a hope then, or a plan, something glimpsed from a mind reaching out to his own. This was real. It was Port-au-Prince, the capital of French Saint-Domingue, and it was burning.

As they drew nearer, the smell of smoke permeated the ship, even down in the hold where Fina was hidden. She waited in the darkness as the ship slid into port with shouts and creaking of masts. She didn't look out again through anyone's eyes: the glimpse she had stolen had told her what was waiting for her, and she knew most of the sailors would be focused on their own work rather than their surroundings now. Instead, when all seemed as quiet as could be expected, Fina carefully unfolded herself from her hiding place. Her muscles were stiff and trembling from her long confinement, and her heart throbbed in her ears.

Once again, she hesitated on the threshold of a ship. It had been nearly impossible for her to enter in the first place; leaving it didn't have the emotional wrench of leaving behind her family on Jamaica, but still her limbs were frozen. The world outside was so unknown and so angry, and she had nothing in the world except Jacob's knife and Molly's love and the promise she had made to find the voice that had started a revolution and bring it home.

The owner of the voice was here. She knew that now, without knowing how except that it was through her magic. She couldn't see through his eyes, but now that she stood on the edge of the island she could feel him in every tree and stone. If she looked hard enough, through battle and bloodshed and civil war, she would find him; then, perhaps, she could bring the war to her own people. Jacob would have gone at once. Clemency would have gone. Molly would not have left the others, perhaps, but if she had come this far to save them, she would not have hesitated to go farther. None of them would have been afraid, as she was. She was the wrong person to be free. And yet she was the only one here.

She drew a deep breath and walked out into the flames.

London

April 1792

In the spring, France declared war on Austria. The threat of it had been hanging over the two countries since Louis's attempted escape, but most never expected it to fall so fast, and still fewer had expected the final push to come from France. It was a war of defense, according to them, after Austria's aggressive overtures the year before. This was true enough. It was also a war of expansion—not of territory only, but of ideals. The Revolution was coming to Europe.

In theory, France moved forward without breaking the Concord. Commoner magic was still illegal in the streets, even though the bracelets were inactive, and it was still illegal on the battlefield. When the rest of Europe sent stern warnings about the frequent explosions of fire and water from the French army, France responded with injured innocence.

We have not broken the Concord, they said. We have no intention of breaking the Concord.

But the Concord is being broken, the various ambassadors insisted. There is clear evidence that Commoner soldiers have unleashed their magic on the battlefield.

It's illegal, France said. Of course, with the bracelets still inactive and the Knights Templar so ineffectual, it becomes very hard to enforce the law. In the heat of battle, things do happen. Soldiers defend themselves. But this does not reflect the official policy of the French Assembly of Magicians. The Concord remains intact.

"Really," Dundas complained to Pitt. "Do they think we're idiots?"

"No," Pitt replied. "They think we're afraid. And we are, aren't we?"

The two of them were in Pitt's office. Outside, the fragile sunlight had hardened into a bitter frost as the afternoon drew on. Eliot and Harriot, both of whom were staying at Downing Street over the session, sat side by side in front of the fire. It would have been a peaceful scene a year or so ago, when the subjects under discussion had been less momentous.

"If we choose to insist that they're breaking the Concord," Pitt said, "then by the terms of the Concord we need to see their actions as a declaration of war upon the whole of Europe."

"The French government can't want that either," Eliot said. "Have they gone mad?"

"No, of course not. The trouble is, this is a war of ideals as much as a war of conquest. There are magicians in that country who have been bound their entire lives. Now their bonds are cut. They would take any excuse to flex their muscles and stretch. The fact that using magic on the battlefield will draw the rest of Europe into the war is the only thing holding them back."

"And if we claim they've done so already and go to war to stop them," Eliot said, understanding, "then they'll have nothing left to lose. And then there's nothing to stop them breaking the Concord."

"Exactly. If we go to war with them for any reason at all, come to that, they'll have nothing left to lose. We need to remain neutral as long as we possibly can."

Harriot spoke up thoughtfully, her chin propped on her hand. "If Britain was to go to war with France, and France does break the Concord—would Britain break it as well?"

"Not if I can possibly help it," Pitt said.

She knew him too well to let him get away with that. She'd had the same political tutelage growing up as he had. "But other countries might. And if they do—if the Concord is broken on both sides—then this becomes a war of magic. We return to exactly the kind of conflict that the Concord was designed to prevent."

"Nobody acting against France will break the Concord unless we do. They'll wait for us to make a move."

"You can't know that, William. Besides, if France does use magic against us on the battlefield, how long can we realistically last without it?"

"I don't know," he admitted. "Which is one more reason why we need to avoid war with France if we possibly can."

"If they cross over into Holland and threaten British interests," Dundas said, "we will have to respond, magic or no. We can't let them tear through Europe unchecked."

"And we've told them that," Pitt said. "With luck, that will be enough to stop them." He paused. "Still. We should probably look at strengthening the navy, just in case."

Harriot caught his eye, and he knew they were both thinking of their younger brother. It had been more than ten years now since James had died at sea, so soon after their father and their sister Hester. His ship had been in the West Indies. The name had been little more than a scrawl on a map and a list of British interests to Pitt at the time; he knew it much better now, thanks to Wilberforce's efforts for abolition, but he still couldn't quite picture the color of the ocean or the strength of the sun.

Harriot looked away first, the memory having come and disappeared like a pebble beneath the surface of a pond. Her gaze fell to Pitt's desk, by his side. "The daemon-stone wants your attention," she said.

Pitt followed her gaze. Sure enough, the black orb was humming softly. His heart sank. It wasn't just that the stone almost certainly meant bad news, though lately it had. The messages had become so frequent lately, and from so far away: he had talked to their ambassador in France twice already that morning. Picking up a daemon-stone once was mildly unpleasant but forgettable, like having to swallow down a spoonful of bitter medicine. The cumulative effect was far worse. It was all too easy to believe, as Wilberforce did, that the stone was doing it on purpose.

"Well," he said, as dryly as he could. "If that's a declaration of war from France, at least we've already discussed it thoroughly."

"That won't help," Eliot said. "All we agreed was that we didn't want one."

"We'll leave you to it," Harriot said, standing. She gave her brother a sympathetic pat on the shoulder as she left.

Either the shadow in the Downing Street stone was growing accustomed to Pitt or he was more practiced at letting it in; this time, his fingers barely curled around it before the cold, insubstantial presence rushed into his head. It seeped into the crevices of his brain like fog against glass and whispered without words. Meaning grew, flowered, and burst in a shower of sparks. Then it was gone, leaving only a chill and a dull nausea in its wake.

Dundas hadn't left with Eliot and Harriot; he was there when Pitt blinked his way back into the room. "Anything of import?"

"Nothing to do with France—or not directly." He shivered, rubbed his eyes, and tried to chase the last of the shadow-smoke from his thoughts. "That was the stone in Manchester—and could have been sent through the usual channels, frankly. There are signs of agitation from the Army of Commoner Magicians, or whatever that chapter calls itself."

Dundas didn't seem reassured. If anything, his frown deepened. "We need to do something about these pro-magic societies. The more powerful France becomes, the more inflamed they get. We don't need what happened in Paris to repeat itself in London."

"I've already told Grenville and the others to hold back on the bill to relax penalties on Commoner magic—I agree it's too dangerous at this point. Fox will almost certainly bring it forward himself, of course, just to embarrass us, but that can't be helped."

He refilled his glass from the decanter in front of him and took a drink. It warmed some of the chill from the stone, but not all.

(It was a terrible thing to bind a powerful shadow against its will, the shadowmancers said. It would serve you. But it would never forgive you.)

Dundas seemed to be hesitating. "Wilberforce is presenting his abolition bill tonight."

"I know," Pitt said absently. He was writing down the message from the stone before it faded from his mind. "We talked about it this morning."

"You can't support it," Dundas said.

It took Pitt a moment to recall his thoughts from the paper in front of him. "I have no intention of doing anything else," he said.

"You know as well as I do that these are dangerous times. This is not the time to advocate for the things that started the Revolution in France—not to mention Saint-Domingue."

"The Revolution in France started over magical reform."

"It started over talk of rights and freedoms. All those revolutionaries were abolitionists of some shape or form. Any talk of the same in light of recent events will do nothing but anger the king and Parliament, and frighten the people of this country. They don't want what happened in Saint-Domingue to happen here."

It was not too different from what Pitt had told Wilberforce himself only months ago, when the Saint-Domingue rebellion had raised the question of whether it was politically expedient to bring the bill forward that session. He still saw the sense in it. But there was a vast difference between advising the bill be stalled and refusing to support it once it was raised. One was strategy. The other was a betrayal.

"Besides," Dundas added, "if we do go to war, we'll need every bit of that revenue from the trade. You can't tell me you haven't made the same calculations yourself."

"I made them. I don't agree that we need that revenue. It would be *useful*, if it came from a less repellent source, but that can't be helped." He cut Dundas off, sharply, before he could reply. "There's nothing more to be said. This isn't a party matter; you're perfectly free to vote according to your own conscience, and I'm free to vote according to mine. On this occasion, I've promised Wilberforce my support."

"Mr. Wilberforce is a very respectable gentleman," Dundas said. "But he is not the people of Great Britain. And you're the head of the British government. Your conscience isn't always going to be your own."

It was a very different debate that night from the one held less than three years earlier. To some, it might not have seemed so. The main actors were the same on both sides, though both sides had strengthened their numbers and their arguments. Much of the evidence was the same, though it had grown and tangled and been elaborated upon over long months in the committee. The arguments were nothing new, nor were the strategies. But Pitt had years of practice in reading the timbre of the room, and it had changed. The spring of 1789 had been a promise: the long, dark winter of the king's insanity had passed; the streets buzzed with outrage over the plight of the slaves; the growing fervor for reform in France was a glow and not a flame. This spring was a threat.

From the visible tension in Wilberforce's tiny frame when he got up to speak, he knew it as well. His voice delivered the facts but imbued them with passion; it felt, as Wilberforce's addresses to the House often did, as though each sentence was a personal plea meant for each listener's ears alone. Pitt had studied rhetoric and oration almost as soon as he could talk. He knew there were speakers more consistent than Wilberforce, with better grasp of allusion and structure—not many, but a few. He was one of them. But he'd never heard anyone with more natural eloquence. Fox, in support, blazed with indignation. The walls chimed.

Yet the other side, lacking the heavyweight debaters, had numbers and self-interest to their credit. Feelings were running high. The Honorable Mr. Quincy, younger son of the Earl of Casterbridge and unbraceleted weather-mage, had been sent from the room during Fox's speech as his frustration manifested in a burst of rain over the abolitionists; one or two of the MPs had come close to less magical fisticuffs. It wasn't a matter of evidence now—the conditions of slave ships had been proven, painstakingly, over the last few years. It was a matter of greed—and, more dangerously, of fear.

"I must acknowledge that the slave trade is an unamiable one," one speaker said, "but I will not gratify my humanity and my honor at the expense of the interests of the country, and I think it is our duty to not too curiously inquire into the unpleasant circumstances with which it is perhaps attended."

Honor. Duty. The good of the country. They were the cornerstones of Pitt's life; they always had been. He hadn't thought he had any intention of withholding from the debate, but perhaps some secret part of him had wondered if Dundas was right, because to hear the argument put so baldly and so callously in the name of everything he believed in fired something deep inside him. He was very rarely angry, in the House of Commoners or otherwise. He was now.

And so, when it was time for him to speak, he stood. It was five o'clock in the morning of a very long night. The stars had burned away, and the candlelight was fading into the gray light of dawn. Dundas next to him gave a warning shake of his head. He ignored it.

He had been talking for almost an hour when Franklin Larrington, member for Millton, shot out of his seat unexpectedly.

"Mr. Speaker," he called out. "Is this really the time for reforms of this kind? Does the honorable member forget that if Britain were to abolish the trade, France would only profit from it at our expense? At a time, I might add, when France's expansion is already looking increasingly dangerous."

The mention of France stirred the gallery and the House, as Larrington must have known it would. It was what loomed in everyone's mind; Dundas and then Larrington had only put it into words. France was indeed dangerous; the times they were living in were dangerous, so dangerous that perhaps trying to do anything more than survive them intact was like trying to remodel a house in the middle of a storm. And yet hearing it, Pitt felt only the same, unexpected shot of defiance.

"I would ask the honorable member," he replied, without missing a beat, "how this enormous evil is ever to be eradicated, if every nation is thus prudentially to wait till the concurrence of all the world shall have been obtained? There is no nation in Europe that has, on the one hand, plunged so deeply into this guilt as Britain, or that is so likely, on the other, to be looked up to as an example, if she should be the first in decidedly renouncing it. How much more justly may *other* nations point to *us* and say, 'Why should we abolish the slave trade, when Great Britain has not abolished it?' Instead of imagining, therefore, that by such an argument we shall have exempted ourselves from guilt, and transferred the whole criminality to them, let us rather reflect that on the very principle urged against us, we shall thenceforth have to answer for their crimes as well as our own."

"That argument," Larrington said, "assumes that enslaving the Africans could be considered a crime in the first place. Consider that they have shown themselves to be depressed by the hand of nature below the level of the human species. They use magic without constraint or care for the natural order of things. They have proven themselves naturally susceptible to our spellbinding. These facts, and the inferiority of their achievements in comparison to those of Great Britain, mark them as our natural slaves."

It was the wrong tactic; Pitt didn't need the muted notes of the walls to tell him that. Larrington could have pressed home his advantage by turning the argument back to France and the Revolution; instead, he'd taken Pitt's lead and left that path entirely. Now they were arguing, once again, on moral grounds.

At once, in a way he couldn't have explained, he was in tune with the House—not the members of Parliament, but the building itself. Its walls reached out to him, waiting and responsive. He knew that they would reverberate to his words with perfect precision. It was one of those moments that he experienced sometimes in the House of Commoners and nowhere else, when everything made perfect sense. His long-suppressed mesmerism flared in his chest, reminding him—as it so often did—that with a single push he could bend the entire House to his opinion. He ignored it, as he always did. But he tried to imbue his words with that same force of will.

"So have many of the honorable gentlemen argued," he said. "I find it difficult, personally, to see evidence that the people of Africa are uniquely susceptible to dark magic in the fact that they are bound by a spell designed to bind them. One point cannot be denied: Africa does not have Europe's great cities, nor her libraries, nor her technological advantages. But think of this. Why might not some Roman senator, reasoning on the same principles, and pointing to British barbarians, have predicted with equal boldness, '*There* is a people that will never rise to civilization—*there* is a people destined never to be free—a people without the necessary understanding for the attainment of useful arts, and created to form a supply of slaves for the rest of the world.' Might this not have been said as truly of Britain herself as can now be said by us of the inhabitants of Africa?"

Wilberforce caught his eye from the independent benches and smiled. They'd been discussing this only that morning—yesterday morning now, rather, for the candles had burned down as he'd talked, and the sun was beginning to rise behind the high windows above him. It was going to be a beautiful day. He kept the answering twinkle from his own eyes as he continued.

"We may live to behold the natives of Africa engaged in the calm occupations of industry, in the pursuits of a just and legitimate commerce. We may behold the beams of science and philosophy breaking in upon their land, which, at some happy period in still later times, may blaze with full luster. Then may we hope that Africa, though last of all the quarters of the globe, shall enjoy at length, in the evening of her days, those blessings which have descended upon us in a much earlier period of the world."

Just then, the dawn was breaking. A shaft of sunlight speared through the arched windows that spanned the wall, causing the wisps of cloud to glow golden, and Pitt suddenly felt the light of it on his face. It was so appropriate to what he had just been saying that it seemed almost made for him.

Two lines from the *Georgics* came suddenly to mind, and he spoke them almost without thinking. "*Nosque ubi primus equis Oriens adflavit anhelis, illic sera rubens accendit lumina Vesper*": And when the rising sun has first breathed on us with his panting horses, over there the red evening star is lighting his late lamps.

It was an easy and obvious allusion by his standards. He'd been trained in them by his father since he was seven. The rest of the House, however, didn't know this, and he heard a few of them catch their breath audibly. The moment felt perfect: words, images, associations, and feeling, all bound together and shot through with a single fortuitous ray of light. He could have kept going, but he realized that he didn't need to. That was it.

Pitt sat down to riotous applause, oddly distant from it but at the same time very satisfied. Soon, he knew from experience, he was going to feel as though he had climbed a mountain; at that moment, he felt only as though he were soaring at a very great height. Surely, he couldn't help but think, after all this, they had done it. The bill had to pass.

And then, to his surprise, Henry Dundas got to his feet beside him.

"Honorable Speaker," he said. "Both sides have spoken their cases very well, and to my mind there is a good deal of sense in the arguments of both. Clearly, this is not a case where both may be ultimately appeased. Might I, however, propose a third course of action, one which sees the concerns of both answered?"

"Proceed, Mr. Dundas," the Speaker said.

Dundas did so.

Pitt turned to Dundas as the House dispersed around them. Dundas attempted a tight flicker of a smile, but it faltered under the cool, hard glare that Pitt was very well practiced in employing at will. In this case, it didn't require a great deal of will.

"I know it's not what you wanted," Dundas said. It was almost an apology. "But it's what I thought best."

"Best for whom?" Pitt inquired, with more than a trace of sarcasm.

The elation from the speech had well and truly faded. Disappointment and fatigue mingled bitterly in its place. "I'm sure not those with interests in the slave market, knowing how little you are influenced by such considerations."

"You were never going to sell it to the House your way, Pitt," the older man said. "You must have warned Wilberforce of that yourself. This is the closest you were ever going to get."

"We'll never know now, will we? Excuse me." Pitt rose, cutting Dundas off before he could respond.

The debating chambers were flooded with sunlight now. It felt like mockery.

Finding Wilberforce by sight, as it turned out, was going to be difficult in the crowds in the halls outside the Speaker's Gallery. Because he was very tired, and his magic still ran hot in his veins, just for once Pitt gave in and concentrated instead on the cascade of bloodlines around him. He ignored the strongest lines of magic—the water-mages, the weather-mages, the shadowmancers whose cold touch reminded him a little too much of the daemon-stone in his office. Wilberforce's bloodline was so very unmagical even for a Commoner that it was like a speck of light through clouds. Because of this, it took Pitt moments to find him by the door, as usual in the company of a swell of people, including a fire-mage and a strong alchemist.

He wondered, just for once, what would have happened if he had used his mesmerism in the House as easily as he used the senses his magic gave him here. The thought was something else he allowed himself only when he was very tired.

Wilberforce, through his poor eyesight and animated conversation with four others, still needed no magic to pick out a friend from the crowd; he saw Pitt at once and waved him over with a brief but genuine smile. The others in question were abolitionists, of course. Hannah More was the braceleted fire-mage he had noticed, and Henry Thornton's indistinct Commoner blood sang out beside her. The third member, the alchemist, was more of a surprise. It was Thomas Clarkson.

There was nothing terribly unusual about the magic: alchemy

was a common enough Inheritance, after all. But Pitt had spoken to Clarkson—often, in the months when Wilberforce had been ill. He would have sworn that Clarkson was a Commoner, with a few strains of latent magic that hadn't awoken. Either he had been astonishingly unobservant, or something had changed that wasn't supposed to be able to change.

"I thought we had it this time," Clarkson was saying. From the sounds of it, it wasn't for the first time. His voice was fired with fury—or perhaps despair. "I really thought we did. Did Saint-Domingue teach them nothing?"

"I think," Wilberforce said heavily, "it taught them to fear our victims rather than pity them."

Pitt forced his attention from Clarkson's bloodlines to his words. "I'm sorry," he said, and meant it. He couldn't have controlled what Dundas did, but he still felt sick with guilt. "We knew it would be a difficult climate, but I did truly think we could do it."

"It's ridiculous," Clarkson said. "All the eloquence was on our side. You two and Fox, united against bankers and traders and disgraced ex-colonels? The walls were going mad."

"Eloquence doesn't always win debates," Thornton said, without quite his usual equanimity. "People want to be safe."

"Safe." Clarkson snorted. "And so we sit safely above the torture chambers, not venturing down to release the inmates, because we're afraid of the screams."

"Go home, Clarkson," Wilberforce said, with sympathy but also a measure of exhaustion. The other man's despair was so palpable it hurt. "There's nothing more to be done here. We'll talk it over tomorrow."

"There isn't very much more to say, is there?" Clarkson said. "It didn't work."

Wilberforce sighed as Clarkson and the other abolitionists left. Without them, he suddenly looked a good deal smaller. "Poor man. He's close to giving up, I think. He's been giving so much energy to this, with so much brilliance, for so long; he'll burn himself up, if we're not careful. Speaking of which, I thought you'd gone home."

"Why would I want to do that?" Pitt said airily. He tried to ignore the pull of Clarkson's magic departing. "It's still half an hour until breakfast."

Wilberforce smiled. "That was the best I've ever seen you. At the end I think you were actually inspired."

"Well, if so, you were inspired from the beginning," Pitt said, though he knew he didn't mean quite the same thing by the word as Wilberforce did. "I meant what I told Clarkson. You have nothing for which to reproach yourself."

"Is it that obvious?"

"Not at all. I simply know that you wouldn't be satisfied with a motion for gradual abolition."

"Gradual! It's morally right to stop the spellbinding, enslavery, and murder of thousands more innocents, but we should do it slowly and think about it some more for our convenience? When Dundas stood up and said—" He drew a deep breath. His usual faith in human nature and divine Providence was being sorely tested, and it hurt. "It wasn't the result I hoped for," he repeated.

"No," Pitt said. "Nor I."

"Thank you for not saying that it was better than nothing."

"I assumed you'd been hearing that all night."

"I've been saying that all night." Wilberforce rubbed his forehead wearily and glanced at Pitt. "I need to cool down before I try to sleep. Would you mind terribly coming for a walk along the Thames with me?"

"Of course not," Pitt said firmly. It was, after all, the least he could do. "I probably need it as much as you do."

"That is a very kind untruth," Wilberforce said at once. "It's the last thing you need. It's eight o'clock in the morning, it's been a very long and hard-fought night, and you've never had any difficulty getting to sleep in your life. You could probably close your eyes and be asleep right now."

This was so accurate he had to laugh. The laugh turned into a yawn, which made his untruth even less convincing.

"In that case," he countered, "it's a good thing that I have no intention of closing my eyes. As I said, it's only half an hour until breakfast."

Wilberforce clearly wasn't fooled, but he just as clearly couldn't bear to go home until he felt better, and he couldn't bear to be alone. Pitt preferred to be alone, almost always, when he was closest to despair; Wilberforce, perhaps because he came closer to the brink than Pitt, needed someone to pull him back.

And he did seem to come back, at least a little, stepping outside into the sunlight away from the eyes and voices of the House of Commoners. Around them, the city was beginning to wake up; there were boats on the Thames, and faint voices calling across the water. The sky was clear blue against London's gray stone.

"Dundas knew you wanted the trade to stop," Wilberforce added as they reached the river. It was murky and stank of human waste and weed in the chill air, but the light caught it and reflected back on Westminster. "What was he thinking? Did he tell you he was going to do that?"

"No," Pitt said, a little warily. His close friendship with Dundas was something of a sore point. Wilberforce liked the Scotsman well enough, and understood he'd been instrumental in Pitt's rise to power. But he couldn't help but notice that Pitt's evenings with Dundas tended to stretch into long hours of drinking and political strategizing, and that Dundas was not very scrupulous about either. "But I knew he wasn't on our side over the issue. I suppose he felt an agreement to abolish the trade gradually is preferable to a straight defeat."

"But it might not have been a defeat had the alternative not given the waverers a way to avoid the issue. If the trade is indeed abolished slowly, it might be worth it, but you know as well as I do that in all probability nothing will be done—and in the meantime we can't move to have the trade abolished again. The issue will be considered settled. Thornton said it was a step in the right direction, but it's really a step the other way."

"I know." Pitt sighed. "I'm not really excusing him this time. Actually, I'm very annoyed with him. He can vote however he thinks best, of course, but in this case I know exactly why he did it, and I know he thought it was for my sake as much as his own. I'm not twenty-four anymore, and I don't need him to protect me. Particularly not at this cost."

That was uncharacteristically bitter enough to pull Wilberforce out of his own depression. He looked at Pitt more closely. "It's not your fault, you know."

"It's nobody's fault," Pitt said, having recovered his equilibrium. "I'll remember that when I've slept for an hour or two. Dundas was trying to do the right thing; that's what people all do, in general."

"Even Tarleton? And Larrington?"

"Certainly not. I did say 'people.'"

Wilberforce snorted, but his smile faded quickly. "You were right to tell us not to go ahead. This was the wrong time. Some of the Abolition Society were concerned about it too, and I told them it was right to push ahead. I've failed them—and hundreds of thousands of others, of course..."

"Stop it," Pitt warned. "We've been thoroughly over the question of who's at fault. You were right to push ahead—I know I told you not to, but I was being a politician. Your principles were sound, and your rhetoric was flawless. There's nothing you can do about how the vote came out. Think about what you need to do next to make this work."

Wilberforce nodded. "Thank you. That's very good advice."

"Well," Pitt said. "I'm used to giving it to myself."

"Do you take it?"

"Always. But I resent myself for being so infuriatingly reasonable at times like this."

Wilberforce's smile was far more genuine this time.

"About Clarkson—" Pitt heard himself say, almost without meaning to.

Wilberforce turned, surprised. "What about Clarkson?"

Pitt shook his head, infuriated with himself. "Never mind. Probably nothing."

"You can't stop there. What is it?"

"I don't think I've met with Clarkson in person since you were unwell. Before the fall of the Bastille."

"No. No, you probably haven't. He's hardly ever in London these days. He travels all the time, giving demonstrations and collecting evidence. I can't remember how many sailors he's talked to, but it's in the tens of thousands. Why? What's wrong?"

"As I said, perhaps nothing. I just...I never noticed he was an alchemist before."

Wilberforce frowned. "He's what?"

"Unregistered, obviously. He isn't wearing a bracelet. But I definitely felt it, just now. I can't think how I could have missed it before. It's almost as if his abilities have awakened—but I've never heard of that happening after childhood. I would have sworn it was impossible."

"How very strange." Pitt saw the exact moment the import of this caught up to Wilberforce. His friend wasn't angry, but shock had almost the same effect on his voice. "You can't mean...We were investigating the idea that the sabotage at Saint-Domingue came from the *opposition*."

"We were," Pitt agreed. "But, as you said, we might have been trying to be too clever. I was rather stuck on the idea that the shadows and the uprising were connected. If they aren't, however, then the culprit is as likely to be an abolitionist as the reverse."

"Clarkson, though? Honestly?"

"You did just say that he was desperate and close to giving up."

"We're all desperate and close to giving up!" Wilberforce protested. "We've been doing this for three years—Clarkson's been doing it for even longer. He's exhausted. It doesn't mean that he's resorted to criminal activity."

"No, of course not. But he's been traveling back and forth to France since '89. And the sudden alchemy in his blood is strange."

"Inheritances strengthen with practice," Wilberforce said reluctantly. "Could that be the reason?"

"It's possible, I suppose," Pitt said, but he wasn't convinced. "When people say that, though, they really mean that the ability to *use* an Inheritance strengthens, not the bloodlines themselves. I've never heard of those becoming stronger."

"Would his abilities now be strong enough to have unlocked the compound?"

"I believe so," Pitt said. "Yes."

Wilberforce was silent.

"I don't mean to insist he's responsible," Pitt said. "I don't know him well enough to judge. But he's your friend, and you're an excellent judge of character, so I'm asking you if such actions would accord with his temperament. If you say they wouldn't, I'll abandon the entire idea."

He meant it. He trusted Wilberforce, both to be honest with him and—more important—to be right. Wilberforce knew everyone, and he knew them all well. And yet it didn't surprise him when Wilberforce bit his lip and looked at the ground.

"He wouldn't have sanctioned the massacre of so many slave owners," he said cautiously. "Or the civil war that's been raging ever since. He's certainly frustrated, but he's not..." He shook his head. "I don't know. Perhaps. I'll see him at the meeting tomorrow evening. Do you want me to talk to him?"

"Tactfully," Pitt admitted, with a faint wince. He hadn't imagined, after the vote, that the day had been about to get worse. "If you don't mind. Even if he did nothing himself, he may know who did."

"If he does," Wilberforce said, "I'm not entirely sure I want to know myself. The Knights Templar did talk to us, you know, when it happened. They talked to me, even though I'm pure Commoner. They're suspicious because so many of us are also behind the magic-registration reforms. I told them we don't do things this way."

"Well, you don't. But somebody clearly does. And I must admit, I'm finding lately that things do change."

"Not the right things," Wilberforce said, with a glance back at the debating chamber.

"No," Pitt agreed. "Not the right things at all."

* * *

The rain had started in earnest as the twelve or so people who had gathered at Old Palace Yard looked over the cargo manifests Clarkson had brought from Bristol. It lashed against the windows behind the drawn curtains and lent a chill to the room that the glowing fire struggled to penetrate.

"Courtesy of a good few hours spent in a pub," Clarkson said. "Sailors are usually willing to talk once you've put a few pints in them. I arranged to tour another ship while I was there as well. They'd tried to tidy it up, of course, but they couldn't hide the berths the size of coffins or the stench belowdecks."

"I remember," Macaulay said grimly. "It feels sometimes like something of their souls stays behind on that ship when they're first spellbound, doesn't it? They sink into the walls."

"Their souls don't go anywhere," Thornton said, with a touch of firmness. Wilberforce knew this was no reflection of a lack of feeling, but his cousin did feel it his duty to keep the imaginations of the more highly strung members from running too wild. Tonight, after their failure the night before, that was needed more than ever. "That sounds like what the plantation owners claim. They're robbed of their freedom and their will. It's terrible enough without being morbid."

"It does feel like that, though," Clarkson said. "Morbid or not, it does."

Wilberforce watched the room as Clarkson talked. Granville and Macaulay, the oldest and youngest members of the committee respectively, sat side by side, listening intently. Hannah More examined the diagram Clarkson had drawn up from the cargo manifests with an expression of distaste.

Most of all, though, he watched Clarkson. He had indeed arrived back in London only yesterday from his travels up north, and he looked exhausted and ill: his face was sallow, and the heaviness of his eyes wasn't burned away by vehemence as it often was. Once or twice he paused to rub his brow, as if overtaken by dizziness.

The annoying thing was, what Pitt had said was true: if Wilberforce told him that he was confident Clarkson would never do anything like what he'd suggested, alchemist or not, then Pitt would accept it. It was how his friend worked. He threw ideas at people who could be considered specialists in a relevant field, and if they declared them to be impossible, he readily agreed and moved on to the next possibility.

The trouble was, however much he wanted to, Wilberforce couldn't say it for certain. Clarkson believed, Wilberforce knew, in freeing slaves. They all did, but for Clarkson the phrase was literal and tangible. For Wilberforce, it was a question of movement toward legal and social change, within the walls of the House of Commoners and the hearts of the people. Clarkson wanted to break chains. It was entirely possible that he might not care what else was broken at the same time.

"They had artifacts on the ship," Clarkson was saying. "From Africa. Beautiful things: carved charms, and blankets. I have some of them here. I thought if we could show the public what the people they were spellbinding are really capable of..."

"Clarkson," Wilberforce said tentatively; he almost didn't realize he had spoken aloud until Clarkson turned. "You were in France about the time of the sabotage to Saint-Domingue, weren't you?"

"Yes," Clarkson said. "I would think so. That would have been back in early '91, wouldn't it? Why?"

"Oh, no reason, really," Wilberforce said, then was instantly disgusted at himself. That was more than a lie; it was a stupid one. "Well, one reason. I was just wondering if you knew anything about who might have done it. You were there when the Bastille was sacked as well."

"What does that have to do with it?" Clarkson said sharply.

"Well, it's when the original magicians were set free," Wilberforce reminded him. "All the fire-mages and telekinetics and mesmers... and alchemists. You never said you met any of them, but I was wondering..."

"If I in fact made a secret alliance with them? And then worked with them to commit magical sabotage on the alchemy in Paris due to be shipped to Saint-Domingue?"

"I didn't say that," Wilberforce said, trying to keep an even tone against the bite of Clarkson's sarcasm. "I just wondered if you knew anything."

"Would it matter if he had?" Macaulay spoke up. "Honestly, I don't see the problem. We want to free slaves, don't we?"

"Not by force," Wilberforce said. It was an old argument. "Not through violent uprising."

"The death toll's in the thousands now," Hannah More pointed out. "Masters, insurgents, women, and children. That entire colony's drenched in blood."

"Like France herself," Granville Sharp said. "I had very high hopes for that Revolution, you know. It seemed to be doing everything we're aiming for: unlocking of bracelets, breaking of chains, all that. But it's already sent Europe into war, and we'll probably be joining it within months."

"You don't know that," Wilberforce said firmly.

"So something went wrong," Macaulay insisted. "Perhaps the compound the saboteur used was too strong, or given to too many or not enough. The principle was sound."

"My feelings exactly," Clarkson said. "They might get it right next time. Wouldn't you approve of it then?"

"How?" Wilberforce asked, beginning to feel irritated. "How can anyone get it right? What could possibly be right about anything that's happening over there? People are dying."

"And you think I caused it, do you? Well, as a matter of fact, I agree with Macaulay: I don't see it would be so wrong if I had. But you have no right to accuse me."

"He didn't accuse you," Hannah More said impatiently. "He asked if you knew anything. It's a reasonable request, given that you were in France in '89 and again at the time of the sabotage."

"And how could I have known anything if I wasn't behind it? How could it matter where I was, if I wasn't involved?"

"Calm down," Granville Sharp said. "All of you. I know we're all tired and out of spirits, but—"

"That's an understatement," Clarkson said. His voice was carefully controlled, but there was fury seething behind it. "All those years of work, just for one more defeat. They didn't even try to say we were fabricating the evidence this time, do you realize that? We showed them exactly what the trade was; we made them acknowledge it. They just don't care. I don't think I can take much more of this."

"And we can?" Thornton demanded. "Wilberforce is killing himself over this."

"Henry, please," Wilberforce said quietly, with a surge of both embarrassment and panic. It was too late.

"Don't you *dare* try to tell me there are others who are doing more than me!" Clarkson hissed, his reserve suddenly breaking. "I've given this my entire life. I've traveled all over England and half of Europe trying to find people to help us. I've gone to places Wilberforce wouldn't dare soil his boots with; I've made deals with people Wilberforce wouldn't dare think of. I've written till my fingers have bled, I've spoken till my words and throat have dried up, I've threatened, pleaded, begged, cajoled, bribed, and broken, and still nothing has changed. Still!"

"Wilberforce says he can—" Thornton started to say.

"Oh, will everybody just shut up about blasted Wilberforce!" Clarkson snapped, getting to his feet angrily. "If I have to hear one more word about the blasted Nightingale of the House of Commoners, I'm going to ship myself to Africa and volunteer myself for the slave market to have an end to it."

Sympathetic as Wilberforce was to Clarkson, that hurt. "You were happy enough to hear about blasted Wilberforce when you wanted a voice in the House of Commoners!" he said despite himself. "I could nightingale to my heart's content then, as far as you were concerned."

"It was my mistake!"

Thornton shot to his feet opposite. "You apologize for that!"

"Why on earth should I? When have any of you ever apologized to me?"

"Wilberforce has done as much for this cause as you—at least as much!"

"And what has come of any of it, apart from everybody now knowing his name?"

"Is that what this is about? Are you jealous?"

"Thornton, Clarkson—" Wilberforce started to say.

"Jealous of what?" Clarkson interrupted, ignoring him. "Correct me if I am wrong, but to my knowledge he hasn't achieved anything! None of us have achieved anything! Four years since we brought this to Parliament!"

"The country is on the brink of war!"

"And that gives it an excuse for the torture and spellbinding of thousands of innocent lives?"

"Oh, for the love of God!" Wilberforce exclaimed, with a sudden surge of temper. "Would everybody please just shut up!"

In retrospect, it was the best thing he could have done. It wasn't for nothing that Wilberforce's voice was one of the most renowned of the House of Commoners; moreover, the unexpectedness of that voice rising in anger against them was enough to make both Clarkson and Thornton blink in surprise and turn to look at him.

Wilberforce took a deep breath, trying to calm both his heart and his feelings. It was only then that he realized he had leaped to his feet and was gripping the table with both hands. "Thank you," he said, with a quiet he didn't feel. Anger, frustration, and hurt were still warring for attention within him, and it was hard to find God in the midst of it. "Clarkson, I'm sorry. You've given more to this cause than any of us. I had no right to imply you were involved, I know. It's just... It's made things terribly difficult, that uprising and the climate in France, and I would like it put to rest."

For a second Clarkson seemed poised to reject the opening for reconciliation, but all at once the anger drained from his face. "No, I'm sorry. I spoke out of turn. You've done as much as anyone could do in bringing this to Parliament; it's not your fault it hasn't worked."

"Yet," Wilberforce reminded him, and was rewarded with a faint, though resigned, flicker of a smile.

"Yet, I hope. But you must admit, with war against France on the horizon, things seem to be more hopeless than ever."

"You can't blame people for being afraid," Thornton said, but in a softer tone.

"I can blame them for letting their fear dictate their actions," Clarkson returned.

"So can I," Wilberforce sighed, then caught himself. "But I will not. It's neither helpful nor kind."

Clarkson snorted, but with less bitterness and more affection. "So says the man who just remembered to say 'please' when having an emotional outburst."

"He used 'to nightingale' as a verb, also," Thornton reminded him. "Mr. Pitt would despair."

That did make Wilberforce smile, despite everything.

Clarkson smiled briefly too, then took a deep breath and seemed to be choosing his words with care. "I do wish Saint-Domingue hadn't happened as it did, even if I can't be sorry that it happened at all. I only hope that next time, as Macaulay says, the alchemist in question will manage things better. But I can't shed any light on the matter for you. I didn't go near the factories where the alchemy is made when I was in Paris last time. I mostly spoke with the abolition movement over there—much good it did."

"It's done a great deal of good," Wilberforce told him. He forced himself to put aside the sick feeling that had risen suddenly in his stomach. It was, after all, not definitive. "You know it has. It's all done good—Equiano's book, Miss More's poems, your demonstrations. People heard it all. Perhaps by next year the situation in Europe will be less fraught, and they'll start to listen again."

"Well," Clarkson said heavily. "We'll see. I have another lecture tour in Manchester next month."

"Good," Granville Sharp said briskly. "Perhaps you can address the Saint-Domingue issue there, Clarkson? Wilberforce is right that it's corroding sympathy for our cause."

"Surely it would be better not to mention it at all, then?" Hannah More suggested. "It's not an image we want paired with abolition in the mind of the public, not with no end to it in sight."

The talk resumed after that, with Clarkson once again animated and vehement. Perhaps rather too much so: his face in the candlelight had the hectic flush of a man in a fever.

It was past three in the morning when Wilberforce knocked on the door of Downing Street—not a polite hour to call, but the meeting had gone very late, and Pitt would be leaving to spend the day in Cambridge in the morning. This couldn't be entrusted to a letter, and it couldn't wait.

Fortunately, the light was burning in Pitt's office window as Wilberforce approached, and though the butler who answered the door was sleepy and nightcapped, Pitt when he came downstairs was still fully dressed.

"I'm sorry to come so late," Wilberforce said once the servant had been sent back to bed. "I hope I didn't wake you."

"Does it look like it?" Pitt asked, quite reasonably. "I'm in the midst of going through the reports from Holland, actually. It's when you come at a respectable time of the morning that you wake me. What's wrong?"

Wilberforce took a deep breath. He told himself it was because he had rushed here, but it wasn't. "I spoke to Clarkson. I didn't exactly accuse him, but he knew what I was insinuating. He was very much annoyed."

"I'm very sorry to hear that," Pitt said with a faint sigh. "Tell him it was my fault, if that would help. It was wrong for me to push you to talk to him without—"

"No, it wasn't," Wilberforce interrupted. "It was him."

Pitt frowned. "Are you certain?"

"Yes. I mean, not really, I suppose...He didn't confess. But he gave it away. Well, he didn't exactly give *that* away—"

"I think," Pitt said carefully, "we should probably sit down and talk this through from the beginning."

The fires in Downing Street were all cold barring the one in Pitt's office, and that was warm at best. The glowing embers gave the room an eerie cast until Pitt replaced the candle on the mantel.

"You might need to draw the chair closer to the hearth, I'm afraid," he said. "I was continually intending to go to bed, so I didn't order the fire kept up. Would you like something to drink?"

"Are you trying to calm me down?" Wilberforce asked with a faint smile.

"Is it working?"

"Yes." It was true: the smile had eased some of the tension in his chest, and he could feel his heart slowing to normal speed. There was a reason Pitt was faintly notorious in the House for making things seem as if they would be perfectly all right. "It is. Thank you."

"Good." Pitt sat down himself. "Though both the apology for the fire and the offer of a drink were quite genuine, of course. So. Tell me about Clarkson."

"He denied he was responsible, as I said. He denied it even though I never actually accused him, in fact, though that's certainly in character for him lately. He was very upset about the last debate—oh." His heart chilled a little further. "Oh...I suppose he would be, wouldn't he?"

"Well, yes," Pitt said wryly. "Of course he would."

"No, but...I think now that he knows it was at least partly his fault—or the fault of the uprising—that the bill failed again. It would make sense."

"Yet he denied that he was responsible. So why do you think he did it?"

"He denied he was responsible," Wilberforce concurred. "He also denied having been near the factories in Paris where the alchemists create the compound. I know he went near those factories—he went inside them, in fact. He mentioned it in a pamphlet he wrote and distributed. Only in passing—talking about the alchemists at work right in the heart of what was supposed to be the Revolution—but he mentioned it. I looked it up after he left my house tonight."

"Still," Pitt said. "There are many reasons why he might misremember that, or even conceal it."

"He knows how the alchemy works," Wilberforce said. "He's talked about that before too, to me—he did so on the day we first met. He's an unregistered alchemist. He was in Paris at the right time, visited the factory, and then denied visiting the factory, far too vehemently. He told me that the alchemist had made a mistake and that he hoped he would do better next time."

"It's still circumstantial."

"Yes. But you think it was him, don't you?"

Pitt was silent for a long moment. "I'm sorry," he said, with genuine regret. "But yes, I do. On that evidence, it seems not unlikely."

"I think I always worried it was one of us." Wilberforce had never seen Saint-Domingue, but it was burning in his head and echoing with screams. "I could too easily imagine... If you had the power to do it—to set free an entire island without all the arguing and researching and persuading—it would be so *tempting*. I didn't think it would be someone I *knew*, even when you told me about Clarkson, but I feared it would be someone trying to achieve the same things as us."

"I know you did. I have to admit, I initially didn't think an abolitionist would do something so misguided. Clarkson's a very clever man, to put it mildly. Even if he didn't care about the fates of the slave owners, even if he thought the lives of the slaves killed in reprisals were their own to give, even if he didn't care for our relations with France... he *must* have seen the political consequences for abolition."

That made Wilberforce laugh, despite everything weighing on him. "Pitt, you've been in politics for twelve years. You must have noticed by now that even very clever people do misguided things without regard for political consequences all the time. Especially when they're frustrated and angry."

"I've noticed," he agreed, with a rueful smile of his own. "But I keep expecting them to stop."

"Well, I keep expecting people to stop chaining up human beings and selling them across the oceans." Wilberforce felt the clouds settle once again on his shoulders. "So I can't criticize. What are we going to do about Clarkson?"

Pitt was silent for a long moment.

"I think we need to have a word with him," he said finally. "Or rather, I do. Clarkson's your friend. I don't see why you should need to be involved."

"And what do you intend to say to him that a friend can't say?"

"I intend to ask him to turn himself in to the Templars. And if he doesn't, I'm very much afraid I might have to have a word with them too."

Wilberforce had known that, really. He'd just wanted to hear Pitt say it. "He'll have twenty-five years in prison for a crime like this."

"At least. But we have no power over that. The important thing now is that we expose this before France does. There are parties in France who want nothing better than to draw us into war: this would be the excuse they need. The destruction of that colony would be seen as an act of aggression against France. And it could be worse than that. It wasn't only an act of aggression; it was an act of powerful magic. If we don't move very, very carefully, the French government could accuse us of breaking the Concord."

"Good Lord." He hadn't thought his heart could sink lower than it had. Clearly there were new depths to plunge. "But... Clarkson isn't a member of the British government. He's a private citizen."

"So are half the people we have currently spying for us in France—so, for that matter, are the people they probably have spying on us. War is never private. But yes, he is. That's the only thing about this mess that might work in our favor. If we can arrest Clarkson, prosecute him, and make it as clear as we can that he was acting alone, we may yet save our relationship with France."

"And what about Clarkson? Are you at all concerned about saving him?" He caught himself. "I'm sorry—"

"No, don't be. I'm concerned about him. I'm very concerned about him. If I could see any way out of this, I promise you, I would take it. But I can't."

"Why do we need to do anything at all?" Wilberforce asked. "I understand your concerns, I truly do. But we could keep France from finding out."

Pitt hesitated, then shook his head. "We possibly could, I know. But I can't take that risk; I couldn't, even under normal circumstances, and in this case there's still too much I don't understand. I don't think we have the luxury of being able to stand by and let things unfold."

"You still think this is connected, don't you? The shadow, the undead, and now this uprising."

"I think something is happening in France, and it's reaching across to us. Perhaps it's nothing more than unprecedented political and social unrest. But perhaps it isn't. As I said, I can't take that risk. Clarkson's already started one war. I can't allow him to start another."

"He didn't start the war in Saint-Domingue. The planters did. The slavers did. Clarkson only wants what we all want."

"We all want an end to the trade in human souls," Pitt corrected. "We don't all want riots, bloodshed, and civil war. That's a fairly important distinction."

"Clarkson didn't want those things either—I'm sure of that, at least. They just happened. They happened because hundreds of thousands of people have been tortured and spellbound, for hundreds of years. It's still happening."

"Yes, and it's our job to stop it in a way that doesn't lead to hundreds of thousands more on both sides tortured and dead. Do we disagree on that?"

"No!" Wilberforce said, with a touch of frustration. Arguing with Pitt could be a very frustrating business. "I don't necessarily agree with what Clarkson did, even though I can't condemn his principles. But we can't change what happened. If he were an Aristocrat, it would be one thing—for all I know it would be a misdemeanor then—but he's an unregistered Commoner magician. You've always kept quiet about Commoner magicians. You know how hard the courts and the church will be on him."

"I'm not suggesting we report him for what he is. I'm saying we need to report him for what he's done."

"It's the same thing, in the eyes of the law. You should know that better than anyone."

"I do," Pitt said, calmly, but Wilberforce saw his jaw tighten. "And for that reason, I also know better than anyone that it's not the same thing at all. Wilberforce, I've just spent the last three days arguing with French diplomats; do you think I wasn't tempted to tell them to do exactly what I need them to do, and have them do it? I could have, you know—if I was like Clarkson and thought that having an Inheritance was the same thing as using it."

"You impose those restrictions on yourself. The law shouldn't need to do it."

"That's exactly what the law needs to do. That's what all laws should do. Impose the restrictions that, if human beings were always moral and rational, they would impose upon themselves."

"Then this law is wrong," Wilberforce said bluntly. He had never said it, not in so many words, but it had been hanging over all their efforts for a long time. "There is no reason moral, rational human beings should refrain from using their God-given abilities just because they were born Commoners and nobody has yet seen fit to elevate them. That's what the Revolution in France is all about, and they're right. You know they're right."

"They're right about a good many things. So are you. But I'm not saying Clarkson should have refrained because he was a Commoner. I'm saying he should have refrained because it was dangerous."

"He made a mistake."

"Europe is on the brink of war. Nobody can afford to make those kinds of mistakes. And yes, before you say it; yes, especially me."

That effectively silenced Wilberforce's protests, and he felt his frustration wither and die. He could never quite understand Pitt's feelings about unregistered magic—how he could fight for change to the laws, even agree that the laws themselves were fundamentally unjust, and yet still hold to them firmly at the most unexpected times—but he knew that they had to do with his Inheritance. In most cases, Wilberforce thought this prevented Pitt from seeing things as clearly as he usually would; sometimes, though, perhaps it let him see things Wilberforce couldn't.

Pitt must have seen Wilberforce relent, because he relaxed himself.

"I'm not saying he should be reported because he needs to be punished." He sounded unusually weary. It was very late at night, but it wasn't that kind of weariness. "I know he'll be punished for what he is, not what he did, and I know that's deeply unfair. For what it may be worth, I don't blame him for what he did. I know he meant well. We can't see all the consequences of Saint-Domingue—for all I can tell, his actions may work out for the best as far as that colony is concerned. But this has gone beyond unregistered magic. This is a matter of war, here and abroad."

Wilberforce said nothing.

"Besides," Pitt added. "I do think he needs to be stopped. If he is indeed behind this, Wilberforce, do you think he'll stop on his own?"

"No." He said it reluctantly, but he didn't need to think about it. "He's sorry for how it turned out. But he's not sorry he did it."

"And that means that sooner or later he'll try again, and he'll try to do it better. It can't be done better."

"I know." And he did know. Thousands of people were dead. There was no way that could ever be made better. He had known that when he had come, or he would have perhaps thought twice before telling the prime minister of Great Britain—although he couldn't quite imagine not telling Pitt anything. He only wished, as he so often did lately, that the right thing to do and the wrong thing to do were always clear and uncomplicated, as they had been that night in Paris when a shadow had dissolved into vapor before his eyes and left the world at peace.

Thomas Clarkson was arrested by the Templars a few days later, and the incident became one of the most high-profile cases of unregistered magic in recent decades. Apart from the sensationalism of the crime itself, interest swarmed around the question of just what Clarkson would have been charged with were he not unregistered. Surely it would be illegal for even an Aristocrat to break a slave spell and unleash a riot in the French colonies, but it was difficult to see how, when there were no rogue shadows involved and the alchemy was not technically dark magic. There was talk of handing him over to the French authorities to let them deal with it, given that the crime had taken place on French soil, but given the state of the courts over there, nobody was quite sure what the outcome would be. Instead, he was charged with illegal magic, failure to report, and destruction of property.

Wilberforce went to the Old Bailey to see Clarkson sentenced, along with Macaulay and Thornton. Macaulay was fuming with anger at the Temple Church; Thornton, at Clarkson. They argued furiously about who was the most at fault—Clarkson for his unwise action, the Knights Templar for their harsh prosecution—until the court came into session, and Wilberforce had an excuse to tell both of them to please keep it down. He had been tempted to snap at them earlier but had managed to remember that they were just upset. They all were.

Clarkson seemed to have shrunk during his time in prison, in a way that reminded Wilberforce with a painful tug of visiting John Terrell in the Tower of London. He had been looking unwell before; now he looked gaunt and exhausted. His clothes were clean and his hair was neat, at least, and his eyes were blazing with defiance, but he couldn't hold back a wince as the guards shoved him roughly into the dock. He was blinking rapidly and tears were on his cheeks, though whether that was the effect of strong emotion or the blinding light after his time in a cell, Wilberforce was unsure. Possibly both.

Wilberforce had not spoken to him since that final meeting. He had tried, after his arrest, but even his Templar friends could not grant him access to the prison. The Knights Templar had been somewhat frosty with him after he had taken up the cause of magical reform. And the tide of public opinion had turned against abolitionists.

The judge, Wilberforce more than suspected, was not sympathetic to abolitionists himself. He could tell by the nod he gave the jeering members of the gallery, and by the particular relish with which he sentenced Clarkson not only to fifty years for illegal magic (at which Wilberforce caught his breath) and ten years for failure to report, but also to a further seven years for damages to be paid for destruction of property—namely, some four hundred thousand slaves belonging to French colonists or their next of kin. Clarkson's face lost all its color—it became not white, but translucent—and he might have collapsed had not the sides of the dock been there to break his fall. The gallery went wild with mixed cheers and protests.

"Fifty years," Wilberforce breathed as Clarkson was dragged away. He was shouting something that was lost in the tumult of the crowd. "That's meant for dark magic causing death."

"Destruction of property," Thornton said bleakly. "They didn't need that charge to inflate the sentence. He'll die in there. They were only making a point."

"They made a point, certainly," Macaulay said. "They're telling us that we're never going to succeed. Clarkson was right: we can't take much more of this."

Wilberforce felt he should probably disagree with this, but he couldn't find it in his heart to do so.

Saint-Domingue

Spring 1792

Fina walked to the insurgents' camp at the Galliflet plantation down a dusty road staked every few feet with the bodies of black men and women. Perhaps some of them had been killed in battle; many, though, were slaves the plantation owners had butchered and left as hideous milestones to warn the rebel armies that they were without mercy.

On the day Fina arrived at the camp, it was ringed with bodies hung from hooks. Many of them were white slave owners; others were black men who had been reluctant to join the revolution. The camp commander, Jeannot Bullet, had tortured them to death and drunk the blood that spilled from their throats. His excesses had disgusted even the most furious of his supporters. A more senior commander, Jean-François Papillon, came to the camp that afternoon and put an end to it. Jeannot screamed and begged for his life before he was shot.

Saint-Domingue had become an island of corpses, and it was tearing itself to pieces.

By that time, Fina was beyond being shocked by cruelty on either side. She was beyond much of anything. She had walked through fire and gunshots and screams; her feet were skinned and bloody, and her limbs were weak with starvation. A piece of falling roof had seared her right forearm at Port-au-Prince as she had flung it up to protect her face; she had barely noticed at first, but by the time she had made it to the north her entire arm burned, and the wound stood out black under her torn sleeve. She walked past the carnage without a murmur, and kept walking. The world around her was a fever dream.

When the guards came, they came like something out of a nightmare.

There was almost no warning. Fina had time to hear a shout, and then fingers locked about her burned arm and wrenched her around. The pain cut through to the bone. Inside, she screamed, but years of showing nothing locked her face still while her vision went white and her heartbeat roared in her ears. Men's faces swam in front of her eyes, shouting in harsh, guttural creole she couldn't understand. They spoke a different language here, one that mingled French rather than English with the African dialects she knew. She stumbled, and the strong fingers yanked her to her feet.

"Who are you?" she heard. The rest was lost in confusion. She fought to answer, but her jaw wouldn't move. It was as though she was under a spell once more. Everything was pain and fear. Her magic twisted in her chest, useless; even if she were to escape her body, there was nothing she could do to save herself. She wondered if this was how she would die, and felt nothing at all, not even relief.

A woman's voice had joined the confusion now, high and angry, as if scolding. It made no sense.

She didn't want to die.

A pair of hands seized her shoulders, and then her feet left the ground. Her head fell back, and all she could see was the pale, dazzling blue of the sky.

Much later, she learned that the men had been demanding to know if she had been sent to the camp to spy on them, and that the woman, Celeste, had saved her life. The glint of green in Fina's eyes, which had yet to wear away even though it had been weeks since she had taken any of the spellbinding compound, had told Celeste that she was an escaped slave seeking help. She had screamed at the men to let Fina go; her voice had alerted one of the camp leaders, who had come and taken her under his protection. He was a slight, wiry man, with grizzled hair and a weathered face, but when he spoke sharply to the men, they stepped down.

All Fina knew was the dull glare of the sun outside dimming into the coolness of a hut, and gentle fingers stroking her head while another set of hands ripped her sleeve from her arm. She wriggled away on reflex, but a woman's voice spoke to her soothingly. A warm gel was smoothed over her arm; she was weak enough and tired enough to flinch at the sting.

"It's all right." A man's voice. She could still barely follow the lilting, rapid-fire creole, but this voice was gentler and deeper than the others. "It will hurt at first, I know, but this will help. What's your name?"

She had to swallow three times before she found her voice, and it was barely a whisper. But the world was settling back into place. A hurricane had swept her up and put her down somewhere new, but her feet were back on the ground.

"Fina," she said. She had a surname—it was the name of the family who owned her plantation. But she would never say it again.

"Did you escape from a plantation in the south to join us? You wouldn't be the first. There's a place for you here, if you want it."

"Thank you." In her exhaustion, she wasn't sure if she said it in his language or her own until his hands faltered on her arm.

"You're not from the south, are you?" he said. "Where did you come from?"

She considered lying. But what did it matter? These people wouldn't return her to her plantation, even if they could—and they couldn't.

"Jamaica." She managed to look the man directly in the eyes, though his face was blurred. "I came from Jamaica."

His face was puzzled, and he opened his mouth to speak. Then a sharp call came from across the camp; his head whipped toward it, and when he looked back, his eyes were distracted.

"Keep the dressing on your arm," he said. "Have something to drink, and rest. Celeste will look after you. Find me if it gets any worse."

She nodded, and he was gone.

Celeste was a sturdy, matter-of-fact woman, about Fina's age but with an easy self-possession that made her seem older. She had come from a plantation where only those with magic had been spellbound, and so the mere act of moving and speaking wasn't the novelty to her that it was to others. Her fifteen-year-old son had been sold into the south a year ago, before the uprising: she had no idea if he was alive, or if, like his father, he had died at his work. She hated the plantation owners, and she was as determined to liberate the island as anyone. But she was also a fierce pragmatist, and she didn't hold with violence against other former slaves. She explained this to Fina as she gave her water in a bowl and tucked a thin blanket over her.

"It's been just as bad up here as it's been in the south, where you've walked through," she said. "The plantations are all burned, so there was no food—we'd have all starved last month without the Spanish sending supplies. They want to help us—they think this is their chance to move in and take this half of the island from the French. But we'll get through. There's no need to turn on our own."

Fina was half-asleep, and the words drifted over and around her like the tide. She forced herself awake, though, to ask, "Who was that man here before? The one who stopped them shouting?"

"That was Toussaint Bréda," Celeste said. "You were lucky he was here. He's kind to prisoners—he's even kind to slave owners."

"Is he the leader?"

Celeste shrugged. "Depends who you talk to. He isn't supposed to be—he's under Biassou's command. Biassou and Jean-François both outrank him. Bullet did too, before they killed him this morning. But Toussaint—there's something about him. His eyes look right at you." She leaned closer, conspiratorial. "He was at the ceremony."

She didn't know the word, but she repeated it carefully without admitting this. "What ceremony?"

"The voodoo ceremony. The night before the rebellion, Boukman called on the loa to give us the strength to break free. Toussaint was one of those there."

"Does he believe in voodoo?" She had already learned that many of the black population in Saint-Domingue worshipped the spirits of their homeland, while others remained faithful to the Catholicism pressed on them by the white masters. Some worshipped both, without troubling themselves about the contradictions.

Celeste snorted. "Him? No. He thinks it's all superstition. But he was there. Perhaps it believes in him. Now go to sleep."

Fina did sleep: the first uninterrupted sleep she had found since she had stepped off the ship and into the inferno of Port-au-Prince. When she woke, it was the early hours of the morning, and the camp was stirring. The ground was hard packed beneath her blanket, and the air smelled of smoke with the faintest memory of hibiscus and oleander. Fina closed her eyes again, deliberately this time, and reached out with her magic.

She reached out with her magic a great deal over the next few days. She'd had a practice, over her long weeks on the road, of hiding and using others' eyes to look at the road ahead, to keep herself safe, and to avoid any confrontations. Now she used it more deeply, to learn the place she had come to and the people she had come among. Her magic couldn't give her people's voices, but she had learned to read the things their eyes picked up, the corresponding flutters of emotion, and even rare glimpses of their memories. She learned, for example, that Celeste's eyes were sharp to pick up on children and the weaker members of the camp so she could help them as she had Fina, but that she also stopped to gaze at sunsets and her heart would uncurl within her when she did. She watched, with her own eyes and with those of other people, as the ill-provisioned guerrilla fighters came back from the borders of the camp streaked with filth, laughing too hard. She watched the supplies dwindle, and the men sicken. She watched, and tried to understand the shifts in power that were taking place.

Most of all, she watched Toussaint Bréda.

She wasn't sure what had drawn her to him at first, other than the fact that he had helped her. But it quickly became apparent, as she moved about the camp, that he was indeed special. He was older than many of the others, for one thing: in his midforties, yet still exuding wiry strength. He was born a slave, yet when the revolts broke out, he had been free and prosperous, with slaves of his own who were now part of the rebellion. More important, he was quiet, stern, implacable. When others raged, he listened, much as Fina did herself, and his eyes were like steel.

And he had been there at the start of the rebellion. He had planned the night the voice had spoken to his people and urged them to rise up. Perhaps he was one of the few trustworthy people who could tell her what she wanted to know. The trouble was, she couldn't decide to trust him.

Instead, she watched him as he rode into camp with the dark, tireless after days without sleep. She listened, as much as she could, as he talked to his men in rapid creole. She reached out to him with her magic as he worked to make medicines to treat the sick. From behind Toussaint's eyes, she saw the details of the aloe plant he was cutting, in startling precision. She felt the fleshy leaves in his hands yield a clear gel to heal the skin; she felt his awareness of the rest of the camp, even though he sat with his back to them all. She felt his purpose, as clear as hers had been the night she left the plantation, yet gentler, firmer, less at the mercy of anger and fear. And yet none of this meant anything solid; she couldn't tell how best to approach him, or if it would be safe to do so. She had survived years of her life through constant, vigilant caution. She didn't know how to break it.

In fact, she might never have broken it, had Toussaint not come to her first.

It had been raining all day, dangerous, unrelenting rain that lashed at the trees and turned the twisted mountain paths into trickles of mud. Celeste and her friend Anne had risked the weather to share the food; Fina had remained behind, preferring to make a bargain with hunger for relative warmth and the solitude of the empty tent. She could survive, she had found over the last few months, on very little food, and she didn't want to be seen to take too much. Despite the help of the Spanish troops, supplies were becoming scarce again. She didn't know how long she'd be able to stay if they ran much lower.

Her companions had already been gone longer than she expected when she heard the rustle of the flap and felt the sting of wind. She looked up, expecting to see them.

"May I come in?" Toussaint asked.

Fina watched warily as he closed the tent flap behind him. He was very small, was her first thought—smaller than he had seemed from a distance, and even from inside his head. His limbs were thin under his blue coat, and his eyes were on a level with her own. His face was wizened and asymmetrical, and his curly hair was shot through with gray. It was a strong, likable face, but difficult to read—a face that invited respect rather than friendship.

"I'm the chief medic," he said, which almost made her smile. Even had she not been hearing his name whispered about the region, she would have known he was more than that. But titles meant little here. The rebels borrowed rank and uniforms from the whites with flamboyant abandon: Biassou had styled himself a brigadier. "We met the day you arrived."

"I know." It look her a while to find the foreign words—she was too focused on watching him, wondering what he would do. Her heart beat quickly, from anticipation rather than fear. "You're Toussaint."

"I am. How's your arm?"

"It's fine." She resisted the urge to glance down at it and kept her eyes fixed on him. "It hurts less."

"Good." He paused. "Your friends tell me that you escaped from your plantation and came to us from Jamaica."

She nodded. She could have said more, but long habit kept her silent. It was different for the others at the camp: they had been enslaved, but they had never had to pretend to be otherwise. As soon as the spell was broken, they had been able to move, talk, scream. Even now, too many years had been spent trying not to show a flicker of an eyelash out of place for her to relax her guard.

Toussaint didn't seem to expect her to speak. He sat down on the ground opposite her, avoiding the steady column of rain pouring through a gap in the tent roof. His eyes watched her, dark and steady, without a trace of the spell-green glints that still lingered in her own eyes.

"You've awoken to your magic," he said. It took her a moment to realize that he had spoken in her old language—her childhood language, the one she and Molly had shared. Had she still been pretending to be spellbound, she would have been lost then. Her breath caught.

He smiled, unsurprised. "You spoke the language on the day we met. But even if you hadn't, I might have wondered. There's a look about you that made me think of my father. He was the second son of an Aradan king. You were born free?"

She had to swallow hard before she could speak. The familiar lilt woke an ache in her chest, unbearably sweet and sad at the same time. "Yes."

"I wondered that too. Magic tends to emerge faster in those who weren't spellbound from birth—though it's really only a matter of time, and degree. Many are awakening to their magic on this island these days, including those who never suspected it."

She avoided the implied question. "Did you awaken to magic when you were freed?"

"I was never spellbound, even when I was a slave." His answer came readily—so readily, in fact, that she suspected he had determined from the start to be open with her. "The family that owned us were kind, as far as that went. They let me grow up without magic restricting me, as long as I did my work—they even allowed me to be educated, as a free child might have been."

"Celeste says you protected the family from the rebellion."

"I did. You don't think I should have?"

"I don't know." She only knew she would never have thought to do it for the family who owned her plantation. "I don't know them."

He nodded as if satisfied. "To answer your first question, I have very little magic of my own—a little weather magic, that's all: enough to call a breeze, or a sunbeam. No healing magic. What I do as a doctor, I do by knowledge alone—from reading, and from what my parents taught me. But you... for you to fight the spellbinding as you did, your magic must be very strong."

There was, she supposed, no real reason for it to be a secret any longer. And of all the people she could tell, from all the watching she had done, he was the best. Still, it was difficult to speak it out loud. She had never even done so to Molly.

"I can see through others' eyes," she said. "Sometimes I can feel what they feel. I can't do anything useful, just see."

To his credit, he didn't react beyond a slight twitch of an eyebrow. "I've never heard of a magic like that. It sounds like a very beautiful gift."

"It does?"

"I think so. I would think it would be a privilege to be able to see through someone else's eyes. To have some sense of how they see the world. Isn't it?"

"It could be," she conceded. "But most of what there is to see is very ugly at the moment."

"It might not always be. Why have you come here?"

"To the camp?"

"To Saint-Domingue."

She hesitated. "I want to free my people. The men and women I grew up with. When I heard about the rebellion here, I came."

"There are insurrectionists on Jamaica as well," Toussaint said. "They haven't yet achieved the uprising that we have, but they may. If you wanted to free your people, then it would have been far simpler and less dangerous for you to escape and join them. Why did you come to us?"

"Because you've succeeded where they've failed. And because—"

She couldn't quite bring herself to go further, even though she had steeled herself to do it. She hovered on the brink, afraid to jump.

"What is it?" he asked. "I might be able to help you, you know."

"I don't know if I can trust you." She shook her head, frustrated, as much with herself as with him. "I don't know who you are."

He considered that carefully; she could see it turning over behind his eyes. At last, he looked up, having come to a decision of his own. "Why don't you look? You have magic that allows you to see people through their own eyes. Look."

"I have," she said. "I can't see that deeply. I'm only on the surface of people's minds—beyond that, it's just glimpses."

"Why don't you try? I'll try to show you."

She stared at him. "You'd let me do that?"

"I don't see how I would be able to stop you." His mouth gave a wry twist, and she wondered if he was as nervous as she was. For him to be willing to take that step, whatever had driven him to her was more than idle curiosity. He wanted something very badly. "But yes. I would let you."

She had never slipped behind someone's eyes when they were sitting directly in front of her, and never when they had known she was there. It would leave her open and vulnerable, outside of her body while Toussaint sat only a few feet away. She felt sick at the thought. But then, she reasoned, she would be inside his head; if he moved to hurt her, she would know as soon as he did. Besides, he could hurt her right now if he so chose, and there would be little she could do about it no matter whose head she was in. They were each vulnerable to the other. Perhaps there was a power in that.

She closed her eyes—not because her magic needed it, but to signal her intentions. Then she was inside Toussaint's head, looking across at herself in the dim, rain-soaked tent.

It wasn't the first time she had been in his head, of course. It was familiar to her, even comforting. She was used to the strength of his wiry muscles, the steady beat of his heart, the way the world sharpened through his eyes. (It was a not a matter of eyesight, she thought, as much as attention. People saw the world through different degrees of focus. Toussaint saw it very clearly.) She was used, too, to the vague shape of his thoughts and feelings. But this was different. They were softer this time, more open—he was marshaling them for her. He might not be able to sense her, but he knew she was there, and he was trying to show her who he was.

She saw herself through his eyes: very small and thin, eyes closed, black hair a matted mess of curls. Fina had never seen herself before, even as a faint ghost reflected on water. Toussaint's eyes rested on her face, with compassion and awe and the slightest trace of fear that he tried very hard to suppress. It made her uncomfortable: she wasn't used to being the subject of such close attention.

She went deeper.

His emotions solidified around her. It was little she hadn't felt before, just stronger—she was pushing against the bounds of her magic. She felt his determination, his conviction, his belief in something far greater and more important than revenge. She felt a past made of the texture of books, the feel of a mother's hand about his own, the flicker of a fire at night. And once, just once, she caught an image: a woman, her face tender and determined, a small tufted-haired baby in her arms and two other children at her side. It was early morning, and there was a carriage waiting to take them away. When the carriage left, her heart wrenched in two.

She opened her own eyes. Toussaint was watching her.

"Are you back?" he asked. There was nothing on his face but curiosity—she supposed there wouldn't be. He would have felt nothing. "What did you see?"

"Who was the woman? And the three children?"

For the first time, she had startled him. "What woman do you mean? What did she look like?"

"About your age. Dark, with a round face, very beautiful. She had a baby in her arms, and two other children at her side."

"That was my wife, Suzanne, and our sons. Placide, Isaac, and Saint-Jean." His mouth softened as he said the names; the corners of his eyes crinkled. He made them almost a caress. "I sent them to safety when I came to join the rebellion. I wasn't aware I was thinking of them."

"You weren't. It isn't like that—I don't see thoughts." She didn't know how to explain the fragments of emotion, or to say that she had latched on to the anguish of being torn apart because it so closely matched her own. All she could say was "You must care about this rebellion very much not to go with them."

"I do care very much," he said. "But it isn't the rebellion itself. It's what I believe we can build afterward."

"What do you want to build?"

It was his turn to hesitate. "You ask a lot of questions for a woman who has already seen inside my head."

"I want to understand what I've seen," she said. "I saw how much you loved your family. I want to know what could matter so much that you would watch them sail away and not go with them."

"We won't be parted for long. I'll see them again very soon." He drew a deep breath. "Very well. I believe we can build a new world here, of a kind the world has never seen. I believe that all of us—blacks, whites, mulattoes—can work together to farm the land and trade for a profit, all as equal partners."

"You want your rebels to work with the people who enslaved them?"

"As free men and women—free to own our own land, wield our own magic, raise our own families. Yes, I do."

Surprise made her outspoken, for perhaps the first time in her life. "You can't. Even if you could make those men and women out there accept it, the whites never would. They hate us too much. Besides, they already have those things. Why would they share them with you?"

"Because this colony won't survive any other way." He had recovered his equilibrium now. His eyes met hers openly. "The whites had those things once; they don't have them anymore. We're not slaves anymore—we're free people, like them. They need to negotiate, and so do we, before this island is no good to anyone."

"They won't." She had never felt more certain of anything. "It's madness. They'll just keep trying to kill you."

"Then we'll keep trying to kill them." He shrugged. "But sooner or later, there needs to be an end to it. What that end looks like is anyone's guess at the moment. I have my preferred end, that's all. And I mean to do all I can to bring it about."

She wasn't fooled by his careful nonchalance. His caution was very understandable—his vision was not likely to be shared by many out there, and many would be actively repulsed by it. Bullet's cruelty had been extreme; his people had turned away from it now, after the first excesses of their revenge. That didn't mean they were willing to work with their former captors, or even those of the same class and color as their former captors. If Toussaint proposed any such thing, he would have very few willing to follow him, no matter how well-liked he was. But she had been inside his head and felt the depth of his conviction. He meant every word.

"Now you know what I left the people I love most for," Toussaint said. "Why did you leave yours?"

She could still have refused to answer. But all at once, she was tired of being afraid. She had been afraid for so long.

"I came here because I heard a voice that night," she said. "I heard it all the way across the water. It wasn't a spirit, or a god: it was a human voice, but like none I've ever heard before. It spoke in your heads. I overheard it, the way I might hear a shout in the next field. It told you to rise up, and take revenge."

Toussaint considered her for a long time. "None of us heard it," he said at last. He was telling the truth. "No one on the entire island has ever, to my knowledge, mentioned such a voice. I certainly never heard anything of the kind."

"But you believe me." For once, she wasn't afraid.

"I do," he said. "You broke free of the spellbinding—that takes truly powerful magic. I believe you. And you've come to look for this voice?"

"Whoever it is," she said, "he must be a very powerful magician. And if he enabled this rebellion, perhaps he could help us in Jamaica too."

"Nobody enabled this rebellion, Fina. We did it ourselves. I saw it form. It was very carefully planned from the beginning by Boukman and the others. The only thing we didn't bring about ourselves was the breaking of the spellbinding, and we knew of that in advance. A letter came from an alchemist in England, advising us that it would take place; we saw the new shipments arrive in the north and knew that if the alchemist had succeeded, it would happen soon. And it did. But we know the identity of the alchemist now. He doesn't have the powers you claim."

"Thomas Clarkson." She had heard the name since coming to Saint-Domingue. "The English abolitionist. It isn't him. The stranger is still here in some way. I can feel him in the soil. Sometimes, when I'm asleep, I can almost see him. If he didn't bring the rebellion about, he shaped it in some other way. Perhaps he still does. I want to know how."

"So do I." She felt she knew some of the expressions on Toussaint's face now, simply by having been inside his head. Like her, he showed his feelings least when he felt most strongly, but his eyes were troubled. "It was a strange, dark night, the night you speak of. As I said, the rebellion was planned. We knew what would happen, and when. But when it came, it was like a storm tearing the island apart. Everything was madness and flames and blood, and when the sun came up, we were standing in a different world."

"Celeste told me there was a storm that night," Fina said. "She said a group of you met, under the guidance of a voodoo houngan. They say you made a sacrifice, and the loa came and took possession of you all."

"There was a ceremony," Toussaint agreed cautiously. "They say that a pact was made that night with the spirits of our homeland. Perhaps it was. I have never had much belief in voodoo, but I was there when Boukman called the loa, and I can't deny there was a power in him that night. But that didn't frighten me. What I saw that night, from both sides, did. That degree of hatred and cruelty, so concentrated in such a short space, was like nothing I've ever seen before."

"The whites have earned our hatred," she said. "And they don't need any reason to hate us."

"That's true. Perhaps it was natural and purifying. And if that's all, then we can hope that it will burn away, and we can start to rebuild on the ashes. But I don't like the sound of the voice you mention, and its message. It sounds as though it wants the burning to continue."

Fina said nothing. Deep down, she wasn't at all sure she didn't want the burning to continue as well.

"I came to see you because I was interested to see if you had strong magic," Toussaint said after a pause. "Now that I know what it is, I'm more interested yet. I have a band of some five hundred men and women, many of whom I've chosen for their magic. Yours could be very useful to us."

She had known something was coming, but she hadn't expected this. "A war band?"

"A very particular kind of war band. I will be honest with you, Fina: I think that Biassou, and almost every other military commander on our side, is fighting this conflict wrongly. We have no order and little discipline—just passion and cruelty. My father used to talk about how Europe is able to do so much harm to Africa, despite the fact that we have free magic and they don't. Part of it is because their officers at least do bring their own magic to the battlefield, of course. Their Concord, as they call it, doesn't apply in Africa, any more than it applies to their treatment of the slaves here. Part of it is that some of their magic is more advanced: their alchemists, for instance, have developed amulets for protection and spellbinding for control that we don't have. We can deal with these things as they come. But the most dangerous thing of all is that they work together like a machine."

"So you want us to fight like them?"

"Not entirely. We need to learn from the commanders from the ancient world, as do the French garrisons that fight us, or they will win. But we also need to find a way to retain our own strengths: free magic, of course, being one of the most important. I think an army that combines the two modes—discipline with ferocity, strategy with magic—will be able to hold this island. To this end, I want as many magicians with us as possible. And speaking for myself, I certainly wouldn't mind knowing what my enemy was seeing before I rode into his view."

She smiled a little, but said nothing. Her heart had quickened.

"I know you didn't come here to fight for Saint-Domingue," Toussaint said. He was watching her face very closely. "But I think we can help each other. I can't tell you anything more about the voice you heard, though I'm very much interested in helping you find it. As for Jamaica—I can do nothing to free your plantation now, as I'm sure you're aware. We're very far from free ourselves. I can't even give you my promise that I will one day help you to free it—the future is too uncertain. But I can promise you that if it becomes at all possible, I will do what I can."

Still, Fina said nothing. She knew Toussaint's war band already—they were handpicked, not for reasons that were readily apparent to others, but they rode out with him often, and they came back alive more often than could be explained by luck. They were in the thick of the deadliest of skirmishes, traversing great distances in a day and appearing where they were least expected. It was a dangerous offer. But then, nowhere in Saint-Domingue was very safe these days. Perhaps the space at Toussaint's side, paradoxically, was safer than most. At least she would have no fears of being thrown out of the camp without protection. More than that, she liked him. She had liked him from the outside of his head; from the inside, she liked him better still. She liked his kindness, his steel discipline, his quiet that was so different from her own. She was a storm of fear and anger behind her still face; Toussaint's stillness went so much deeper. It was comforting, in a world turned to noise and chaos.

"Would I have to go into battle?" she asked.

"I don't think so," he said. "The way I see your magic, it would be of far more use outside the battlefield. You could tell us the positions of the enemy long before they come into view, give us the shape of enemy terrain without needing to ride it—even give us some glimpses of the enemy's strategies, if we're fortunate. I don't think I need to ask you to stand by my side—if I do, then you'll have fair warning of it, and I'll accept your refusal without question. I'd like you to promise me something in return, though."

"What is it?"

His mouth twisted ruefully. "Please stop looking through my eyes from now on. Your magic is your own, to do with as you please. But I would rather not have to avert my gaze from private moments."

Heat rose in her cheeks, but her smile grew more certain. "I promise."

"Thank you. I'd like you to promise me something else, as well."

She waited.

"If you ever hear this voice again," Toussaint said, "tell me at once."

Perhaps, in the end, that decided her. "I will," she said. "And I'll join you, as you've asked. But I have a condition of my own, aside from your promise to help Jamaica."

"What is it?"

"If you ever hear the voice yourself," she said, "you will tell me too."

Paris

August 1792

News of Thomas Clarkson's conviction caused a stir in the French Assembly of Magicians. For a while, it looked indeed as though France could declare war on England, despite the British ambassador's assurances that the revolution on Saint-Domingue had been wholly unsupported by the British government. If the warmongers had been able to blame anyone other than Clarkson, perhaps they would have done it. But Brissot, still the strongest proponent of war in the Assembly, was also president of France's abolition society—which, moreover, he had founded after visiting Clarkson in London. The society had never been very successful, and was largely inactive now, but it would still look very strange for the Girondins to demand retaliation for an act committed by Brissot's friend in accordance with his own principles. Besides, the Girondins were cautious about free magic. They wanted to declare war on Britain, but not in a way that might entail the breaking of the Concord, as accusing the British government of an act of magic against France would almost certainly do.

Robespierre was inclined to think the Saint-Domingue rebellion was indeed supported by the British government, but for once he wasn't inclined to argue. He had emerged as the leader of the antiwar movement. Despite having no official presence in the Assembly, his voice was one of the most powerful in France. He and Brissot had been friends not so long ago; now they were carrying out an exhausting, dragged-out war of public opinion by speech and by pamphlet.

The worst of it was that Robespierre was still doing so with very little mesmerism—enough to keep him in the public eye, but not enough to change things. His benefactor had not budged on the death of the king.

"You want to end the warmongering and turn France's energies elsewhere," his benefactor said late one night. "You won't end it by words."

"I might," Robespierre said. "If you gave me more magic."

"You won't. The king himself has written to the major European powers in secret, asking them to invade and reinstate him. He won't let the war stop as long as he has a say in the matter."

"I know." Robespierre had no proof of this, but he believed it was true, and for him that was the same thing. "I've told everyone that. They don't believe me—at least, not enough of them."

"If we lose the war, with France as it stands, we'll have a monarchy again. Everything you've achieved will be lost. You know this."

"I know," Robespierre repeated. He folded his arms tightly and tried not to shiver. The garden in his dreams was always so cold now. Presumably, that was his benefactor's anger. It seeped into his bones and stayed there throughout the hot summer's days.

He still wasn't ready to overthrow the monarchy, much less kill the king. He was the Incorruptible. The power he held was based on his own image of himself as a pillar of virtue. The idea of committing an act of violence against the royal family was unthinkable. But he found himself looking more closely at people who might think of it. In particular, he started to look at Georges-Jacques Danton.

Danton had been a lawyer in the city before the Revolution came, more successful than Camille, better connected than Robespierre. He was officially an unmagical Commoner, but the Knights Templar had been looking askance at him for years. He simply didn't seem quite canny. For one thing, he was the largest and ugliest man Robespierre had ever seen. His colossal frame took up the space of two men; his barrel chest could broadcast with the volume of three. When he was a child, his face had been ravaged by smallpox and a series of wild animals, but it could hardly have been pleasing to begin with. Periwinkle-blue eyes peered out from under a coarse brow amid a landscape of scars and crevices. His ugliness had a fascination that mere good looks could not hope to match; combined with his booming voice and sharp intellect, it made him hypnotic. He could play a room like a finely tuned violin.

"Part minotaur," Camille had decided one night as the Jacobins assembled. "That has to be it. He ought to be living in the catacombs somewhere."

"There's no such thing as a minotaur," Robespierre had scoffed. "They don't exist."

"Danton!" Camille had called immediately across the room. "Robespierre thinks you don't exist."

"I don't," he called back, drowning out half a dozen other conversations in the process. "I am a figment of his imagination. You can only see me because you're seated close to him right now."

"I will never leave his side," Camille vowed.

Robespierre had stiffened at the teasing, but smiled reluctantly. It was hard not to smile at Camille, even when he also wanted to strangle him. "You'd better not."

In fact, the three of them had become very closely allied as the political wheel in Paris continued to turn. They were an oddly matched set, but they complemented each other: one bull-like and daring, one lightning fast and playful, one tightly wound and meticulous. All three had been consigned to pulling strings behind the scenes with the advent of the new government, but all three did it very well. When they pulled together, they could shift mountains.

The summer after the Assembly declared war on Austria, Lucile Desmoulins went into labor with the couple's first child. Robespierre and Danton talked the military threat over as they waited in the Desmoulinses' villa, trying with increasing futility to distract Camille from the muffled cries and voices coming from upstairs. Robespierre had come from the Jacobins to see if he could help and had found

Danton already there; it was well into the small hours of the morning, and the candles were burning low.

"This is exactly what the king wants," Robespierre said, over the sound of footsteps overhead. "He's urged the Assembly to make war because he thinks we'll lose. He *wants* France to be defeated, and Austria to reinstate him. I told them this at the time. They're just all too blinded with the idea of increasing France's wealth and territory to listen."

"To be fair," Danton said, "the essay in which you told them was twenty pages long. I didn't get through all of it either."

Robespierre ignored this remark. "I have nothing personal against Brissot—we used to be very good friends, and I know he's a fervent Republican ideologically. But he hasn't been one in practice lately."

"*I* have something personal against Brissot," Camille retorted, to Robespierre's relief. He hadn't been sure Camille was even listening. His friend hadn't stood still since Robespierre had come in; sitting was apparently out of the question. "And he was one of the chief witnesses at my wedding. He said I only call myself a patriot to insult patriotism."

"You said far worse about him."

"I did," Camille said, not without pride. The article in question had taken Paris by storm with its savage humor. "And I meant it. It's Brissot's people who are to blame for the fact that we still don't have freedom of magic, too. I can't believe they still call themselves the Assembly of Magicians. There's hardly a magician among them. They're afraid of us. They say they want free magic, but what they really mean is that they want to limit the powers of the Knights Templar. They don't want us to actually use it."

Danton laughed. "When has anyone stopped you from using magic in the last three years?"

"It's a matter of time, as long as the bracelets are still on. The only reason they've left it so long is because not having officially declared magic illegal again is useful on the battlefield—and because they're afraid of what we can rouse if they came out and bespelled us again. They don't want another Champ de Mars."

"This isn't what the Revolution was meant to be about," Robespierre said. A sharp cry came from upstairs; he raised his voice determinedly. "We're supposed to be liberators."

"For that matter," Danton said, "there was a point where we were meant to be a republic. Camille, for God's sake, will you stop hovering uselessly at the door? You look like you're threatening to take flight."

"Leave him alone," Robespierre said—reflexively, as he had to far less sympathetic bullies during their schooldays.

"I might, in fact, be about to take flight," Camille said. His usually sun-browned face was white as milk. "Or burn up. Or fall apart. God. I can't be a father. Why didn't one of you stop me?"

"I hate to disappoint you, Camille," Danton said, "but neither of us was there at the crucial time."

"I don't know what I was thinking."

"You? You weren't thinking. Your brain does remarkable things, Camille, but nobody ever calls it thinking."

"What do they call it?"

"They don't. People have better things to talk about than your brain. There's a revolution in progress."

"I don't believe, for you, your brain has anything to with it," Robespierre said thoughtfully. It wasn't the moment, but the notion had come to him. "I believe you think with your nerves. Or with your magic."

"Certainly," Danton said, "your brain had nothing to do with it nine months ago."

"Oh, don't be coarse," said Camille, who said far worse things several times a day and sometimes in Latin. "Why do people think it's so amusing when your wife is having a baby?"

"My wife has had three," Danton said. He was only a year older than Camille—a year younger than Robespierre—yet always seemed to have lived twice as long. "I know it's not amusing. Nothing about the situation is amusing, apart from you, and that's not situational."

"Can't you find another wild bull to annoy instead?" Camille said, but he was smiling faintly. Robespierre couldn't help but feel a stab of jealousy. Danton's teasing, after all, had helped. Robespierre had known Camille so much longer, and yet all that came to his own tongue were unhelpful commonplaces.

"All will be well," he said, awkwardly. "You'll see."

"Thank you," Camille said. He ran a distracted hand through his hair and sighed. "This door isn't working anymore. I need to momentarily hover by the stairs. Nothing personal. Please continue to talk amongst yourselves."

Uneasiness descended over the room when Camille left. The truth was, Robespierre wasn't entirely sure of Danton, and he knew the other man felt the same about him. They were too different: Danton's pleasure-loving pragmatism was entirely alien to him, as he suspected his own quiet asceticism was to Danton. The gulfs of understanding between them were too vast without Camille to help traverse them.

"How long does this usually take?" he heard himself ask, and mentally kicked himself. Danton already thought he had far too little experience with the realities of life. But he'd been awake for a very long time; his mental energies were flagging. He found this sort of thing more draining than a thousand political arguments.

Fortunately, Danton's thoughts seemed to be elsewhere. "Oh, hours. Days, sometimes. But I don't think Camille will have so long to wait. You were right, you know."

Robespierre tilted his head. "About?"

"This war playing into the king's hands. I'm not so certain that Louis is mentally capable of that kind of deception, but some of his generals are. It would be all too easy for them to turn on us and let Austria in."

"It's a matter of time," Robespierre agreed immediately. He sat forward in his chair. "We need to put a stop to it."

"The war?"

"The war. Brissot's domination of the Assembly. The king's influence on government."

"The king's relatively harmless now."

"It's not about the king as an individual. It's about the monarchy as an institution. And in that light, the king and his supporters are hardly harmless." He wondered briefly why that sounded familiar. He had so many hours of political discussion every day now, and had for so many years. "They aren't harmless for exactly the same reason the bracelets aren't harmless. Because as long as they're still there, we haven't shrugged them off. We aren't free of them. They're waiting, until the wheel turns and people relax their guard, and then they'll tighten their grip again."

"I can't imagine you ever relax your guard," Danton said. "Look at you. It's almost dawn, you've been arguing ideology all night, there's a child being born upstairs, and you look as if you've just been starched, cleaned, and pressed."

Robespierre ignored this. "It all went wrong after the king's flight. After the Champ de Mars massacre. The wrong people came to power and made all the wrong concessions."

"And what do you propose we do about that?"

Robespierre said nothing. The truth was, he'd been told what to do about that. He was still told, every night.

"I agree with what you're saying," Danton said into the silence. He leaned his bulk back against the cushions and put his feet up on the cold grate. "But we're already arguing until we're hoarse every night of the week. I don't see what more there is, short of storming the palace."

It was hard to explain what came to him then—whether something stirred in his head, or the idea simply presented itself too perfectly to ignore, or whether he was just tired and ready, for once, to compromise. But mesmerism kindled in his chest unexpectedly. It was the first time it had awakened of its own volition. His necromancy was often alive in his veins; even with his benefactor's help, his mesmerism always needed to be drawn on deliberately, and lately it had been a reluctant child dragging its heels at being put to work. Slowly, he removed his spectacles and met Danton's gaze.

"Someone could do that," he said. And for the first time in months his benefactor's magic joined with his own and infused the words with all the force of a command.

"Someone could do what?" Danton asked. He was looking at Robespierre very closely.

"Take the palace by force. It could be done. It would just take the right person, at the right moment."

"I can't imagine you're speaking of yourself."

"Of course not. I don't want to seize power. I'm not speaking of anyone at all, really. But I suppose it would be someone capable of rallying a crowd and leading a charge. Someone used to being heard."

Danton's periwinkle eyes, surprisingly light and clear in such a ruined face, held Robespierre's. Robespierre looked back at him. He was no longer tired or uncertain. Mesmerism was a tongue of flame licking through his blood. It was exhilarating.

"They'd have to take control of the Hôtel de Ville as well," Danton said slowly. "If they were to have any bargaining power."

"They would," Robespierre agreed. "And from that position, with the king gone, they would be perfectly placed to institute any form of government they so chose. As long as the king was out of the negotiations."

It wasn't as though Danton hadn't thought of it himself—or, if he hadn't yet, he certainly would have soon. It wasn't as though Robespierre had told him to actually kill the king. For that matter, it wasn't as though Danton was entirely under his power: he was far too strong for that. But words unsaid hovered between them like a fog. From upstairs, there came the thin, bewildered wail of a baby crying.

Danton and Robespierre were still considering each other when Camille burst into the room.

"I have a son," he said without preamble. "Horace Camille Desmoulins. You have a godson, Maximilien, but I think you'll forgive me the greater claim to immediate inebriation. You hardly drink anyway."

Robespierre blinked, his attention diverted. "A godson?"

"Didn't I ask if you wanted to be godfather? I was supposed to. If Lucile asks, you accepted last month. You do accept, don't you?"

"I—yes. Yes, of course." A warmth very different from mesmerism blossomed in his chest. For a moment, he forgot all about the king. "It would be an honor. Congratulations."

"Yes, congratulations," Danton added sincerely. The teasing had gone from his voice. "It's wonderful news. I assume Lucile's well?"

"She's well. The baby's well. Everything is completely wonderful. Apart from, you know, politics and war, but we'll fix that." He sank down onto the couch, quite suddenly. "My God. I'm exhausted. I think I'm crying a little too, but there you are. What time is it?"

"Almost dawn," Robespierre said. The air coming in from the open window promised a long, hot summer's day. He didn't look at Danton, and Danton didn't look at him.

It never even occurred to anyone that Robespierre might want to help orchestrate an act of mob violence. Nobody remembered, now, that he had been at the Bastille; if Camille did, he was astute enough not to mention it while Robespierre was clearly choosing to conceal it himself. And Robespierre, after careful consideration, did choose to conceal it. His role in the fall of the Bastille was too dangerous to be revealed, in his opinion, even as he praised those involved to the heavens. He had flooded a crowd with mesmerism on that day. He had raised the dead. That was, after all, still illegal, and he was the Incorruptible.

And so over the next few weeks, as Danton and Camille began to spend more and more time in discussion away from Robespierre, and whispers began to pile up in corners, Robespierre both listened and didn't listen. He heard the shapes of plans without asking for the specifics. He knew without knowing what he had set in motion. This was nothing new. His friendship with Camille had always been dependent on not asking for details that Camille would cheerfully have supplied but knew better than to volunteer. It wasn't hypocrisy, or he didn't think it was. It was just another way of staying clean.

Perhaps Danton understood this better than Robespierre gave him credit for. At the very least, on the evening of 9 August, when the two of them met by chance on the street, his cheerful voice held a trace of condescension.

"There should be a few bells ringing tonight," he said. "If I were you, I'd bolt the doors and stay inside. It might get dirty out here."

As night fell that evening, the bells from the churches began to ring.

Robespierre heard them as he sat at the dinner table with the Duplays; he looked up sharply and saw Éléonore, opposite him, do the same. Maurice set down his fork and got to his feet.

"Is that—?"

"Yes," Robespierre said. He spoke calmly, but his chest tightened. "It's starting."

The bells rang throughout the night, a slow, rhythmic, all-consuming call to battle. At the Dantons' house, Lucile Desmoulins walked her infant son up and down, jiggling him comfortingly as he bewailed the constant noise. Her own tears probably did little to help. Only that evening, she had been filled with high spirits, knowing that if she didn't laugh, she would cry. She couldn't laugh anymore, and so she was crying. It all seemed too real, suddenly, and too impossible.

The parlor swarmed with revolutionaries: Danton, Camille, and others, who had named themselves the Insurrectionary Commune. With the exception of Danton, they all wore bracelets; many, Camille included, were already showering the air with practice bursts of magic in a state of nervous bravado. They also, more practically, all wore pistols. Gunfire tended to outweigh most abilities, unless the Inheritance was exceptionally strong. Danton's wife, Gabrielle, sat watching in quiet misery. Lucile knew her well and generally liked her, though she found her lacking in imagination. Normally she would go to her, but this time she held back. It struck her suddenly that she didn't know whether she should comfort her or be comforted. She had never been good at the former and wasn't sure if she could bear the latter. She felt faint and sick.

The Tuileries was not like the Bastille. Louis XVI, however weakened, however vulnerable, had armies loyal to him: the Swiss Guard made up the bulk of the defense, but he had a small personal guard, and a number of the National Guard would fight for him rather than the insurrectionists when it came to it. He would not go down without a fight. There was going to be death on both sides.

"Not many on the street yet," Camille said to Danton.

"Give them time," Danton said. "They can all hear. They all know what it means. And all of Paris is with us. They'll start coming out soon." He yawned. "I might get some sleep for an hour or so before it starts. It's going to be a long night."

Lucile waited for him to go, then quietly took Camille aside. "I don't want you to die," she said. Even put so bluntly, it sounded artificial to her. She had read too many romance novels, and now tonight everything she said was an echo of a book rather than real life.

To anyone else, Camille might have declared, like a romance hero, that he was happy to die in the service of the Revolution. He didn't say so to her. He had been saying such things less and less of late, since their marriage, since the birth of their child.

"I won't," he said instead. He looked white and strained, and utterly alive. "I'm not going to die. If it makes you feel better, I promise I won't leave Danton's side. We'll look after each other."

That shouldn't have been reassuring, given that Danton's side was likely to be in the heart of the danger. But Danton was so solid, so sensible, and so cheerfully interested in his own self-preservation that somehow it was.

"Madame Robert says that if her husband dies, she'll kill Danton," Lucile said, lowering her voice further as she looked sideways at the wife of one of the other revolutionaries. "I won't let her; I'll protect Danton and his family at all costs. But if you die, I think I'll probably kill *someone*."

"Well, make it someone with a title," Camille advised, then kissed her quickly. He must have tasted the tears on her face. "Oh, Lolotte.

You shouldn't love me so much, not if it's going to make you so unhappy."

It made her smile weakly. "As if it was my doing! You were just a boring failed lawyer when I first met you. I had no intention of falling in love with you. You just wouldn't leave me alone." Her own words caught up to her, and she held him close. "Please, please don't leave me alone. Be careful."

"I will," he said. She knew he wouldn't be.

By the early hours of the morning, twenty thousand Commoners were assembled outside the Hôtel de Ville. They were armed with rifles, with pikes, with their own magic, and their blood was up. The relentless gong of the bell could barely be noticed anymore: it seemed to have sunk through the pores of the crowd and blended with its heartbeat. At the Tuileries, the king had been rushed to the safety of the old riding school, where the Assembly had gathered to argue furiously about what to do. They heard the approach of the crowd from a long way away. It sounded like the wild hunt of legend, a thunder of footsteps and a baying for death.

As the dawn began to tint the sky, Lucile Desmoulins curled up by the window at the Dantons'. She no longer cared about sounding artificial, as though quoting from a romance. She was in one.

What will become of us? she wrote in her journal. *I can endure no more. Camille, O my poor Camille, what will become of you? I have no strength to breathe. This night, this fatal night! O God, if it be true that thou hast any existence, save the men who are worthy of thee. We want to be free. O God, the cost of it!*

All that morning, the palace was a battlefield.

It wasn't until afternoon that Robespierre emerged from the Duplays' house, where he had spent the long night and day. The Duplays protested strongly that the streets were still in chaos, but he couldn't stand to be within those walls a moment longer. He had slept fitfully that night, and worked more fitfully still that day, half expecting at every moment that his friends might send for him. There had been no word. His curiosity at last burned away his fear.

"I just want to go around the corner and look," he told Madame Duplay. Babette clutched his arm in a death grip; he disengaged it gently. "I'll come straight back."

The trees in the Tuileries had been the yellow green of late summer when he had walked down the streets only yesterday: as he turned the corner now, they were red gold, and many littered the ground. Autumn, come early—the aftereffects of strong weather magic. He remembered the way the wind had whipped and wailed past his window that morning. It had gone now. The trees stood tall, eerie in their straight military lines.

Around them was a scene of carnage. The gates of the Tuileries lay in ruins: blasted apart not by stonemancers this time, but by cannons. The walls, the gardens, the streets, the palace swarmed with thousands upon thousands of people. It resembled nothing so much as a nest of ants covering a human corpse.

There was a terrible smell in the air, of smoke and ash and charred flesh. His necromancy, so active these days, writhed inside him, but he didn't need it to tell him what was burning on the bonfires that littered the grounds.

"It's over," he told the Duplays. "We won. The palace is ours. But don't go out quite yet."

He stopped by Camille's house on the way to the Jacobins that evening. The house was shut up, but he managed to catch his friend there. Camille had stopped by only to wash and change his clothes before going out again; his family were staying with friends across town. Lucile had refused to return to the Dantons' that night, exhausted as she was, yet she insisted their own home wouldn't be safe.

"I think she's probably being irrational," Camille said. He was pale and half-drunk with fatigue, yet still talking brightly. Perhaps a little too brightly. "But I'm feeling irrational myself. I think it comes of overthrowing the monarchy on an empty stomach."

"She must have been very worried about you," Robespierre said, and felt the familiar twinge he couldn't quite name. Lucile's revolutionary leanings were more romantic than ideological, yet somehow their marriage struck Robespierre as the kind that could be forged only in the same smithy as revolution: fiery, tender, exultant, equal parts soul and intellect and animal heat. It made him wistful without knowing why.

"Very," Camille agreed, with more seriousness. "I was worried about me too, here and there. I promised her I would stay close to Danton, but I'm not sure that close to Danton was the safest place to be. I certainly think I was protecting him more than he was protecting me. I had the air around us thick with shadows by the end."

"And set a few things on fire, no doubt," Robespierre said.

He meant it lightly, but his friend's face went quiet. Robespierre, too late, remembered the bodies of the Swiss Guard amid the premature autumn leaves.

"There was some fire," Camille said at last. He flicked a spark at Robespierre and managed a quick smile. "That's about all I have left, I think. It was a long night, and a long day after it."

"How many dead?" Robespierre asked, as neutrally as he could. He had heard varying reports.

"I didn't count personally. There were nine hundred guards; I think our forces must have killed most of them. I don't quite know how we managed it. We had more magic on our side, of course. Perhaps that was it. It was a massacre, afterward. A lot of screaming. And yes. Burning. I saw Suleau hacked to pieces by the crowds. Do you remember him? He was at school with us. Royalist, of course."

"Camille..."

"It was glorious, really," he interrupted. "The royal family have been taken prisoner—real prisoners, this time. France is in our hands. We won. I just need to get the smell of smoke out of my lungs."

Robespierre remembered, suddenly, the day the Bastille had fallen. Not the parts he usually remembered: the magic and the crowds and the stone shattering into a fall of dust. He remembered instead getting home—to his dark rented rooms, not the warm haven of the Duplays'—and taking off his jacket. There had been a splatter of blood on his shirt cuff—not his, and not particularly large. It could have come from anywhere, or anyone. But for some reason, he had panicked. He had torn the shirt from him as though the touch of it was toxic; his flesh had crawled; he had scrubbed at his hands again and again, shivering convulsively with cold or horror or something else.

"I hope you didn't take it amiss that I wasn't there," he said awkwardly.

"What could you have done?" Camille said. It was perhaps a little too dismissive for Robespierre's liking. "It was pistols and magic and corpses. Not your sort of revolution at all. It would have wounded your delicate sensibilities."

His pride, always sensitive, flared. "I'm not as squeamish as you think I am."

"How squeamish do I think you are?" Camille held up his hands before Robespierre could reply. "I didn't mean that. Nobody expected you to be there, Maxime. It was Danton's show. And you would have got yourself killed venturing near the Tuileries today—which might have been an effective piece of martyrdom, come to that, but we didn't need any more martyrs. You're more valuable alive."

"So are you and Danton," Robespierre pointed out.

"I know it. That's why we're both alive." He yawned hugely. He had managed to snatch only a few hours of sleep the night before, most of it leaning against Lucile's shoulder. "If you want to help next time, you can take care of your godson."

Robespierre was placated by that. He realized that part of his irritation had been borne of jealousy of the closeness that had grown between Danton and Camille and that, after today, would doubtless continue to grow. But it was not Danton who had been primary witness at the wedding of the Desmoulinses, or who had been named godfather to little Horace Camille. That, amid all the politics and heads on pikes, still mattered.

"Is he well?" he asked.

"Mm. He woke at the sound of the tocsin bells last night, like a true revolutionary, but he slept through the sound of violent uprising this morning, like a true politician. Could go either way. Either way, he should make an orator, judging by the strength of his lungs."

"The France in which he'll grow up will no longer need revolutionaries," Robespierre said. He had already disregarded the disquieting memory of the Bastille. He was bursting with hope and purpose. This, finally, was it. "It may not even need politicians or orators, of the kind you're thinking. It will be a republic. Moral, virtuous, incorruptible."

"Normally, I would say that sounds rather dull," Camille said. "But tonight, I'll take it."

Paris

September 1792

The fall of the monarchy changed everything.

That night at the Jacobins, Robespierre stood and gave one of his greatest speeches yet, praising the attack as the promise of the fall of the Bastille come at last to glorious fruition. He knew his words were laced with mesmerism, but he could barely distinguish the glow of magic in his chest from his own exultation.

"In 1789," he said, "the people rose up to overthrow a prison. Now, in 1792, the people have risen up to implement a new world. In 1789, we were a revolution. Now we are a republic."

The Jacobins cheered.

The French Republic of Magicians, at last, had been born.

Things began to happen after that. Once again, mob magic was alive on the streets of Paris. Aristocrats attempted to flee the country in droves: many were stopped at the border and imprisoned for treason. It was announced that a new government would be elected: elected, for the first time, by any Frenchman over the age of twenty-five, regardless of class, occupation, or magic. The Assembly, with its conciliatory ways, had lasted only a year.

Robespierre's younger brother Augustin came from Arras to run for office, bringing Charlotte with him. There was little time to prepare for their arrival: their carriage pulled up at the Duplays' with barely a day's warning. Robespierre came through the courtyard to be rewarded by the sight of his two siblings, hot and flustered from the long journey, and the ecstatic greeting of his dog Brount, who had made the journey with them.

"Maximilien!" his brother called. His young face, like Robespierre's own but rounder and more good-natured, was alight. "We're together at last!"

"It's so good to see you, Maxime," Charlotte said sincerely—then, when he took her hands to welcome her, added with a frown, "You've been biting your nails again. I warned you about that."

For a fortnight or so, Robespierre dared to think it might all work. The king had not been killed in the attack on the palace, it was true, as the darkest, guiltiest part of his heart had hoped. It had not stopped the war, though he hoped the change of government would bring about peace faster. But the uprising was over, and they had won. He had achieved some measure of what his benefactor had asked, and he had done so without compromising his own reputation. Surely that would be enough.

But the violence didn't stop with the fall of the palace. In early September, as elections for the new government reached their summit, news came to Paris that Prussia had invaded the outskirts of France, seeking to place the king back on the throne. It threw the Commoners of Paris into a panic. In their panic, they turned to the prisons filled with Aristocrats and royalist sympathizers and Knights Templar. These people were all potentially dangerous; if an invasion came, any one of them could conceivably give aid to the enemy. And so, one by one, they killed them.

Makeshift tribunals were set up to sort the enemies of the people from the innocent, but in practice few were spared. Judges rushed prisoners through the courtroom into the yards outside, where hordes of Commoners were waiting and baying for blood. Magic, it turned out, could be used in creative ways by those with a mind to it. Bodies were set on fire; severed limbs levitated in an ever-growing constellation above the prisons; men and women drowned on dry land. The

British ambassador, writing to Pitt at Downing Street, reported only "circumstances of barbarity too shocking to describe."

One of those killed was Marie Antoinette's friend and cousin by marriage, the Princess de Lamballe. She was torn apart by a mob, and her head was mounted on a pike. The Commoners took the head to a local barber; amid a host of knives and grins, he styled her beautiful golden hair, and it streamed behind her head like a banner. Marie Antoinette hadn't been content to watch then. Her fire magic had blazed from the palace. The trees had burned; several of the mob had gone up in flames. But it had done no good.

It was said that Danton and his government, Camille included, were masterminding the slaughters for their own ends. Danton himself gave no sign of this, but certainly he didn't move to help the victims.

"To hell with them," he said, or was reported to have said. "Let the prisoners take care of themselves."

Robespierre didn't know what Danton's involvement was, or Camille's. He tried not to look or to listen. He was very busy. The formation of the Republic meant he was once more eligible to serve in office, in what was going to be called the National Convention. He needed to campaign; more important, he needed to work behind the scenes to ensure the elections themselves went smoothly. But one day, walking home, he passed a group of men playing chess outside the Conciergerie. His eyes lingered just a little too long, perhaps hungry for a scene of normality, and he saw that the board was set on a mound of mutilated corpses. At that, bile rose in his throat. When he reached the Duplays', he was still pale enough even by his standards that Éléonore stopped short.

"What's wrong, Maximilien?" she asked in alarm. She had been painting a self-portrait for her art class: one day, she hoped to make a living as an artist. She dropped the brush in a hurry.

He managed a smile for her, as he would have for his sister. "Nothing. Nothing at all."

She wasn't fooled, just as Charlotte wouldn't have been. Her concern was softer but no less determined. "It's something. You're shaking. You saw something, didn't you? We all see things we don't want to these days. Was it someone you knew?"

"No," he said, though it might have been. People all looked the same with no heads. "It just took me by surprise. They were counter-revolutionaries, I suppose. For all I know, they were Prussian agents. I don't know why it should bother me."

"Because you're not like those people out there. You're kind. Too kind, perhaps, for what you have to do." She hesitated. "Do you want to stop it? All the killings? You could, you know. People listen to you; they respect you, really, more than Danton."

"I don't think I could stop this," he said. "Danton isn't even trying."

"Do you want to?"

"I don't know." He looked over at the canvas, where the unfinished self-portrait watched him with unfinished eyes. She'd made them a touch darker than they were in life.

"*Can* we stop it?" he asked, in the garden of his sleep.

"Do you want to?" his benefactor said, in a horrible echo of Éléonore. He had been in a better mood since the monarchy had fallen, but Robespierre suspected he was still not content. "You asked for the voice of the people. Well, this is the voice of the people. This is what they want."

"They don't know what they want. They're angry. They're not thinking clearly."

"So your idea of Rousseau's social contract is to supply the people with what they *would* want, if they were thinking clearly." His benefactor shook his head, amused. "I do enjoy your ideological gymnastics, Robespierre. But it's you who has failed to think. You need mob violence. You would have nothing without it. The storming of the Bastille. The attack on the Tuileries."

"Those were different. Those had purpose."

"So does this. These prisoners are too dangerous to be allowed to live. France is facing invasion."

"Some of them are dangerous, perhaps. But this is mass slaughter. There's no real judicial process; it's all just a mess."

"Then you don't want to stop it. You want to give it order. You can't stop the people from exacting revenge. It's human nature—true human nature, not that nonsense in your Rousseau. Your mesmerism could never be that strong: you'd have to control all of France from your study, day and night. But you can use their anger. It could be a weapon."

"How?"

"You're an intelligent man. Work something out. But do it quickly, and do it decisively. Danton has surpassed you, since he delivered the country from the monarchy."

Against his will, he felt again that sharp, insidious stab of jealousy. "I did that. Danton wouldn't have moved on the palace without me."

"He doesn't know that. Nor does anyone else. I thought that was what you wanted."

It was, of course. He didn't even want to know it himself; he wasn't sure it was even true, because he didn't want to be sure. Perhaps Danton had needed no encouragement. But still…

"We can do something about Danton later," his benefactor said. "The palace was stormed and taken. On the whole, your move worked. But you need to gain ground, and do it fast."

"I don't want to do something about *Danton*," Robespierre said, with a jolt of alarm. "For all his faults, he's a patriot. I consider him a friend. We share a vision of France, at least in part."

"You don't want to," his benefactor agreed. "Yet you know you may have to. As I said, you're an intelligent man." He paused. "And yes. You *can* stop the killings, if you want to. You can stop a good deal more than that. You've tried to keep your hands clean by letting Danton do it his way. It hasn't worked. You need to do it our way."

"And what is our way?"

"I told you. It starts with the death of the king. You need to impose order. He's in your power now."

In his sleep, Robespierre tossed restlessly. "It's not my decision."

"But the people listen to you now. They trust you. If you tell them to kill the king, they'll do it in the end."

Robespierre struggled to put his feelings into words. "I've always hated capital punishment. It's wrong."

It was beginning to sound weak to his ears: more like a matter of taste than a moral precept.

"You've always hated injustice," his benefactor said. "The monarchy has been at the heart of it for generations. It's no betrayal of your principles to see it dead."

"It would mean war with England. They've been holding back thus far. They won't be able to look the other way if we do this. And it will be a war of magic, sooner or later."

"Then we'll be at war with England, and it will be a war of magic. It was inevitable in the end. We're already at war with half of Europe."

"I've always been opposed to that war as well. I hoped to end it."

"Back when it was still the king's war, a war of tyranny. Without the king, this will be a war of free people defending their ideals. A war of liberty. If it's the price we have to pay for liberty, is it so great?"

"Why does it matter to you?" Robespierre asked, with a flash of insight. He so rarely questioned what his benefactor wanted, or why he asked what he did. In some ways, he wasn't a person at all, just a dark figure in his mind who voiced things that Robespierre himself would never dare. But he wasn't just in Robespierre's mind. He existed somewhere in the world. And he had an agenda of his own. "What do you want?"

"I told you. I want France freed from the monarchy."

"Yes, of course. But we've deposed Louis, and still you're not content. What does his death gain for France that his deposition doesn't? You must have something in mind."

His benefactor fell silent. "I want the monarchy destroyed," he said eventually, "because it threatens France. But I also want the king destroyed because I intend to set another in his place."

"Another king?"

"No more kings. Another leader. Someone who will lead France to its natural destiny."

Robespierre's heart quickened. "Is it me?" he asked bluntly. "Is that what this has been about?"

"Would you like it to be you?"

"You think I want power. I don't, not for its own sake. I never have. But I want the France in my head. The France where all are free, and equal, and at peace. To bring that about—yes, I would be that leader."

"Then," his benefactor said, "you need to do what is necessary. Besides, Robespierre, you do owe me."

The garden dissolved after that; a moment later, Robespierre opened his eyes to his sloping bedroom ceiling.

He lay there, staring up at it, for a long time. His thoughts circled, backtracked, swarmed. The occasional scream drifted in from the night outside, and the clash of pikes.

By the time the results of the elections came in, the violence had ended, or perhaps there was nobody left to kill. The National Convention was made of 749 deputies from all over France. Danton was elected the second of Paris's twenty-four delegates; Camille was the sixth. Robespierre's brother, Augustin, was—to Robespierre's surprise and pleasure—nineteenth. Robespierre was first.

It was at the opening of the first National Convention that the bracelets were finally removed. Danton and his temporary government had insisted upon it from the moment they took the palace, and nobody left dared to oppose it. The last of the Knights Templar had either fled the country or been killed in the September massacres. Anybody who attempted to assume their role, at this point, would have been quickly made to join them. Magicians had taken the palace and liberated France from the monarchy at last. Support for free magic had never been so strong.

The moment when the clasps unlocked and the air resounded with the thud of metal hitting the ground was among the most beautiful of Robespierre's life. For the second time, he could almost wish he had a bracelet, just so he could watch it fall.

Camille didn't wait for his to fall; he wrenched it off before it was even fully open, and flung it across the room so hard it chipped a column and spun sideways into the crowd. There were mixed cheers and laughter from the people—and, probably, a cry of pain from whoever had been hit by it at full speed.

"We did it," he whispered to Robespierre as they filed in with the other delegates. He was trembling. "We actually did it."

Robespierre didn't remind him that there was far more work to come. Camille knew that. He looked down at his friend's bare wrist, blanched and scarred from thirty years of burning metal, and gave a rare smile. "We did it," he agreed.

Robespierre was indeed an intelligent man. He had learned two things from the September massacres. First, the people could not be held back from their desire for blood, and this being the case, it was best that the government distribute death so that it could be sated without mass slaughter. He still hoped that France could free itself from the death penalty entirely, but plainly the time was not right. Second, as long as there needed to be death, such death could be used as a weapon—but not as Danton had used it, looking the other way and leaving it to chance and the whims of a mob. That caused more suffering than it prevented. There would have to be another way.

Under the old regime, a swift execution by beheading was reserved for the Aristocracy. Commoners were hung, often after long and pointless torture. That could not be the case under the Republic of Magicians: if there must be capital punishment, Robespierre proposed in the Convention, it should be democratic, easy, and painless for all. Death by the sword was too messy and inefficient for large groups, when the slightest wriggle of a shoulder could send the blade glancing off the base of a skull or into a spine. Fortunately, technology had progressed as rapidly as ideologies.

Almost at once, the guillotine was set up near the Tuileries, at what was now being called the Place de la Révolution.

After that, Robespierre set about planning the death of the king.

London

October 1792

When the ripples of the monarchy's downfall reached England, they stirred a contradictory swirl of public emotion. The conservative were horrified; the radical were filled with violent exultation. Fox and his party sent public letters of congratulations to the French government; the Aristocrats among them fired off bursts of magic from their club, which were legal but considered in very poor taste. Many who had supported the Revolution now turned against it. Others, already angered by the government's rejection of magical reforms the year before, turned toward it.

All these reactions, from Wilberforce's point of view, were equally dangerous. His hopes of turning the House around to anything that looked like abolition or reform dwindled with every angry shout.

He had been struggling against overwork and despair since Clarkson's arrest. This, apparently, was a weight too far. One morning he woke from broken sleep with his old wound twisting viciously, burning with fever and too weak to rise from his bed. Thornton insisted he go to Bath, where he could seek treatment at the famed magic springs; the prospect was made more enticing by Hannah More, who invited him to come and recuperate with her afterward in nearby Mendip.

"You'll love Mendip," Eliot coaxed him at his bedside, having visited Hannah More there himself the year before. "Cheddar Gorge is one of the most spectacular natural wonders I've seen outside the Lake District. When you're feeling strong enough, you can get them to show you around. Harriot and I would come too, if it weren't for the child, you know."

Eliot's offhand tone made Wilberforce smile, despite the icy tendrils shooting up his side. "Oh, are you two having a child, Eliot?" he asked, mock sincere. "Really, you should have mentioned it before."

"Oh, shut up," Eliot said, but he was grinning. "When you finally find the time to marry and start a family, you'll talk of little else yourself. Honestly, Wilber, get out of London before you kill yourself. You'll be with like-minded people the entire time, so you can discuss the slave trade as much as you like. Pitt and I can keep you informed of everything that's happening in town. And you know you'll be of no use to anyone in January if you're not stronger."

This last was undeniably true.

Cheddar Gorge, when he was well enough to walk it, was indeed glorious: a massive split in the land, draped over with rambling woods and flowers, with rare wildlife teeming in every crevice. Yet Wilberforce couldn't help noticing the more common scraps of life: men, women, and children scraping together a living in the gorge, starving and ill. Most were living in tumbledown shacks; many were living in caves.

Braceleted Commoners, mostly, the guide told him. In the nearby villages, there was a strong prejudice against employing them; since the French Revolution, in particular, it was thought to be unsafe. Their eyes, watching him resentfully as he toured the scenery, haunted him that night. For the first time since Clarkson's arrest, something kindled in his chest. It was a familiar flicker: not quite anger, but purpose. Or perhaps it was a promise.

"Something needs to be done for those people," he told Hannah More at breakfast the following morning.

"What do you propose?" she asked at once. She, like Wilberforce, had no patience with people who claimed a thing needed to be done without doing it themselves at once.

"Well. They need decent clothing, food, and houses. They need a school."

"Many would say that Commoners of their status don't need to learn to read and write. That, in fact, it would be dangerous for them to encounter the kinds of ideas that inflamed Paris."

"I know you don't think that. Nor do I." He paused. "I think the magicians among them need more than that, in fact. I think they need rudimentary magical theory."

He watched her closely as he spoke. She and her sister were, after all, the leading scholars of magic outside of the Knights Templar.

Her eyebrow quirked. "Now, that would certainly inflame public opinion."

"If Commoner magic is ever made legal, these are the men and women who will wield it. They'll need to know how to wield it safely, and ethically, and to the best of their abilities. That time hasn't come yet. But I see no reason why they shouldn't be ready for it when it does."

"Nor do I," she said. "You know I've always thought that. But what you're talking about will cost money."

He smiled. "Fortunately, as I was told in my youth, money is something I have. If you and your sisters are willing to arrange the particulars from here, I'll fund anything you need."

They set to work that same day. And, for the first time in a long while, the world began to make sense again.

In the midst of it, he received a letter from Pitt. Harriot Eliot had died from fever five days after the birth of her little girl. The news had nothing to do with kings falling and countries at war. Women had children all the time; they died bringing them into the world all the time. It was perfectly natural, and devastating.

Wilberforce called in at Downing Street almost as soon as he returned to London—in the evening, after dinner, so as not to put the house to the trouble of finding food for him. Pitt met him in the library, where the firelight dappled across the worn volumes of Milton and Shakespeare and Virgil and Horace. He managed only a flicker of a smile. Pitt tended, even when exhausted, to be lit from within with energy and optimism; now heaviness had settled over him like fine dust. There were new lines around his eyes, as though his face had hollowed or collapsed, and he moved as though not quite certain of the world he was in.

"I'm so, so sorry," Wilberforce said, without preamble. "Truly. But she's with God now."

He longed to say more, but he knew well enough that trying to force God onto people who were grieving could do more harm than good in some cases. He also knew Pitt well enough to know that he was one of those cases.

"Thank you," Pitt said, and did seem to mean it sincerely. "I'm glad to see you looking so much better. I hope Bath was restful?"

"I started a school," Wilberforce said. "For magical Commoners."

"Of course you did." He sank down in his chair by the fire; Wilberforce sat opposite. "Eliot's in his room, I'm afraid; I've just come from him. I managed to get him to venture downstairs for dinner last night, but today he hasn't left his bed. I'm very concerned about him. I hope you'll go up and talk to him."

"Of course I will." It was what he had feared. Eliot had never been the sort to take bad news well; a loss like this might destroy him. "Poor Eliot. Does he want to see me, though? I don't want to disturb him."

"Please, disturb him—or at least distract him. He needs it badly. I'm doing my best, but I suspect I'm too close to this to take him away from it. Try to convince him to take an interest in his daughter, if you can. Right now, he blames her, and is trying not to. If he actually spent some time with her, I have no doubt he'd fall in love completely, and it might save him."

"I have no doubt either." Eliot loved children. When Pitt's other three nieces came to town, Eliot played with them as rambunctiously as Wilberforce himself. "The baby's well, then?"

"Thriving, thank God. She's a beautiful little thing. I'm taking her out to my mother as soon as Eliot can be left alone. You can see her, if you'd like. She's somewhere about this awkward house—a nurse is attending to her. She's pure Commoner," he added, as though Wilberforce had asked. "Not even a strain of mesmerism. She's in no danger."

"I'm so glad." He paused. "And you? How are you feeling?"

"I hardly know, most of the time," Pitt said tiredly. He glanced at Wilberforce. "It's growing easier. I've been able to resume work. I slept better last night than I have since it happened. I know time is very kind in cases like this."

"In other words," Wilberforce said, "you feel terrible."

The flicker of a smile was real this time. "How did you know?"

"You look terrible."

"Tactful. Thank you."

"I mean it in a sympathetic, concerned way, I assure you. A way that implies that I'm very much hurt on your account and on Eliot's, and if I can do anything, ever, at all, to make it any better, please don't hesitate to ask."

"I know. And thank you for that, as well." He fell silent for a moment; when he spoke again, he sounded more like himself. "It's far worse for Eliot, of course. I've been through this before. My older sister died a few years ago; my younger brother died the same year; my father died not long before that. This has been the hardest in some ways, given that it happened under my roof, but it's horribly familiar. Eliot lost his wife."

"My father and two of my sisters died when I was still a child," Wilberforce said, though he knew it wasn't quite the same thing. He loved his family, but he had been sent to school young; in some painful respects, he barely knew them. "I don't think it's ever easy. I'll go up and see Eliot now, shall I?" He hesitated. "Before I heard about Harriot, there was actually something I wanted to talk to you about. If it's not too terrible of me—"

"No, please. Believe me, I would far rather be thinking about business than remembering other things. You might find my thoughts working rather slowly, for which I apologize."

"Your thoughts have never worked slowly in your life. I just wanted to talk to you about Clarkson."

"Yes." Wilberforce watched him pull together a version of himself then, painfully, as someone might pull on a familiar garment when their ribs were broken. "I was very sorry to hear the Knights Templar insisted on the Tower for him. Is he well?"

"As well as can be expected. We've done all we can to make sure he's comfortable. But the Knights Templar are making difficulties about his classification. He was tested at birth, you see, as a pure Commoner; that's not unusual, as you well know. He tested strong alchemist upon his arrest. But he was tested again in the Tower—they were very thorough. He's certainly an alchemist. But they now say his ability isn't strong enough to have done what he claims. It's practically latent, according to them."

Pitt frowned. "But they don't think he's innocent?"

"Not at all. He confessed. But they think he has an accomplice whom he's protecting. They questioned him, under mesmerism; he maintained he was the one who carried out the alchemy."

His interest was no longer forced. "Why wasn't I told about this?"

"You will be, probably, too late and buried at the bottom of a list of other issues. You know what the Knights Templar are like. Clarkson wrote to us in Mendip, or I wouldn't know myself. They're investigating all of us again—the Abolition Society. I am all but positive that Clarkson is the only one of us involved in Saint-Domingue, but I'm a little concerned about—"

"Yes, I quite understand. The Temple Church are not your strongest supporters at the moment. I'll have a word with the Knights Templar about persecuting your society without evidence, of course."

"Thank you. And Clarkson? Are they right about his abilities, or was that just an excuse to investigate us further?"

"I doubt the latter. The tests are a matter of scientific record; they couldn't simply make up the blood results. As to the former..." He fell silent. The flames danced in the grate as he looked at them without seeing them.

"I'll go and see Eliot," Wilberforce said when the quiet had stretched out a little too long.

Pitt blinked, coming back. "I'm sorry. Yes, please do. I'll think about it while you're gone." He smiled wryly. "Slowly. I did warn you."

Eliot, as Pitt had also warned him, was in a miserable state, although he did seem genuinely pleased to see Wilberforce. He was out of bed, but only just: the covers were in a mess, as was Eliot's fine ginger hair, and his nightshirt hung rumpled about his slender frame. His eyelashes quivered with unshed tears. It wrenched Wilberforce's heart, as Pitt's quieter grief downstairs had. He couldn't help but think that it wasn't fair.

"I know," Eliot sighed when Wilberforce carefully brought up the topic of his daughter. "I'm failing her. I just—I don't have any feelings left anymore, for anything."

"You will," Wilberforce said. He meant it, but he felt the inadequacy of the words keenly. "It will get easier."

"But what do I do *now*? You tell me, Wilber: How am I supposed to live now? Oh, I know I have things to live for. My daughter, my friends, helping you abolish the slave trade, helping Pitt run the country...Those are all important things. But how am I supposed to...physically live through them? How am I supposed to bear her absence, every day, with only the promise—or the threat—that I will one day forget her?"

Wilberforce shook his head, hating his own helplessness. "I suppose by holding to the knowledge that Harriot is with God, waiting for you, and that everything, however painful, is part of a much larger plan for us all. And that the God who planned it loves us all very much and would never test us with something we can't, in the end, endure."

"Do you actually believe that?" It wasn't an incredulous question, or a scornful one; he genuinely wanted to know.

"Oh yes," Wilberforce said. That, at least, he could answer. "I do."

It was late when Wilberforce came downstairs; he was weary himself by then, and the old knife wound twinged at each step. Pitt was sitting by the fire, where he had left him. His eyes, still directed at the flames, had the misleadingly vague look that indicated serious thought.

"Eliot's a little better," Wilberforce said, sitting down opposite. "He's eaten something. We had a good talk, and he's going off to sleep now."

"Excellent," Pitt said, slightly absently. "Thank you. I don't think he's slept all week. What did you talk to him about?"

"Religion."

"I see. Well, that would put anybody to sleep." He caught himself at once; his head snapped up. "Dear God, I'm sorry. I didn't mean that."

"Yes, you did," Wilberforce said. It might have stung at another time; in the wake of his talk with Eliot, he felt perfectly at peace, and only a little sad. "It's all right."

"No, it isn't. I wasn't thinking."

"I know." It was very rare for Pitt to hurt anyone, outside the pitched battles of the House of Commoners. Wilberforce was the one whose emotions could carry him away. Pitt's temper and wit were usually perfectly within his own control. "You're tired, and you're grieving. It really is all right. And I know you don't understand."

"If I don't understand your beliefs," Pitt said, "I understand your feelings completely. There are things that matter to me as well. I don't like people to sneer at them."

"I know," Wilberforce repeated. "Honor, duty, country. Balance sheets." He said the last with a twinkle and, to his satisfaction, was rewarded with a soft laugh.

"Well," Pitt said, "you can sneer at balance sheets a little. But not exceptionally well-balanced ones. I really do apologize."

"And I really do forgive you." He smiled. "We evangelists are very good at forgiveness."

"Oh, do shut up."

They sat for a while in silence—companionable silence that felt very restful after the constant stream of communication Wilberforce had maintained with poor Eliot. He suspected, looking at Pitt, that his friend was working something through in his mind, and as usual he was prepared to wait for it. The firelight danced, and he stifled a yawn. He'd had a long journey that day.

"I'm sorry," Pitt said abruptly, "but I've been turning it over, and it makes no sense. Clarkson was not an alchemist when I met him. It was already very unusual for his magic to awaken so late in life. And now the Knights Templar are saying that he has *some* abilities, but not the extent required; and yet when I spoke to him outside Parliament that night, the extent of them was exactly what I noticed. By your account, it's as if his magic was awoken, used, and put almost but not entirely back to sleep. That's more than unusual, it's impossible. Inheritances don't work that way."

Wilberforce took a moment to wrench his thoughts to the problem. "But what does?"

"I don't know. Some kind of dark magic, I would assume, but if so, it didn't come from Clarkson. You can't, with no magic, work a spell to give you magic."

"Which means," Wilberforce said, "that it came from somebody else. Somebody, perhaps, whom he met in France, at the time the Bastille fell."

"It's very likely. Whatever it was, I think I need to talk to Clarkson again, in private. I'd be very grateful if you'd accompany me."

"I'd be very happy to," Wilberforce said, and meant it. He had been wanting to look in on Clarkson, and he was immensely relieved to see Pitt coming back to himself. "When?"

"Now? Would that be convenient?" Pitt was already standing. "I'd like to deal with this as soon as I can—and, I have to admit, I really do need to get out of this house. I realize it's late."

"No matter—I don't have any other appointments tonight. But the Templars already questioned him, you know. He couldn't lie—not under mesmerism."

"He couldn't," Pitt agreed. "But they may not have been asking the right questions."

* * *

By the time Wilberforce and Pitt got out of the carriage and instructed the driver to wait for them, it was almost ten o'clock, and the Tower of London stood like a pale monolith against the cold night sky. Clarkson had obviously been told that he had visitors, because he was standing in the center of his cell, waiting to receive them, when the Templar unlocked the door and opened it for them. He was dressed, but barely, and he was rumpled and bleary-eyed with sleep. His hair had grown longer and more grizzled and now hung loose about his face.

"There'll be a guard outside," the Templar told them. "He won't be able to hear what you're saying, but if you knock on the door, he'll let you out."

"Really?" Clarkson said. "Is that a promise?"

"Provided the prisoner is standing well back from the door, of course," the Templar added, without looking at Clarkson. He might have been hiding a smile. It was difficult to tell in the light.

"Thank you," Pitt said to him, and the Templar inclined his head and left.

Clarkson turned to them as the door closed. "Wilberforce," he said. There was an understandable note of curiosity in his voice. "Mr. Pitt."

"Clarkson," Wilberforce returned, a little apologetically. "How are you?"

"Quite well, considering," Clarkson said, dryly. "This is an unexpected honor."

"We have something very important to ask you," Pitt said.

"Are we disturbing you?" Wilberforce asked. "We could perhaps come back at a more convenient time."

"Exactly how full a calendar do you think I have?" Clarkson reminded him, with a wry glance at the cell about him. "I suppose if *you* were confined to the Tower of London, you would have regular dinner parties and guests staying over all the time, but in my case...Not at this time of night, no. I am not otherwise engaged." He gestured, with some irony, at the wooden table and chairs. "Well. Do sit down."

Wilberforce had been a regular visitor to Clarkson's cell during the months of his imprisonment, as had many of the major abolitionists: it had been difficult to gain access at first, but they had persisted, and the Knights Templar had gradually become more lenient. As cells in the Tower of London went, it was fairly comfortable. Unlike poor John Terrell, who had lived in poverty and therefore filth and deprivation, Clarkson had both a little money and a good deal of sympathetic friends to ensure that he was provided with clean bedding, decent food, clothing, furnishings, and perhaps most important in Clarkson's eyes, books and writing materials. His work for abolition had suffered from his inability to travel, but he had been no less tireless in the pursuit of it. He seemed to have eyes, feet, and voices in most of the major ports in the country, and what they brought him quickly evolved into passionate diatribes against the trade and pleas for its victims that, equally quickly, found their way into bookstalls all over England. Among many of the abolitionists, Clarkson's so-called crime had raised him to heroic status; even those who disapproved of him could not deny his commitment. Clarkson was too brilliant a writer and speaker to be confined by mere prison walls.

Still, those same prison walls couldn't be ignored entirely, especially as the days grew colder and shorter. The cell was chilly and damp in the autumn night, and there was scant light from the one window even by day.

"You may as well have something to drink," Clarkson said. "As I said, I don't have a good many visitors to share with. Some kindly soul who admires my pamphlets keeps sending me bottles of Madeira. I'm not sure why—they could only have a detrimental effect on the pamphlets. Perhaps they're trying to give me the chance to drink myself to death."

"You know there's still a chance of your sentence being shortened or overturned," Wilberforce reminded him, "if we push through the magic reforms we've been aiming for."

"Yes," Clarkson agreed, with what could almost have been fondness. "If you do that. Well, you'd better hurry. I only have fifty-six and a half years left as it is."

He gave Pitt a less-than-friendly look as he spoke. In theory, he accepted that Pitt had had no choice but to hand him over to the Knights Templar, given the situation with France; in practice, there was a certain coolness in his attitude toward the prime minister.

"So," Clarkson said as he sat down and picked up his glass. He didn't drink, but looked at them cautiously from over the rim. "How can I help you gentlemen? I'm assuming this isn't a social call?"

"You assume correctly," Pitt said.

Clarkson nodded, his heavy-lidded eyes veiled. "Then I assume it touches on abolition?"

"It does," Pitt said. He sat forward. "This *is* an unsociable hour, I agree, so I'll come straight to the point despite the reproachful looks Wilberforce is shooting at me. I think we'd both prefer it. Mr. Clarkson, we have reason to believe that you met someone when you were in France—someone, moreover, capable of enhancing your latent magic into something powerful enough to start a revolution. We suspect you made a deal with this person. If you care at all about your cause, please tell us what it was."

They hadn't discussed the possibility that Clarkson had made a deal with someone, not openly. But it was, Wilberforce knew, what he himself had been dreading. He should have realized it had occurred to Pitt also.

Clarkson looked at them, his eyes widening, and Wilberforce's heart sank. There was no comforting bewilderment in that gaze, only fear and surprise. If he had actually said "How did you know?" he could not have said it any plainer.

"Please, Clarkson," Wilberforce said, adding his gentler voice to Pitt's. "It could be extremely important."

"Don't talk to me as if I were a child, Wilberforce. What makes you think I made any kind of deal?"

"The way you reacted when Pitt said you had," Wilberforce said honestly.

Anger flickered into Clarkson's eyes then. "And by what right does Pitt accuse me? He's already had me committed to this place for the rest of my natural life. I haven't seen any sign of him concerning himself about the fates of the slaves since I've been in here."

"He does!" Wilberforce protested. "I've told you many times."

"I do," Pitt agreed, more calmly, "but that doesn't matter. *You* care about their fates. And we're afraid you might have done something to jeopardize them. If it matters to you, you may also have jeopardized the country."

"I certainly haven't!" Clarkson denied hotly. "You don't know what you're talking about."

"No, he doesn't," Wilberforce agreed, before Pitt could reply. "Neither of us do, and it's very important that we do. Please."

Clarkson seemed about to argue back but stopped just in time. "You say it's important to abolition?"

Wilberforce nodded vigorously.

Clarkson hesitated a little longer, then shrugged elaborately and took a drink from his glass. "I suppose it doesn't matter really." He ran a hand through his prematurely graying hair, sweeping it away from his face. "It's done now. You can't stop the rebellion in Saint-Domingue. And the Templars can hardly put me in *more* prison."

They waited.

"It was the first time I went to Paris," Clarkson said. "July '89."

"When the Revolution broke out?" Wilberforce said.

"Exactly." He smiled a little. "I wish I could tell you what it was like. The life of it! It was a riot of noise and colors and ideas and liberty—you only had to go out on the streets to feel drunk with it. And there was hope too—the kind we'd just had beaten out of us in the House of Commoners. Real hope that anything was possible and that the world could change for the better. You would have loved it, Wilberforce."

Wilberforce smiled faintly himself. "I think you overestimate my bravery."

"That was when he came to me," Clarkson said. "Right in the middle of all that passion and idealism. I actually thought at the time he might have been one of the illegal magicians released from the Bastille, but I suppose he couldn't have been. If the Knights Templar had ever found him, they wouldn't have stopped at locking him up."

"He came to you?" Wilberforce said. "You mean he approached you, in person?"

"No," said Clarkson thoughtfully. He frowned. "No, now you mention it, he didn't exactly do that. And yet I saw him. I was asleep, but it wasn't a dream. I was standing on the streets of Paris, and he was standing before me. There was a mist over the cobbles, but a wind was blowing, and it brought with it the smell of blood and a sound like a battle a long way off. And then he came."

"Who?" Wilberforce asked.

"He never told me," Clarkson said. "But he knew who I was, and he knew of our recent defeat in the House of Commoners. He told me he wanted the slaves liberated as well. He asked for my assistance."

"What kind of assistance?"

"He wanted my help in sabotaging the factory in Paris. As I said, he knew who I was. He told me there was a latent strain of alchemy in my blood, and he could ignite it. He needed me to alter the alchemical magic in the compound, smuggle it into the factory, and send it out on the way to the Caribbean."

"And you agreed?"

"Of course I agreed!" Clarkson retorted, with just an edge of defensiveness. "I knew the situation on Saint-Domingue; there isn't a lot I don't know about the trade in human souls. Hundreds of thousands of people locked in their own minds as their bodies sickened and wore out. Most of them brought in from Africa don't survive beyond two years; those who do are regularly beaten, tortured, and humiliated with cruelty shocking even by the usual standards of slavery. Of course I was going to agree. It was an opportunity to free them."

"That's what we were doing in Parliament," Wilberforce pointed out, though without much heart. "We're still doing it."

"Without success," Clarkson said bitterly. "We may never succeed. And even if we do, what good would it be for those already enslaved? We're only aiming at the slave trade, not the practice of slavery itself.

That's another battle, and I doubt any of us will live to see it. Those individuals were suffering at that very moment, and this was their only hope. But we've been through this. You know my feelings on the subject, and I know yours. Whether it was a mistake or not, I did what I did. A good many people are dead because of it, and a good many people are free."

"I know." They had, indeed, been through it all before. Sometimes, in his more hopeless moments, he even believed that Clarkson was right.

"It took me over a year to perfect the magic," Clarkson said, "even though he told me what to do. I knew I had a latent thread of alchemy in my blood—the Templars had noted it at birth, though it had never been awakened. Even when it was, it wasn't anything special on its own. If I'd been an Aristocrat, I probably could have been schooled to use it to the point where I could transmute fairly basic compounds by formula. Little more than mundane chemistry, really. But the visitor did far more than simply awaken my magic. He reached into my blood and set my magic on fire. When I worked, using the samples of the compound I had, I could feel him in my mind, and at once I could see every atom. With a touch, I could shape it, change it—I could even reverse it, so that it became its own antidote."

"That compound's meant to be unchangeable," Wilberforce said. "They lock it in place."

"It almost was. As I said, it took over a year of practice, every night, every minute I could snatch from my other work. I was constantly exhausted, and my health started to break down over the last few months, but I kept at it. And then, one night, the compound shifted under my fingers, and it became what I wanted it to become. It took a few more weeks to arrange a visit to the factory in Paris where the alchemy is made. When I did, though, the opportunity was easy to find. The compound was already crated, waiting to be sealed and shipped out. I reached inside one of the crates, and I changed the whole shipment in one burst of magic. The compound became a formula to break the spellbinding."

"The whole shipment?" Wilberforce's eyebrows shot up. "That should have killed you."

"It almost did. But I told you, I had help. It was like a wave rippling from my fingertips. My only worry was that the elements making up the crates would change under it as well."

He spoke carelessly, but Wilberforce remembered how white and haggard he had been after that visit. He and Thornton had remarked on it sympathetically to each other. How could they not have done anything more? "Are you still in contact with him? I mean—"

"I know who you mean. No. The visitor withdrew from me when I was convicted, and took his power with him. I have only my own very weak alchemical abilities now. I suppose he had no further use for me. I couldn't help you to find him, if that's what you mean. I never even saw his face."

"And that was all it wanted?" Pitt said. It was the first time he had spoken in a while. "Your help for Saint-Domingue?"

"He asked me to free slaves," Clarkson repeated. "What would you have done?"

"Did you know what it was? The figure who came to you. What was it?"

Clarkson looked at him. "He never said."

"But you knew."

"How could I?"

"Don't lie to us, Clarkson," Pitt said, and Wilberforce glanced at him with alarm. His voice was very low and quiet, and his eyes were blazing. Mesmerism was supposed to be impossible to detect except by those who had made long study of it. Wilberforce had made no such study of magic, but he had made a study of Pitt over several years, and he knew what he was seeing.

Clarkson couldn't have known he was being mesmerized, but Wilberforce saw him swallow hard as he struggled against it instinctively. "You have no right to ask me. It isn't your cause."

"It's my country," Pitt said. Magic crackled in the air around him;

Wilberforce, next to him, felt it like a heat wave. "And you will tell me what you've done to it."

"Pitt," Wilberforce warned softly.

For a second, Pitt's eyes remained fixed on Clarkson. Then, all at once, Wilberforce's voice reached him. He glanced away, both mesmeric fire and fury draining so swiftly from his face that he seemed to lose all color, and caught his breath with a shudder that only Wilberforce heard.

"Excuse me," he said, without looking at either of them, and he stood and left the cell. The door opened for him from the outside, then closed again with a dull thud.

Wilberforce's first impulse was to follow him, but he turned to Clarkson instead. The abolitionist looked understandably shaken.

"Is he right?" Wilberforce asked. "Did you know?"

Clarkson hesitated, then shrugged. "It was a blood magician." He rubbed his eyes tiredly. "A vampire. Yes, I knew."

The world rang dizzyingly in Wilberforce's ears. When he breathed again, it had settled into something unfamiliar and strange.

"How?" he managed, at last. "How did you know?"

"What else could have felt the magic in my blood? Of course it was a vampire. I didn't care. Blood magic. It's an Inheritance like any other."

"It isn't." It was what Pitt had been trying to tell him for years. He realized that when he contradicted his friend, he hadn't been honest. "It requires human sacrifice."

"So does slavery!" Clarkson retorted. "A lot of it. I want those slaves freed. I always have. That's all I want. If a vampire is an enemy to the slave trade, there's no difference in my mind between that vampire and yourself."

"You can't believe that. You're one of the most principled people I know."

"Yes. And I was willing to sacrifice my honor and my principles for the lives of hundreds of thousands—more than willing. For all the praise and all the blame they heap on your head, Wilberforce, you can't say the same."

"No." Wilberforce felt very tired suddenly. "No, I can't."

Outside the Tower gates, the night sky had clouded over; a chill mist rose from the Thames, and the lights burning across the river from the South Bank were cloaked in fog. The street was very quiet. At first, Wilberforce was afraid that Pitt had already left, but he quickly caught sight of him, standing a little way off beside one of the trees that overhung the river.

"Wilberforce," Pitt greeted him without turning around, which Wilberforce thought was probably a bad sign. At any rate, he couldn't have done it without senses that were very enhanced.

"Good evening," Wilberforce replied as cheerfully as he could, drawing nearer. Up close, his friend's tall, angular frame was unnaturally still even for him. "Or morning, rather, I suppose...Are you well?"

"Perfectly," Pitt replied, in something that was almost his usual voice but too tight. He took a deep breath. "Could you just...talk to me for a moment, please?"

"What should I talk about?"

"Anything. Anything human and ordinary."

"Ordinary." Wilberforce thought frantically. "You already know about the new house out at Clapham, don't you?"

"It doesn't matter. Tell me about it."

"Thornton has his heart set on inviting as many as possible of the evangelicals and abolitionists to join us out at Clapham. I wrote to him about the school Hannah More and I set up, with her education and my income, and it's made him even more excited. He thinks that so many of us working together, using our skills and ideas and strengths—who knows what good we might be able to do? Macaulay's coming, and I just spoke to Hannah More about her buying a house out there as well. Thornton still loves showing complete strangers around the library you designed for him, by the way. He tells them all that he was so lost as to what to do with the space, the prime minister of Great Britain had to kindly step in and help him."

"That's very tactful of him," Pitt said, in something far more like his usual voice. "I think I actually just dropped so many wistful hints about libraries that he took pity on me." He shivered, just once, and relaxed. "Thank you. When does everybody plan to move in? Do you know yet?"

"What happened in there?"

For a moment Pitt looked as if he wouldn't answer. Then he sighed. "I made a mistake. I haven't done that in a very long time. I won't do it again."

Wilberforce wasn't quite sure what to say. "It was understandable, just this once. We needed him to talk to us."

"Understandable," he conceded. "But unforgivable. Thank you for intervening, and please stop me if you ever see anything like that again. I sometimes think 'just this once' is the most dangerous phrase in the English language."

"I promise to stop you. But I think you're rather hard on yourself. You've just lost Harriot, and I know you're very worried about France, whatever you say. Magic is almost impossible to control when feelings run high."

"That makes it rather worse. I'm the head of the British government. I can't very well go about unleashing dark magic every time I'm less than composed about something. Did Clarkson tell you anything more?"

Wilberforce accepted the change in subject without comment. "You were right," he said. "He knew what spoke to him. It was a vampire."

Pitt nodded without surprise.

"You already knew, didn't you?"

"Not before we came—I had no idea that vampires could awaken bloodlines, only sense them. I knew when Clarkson described the way it came to him. It's called nightwalking. It's a vampiric manifestation.

They can converse with other minds while they sleep—sometimes only with words, sometimes with images as well."

Despite everything, Wilberforce felt a flash of interest. "Can they really? Have you ever done it?"

Pitt smiled. "No. I've only read about it."

"That's a shame. It sounds fascinating."

"That's because you object to abandoning conversations occasionally in order to sleep."

"I do so only *very* occasionally. It's very late now, and we're still conversing." He grew more serious. "So a vampire has been born in France and somehow escaped the Knights Templar. I suppose there's no reason why that shouldn't happen. It happened here with you."

"This one seems to have a stronger strain than I do. Or possibly he's just more diligent about learning how to use it. This *does* cast a new light on one thing."

"The undead." Wilberforce had thought of it too. "Necromancers used to raise the undead for the vampire kings, hundreds of years ago. The knowledge of how to do so died with those kings. It can't be a coincidence that an undead has appeared at the same time as a practicing blood magician. And it also helps explain why King George's magic turned in on itself so violently when the undead was created."

"An aspiring vampire king employing that kind of magic in France would certainly constitute a supernatural threat against Britain—the kind a mage-king's powers are said to respond to. I know that's viewed as superstition these days. But it's been a very long time since there's been cause to test it."

"Not since the end of the Vampire Wars." Wilberforce hesitated. "We've assumed this is a vampire with a bloodline like yours, who manifested recently. There is another possibility. Full-blooded vampires are more or less immortal. In theory, if a vampire survived the Templars' massacre, and he is killing to survive, he could have lived a long time."

"It's possible. I just can't believe anybody survived that massacre.

The Templars were very thorough. They recorded each death—all the noble vampire families were accounted for. And if one of them somehow escaped and has been in hiding for over three hundred years, it seems strange he should reveal himself now." He shook his head. "It's possible. Either way, we need to deal with it."

Wilberforce wasn't entirely satisfied with that answer, but he let it go for now. "Can we warn the new French Republic of Magicians?"

"I doubt they would give any credence to it. At the best of times, it would be the hearsay of an English prisoner, probably calculated to deflect responsibility for his crime. At the moment, I doubt they would trust me to tell them that the sky is blue."

"Well, it isn't. It's gray."

"*You* don't trust me to tell you that the sky is blue. For your information, the *clouds* are gray. The sky is blue somewhere behind them. Or will be, when the sun comes up."

"There's probably a metaphor in there."

"I certainly hope not. The weather-mages have predicted rain and cloud for the foreseeable future. I deny your metaphor. And the French, by the way, are going to deny any vampiric involvement in Saint-Domingue. They've just changed governments. I hope that this new one will be less aggressive than the old, but everything points to the opposite. They are not interested in assigning blame for Saint-Domingue to anybody but us. More important, anything too overt would warn the vampire that we know about it. It will go deeper into hiding. We might never find it."

"In short, then, we need to find him ourselves. But he will be well hidden."

"If it can nightwalk, it could have been thousands of miles from Clarkson while it spoke to him. Probably in France, though. Vampires tend to stay within their territories."

"Is that why you've been promising to come spend the summer in the Lake District with me for years, but never seem to get any further than Bath?"

That finally surprised a laugh from him. "No, that's because I've been unfeasibly busy for the past ten years. I don't have a territory."

"It might not agree with you on that." The thought had come to him, unbidden and unwelcome. "Pitt. Is there any chance it knows about you? What you are, I mean?"

"I have no idea," Pitt said. "I suppose it might. Whether it cares is another question. I'm hardly a threat to it, on a supernatural level."

"But you could be, under different circumstances. And it may not be willing to risk that you won't be. That first shadow, the one in Rheims—you said it was looking right at you."

"Possibly," Pitt said, cautiously. "Though it was only a shadow, such as anyone might have summoned. The undead that stabbed you was almost certainly sent by our enemy—vampires have always been linked with the undead. But that didn't appear until later. Nothing very much happened in '83."

"Quite a lot happened in '83. You became prime minister of Great Britain. And immediately before that, you came to France. You came into its territory. And it saw you."

"This isn't about me visiting France in '83," Pitt said, rather too firmly. "It can't be."

"Why not? Isn't that how vampire territorial wars have always begun? With an infringement, and a challenge?"

"I didn't issue any challenge."

"No. But perhaps it's issued one to you."

"There haven't been any vampire territorial wars for hundreds of years."

"There haven't been any *vampires* for hundreds of years. They were wiped from the face of the earth, and any subsequent aberrations were killed at birth. Now this one's appeared. And at the same time, so have you. I know you're not a pure vampire," he added quickly, before Pitt could protest. "I know you're not a practicing blood magician. I know you don't see yourself, or this country, that way. I'm just suggesting we keep it in mind as a possibility."

"I'm not sure I want that possibility in my mind. I want to be able to sleep sometime in the rest of my life." He shook his head. "I'll see what records the Knights Templar have of any vampire bloodlines left in France. My bloodline's on record, after all—perhaps we'll find where this one might have emerged."

"We didn't have any such luck finding the necromancer."

"For now, it's all we have. We need for it to make a mistake, or we need to look for one that it's already made."

"What if it hasn't made one?"

"Everyone makes mistakes."

It was a hopeful statement, in context. But the night was very dark, and applied to other things, it didn't sound so very hopeful.

"The new house out at Clapham," Wilberforce heard himself say. "That's one thing I talked to Eliot about tonight. He wants to move out of Downing Street and come and live out there with us, with his new daughter. To convert, I suppose you would call it. He thinks—well, he thinks it might help."

Pitt, understandably, took a moment to work out what on earth Wilberforce was talking about. "I see. Well. That explains why you were discussing religious consolation, I suppose."

"I hope you don't mind."

"Why would I mind?"

He didn't know, really, except that Downing Street had seemed such a poisonous labyrinth that evening, and he didn't like to think of his friend being drawn deeper into the middle of it alone. Except, perhaps, that since he had found God, it seemed that he, and now Eliot, were being drawn somewhere else entirely, and he knew that it was one place Pitt had no idea how to follow them to. Except that he was afraid.

"I don't know," he said instead. "I suppose you wouldn't... May I ask you something?"

"Of course. Anything."

"In there... If you had done what you did to Clarkson in the House on the day of one of the abolition debates..."

"Could I have forced the House to vote our way?" Pitt didn't seem surprised at the question. "Yes."

"You know that for certain?"

"For certain, no. I've never done anything of the kind. But in theory. It would be a considerable strain on the elixir, of course; a true vampire fueled by human blood could control entire countries, but I'm neither. I'm still not feeling very well from those few seconds of mesmerism with Clarkson, to be honest. Even so—what was our margin last time? Seventy-five?"

"Exactly. If you were to influence, perhaps, eighty people..."

"I could do it."

"Really?"

"Really." He paused. "Are you asking me to?"

"No," Wilberforce said. He hated himself for the brief second's hesitation that preceded it. "Of course not. No. That would be wrong."

"Would it?"

"Of course it would. You can't force your will on another human soul, without their consent. It's not how government works. It's not how free will works."

"And so the cost of free will is thousands suffering and dying?" It was difficult to tell how bitterly that question was intended: the tone seemed merely curious.

"Always," Wilberforce answered. "Since the fall of man. You can't be held responsible for that."

"Only since the fall of man." A trace of amusement crept in. "Tell me, is it comforting to have such a wide view of things?"

"Of course it's not comforting. It's absolutely terrifying. If you find it comforting to see the entire world as a battle between good and evil, with every action you take reverberating through time like ripples in a pond, then you are clearly doing something very wrong. Except every once in a while, then it is, yes." He hesitated. "What would you have done if I had said yes? If I had asked you to do it?"

Pitt smiled. "You never would."

* * *

Wilberforce went to the Temple Church himself the following day. Frederick Holt had finished his service in the Tower of London—he was a research cleric now, mostly working on the projects of higher Templars like Forester. He sighed when he saw who was waiting for him. "Oh no."

"Frederick," Wilberforce greeted him, undaunted. "It's wonderful to see you too. How are you? Has your cat had her kittens yet?"

Holt had to smile reluctantly. "Last week, as it happens, thank you for asking. Three tabbies and one black, all well. If this is about Clarkson, Wilber, I really can tell you no more. His bloodlines are the least of our troubles now—and you're under investigation yourself, after what you and the More sisters began in Mendip."

"If you mean the school, there's no law against Commoners being educated in anything—including magic, as long as they don't practice, and your bracelets see to that. And I haven't come about Clarkson. I wanted to know if there were any records of vampire bloodlines left in France."

His school friend looked startled but recovered remarkably quickly. Anyone who dealt with Wilberforce was used to how wide-ranging and eclectic his interests could be. "Well, to begin with, there are few records of any kind from France anymore. They were destroyed with the Bastille, or not long after. But I can almost promise there were none to start with. The Templars in France were even more thorough than here. I don't think they've ever had a child test for blood magic after the war. You don't intend to start campaigning for the rights of the illegal magics, do you? It isn't worth it. Particularly not in the case of blood magicians. There are almost none left, and they'd die in any case unless you want to murder to keep them alive."

Wilberforce held back from mentioning the elixir. It wouldn't help, and it risked betraying Pitt. The vampire strain in that bloodline was no secret, nor was Pitt's friendship with Wilberforce. "Not at the moment. But you must have older records from France? Records that were copied into the books before they were destroyed?"

"Perhaps. They'll be old, though—and they won't tell you anything important."

They probably wouldn't, it was true. But it would be a place to start. "Thank you so much. I really do appreciate it."

"I haven't promised to look them up for you yet," Holt protested, then smiled ruefully. "But I will. Just don't ask me for anything else. I mean it, Wilber—you really do need to be careful these days. The Temple Church are very nervous about your kind—reformers. They're afraid of what happened to us in France."

"So am I, believe it or not," Wilberforce said. "And I'm very much afraid that the Temple Church are the least of my concerns."

Paris

Winter 1792–1793

Robespierre was very pleased that Charlotte and Augustin had come to Paris, of course, but it did present difficulties. The Duplays assured him that his siblings were welcome to come and live with them; though there were no more upstairs bedrooms, they cleared two rooms for them on the ground floor. (For Brount, they found a basket, and he ignored it entirely and slept at the foot of Robespierre's bed.) Augustin was perfectly happy with this arrangement; he got on well with the family and was too excited to be in Paris to question particulars. Charlotte, however, did not approve of the Duplays. Robespierre had enough good sense to realize that she was jealous of the place they had gained in his heart and his life, but not enough to know what to do about it.

"It's not good for your reputation," she said as he sat at his desk writing out notes for the Convention that night. "Living with a carpenter's family. You should have your own lodgings, in a better part of the city."

"If I notice my reputation start to suffer," he said, "then I'll consider it. I promise."

"You won't notice. You never do. They're using you, you know. They clearly gain by association with you. And I'm sure Madame Duplay intends for you to marry her eldest daughter."

"What would be wrong with that?" he said, as carelessly as he could. He and Éléonore had found the time to go for a long walk that day through the Champ de Mars, and he was sure that Charlotte had noticed. "Perhaps I intend to marry her as well. It's absurd to think about it now, though. I'm far too busy."

"Everyone will say she's your mistress. I'm sure they do already."

He knew they did. She wasn't, in fact, though she would often come up to his rooms to talk to him, as did Babette, but in Éléonore's case there was something in her friendship other than strictly sisterly. It hung between them like a promise, or a door; a word or look from him would unlock it, but until then she seemed content to leave it closed. Robespierre himself wasn't sure how he felt about it. He was very fond of Éléonore, and when he had time to think about it, he liked the idea of marrying her. Charlotte was quite right that Madame Duplay undoubtedly intended it. But he could never be sure how much of his feelings were for Éléonore herself, and how much were for her family. He had lost his own parents very young, and while he loved his siblings, the Duplays' uncomplicated warmth filled a hunger in him he had never realized was so deep and so aching. Éléonore was something between a sister and a lover to him, just as Maurice and Madame Duplay were something between parents and friends. He couldn't help but wish he didn't have to work it out—especially when Charlotte was going to be so difficult about it.

"If she and her family have no objections to the rumors," he said, "then neither do I. Nobody with half a brain would believe them. How could I take Éléonore as my mistress under her family's roof, with her parents asleep in the next room?"

"They wouldn't mind! This is Paris."

"Charlotte, please, I'm sorry you're upset, we'll talk about it later, but I really do need to work now. I have to say this to a hall of people in an hour or so."

She sighed. "They make too much of a fuss of you, Maxime."

It took him a moment to realize she was waiting for a response. "Who do?"

"The Duplays. It's my fault, I know. I made too much of a fuss of you back in Arras. You became too used to it. But it's not good for you. If you don't watch out, you're going to become horribly conceited."

She left with a flourish before he could work out if she truly expected him to be motivated to leave a family that loved him for the promise of being more roughly treated by his own.

Those were domestic battles. The battles in the Convention were far more serious.

The political landscape of the National Convention of the Republic of Magicians was a landscape in more than one sense. The Mountain, Robespierre and Danton's faction, sat at the high end of the benches. They were far from a united party. Robespierre's supporters and Danton's were really two separate groups, Robespierre's having followed him from the Jacobins and Danton's from his own club; this, for now, mattered very little, while their plans accorded so well and any allegiance to one or the other was purely personal. More troubling to Robespierre were the undesirable elements of the Mountain, those who gave their party a rather disreputable edge: Jean-Paul Marat, a druid strikingly disfigured by a curse that had gone awry, whose aggressive rhetoric chilled the blood of the most hardened Republicans; and Jacques Hébert, a fire-mage whose pamphlets were written in the language of the street and called for violence in the filthiest terms. Yet they were all loosely held together by their opposition to the war with Austria, their Republican fervor, and their determination to see the king dead. They were also overwhelmingly Commoner magicians; perhaps Camille's presence saw to that. The exceptions, or so the public believed, were the Mountain's two strongest speakers, Danton and Robespierre. In Robespierre's case, of course, they were misled.

Across the room were Brissot's supporters, the Girondins. They supported the war with Austria and had nearly all opposed the total freedom of magic that had won the day; even now, while they supported many of the same reforms as the Mountain, they sought to limit the magicians' legal rights. They were also suspected of being sympathetic to the king, or at least not actively intent on his death. All these things, according to the Mountain, made them the enemy.

Between the two groups, uneasy and perpetually undecided, lay the Plains. They, according to Robespierre's benefactor, did not really matter. Robespierre kept an eye on them all the same.

The Convention met every afternoon, to debate the issues of the ever-shifting political situation, rule on policy, and discuss the war currently raging on the borders between France and the Low Countries. At least, that was the theory. In practice, they tended to spend most of the time fighting with each other. Most of these fights were verbal, punctuated here and there by outbursts of magic from the Mountain that inflamed the Girondins further. Politics had become a lot more dangerous since the early days of the Revolution. Every so often, the conflicts would escalate into physical brawls: low-level magic and fisticuffs, mostly, but once or twice there had been flashes of knives and pistol shots discharged into the air. Camille, in the middle of a particularly provoking oration, had been unceremoniously decked across the room by one of the Girondins; he had sent a few flames in their direction at other times himself. At times, Robespierre had to admit, having Danton's powerful presence on their side felt less a political advantage and more like having the friendship of a school athlete when crossing a playground populated by bullies. The public crowded into the stands to watch and cheer in delight at each burst of violence, which gave the new Republic the frisson of a Roman arena.

In November, they met to decide the fate of the king of France.

It was the first time Robespierre had been seen in the Convention for a month. His benefactor's support had returned to him wholeheartedly since the rise of the Republic, with the consequence that the mesmerism pouring from him had been almost too much to bear. It was like holding a burning coal in his chest. After weeks straight of it, he had started to find it difficult to breathe; finally, after one marathon session, he was so chilled and so weak that he had been forced to curl up in bed and stay there. It had frustrated him at the time, not least because Charlotte had taken advantage of his weakness to move him from the Duplays' to a house of their own. Yet the reception he received now almost made him feel it had been worth staying away. His supporters rushed to cheer him, but it was in some ways more gratifying to watch his enemies' looks of loathing and fear.

"You're quite certain you're ready for this?" Camille asked as Robespierre took a seat beside him.

"Certainly," Robespierre said. "I feel much better."

"I didn't mean that—you look rather pale, but you always do. I mean the king. Are you truly ready to push for his immediate death without trial? It's only that I used to talk about hanging Aristocrats from lampposts and tearing out their entrails, and you used to say, 'Stop it, Camille, were you raised in a barn?' "

"I'm truly ready. It isn't murder if we do it in the name of liberty."

"It certainly is," Camille said. "I don't see the point of calling it anything else. If you can't face the thought of murder, then you have no business calling for bloody revolution."

The thought was disquieting. He was afraid it might be true and yet felt it couldn't be. "You didn't come to visit me in the last few weeks," he said, mostly to change the subject. He tried to keep it from sounding like a rebuke.

"I know. I'm sorry—we were busy. Honestly, Maxime, your sister doesn't want me there. She keeps looking at me like she thinks I should brush my hair."

"In fairness," Danton said, turning in his seat, "that's neither a hanging offense nor a minority opinion."

"I've moved back to the Duplays' now," Robespierre said. "They've insisted on it."

"No wonder you're feeling better," Camille said.

Robespierre smiled, but couldn't shake his growing sense of disquiet. He wasn't at all certain that he was ready to face any kind of murder.

Don't you dare falter now. The voice made him jump: it was only the second time he had heard it in his waking ear.

Fortunately, it was on that day that Antoine Saint-Just delivered his maiden speech. Robespierre had met the twenty-five-year-old in person only recently, but the two of them had been corresponding for years; he had written to Robespierre to introduce himself as he embarked on a career in politics. Something about the young man had interested him, quite apart from his flattering reverence for Robespierre himself. At the time, he had just been released from prison, not for magic or any revolutionary activity but for stealing from his own mother. While in prison he had made his name by writing a long, obscene poem and dedicating it to the Temple Church. And yet there had been no hint of this disreputable background in his address or his ideas, in that letter or since. It was as though he had come through the Revolution a new man, with his misdeeds melted away and only a hard, intelligent core remaining. Still, Robespierre and the Convention were not prepared for the effect of his speech. He was strikingly handsome, dark-haired and marble-faced; his voice had a clear ring that reminded Robespierre of Camille on the day the Bastille fell. He was a shadowmancer like Camille, for that matter; whether by accident or intent, the shadows of the room danced around him in patches of gray as he spoke. But he had none of Camille's fire in his magic or in his manner. He was pure ice, and yet he burned just the same.

"I say that the king must be judged as an enemy," he said, "that we must not judge him so much as combat him. For myself, I can see no compromise: this man must reign or die. *No one can reign innocently.*"

There was an intake of breath at the last. It seemed that in the midst of so much confusion and doubt, someone had found some elemental truth that outweighed all other considerations. Robespierre's head cleared suddenly, unexpectedly. At once, he could see his France again. Saint-Just could see it too.

("God, did you see him after that speech?" Camille snorted as the two of them sat together later at the Jacobins. "He carries his head about on his shoulders like a sacred host."

"Oh, shut up, Camille," Robespierre said. "You do talk nonsense at times.")

By the time Robespierre stepped up to speak, he felt fully recovered in both body and soul. The king was the enemy. They were at war. The Revolution had been his trial; it had sentenced him to death. Different laws applied—yes, and a different morality, if that was what it took. Just for now.

"This is not a question of legal justice," he said. The magic inside him scorched. "We can have law later. This is a revolution. A people does not judge as does a court of law. It does not hand down sentences; it hurls down thunderbolts. It does not condemn kings; it plunges them into the abyss. Louis must die because the nation must live. He must die to nourish in the spirit of tyrants a salutary terror of the justice of the people."

"Is that what you and your kind did this September?" The speaker was a Girondin; Robespierre thought it was Roland, the rather fussy minister of the interior, who had risen to authority largely through the machinations of his brilliant wife. The disadvantage to pushing up his spectacles to allow his mesmerism to spill forth was that his audience became a hot, flesh-colored blur. "Hundreds of innocent people were butchered while you and Danton stood by and profited—"

Robespierre stood in the wave of protests and jeers that drowned out Roland's words, and felt oddly above it all. He had made his peace with the events of the autumn now. Indeed, it seemed strange that anyone would bring them up.

"You complain that innocent people have died this September," he said when he could. The room quieted to listen. "One or two were innocent, perhaps, and we should grieve for them. We should grieve also for the guilty victims, reserved for the vengeance of the laws, who fell beneath the blade of popular justice. We can even grieve for the king when this has all passed. But let this grief have an end, like all mortal things. Weep instead for the hundred thousand victims who died under the old regime; that is where our sympathies need to be. You complain that I have committed illegal acts. Of course I have. We all have. The Revolution is illegal. The fall of the Bastille was illegal.

The formation of this republic was illegal—as illegal as liberty itself. Citizens, *do you want a revolution without a revolution*?"

He believed it. The crowds knew it. The magic in him surged, but perhaps he didn't even need it.

It was a long, hard fight to have the king executed. Even the combined power of Saint-Just and Robespierre was not enough to persuade the Convention to kill the king outright, only to put him on trial, and the trial dragged on for weeks—weeks of noise and public spectacle, weeks where Robespierre began to feel he was blazing with mesmerism every waking moment. Camille's pen blazed with the same fervor: vicious, clever, deadly. Saint-Just became a constant visitor to the Duplays', running up the outside staircase that led to Robespierre's room at all hours of the day and night. Even at the last, Louis's fate came down to just a handful of votes. It was all it took.

Once, as a young lawyer back in Arras, before the Revolution or his benefactor or the war, Robespierre had served as a justice on a capital case. It was nothing to do with magic or politics, just a common murderer, a barrel maker who had clubbed his brother over the head in a brawl over a woman. The punishment for such an offense was execution: not the clean decapitation reserved for the Aristocracy, but slow, excruciating death by hanging, while the same crowds who now flocked to the guillotine talked and laughed and pointed out the stages of his dying. There was no doubt of his guilt. Robespierre's job was merely to pass the sentence.

Robespierre lived that death in his mind a thousand times before the man was condemned to it. For two days before the trial, he had neither eaten nor slept, but paced the house in a black fog of dread. Right until the last moment, his brain had raced, scrambling for anything, any excuse at all, that would enable him to save his principles and the man's life. Yet when it came to it, he had sentenced the man to death. His hand had shaken when he had signed the warrant, but he had signed it. He had collapsed at home afterward, shivering and retching with nothing to bring up, but he had returned to work the next day. He had thought it would destroy him, but he had lived.

"For God's sake, Maximilien," Charlotte had sighed as she brought him a hot drink and shooed Brount from his bedroom. "The man was a criminal. You did your job. You do get worked up over nothing."

This time, as the king was wheeled past the jeering hordes to his death, Robespierre knew better than to get worked up. He breakfasted at home that day with the Duplays. If he ate less than usual, nobody commented. Madame Duplay kept the talk on small matters, and everyone seemed relieved to follow her lead.

Babette came downstairs last. At twenty, she was lively, scatterbrained, and warmhearted; she paused by Robespierre's chair to give him an extravagant hug.

"It's so good to have you back home!"

He laughed and wriggled free playfully. Fortunately, Charlotte wasn't with them. "I've been back home for weeks."

"And it's still good to have you here."

"Still? I'm glad to hear it. When does it stop being good?"

"When you do. I'll let you know."

"For goodness' sake, Babette, let the poor man eat," Éléonore said, with an amused glance at Robespierre. He felt that pleasurable stir in his chest and wondered, not for the first time, if it was really only familial love he had missed over the winter.

Babette slipped into her chair and glanced at the door. "There are a lot of people out there on the streets this morning," she observed. She helped herself to toast. "What's happening out there?"

Robespierre's amusement died abruptly; he saw the same happen in Éléonore's eyes. "Something you shouldn't see," he said, and got up to close the door that led to the courtyard.

London

February 1793

Shortly before Saint-Domingue, Pitt had stood up in Parliament after almost a decade of careful management of the Treasury and—Wilberforce suspected not without understandable pride—had been able to declare that Britain was enjoying almost unprecedented prosperity. Taxes had been cut, national debt paid off, and Pitt had announced that it was feasible that within fifteen years Britain would be entirely free of debt. He had added that of course it was impossible to predict what crises might arise in fifteen years, but that unquestionably there was never a time in the history of the country when they might more reasonably expect fifteen years of peace than at the present moment.

Wilberforce had reminded Pitt of this statement not long ago, and teasingly asked him for an explanation.

"The explanation, Wilberforce," Pitt had said, "is that I was talking complete nonsense, and somebody should probably have clubbed me over the head with my own budget as soon as I sat down again. In future, that duty falls to you."

He said it with a smile, but it was tight enough that Wilberforce suspected he had been rather tactless.

On the Continent, things were growing darker. The stories from France were alarming: news of riots, and massacres of innocent prisoners by jeering mobs, and the violent overthrow of the monarchy. Against popular predictions, France had not settled after its latest transformation, but had transformed overnight into an engine of conquest, tearing across Europe, assimilating new territories. Pitt and the government had at last sent the French Republic of Magicians a warning that if they didn't confine themselves to their own region, they would be posing a serious threat, and Britain would have to respond accordingly.

All in all, Britain seemed to be heading deeper and more inexorably into war with every passing day, and Wilberforce was deeply troubled by it. This was because the prospect of war was troubling, of course. But he was also troubled that Pitt was not troubled, at least not visibly. Of course, Pitt was not often visibly troubled. It was something that had always frustrated Wilberforce in his efforts to judge what his friend had to be feeling at moments of political crisis; even when talking seriously about matters of importance, he rarely seemed anything less than reassuringly calm and perfectly logical. Wilberforce could agonize for hours over the morality of different courses of action; Pitt seemed to take the most momentous of decisions entirely in his stride. It was not surprising that he treated the prospect of open conflict with Europe with the same equanimity. But he couldn't help but wonder if something had shifted in Pitt's calculations since the night they had learned of the vampire on French soil; if, perhaps, the conflict had ceased to be a national matter and become, in some peculiar way, a matter of honor. What was perhaps most troubling of all was that Pitt might not have even realized this.

"It's not that I think the administration is to *blame* for the state we've come to," Wilberforce explained rather miserably to Thornton as they took their seats in the House of Commoners. "I know how much they want to avoid war. I just don't think the government have acted quite as I would have acted, at all points."

"I heard you pacing upstairs last night," Thornton said. He and Wilberforce were still sharing the massive house at Clapham; by now, as Thornton had hoped, it was the center of a rapidly growing community of evangelical reformers. "I thought about coming to see if I could help, but I didn't want to disturb you."

"I'm a little concerned as to how to phrase my objections to the war in a way that doesn't seem to criticize Pitt," Wilberforce said. "I was up for a good deal of the night trying to work it out. Then I was just up. I dozed off in my chair about six and woke up with a very sore neck and my head stuck to one side three hours later. I'm not sure it's entirely straight yet."

Thornton looked him briefly up and down. "As usual, head on straight and heart in the right place," he assured him with a smile. The Speaker was calling the House to order at the front of the room. "Which is, also as usual, right out on your sleeve. Pitt won't be hurt. He doesn't want a war either: he simply thinks that after all one might be inevitable. Your principles are the same; you merely disagree as to practice. And it isn't as though you haven't made your position clear from the beginning."

This was true, of course. It was also true that Pitt had made it clear, long ago in a different time, that if Wilberforce were to speak against him, it wouldn't touch the friendship between the two of them. He was an independent MP, with his own conscience to follow. But it had never happened before.

Pitt stood first to outline, in regretful but firm terms, the necessity of opposing France's advance on Europe. "Britain has pushed, to its utmost extent, the system of temperance and moderation," he said, "but has been continually slighted and abused. France has trampled underfoot all laws, human and divine. She has at last avowed the most insatiable ambition, and greatest contempt for all nations, which all independent states have hitherto professed most religiously to observe; and unless she is stopped in her career, all Europe must soon learn their ideas of justice, law of nations, models of government, and principles of magic, from the mouth of the French cannon."

Wilberforce listened and felt cold. He sat there still as Fox argued passionately in the defense of the Republic, then as Dundas stood to refute the opposition. He waited, heart pounding, for his opportunity to speak.

When it came, however, he was startled to be interrupted in the act of rising to his feet by Eliot's voice whispering his name. Wilberforce, from sheer habit, checked his motion.

"Just a moment!" Thornton called out to the Speaker.

Eliot slid into the seat behind them, his face flushed and awkward. "Sorry, Wilber," he whispered back. "But I've just come from Pitt. He asks you not speak against the war at the moment. The situation's too delicate—for opposition to come from you rather than Fox's people might do irreparable mischief."

"What sort of mischief?" Wilberforce asked, with a guilty glance at the waiting House. Mischief to the war effort, after all, was exactly what he aimed to cause.

Eliot shrugged helplessly. "He's asking you to trust him. He swears you'll have another chance to address the issue before anything happens."

Wilberforce hesitated, torn between his genuine desire not to make things difficult for his friend and his annoyance at Pitt for using that desire to silence him. Then he glanced over to the government benches and without warning caught the prime minister's gaze. Pitt shook his head very slightly, his eyes holding a plea but also an unspoken trust that the plea would be answered. Neither plea nor trust could be resisted. With resignation, Wilberforce held his gaze just long enough to give him a hard look, then looked to the Speaker.

"Never mind," he said. "Forgive me." He sat down again.

A member of the opposition spoke instead—not Fox for once, but a pale young MP from one of the southern constituencies. Like Fox, though, his objection was largely regarding the purity of the French ideals of justice and liberty, and the lack of a threat they posed to Britain if properly appealed to.

"I'm aware of their ideals," Pitt replied, getting to his feet immediately, "and I had nothing but sympathy for them at the dawn of their revolution."

Whatever he would have argued swiftly became a moot point: at that very moment, the daemon-stone that sat by the Speaker's chair began to hum.

Wilberforce turned to it in surprise, along with almost everyone in the room. There had always been a daemon-stone in the House of Commoners, so that a message could be sent from Parliament to the king in times of direst need. But it was a tradition rather than a true necessity. Wilberforce could never remember it being used during a sitting. And certainly it had never in living memory been used to receive a message.

"Who answers a daemon-stone in the House?" Thornton whispered to Wilberforce.

"I haven't the slightest idea," Wilberforce responded, bewildered. "There must be a protocol, but I've never heard it mentioned. Pitt probably knows. I doubt the Speaker does."

The same idea had clearly occurred to Pitt. "Mr. Speaker," he said, "would you like to accept and read that message, or would you prefer the responsibility to fall to me? It's bewitched to respond to one or the other."

"Proceed, by all means," the Speaker said, sounding a little flustered.

Fortunately, despite the disuse into which the House daemon-stone had fallen, the desk near it was still well stocked with paper and ink. Pitt took up the quill in his right hand, hovered it over the paper at the ready, and took up the humming stone in his left. Because he was looking for it, Wilberforce saw the brief shiver as he did so—Pitt had told him once that he felt touching a daemon-stone as a handful of snow down the back of his neck—but nobody else would have thought anything amiss. Their eyes were fixed on the paper as the stone hummed its message and Pitt's hand filled the page with his small, neat script.

It was a relatively short message. Without warning, the daemon-stone fell silent again, and Pitt came just as suddenly out of the necessary trance. He was still blinking to clear his head as he read the paper.

"What does it say?" someone demanded; it might have even been someone from the visitors' gallery. "Is it from His Majesty?"

"It's from Paris," Pitt said slowly. "The French Republic of Magicians have executed their king."

★ ★ ★

The next day, they were at war with France. Pitt stood up in the House of Commoners and read out the message from the king—as always, clearly, calmly, and with unimpeachable dignity. France had declared war on England only hours ago, presumably with the knowledge that England would declare war on France if they did not get in first. The French Republic of Magicians was, in their own words, fighting for the principles of freedom of magic for all classes, races, and creeds.

"Freedom of magic? Does that mean they've broken the Concord?" someone called, completely in breach of House protocol.

Pitt nodded. "Yes. It means exactly that. From now on, the French army have given their Commoner soldiers permission to use magic on the battlefield. We have not, of course, extended that permission to ours. This is not a war between magicians. But France has broken the Concord, and we are at war with them."

The news was greeted with a rustle of whispers. It was as though a stiff breeze moved through the House, shaking but not dislodging. Most, deep down, had expected nothing less.

Wilberforce remained quiet. Apart from the chill that had settled over his heart at the thought of war, he couldn't shake the memory that Pitt had sworn he would have a chance to voice his objections before such a war was upon them. It wasn't Pitt's fault that it had happened otherwise. He couldn't have known. But it was the first time a word had ever passed between them and been broken.

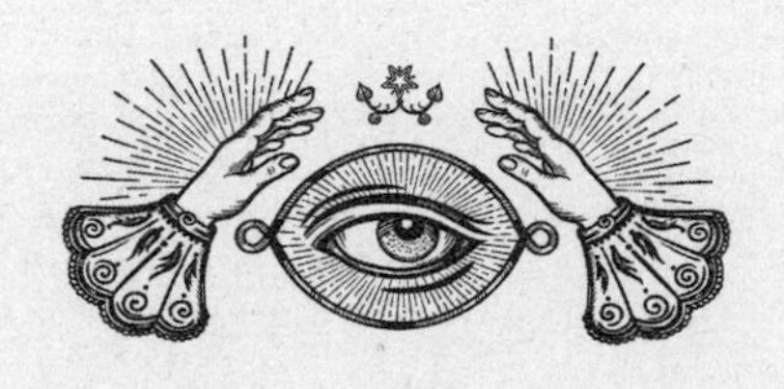

PART THREE

TERROR

London/Paris/Saint-Domingue

Spring 1793

Pitt did not, at first, know anything about war. His father's tactical brilliance had led Britain to glory during the Seven Years' War with France, but that had been over before Pitt was four; his own childhood training had been in oration and government, and his young mind, though it had grasped eagerly at everything it was offered, had memorized accounts of classical battles for their rhetorical flourishes rather than their lessons on strategy. His elder brother had been a soldier before Pitt had appointed him first lord of the admiralty; his younger brother had died in the service of the navy before Pitt had become prime minister. Pitt himself had never seen a battlefield. He didn't see this as necessarily a problem: for better or worse, he was used to the idea that he could learn anything he turned his attention to, with enough study and effort. Other people were used to this idea too, or they were just content to let responsibility fall to him. Either way, they didn't question it.

He was thirty-three, and he had led the country for almost a decade. Now the country was in the midst of war, and it was his job to lead it through that as well. He had never wanted to do any such thing; the thought, if he were more honest with himself than he cared to be, was a cold lump in his chest that he had to repeatedly swallow back down. But it was his job. More than that, it was his duty.

Austria and Prussia had been at war with France already; Spain, the Kingdom of Sardinia, and the Holy Roman Empire joined swiftly afterward. It took very little negotiation for them to agree to join with Britain in a loose alliance against the French Republic of Magicians. It took more persuading for Austria in particular to agree not to break the Concord in the process; fortunately, they needed the finances from Britain more than they needed magic. Their main priority was to force France to return to a monarchy—a priority that many of Pitt's ministers, as well as King George, shared. Pitt was less convinced.

"The French monarchy were too oppressive for too long a time," he said. "I think we can work with France if they choose to stay a republic, under a different government. What we can't work with is the breaking of the Concord. Whatever else happens, we need to push France back into its own borders and force them to swear to the Concord once more. As far as I'm concerned, they can have unpoliced magic within their own country if they want. They can even break with the Knights Templar again if they want—God knows I want to often enough. They absolutely cannot bring magical warfare back to Europe."

"We might find it difficult to stop them without breaking the Concord ourselves," Dundas said cautiously. His Scottish accent had a knack for making unpleasant truths as unpleasant as possible. Since his appointment as secretary of state for war, this trait had grown more pronounced. "The French are actively enlisting magicians now. Our own men will be at a disadvantage without magic of their own."

It was very similar to what Harriot had said, in the same office, when the question had still seemed hypothetical. Eliot had been there too then; he was still in the government, but his health had suffered since Harriot's death, and Pitt hardly saw him since he had moved out to Clapham. A lot had changed since that day.

William Grenville, foreign secretary, raised his milder voice. Since the start of the war, he had been in constant communication with their spymaster in Switzerland, and he and Pitt were working to smuggle at least one of the valuable daemon-stones into Paris itself. It meant that his opinion of French affairs held serious weight; perhaps as a result, he held a more lenient view of the Republic of Magicians than most. "I don't believe the French have found much advantage yet from Commoner magic on the battlefield. They need to invent new strategies entirely to make use of any skills their soldiers have, and they've rushed into war too hastily to do that. Fire-mages and mesmers are no match for cannon and gunfire in the heat of battle."

"Which is why we need to push into France as quickly as possible, before they refine their strategies," Pitt said before anyone could disagree. "Fortunately, our allies are already making that move—they only need our support."

"I think we can do better than that," Grenville said. "France is not a united country at the moment. There are many regions right now with groups loyal to the monarchy. If we can support them, they'll rise up. At worst, the Republic will be forced to expend resources dealing with them. At best, they'll be able to help us enter into France on the coast."

"The navy are ready to offer support," Pitt's brother, the Earl of Chatham, said, to Pitt's relief. He loved his elder brother and had faith in his competency, but his appointment had been made in peacetime, when the role had mattered less. Chatham was going to come under far heavier scrutiny these days, and there were already rumors that he wasn't particularly suited to the role. "It's in the best shape it's been for decades. But if we're going into battle with magic, we *do* need to look at protecting our ships from stray spells as much as we can."

"Which means amulets and alchemists," Dundas sighed. "Which means more expense."

"Expense is my worry," Pitt said. "Give me an estimate of what you need, and I'll work it out somehow."

That, at least, he could do in his sleep. It was comforting the way that some things never changed, and numbers were one of them.

"Are protective amulets allowed on a battlefield, under the terms of the Concord?" Grenville mused. "There was dispute, in the Seven Years' War, if they came under the heading of—"

"I don't care," Pitt said frankly. He was determined to take as objective a view as possible to magical warfare—to warfare of any kind. But James had died in the service of the navy; it was difficult for him to be objective about that. The line had to be drawn somewhere.

"You started this, in a way," Dundas said.

Pitt took a moment to realize he was being spoken to. "What did I start?"

"Commoner magic as self-defense. Commoner magic in defense of others. Your bill, eight years ago—I warned you, at the time. It won't take long before the soldiers demand to know why they can use magic to defend themselves on the streets and not in the heat of battle."

"They have every right to demand to know." He kept his voice light but let a note of warning creep in nevertheless. "I have no problem whatsoever with telling them exactly what I told you."

"You might not be too popular with them."

"Fortunately," he said with a smile, "that, too, is my worry and not yours."

"Do you think it's right," Grenville said, out of the blue, "to conduct all our war meetings as late at night and as drunk as we do?"

"I absolutely refuse," Pitt said, "to worry about that."

The Allies moved on France in a swarm from all sides. Spanish armies moved on the Pyrenees; Sardinia swarmed across the Alps. The Austrian forces moved deeper and deeper in Valenciennes. Meanwhile, the British naval barricade moved to starve France into submission, while its agents worked within its borders to fan the flames against the Republic of Magicians.

Pitt lived in a daily cloud of dispatches and daemon-stones, all relating to the movements of troops and ships thousands of miles away. He worked with Grenville to find and support pockets of resistance within France, in the hope that this might give them a foothold in French territory. He worked with his brother to organize naval operations. He and Dundas schemed later and later into the night. As the months went by, it became normal to be constantly behind on work, correspondence, rest. His magic began to stir in his blood, trying to help him through the parade of meetings and parliamentary sessions.

By the end of most nights, his head throbbed, his stomach spasmed painfully, and London's bloodlines were a dizzy swirl in his senses; by morning, either elixir or sleep had done its job, and he felt better, or close enough. He didn't mention this to anyone; it felt ridiculous to talk about being overworked when the work in question sent men to death and agony. Instead, he found himself telling half his cabinet to send him their work because he was relatively unoccupied. He had no idea why he always did this, or why everyone always seemed to believe him.

"It's very simple, actually," Wilberforce told him one afternoon as they walked through St. James's Park. "You think that if *you* have too many things to do, everyone else must as well, and they're probably not doing them correctly."

"That can't be it," Pitt objected, with the uncomfortable feeling that it might be at least part of it. "I wouldn't put people in office in whom I didn't have confidence."

"Perhaps. But you have still more confidence in yourself." He laughed at Pitt's expression. "Well then, if you don't like that hypothesis, try this one: when the government is suffering, you don't feel right if you're not suffering more than anybody."

"But I'm not suffering. I'm working. I've never suffered in my life. Oh well, never mind," he added quickly, before Wilberforce could reply. "It should all be over in a few months."

"Are you truly confident about that?" Wilberforce asked, more soberly. "Or is that something you're trying to convince the House?"

"Truly—I wouldn't go anything like that far in the House of Commoners. But to you, in private: wars are a matter of resources. France is expending theirs faster than they can sustain. We can calculate almost to the day when they will need to give in and negotiate."

"I'm not sure war works quite that logically," Wilberforce said. "I don't recall Achilles or Priam having a chancellor of the exchequer to advise them on finances."

"I daresay someone was giving them some thought," Pitt said dryly. "It's just not good manners to mention them in an epic."

Wilberforce smiled, then hesitated. "Dundas told me you'd agreed to send the navy to capture Saint-Domingue after all. Is it true?"

"Yes, it's true." Pitt said it as neutrally as he could. "For that very reason. When the planters asked for our help at first, the risks weren't worth the reward. Now, if we can take that colony from France, we can increase our revenue and diminish theirs at the same time. The war could end even faster."

"But the French don't hold Saint-Domingue. The rebel armies do—at least part of it. And Britain still upholds slavery. If we take the colony, Saint-Domingue will be back where it began, and no hope of anything good will ever come from that rebellion."

"I'll worry about that once the war is over, I promise. For now, the priority is to force France's surrender as quickly as possible. The longer this war goes on, the more difficult it is to keep the magic all on one side."

Wilberforce was clearly not convinced, but he let it pass. "Well," he said, "let's just hope France is working from the same balance sheet as you. And that you don't start to suffer. I wanted to tell you that I received a letter from Holt today—my friend in the Temple Church. He's finally found a record of the last known vampires in France. He was right—they are rather a way back. In fact, all he has is the complete list of every blood magician killed in the Vampire Wars."

"Good God. That sounds like long and gruesome reading."

"It is, rather. The rest of the records pertaining to France burned with the Bastille. I did think, though, that it might be worth searching for records of anyone surviving descended from those families. It's unlikely to be profitable, I know, particularly since we'll only have access to British records given events overseas. But..."

"It's certainly worth attempting. I just don't know when either of us will find the time."

"Fortunately," Wilberforce said, "I happen to be living in the midst of some of the cleverest and most hardworking people in the country, present company excepted of course, and they are all very good at research. If I give them several names each, they'll find time to look."

"What will you tell them?"

"That I want to investigate the possibility there was a vampire in Europe involved in the Saint-Domingue uprising, which is perfectly true. They already know Clarkson was approached by someone claiming to be a blood magician on the night the Bastille fell. We don't have any secrets from each other." He glanced at Pitt. "Except for yours, of course. That one isn't mine to share."

"Thank you. I do mean that." The wind gusted past them, dusted with a light speckle of rain. Wilberforce shivered a little but ignored it dutifully. Pitt knew very well that they were outside because he hadn't left London for far too long, and the park was the closest there was to trees and grass, and he was grateful for that as well. "Let me know if you discover anything."

He had to leave after that. Grenville had received word about a counterrevolution in Toulon, on the French coast, and they needed to investigate the hope of sending soldiers to help them take the port.

That night, Robespierre met his benefactor in the garden. He had thought the meetings would become more pleasant now that he had done what his benefactor wanted and killed the king. It didn't seem to work that way. The skies glowed with red light, and the wind that cut through the grass was ice-cold.

"The war isn't going well," Robespierre said. It was something he would never have said in the Convention, but it was true. "I know it was inevitable that England would rise against us if we didn't rise against them first. But bringing them into the conflict might destroy us. We barely have control of our own country, and there are too many against us."

"Not if you do what I ask of you."

"I did what you asked of me. I killed the king. We broke free of the bracelets. We brought magic back to the battlefield."

"You brought *some* magic back to the battle," his benefactor corrected. "It's a beginning. But you're still holding back."

Robespierre barely heard him. "I thought it would be different once we broke the Concord. I thought it would be like the fall of the Bastille, when Camille unleashed his power in broad daylight and the prison fell before our anger. It hasn't worked that way."

"You need more soldiers."

"We've conscripted all the magical Commoners we can muster from the provinces. Hundreds of thousands of them are ready to be sent to the front. The problem is that they don't want to go. They may desert before they—"

"I'm not talking about Commoner magicians. Commoner magicians are well enough, but they're not yet skilled, and your generals aren't clever enough about how to use them."

"I don't understand," said Robespierre.

"Yes, you do." His benefactor sighed. It was difficult to tell, when his face was always in shadow, but Robespierre thought he'd been sounding tired lately. If so, he wasn't alone. "I wish you wouldn't lie to yourself. It's so time-consuming."

"I'm not lying. You said it was impossible to lie in here."

"To me. You can still lie to yourself in your own head. You know what I need of you. It's why I chose you. Surely you haven't forgotten. That night, before the Estates General. Before any of this."

Robespierre shivered. "Of course I remember that night. But what good would that do now? One undead? I don't even know what you did with the first one—"

"Not one undead. Hundreds of undead. Thousands."

"I don't—"

"Stop it." The voice was uncharacteristically sharp. "I told you I chose you for your necromancy, did I not? This is what I chose you for. I want you to create an army of the dead."

For a long, long time, Robespierre did not speak.

"It's what will save us," his benefactor said. "You know it's true. An army with the strength of men but the invulnerability of shadows, who cannot be killed, and yet who can kill with the precision of the most skilled human soldiers. A single undead, properly commanded and armored, could destroy hundreds of enemy soldiers on its own—thousands. An army..."

"There hasn't been an army of the dead for hundreds of years," Robespierre said hoarsely. His chest hurt. "Not since—"

"Since the Vampire Wars. Since the Concord was formed, and dark magic was outlawed, and necromancy—and vampirism—became punishable by death. What do you think breaking the Concord was ever about?"

"I thought it was—it *is* about freedom of magic."

"This is freedom of magic. This is what a war of magic looks like. Robespierre, you talk about Camille's magic, that day at the Bastille. You talk about how beautiful it was. You need to understand the beauty of your own. You're far more powerful than him. Your magic burns in the dark, glorious and cold. This is your birthright."

"You helped me hide that birthright. When I did what I did for you that night, you told me that nobody looking for a necromancer would find me. You said you had removed my mother's arrest from the Templar records, and none of the Templars who had been involved were still alive."

"You were a petty lawyer in the provinces then. The Knights Templar still held power in France. Things have changed."

"And where would we get the dead? For them to be suitable, they'd have to have died in a particular way..."

His benefactor looked at him. "You know where."

And he did. The worst part was, he did. "I won't do it," he said flatly. "Not that."

"And why not that? Why not, after so much?"

"I am not your pawn!" The flare of temper was a relief; it burned his fear away. "I don't serve you. I serve the people of France."

"You served me in Arras, before you were appointed to the Third Estate. You served me because you needed my help, if you were to ever be in a position to serve France. In return, I gave you your mesmerism. I gave you your position. I gave you your Republic."

"And I don't regret it. But what I did that night—it was *evil*. I felt it. I won't do it again."

"Positions change very quickly these days, Maximilien Robespierre. It would be a simple matter to shift yours."

The words came with a stab of pain behind his eyes. It threatened to bring him to his knees; Robespierre gasped and staggered. He didn't know whether it had been accidental or on purpose.

"Do it," he said through gritted teeth. "If you want to. But you didn't before, when I defied you for so many months. When I refused to kill the king. I think you need me where I am now."

"I do. But I needed you for precisely this. I raised you to power, I helped you break the Concord, specifically so that you would be in a position to give France the army it needs. From now on, you're useless to me without it."

"I don't think I am. I think that whatever you are, you care for France as much as I do, and you know I can bring her to greatness, army of the dead or not. I am willing to take the chance that I am wrong."

"Are you, indeed?" his benefactor said. "Because you *are* wrong. And I am not willing to take that chance."

There was enough threat that Robespierre's confidence flickered. And yet if he gave in on a principle because he was afraid, then what was he? "I killed the king," he said again. "Because you asked me. I raised a republic in his place. Surely that's enough."

"It's not why I chose you. I could have used any half-decent mesmer to accomplish that. I needed a necromancer. I need an army of the dead."

"I won't give you one. Besides—" He broke off, but his benefactor heard his hesitation. He pounced at once.

"Yes?"

"The Girondins would never allow it," Robespierre said. "I don't mean that I don't have moral objections myself—I do. But if I put forward that proposal—they'd never allow that kind of dark magic. They're still trying to reverse the breaking of the Concord."

"You have power enough in the Convention to overcome their

objections. Particularly if Danton supports you, and I suspect he will. And I can help you."

"I can't mesmerize half the Convention—not on something like this. I think they're beginning to suspect me as it is."

"Mesmerism isn't illegal anymore."

"But I've been using my magic on the Assembly and on the Convention for years, in secret. I've been using it on the crowds. I've even used it in the Jacobins at times. It doesn't matter what's legal or illegal—they won't stand for that. It will invalidate everything I've ever done for the Republic—all the principles I've tried to instill in it, all its virtues, all its achievements. They'll kill me as a traitor to France. They want me dead already."

"You really are afraid of them, aren't you?"

"I'm afraid of everyone. If you seek to shame me with that, you won't succeed. There are plots and conspiracies everywhere these days. It's only by being afraid that we'll save the Republic."

"Very well." His benefactor was not angry anymore. The stabbing pain in Robespierre's head had dissolved. It left him sick and short of breath. "The Girondins are your enemies. They would prevent you from bringing dark magic back into the world. They would kill you, if they could. I accept this. So if we were to deal with them—"

"Could we?" Robespierre asked. He felt, unexpectedly, a rising hope.

"Of course. I should have thought of it sooner. You need greater power in the Convention: removing the Girondins will leave the Convention solely in the hands of the Mountain. It will keep you safe. And it will leave the path free for us to fight the war in our own way."

"I don't promise to give you an army of the dead," Robespierre said quickly. "I'll champion the cause of free magic, of course. But I don't promise that."

"Breathe, for heaven's sake," sighed his benefactor. "You get so agitated. You won't create an army of the dead. But you want me to help you destroy your political enemies?"

"They're the enemies of France as well." In the last few weeks, he had developed a nervous twitch in his left eye; it was spasming now, painfully and distractingly. It seemed unfair, when this wasn't even his physical body. "They're hampering the war effort—after starting the war in the first place. If we can just start to turn the tide of public opinion against them..."

There was a pause, and when the voice came again, it was tinged with something not unlike amusement. "Very well, Robespierre. I can afford to wait a little longer. We'll play it your way for now. Enjoy your revolution."

Robespierre woke, with heavy eyes and aching head, to a pounding at the door. The Commoner magicians outside of Paris had risen against the new conscription laws, and the rioting was raging out of control. Civil war had broken out in the provinces.

The Revolution was not going well either.

Thousands of miles across the ocean, Fina woke too. It was still dark in the West Indies; her eyes met only the dark sky above her head. But for a moment, she had been in a garden, listening to the voices of two men. They had spoken a language she didn't understand, and yet the meaning was clear—as it had been almost two years ago, when that same voice had called out to the enslaved men and women of Saint-Domingue and urged them to take revenge. Her magic curled inside her, fragile and strange. She lay awake a long time.

Paris

June 1793

By summer, the Allied powers were beginning to encroach on the French border. The regiments of French magicians, inexperienced in the use of the power suddenly at their fingertips, tended to fire useless magic in a panic while the generals barked commands. Many of the soldiers were conscripted, disillusioned, and fed up with the promise of liberty, which had amounted to worse than the oppression of the old regime. Many of the provinces, including the major ports, were outright royalist and were more than willing to accept the support of the Allies to help take back France. They refused to use magic, in solidarity with the Templars and their allies, but there were other ways to kill.

In Paris, by contrast, war fervor ran high. Dissatisfaction centered instead around the Girondins, who were coming to be seen in the same light as royalists and anti-magic sympathizers. In light of the revolts in the provinces, Robespierre found himself forced to call for more and more arrests of Aristocrats, and tighter and stricter controls against the counterrevolution. The Girondins preached moderation and a reduced use of magic. It didn't take much mesmerism, as it turned out, for Robespierre to have the people jeering at them in the street. The pamphleteers were quick to leap on the public mood: Camille first, with his playful, savage, classical allusion; then Hébert, with his coarse humor pitched at the barely literate. Marat joined in, and the people swarmed. It was almost frightening how fast the flame took and how bright it burned. He wondered, not for the first time, what other powers his benefactor had besides that which he shared with Robespierre. Surely his own mesmerism alone couldn't have accomplished so much.

He met Madame Roland one night outside his front door as he and Duplay returned from the Jacobins. She was the real power behind her husband, and indeed behind the Girondins: brilliant, educated, daring. Her sharp face was pale in the light from the courtyard.

"Congratulations," she said to him. "The mob destroyed another of our press shops this morning."

"They don't like what the Girondin journalists have to say," Robespierre said evenly. "I'm not responsible for that."

"Aren't you? Jean-Paul Marat would be happy to claim responsibility. His own journals have been tearing into us since spring. And your Camille has been in fine form."

"I have no control over Marat—and Camille writes what he likes."

"So you deny you're trying to destroy us?"

Maurice Duplay, at Robespierre's shoulder, made a convulsive move forward; Robespierre put out a hand to stop him. "I don't deny that I oppose you," he said to Madame Roland. "I never have. Your policies are dangerous. We have no place for moderates anymore, and no place for those attempting to quell the use of magic. I've made no secret of this."

"I don't know what you are, Robespierre," Madame Roland said. "And I don't know what you're doing. But rest assured, I will find out."

"Leave him alone," Duplay snapped.

"You could have asked," Robespierre replied. He managed to keep his voice quiet, even cold. "I'm a patriot, and I'm trying to save my country. Anything else is immaterial."

"Is it?" she asked. "Are you sure about that?"

The people were scared, again. And, as Robespierre had learned the previous September, when people were scared, they wanted somebody to blame. Really, he shouldn't have needed the September massacres to teach him that. He was scared too.

⋆ ⋆ ⋆

"I'm going to call for a revolt against the Girondins," Robespierre said to Camille. They were in the garden at the back of Camille's house, but he still kept his voice low. Lately, he had felt ears and eyes trained on him everywhere. From the house drifted the high, clear notes of a piano: Lucile, practicing. "I'm going to call for those loyal to us to rise up and expel them from the Convention."

"Excellent," Camille replied promptly. He was obviously not surprised, but his eyes kindled. "What do you need me to do? I can talk to Danton, if you'd like."

"I think I should do that myself. You're doing enough already. You took Brissot to pieces in that pamphlet you wrote."

"Oh, that." Camille looked almost embarrassed. "That went further than I meant it to, really. I was just angry. Brissot called me names and questioned my republicanism, in public. I mean, really. He should have known better."

"Well, it worked, whatever you intended. Just...keep the public feeling moving against them. Keep dredging up the past. Keep stirring."

"You say that as if I ever did anything else. Really, Maxime, well done. It's long past time."

Robespierre wondered, as he often did, if Camille even remembered that Brissot and several other Girondins had been guests at Camille's wedding only two years ago.

"They don't care about the good of the people," he said. "They don't care about virtue. They didn't want the death of the king; they didn't want the removal of the bracelets; they didn't want to break the Concord. They aren't willing to do what it takes to bring about a free Republic."

"You don't need to rehearse on me. They want to reinstate testing at birth—as if there could ever be an innocent reason for having a record of Inheritances! The problem is, they're unmagical Commoners, almost to a one. They're afraid of us."

"Danton's an unmagical Commoner as well," Robespierre pointed out. He forgot to add the lie that so was he.

"Oh, Danton," Camille said, careless. "He's a demigod."

"I thought he was a minotaur."

"There's another revolt coming. I'm promoting everyone I like to demigod. Don't be jealous: you can be one too."

"I just want to be a Republican."

"You're certainly that." He looked at Robespierre a little closer, and his face softened. "Are you all right? You *are* doing the right thing, you know. Don't listen to me being flippant. I mean it. Things are going wrong, and we need to keep fighting."

"I know." He knew he didn't sound convincing. "Listen, Camille—in the course of your writings, do you think you can find some accusations to level at Madame Roland?"

Camille snorted. "Can I find some accusations? Can you find your glasses on the end of your nose? Can my wife find a reason to love me?"

"Can she?"

"If she can't, she can make one up." Camille's laugh, it came to Robespierre, still had exactly the reckless quality from their school-days, no matter what else had changed. "And I can do the same in answer to your request. Leave it to me. Go call for an uprising."

Robespierre barely closed his eyes that night before he opened them in the garden. His benefactor stood waiting. The sky was red as blood.

"Help me," he said.

"I never stopped," his benefactor said.

At the Jacobins the following evening, Robespierre addressed the chamber of magicians and revolutionaries with mesmerism burning hot in his blood. He had already spoken against the Girondins in the Convention that morning, and thrown the room into chaos. That had, in some ways, been only the setup for this.

"Today," he told the hundreds of waiting ears, "I stood up in the Convention and demanded that the Girondins stop slandering us and our supporters. I demanded that the journalists in their pay be silenced in their attempts to pervert the will of the people. I demanded that we increase our efforts to exterminate the Aristocrats, who are still everywhere, and whom the Girondins are defending." He had to raise his voice over the building cheers. "As we suspected, they spurned my requests. The Girondins and the conspirators have too much control. France is at a crisis. It is being destroyed from inside that very room. Citizens, I cannot do any more. Unless there is a revival of public spirit, unless the patriots make one last effort, then all we have achieved will be lost. Virtue will disappear from the face of the earth. It's time to decide if you truly want to save the human race."

The Jacobins erupted into chaos. Not since the formation of the Republic had the room been so filled with revolutionary fervor. It almost hurt.

The following day, a horde of Parisian petitioners pushed their way into the Convention. They wore the red caps of Commoner magicians—though the likelihood of them all possessing Inheritances was remote. Many brandished pikes and pistols; others crackled the air with what was now being called mob magic: lightning, fire, water, anything visible and dramatic. They demanded the removal of the Girondins from the chamber. The Girondins did not go quietly.

"The rest of France will never stand for this," one of them shouted. "If the magicians of Paris rise against the national representatives of the Republic, the city will be annihilated. Future travelers will seek along the shores of the Seine whether Paris had ever existed!"

Robespierre stood amid the angry shouts. He was small, pale, meticulously dressed. In that room of mob violence, he looked like an anachronism. Yet the crowd were with him. "The people have spoken," he said. "You no longer speak for them."

"The people are echoing your words." This was Roland, white and defiant. "My wife was right. She said you were a magician and you would enchant them all."

It was the accusation he had feared for a long time. It had come too late. "It's precisely that irrational fear of magic that brought you to this," Robespierre said. He had to raise his voice over the noise from the Girondin benches. "This is the Republic of Magicians. This is a country of free magic and free people. There is no place in it for people—"

"Enough!" someone demanded. "It's the same thing again and again. Conclude!"

"I do conclude!" he snapped. "I conclude against you! You who wanted to condemn those who brought about the fall of the monarchy, who tried to save the tyrant king from death, who stood against the rights of the people to use magic freely in peace or in war—you who are the enemies of the Republic. My conclusion is the same as that of the Commoners of Paris who stand here today with their petitions: it is to accuse you of all that is most vile and corrupt."

He turned to the Commoners.

"We know what to do with tyrants in France." He was burning with magic, hotter than he had ever burned. It would destroy him if it lasted much longer. For now, it was exhilarating. "We rise up, and we destroy them. Rise up now. Destroy them."

The insurrection lasted two days: two days of stifling heat, and cannon fire, and the unrelenting chime of the tocsin above the Hôtel de Ville. Marat, his skin blistered and disfigured by his self-begotten curse, clambered up the tower to ring the bell himself, and call out to the people in his hoarse croak. The Girondins barricaded themselves inside the Convention headquarters, and a mob of forty thousand beat at the door.

Robespierre was not there on the streets. He had meant to be this time: this time, after all, he would have been no revolutionary against the established order, but an elected member of France's government, with the people behind him. But the effort of mesmerism in the Convention, coming after so many months of constant magic, had burned him up from the inside; receding, it left a chill like ice. He spent the riot curled up in his room at the Duplays', shivering and exhausted, about which Camille ridiculed him mercilessly when he dropped by that night.

"Whoever heard of reporting sick to your own uprising?" he said, dropping onto the end of the bed, where Brount slept. He was artfully disheveled from the streets and carried with him an air of summer dust and violence and unlawful magic. "You can't call for a riot and then go to bed. It's like getting married by parcel post—or divorced."

"I'll remember that next time," Robespierre said.

"Next time it'll probably be your turn for the receiving end. You'll have to send your apologies to the guillotine."

"Oh, stop it, Camille," he sighed. That possibility was too close for humor; hopefully less close now than it had been, with the Girondins discredited, but he didn't know. Some part of him that he didn't want to acknowledge was glad that he had not been in the midst of danger. "Please. I'm tired, and I'm cold. Just tell me it went well."

Camille softened. "It went wonderfully well. Marat was in fine form. Hanriot had sixty cannon placed around the Convention. The crowds turned out in the tens of thousands. All the Girondins have either fled the city or been arrested. Oh, and Roland's wife is in prison—refused to flee when her husband did, or something. You seemed worried about her. The Republic is ours—yours and Danton's, really, the way things stand."

" 'Ours' will do. I don't want to be a dictator. I just want France to be safe."

Camille started to reply, then stopped. Something Robespierre didn't understand crossed his face. But when he spoke again, he sounded the same as before. "Well, for that, you probably will need to get out of bed, I'm afraid. Will you be back at the Convention tomorrow?"

"Yes. I'll have to be. There's going to be a lot to discuss."

"Good. Otherwise, I'd have to take power in your place, and I hate public speaking." He took Robespierre's hand and frowned. "You *are* cold, aren't you? Here, hold still."

Flames flickered around their entwined fingers—warm, yellow, gentle, not at all like the sparks that had lit a revolution or the scorching heat of his benefactor's mesmerism. It felt like stepping into a sunbeam on a winter's day. He sighed.

"Better?"

"Yes. Thank you." Even when Camille withdrew his hand and his magic, the lingering warmth remained. The ice in his chest melted a little. "I wish you could have done that back when we were in school. It was always so cold, remember?"

"God, yes. Those huge drafty halls. Out of bed at half past five, prayers at six, scripture at quarter past, mass at half past ten, and all the while the air was icing over. And they wondered why we grew up wanting to burn the world."

Robespierre smiled sleepily. "Do you really think that was it?"

"Of course not. It was the learning, really. That library, with its volumes and volumes of Cicero. We were educated in the ideas of Rome and Athens and in the pride of republicanism, and we were living in the reign of a Claudian or a Vitellius. How did they expect us to admire the past without condemning the present?"

"You're writing a pamphlet in your head now, aren't you?"

"That's how you know I mean it." Camille bounced to his feet, causing the bed to jump and Brount to yelp in alarm. "Get some rest while you can. It's a big day tomorrow."

There had been a lot of big days in the last few years.

Power was entirely in the hands of the Mountain now. Within six days, the constitution that had been tossed back and forth between the Mountain and the Girondins for a year had been drafted, finalized, and set down as law. It was, as Robespierre had intended, the most democratic constitution the world had yet seen, and everybody knew that it was his. All men, regardless of class, were allowed to vote. State education and welfare assistance were promised to all. Total freedom of magic was acknowledged for the first time as a right of blood, regardless of class, race, or sex. After three exhausting years, the France in his head at last existed on paper and in law.

Unfortunately, as Robespierre pointed out, it was too dangerous to put into practice quite yet. All this scheming and rioting had not changed the fact that the rest of the country was in revolt, and the rest of Europe battered at its gates. Until the country was at peace, France remained under revolutionary law. And so the Committee of Public Safety was formed, designed to protect France from her own unrest and insurgencies: a committee with the ability to judge, sentence, and condemn any who threatened the beautiful future upon which the ink was still drying.

One of its first acts, incidentally, was to officially declare William Pitt an enemy of the human race.

Saint-Domingue

August 1793

Fina sat in a tent in the heat of a Caribbean summer afternoon. Outside the cloth walls, the camp was all but empty; a pot sat over the remains of a cold fire, and the ground was jagged with the prints of bare feet. Fina's eyes were closed, her legs tucked up beneath her. She breathed rapid and shallow; every so often, a muscle in her shoulder twitched.

Behind her eyes, a battle raged.

Toussaint was no longer a chief medic, or any other invented title, and he was no longer a subordinate of anyone. Like many of the other rebel leaders, he had made terms with the Spanish against the French—as Celeste had told Fina months earlier, the Spanish San Domingo was very interested in working with the rebel armies across the border in exchange for a share in French Saint-Domingue. He had not done so as a subordinate of Biassou, however, but as an independent leader of six hundred soldiers who were widely known as the best and cleverest fighters in the region, and the Spanish had named him a colonel. Most of Toussaint's army had been slaves or free blacks, but many were white officers and republicans. Many, Fina among them, were magicians. This was not so remarkable; what was remarkable was that he had found ways to incorporate this magic into the rigid structure favored by the French military. He kept his forces low enough to learn each magician's individual strength, and he organized his troops into units of sixteen. Each unit balanced regular fighters with one or two magicians; they drilled mercilessly, so that each learned how to best use their unit's particular magic and could do so without thought. When they charged into battle, they charged out of nowhere, fire and water and storm mingled with the flash of guns and swords.

Fina was outside those tight-knit units. In body, at least, she was outside the battles. Her work came before each conflict, and she worked with Toussaint alone. At his side, she would close her eyes and project herself behind the eyes of the enemy commanders; she could, in this way, tell him the lay of the battleground, the size and strength of the forces they were to face, and their state of preparation. She had come to know the faces of many of the French commanders by sight and could report their presence at each base. Sometimes she even saw plans and dispatches; she couldn't read, but she had a good memory and could trace out what she saw. She could make their enemies spy on themselves.

That morning, it had seemed that her work had been for nothing, and the battle had been over before it began. She and Toussaint had been discussing the number of ships docked in the port when Dessalines, Toussaint's lieutenant, had come with unusual haste.

"A messenger just came from the south," he said. "The commissioners have just declared slavery abolished in Saint-Domingue."

Fina's breath caught. She glanced at Toussaint quickly and was surprised to see him unmoved.

"Did they say on whose authority?" Toussaint asked.

"Their own, presumably. Sonthonax made the proclamation." That sounded likely; of the two commissioners sent to Saint-Domingue from France at the start of the rebellion, Léger-Félicité Sonthonax had become a particularly strong advocate of the black population. The rights he had granted slaves in the south had earned him the animosity of the white colonists, many of whom had subsequently left the island in droves. "But they're the representatives of France on the island."

"It changes nothing," Toussaint said. "We go ahead as planned."

Fina exchanged a look with Dessalines, whose face mirrored her own confusion. "But if slavery no longer exists—" she began.

"The commissioners say that slavery no longer exists," Toussaint corrected. "They have no power to make it true. It would need to be confirmed by the National Convention in Paris, and they'll never allow it. They need this colony now to support their war with Europe. In the meantime, things will go on as they ever have. If we want freedom, we need to take it for ourselves. Is the army ready?"

Dessalines smiled. Fina didn't know him very well, but he had never shown any interest in showing mercy to the plantation owners. "It is."

"Then tell them to prepare to move on Fort Dauphin."

Fina waited until Dessalines had moved away. "Are you sure? Perhaps the Convention will support their ruling. Perhaps they have already."

"If I hear that's the case, I might reconsider." The sternness faded from his face as he turned to her. "I hope it is. But for now—it's taken a long time to build a relationship with Spain. I won't throw it away on so slight a promise as the French commissioners can give. As it is, I suspect this comes from Sonthonax alone. He means well, but he has it in his head that he can come in and save us, and he doesn't understand the way this country works. It's dangerous."

It made sense, of course. Toussaint always made sense. But deep down, she couldn't help but feel a stirring of disappointment. She understood why Dessalines had smiled. He wanted revenge, and for him that meant death. But there were different kinds of revenge, and she was sick of death. Perhaps it would be better for France to admit they were wrong and have to surrender to their former slaves.

But Fort Dauphin, at least, was not surrendering.

Her part in the conflict was over: she had given Toussaint the surrounding area's weaknesses and strengths, and he had taken advantage of both. In theory, she could rest now, and wait for the army to return or not. But instead, she closed her eyes, found her magic, and reached for the battle. She found the town at once, a surge of panic and confusion and flame; she cast herself behind the eyes of the combatants on both sides, throwing out her power at random and not much caring whom it ensnared. They would feel nothing, beyond perhaps a sense of something uncanny that they had no time for in the midst of combat. She couldn't enter Toussaint's head—she had promised him, and she respected that promise. But for reasons she couldn't quite explain, she needed to watch over him.

Fort Dauphin now was a ball of fire. Men and women fought in the ash. The man Fina inhabited now was white, his arms clad in the French uniform as he brought his rifle up to fire. His muscles burned, and the heat throbbed in his skull. His ankle stabbed faintly with every turn—an old injury, or a fresh one, she couldn't tell. Dessalines cut his way through a handful of men; a French soldier rushed toward him, sword waving, then fell back gasping. Dessalines's magic inflicted pain at a glance. It was harmless, but crippling. Nobody had heard of an ability like it, but then nobody had heard of an ability like Fina's either.

In Toussaint's mind, battles were always clear lines—she didn't need to actually enter his head to see that. He explained to her, when he had time, the reasoning behind each attack and strategy. Through others' eyes, battles were a dust-filled, chaotic mess. They frightened her—not just the flash of blades and the spill of blood, or the faces distorted by silent screams, but the rage and bloodlust bubbling beneath the surface of those whose bodies she inhabited on both sides. It was primal and dangerous, like the magic that spilled from the unknown voice she had come to find. It frightened her because she had felt it in her own veins, the night that Molly died.

Toussaint.

Fina saw him through enemy eyes, mounted on his black horse, Caesar. Although there was no sound through her magic, his mouth was moving, and her mind supplied his voice urging his people into battle. The man whose head she inhabited brought up his rifle. His muscles were hesitant, his view wavering. It wasn't just that Toussaint was too far away for a clear shot. He was afraid. Fina felt the roar of his heart, and her own exulted. He wouldn't fire.

And then she saw the other Frenchman. He was at the back of the same low wall that sheltered the soldier Fina inhabited. Fina could see him easily: he wasn't hiding from his own army. But Toussaint, looking out to the battle, hadn't seen him. And the man was carrying a rifle.

No.

Toussaint whirled Caesar around tightly, so that his face came into view through the haze. His eyes were narrowed against the noise and the smoke, and his jaw was set. His face was distorted by the hatred of the man she inhabited, but it didn't matter. Fina knew it.

He couldn't die. Not now, not like this. He couldn't.

The white man brought up his rifle. A few miles away, cross-legged in a tent, something happened inside Fina's head, or her heart.

She remembered being six, in the hold of a ship, screaming in her head and knowing she would never scream aloud again.

She remembered being twelve, watching the bandits from the hills storm the plantation, screaming in her head for them to see her and take her away.

She remembered her friend Augustus, whirling without warning to strike the overseer. They had taken him and burned him alive. He had not been able to scream either.

She remembered Molly.

She was free of the spell now. Her army was taking the town of the enemy. And she had come into her magic.

She didn't let herself think. There was room for only magic in her head, no room even for that, as it spilled out of one man and caught the other like a net. Her surroundings blurred, roared, then settled into the view from the rifleman's eyes: the sight of the rifle, pointed at Toussaint as he sat with naked saber drawn on the back of his horse.

"No!" she cried, and was surprised to hear her own voice. "No, no, *no*!"

The man stopped. It might have been to aim before firing, but she could see the barrel, and it was not quite there. An inch away, less; it might still hit, even kill, but the man's finger was loose about the trigger, and the rifle was not where he wanted it to be. Besides, she could feel him. Beneath the surface, behind his eyes, she felt the man's confusion and fear as he struggled to move. His biceps strained uselessly under his jacket; his teeth gritted; his eyes widened. She remembered the feeling well. She had felt it every day of her life from the age of six to the age of twenty-seven.

"Stop it," she said. "Stop it right now."

Her hold lasted perhaps five seconds, if that. In that time, Toussaint turned his horse; she saw his familiar face meet her eyes, which weren't really hers at all but the rifleman's. With barely a flicker of alarm, he dropped the reins, drew his pistol with his left hand, and aimed. Fina heard the concussion, felt the hot sting of shot, and gasped. The man's chest shattered in an explosion of pain. He fell; she fell with him. The ground beneath them was slick with blood.

As the rifleman's eyes grew dim, the wooden gate to the east of the town shattered with a shower of hot ash and sparks. Fina ducked instinctively, covering her head and squeezing her eyes shut. When she opened them, her tent awaited her. She fell to the ground, shaking, exhausted, exultant. Even from there, she could hear the sounds of gunfire and swords and screams.

That evening, Toussaint addressed the crowds of free blacks and slaves that had gathered in the square of Fort Dauphin. His voice rang out, strikingly deep and resonant from such a slight frame.

"Brothers and friends, I am Toussaint Louverture; perhaps my name has made itself known to you. I have undertaken vengeance. I want liberty and equality to reign in Saint-Domingue. I work to bring them into existence. Unite yourselves to us, brothers, and fight with us for the same cause."

It was the first time he had used the name Louverture: "the opening." Nobody quite knew what it meant, but they all listened.

Fina didn't see Toussaint until the following night. The troops returned in the late afternoon, but Toussaint himself had many to see and talk to before he had time to spare for her. She found him at last under the leaves of a stubby palm tree, in a gully on the outskirts of the camp. Caesar was tied to one of the branches; Toussaint groomed him with sure, firm strokes. The horse's coat gleamed black in the soft darkness.

"I did it," she announced without preamble. She expected Toussaint would know what she meant, and she was not disappointed.

"I thought you did." If he was exhausted, as he must have been, it showed only in a faint sigh as he straightened to look at her. His mouth twisted into its familiar smile. "At least, when I turned and looked down the barrel of a rifle, with an enemy frozen behind it, I suspected I was seeing the touch of somebody's magic. I also suspected it was somebody who liked me."

"I could do it again." Fina slid the rest of way into the gully with a scree of pebbles, causing Caesar to snort in alarm and toss his head. She laid her hand on his nose to calm him. "I know the feel of it now."

"Good," Toussaint said. "We might need it."

He was so much less excited than she had expected that she wondered if her own excitement had less to do with tactical advantage than it did with personal revenge. Her revenge hadn't been the man's death; that had been terrible. But she had been told to stop so often, and forced to obey first by magic and then by fear. Now she had made someone listen to her.

But even if that were the case, there *was* a tactical advantage to her magic—there always had been, and it had just increased. And she had saved Toussaint's life. Under normal circumstances, some excitement was surely warranted.

"What is it?" she asked. "Do you think we should treat with France after all?"

Toussaint looked surprised, then rueful. "No, not that. I meant what I said yesterday: the commissioners can't be trusted to bring about the end of slavery."

"Then what is it?" she asked. "You're worried about something."

"Didn't I tell you to stay out of my head?"

She smiled, knowing he didn't mean it. "I don't need to be inside your head. It's written on your face."

"It isn't, you know." He sounded thoughtful. "At least, not for most people to read."

"Well," she said with a shrug. "I suppose I know what faces look like when things are going on behind them."

There was another, softer brush on the ground next to them; Fina picked it up and joined Toussaint at Caesar's side. She ran the bristles gently over the horse's neck, tracing the arch of the strong muscles underneath. Fina had never known any horses before coming to Saint-Domingue; she had learned how to ride through slipping behind the eyes of some of Toussaint's men, and now she felt at home with them. Her magic couldn't reach inside animals' heads, but she stretched out her magic to Caesar all the same, like a caress. She felt something flicker, as though on the tips of her fingers: a gray-white world, and contentment.

"My worry is what will become of the land we've gained," Toussaint said after a while. She turned to him in surprise—not at his words, but that he had spoken in their shared language, as he rarely did these days. "When we rode back today, I saw swaths of sugarcane fields lying unharvested. We need to go back to working them, exactly as we did before they were liberated. I've given instructions about this, many times. But too often, people won't listen. They don't understand that freedom doesn't mean freedom from labor."

"They understand that they need to grow food for themselves and their families," Fina pointed out, in the same language. The familiar tongue made her bolder than usual. "But you want them to work the same hours and produce the same harvests as they did when they were slaves."

"This was the richest colony in the Caribbean before the uprising. It could be again—only this time not for the white plantation owners, but for us. If we can produce the same crops we always have, then we can trade with England and America and Spain. We can prove to France that a colony doesn't need slavery to be successful."

"I don't see why we need to prove anything to people who don't even think we're human."

"Well. It would be helpful in forcing them to come to terms with us." He said it lightly, but she didn't smile. It was too close to the truth. "It isn't about proving what we can be. It's about *becoming* what we can be. Saint-Domingue can be a nation, if our people would just let it."

"They don't see the same Saint-Domingue you do," Fina said. She was learning, now, how to read the differences between what various eyes saw and the various feelings those sights stirred. "When they look at those fields, they don't see crops that need to be harvested. They only see a place they hate, and that hated them back."

"And do you see it?" It wasn't a plea for understanding; he sounded merely curious. But he wanted to know. She thought carefully before she responded.

"I see a lot of Saint-Domingues, through a lot of different eyes," she said. "I like what you see. I want to see it too, I really do. But I was never a slave here. If you asked me to go back to my old plantation, as a free woman, and work it exactly as I used to for the good of your vision, I'm not certain I could do it."

Toussaint nodded. "You saved my life today," he said, as though it were a reply. "I won't forget it."

"It was nothing special." Inwardly, she glowed. "It was a battle. Probably many people saved your life, at many points."

"And I hope I won't forget any of them. But in particular, I won't forget you. You broke the bounds of your magic for me."

"I don't really know the bounds of my magic." It was something she thought about often but had never voiced. "I've never seen magic like mine, even now. In our army we have mesmers, and fire-mages, and alchemists. You have weather magic of a kind, even if it isn't very useful."

"Thank you," he said dryly.

"But what kind of magic is mine? Why hasn't it been seen before?"

"You're still asking your magic to answer to a name," Toussaint said. "Magic doesn't belong to categories. Mesmerism, fire magic, weather magic—those are terms invented by white men, who like to bind things. Magic can't be bound. And the names they have are the kinds of magic common in Europe. Africa has its own kinds of magic—and because they're not recorded in the same way, they seem more mysterious to Europeans." He straightened and stretched his shoulders. "Still. I have a theory about you—and about Dessalines, whose abilities also defy categories."

She tilted her head to look at him. "What is it?"

"You two were both spellbound from a young age. We can't know when Dessalines's magic awakened, since it didn't show until he was freed, but I would guess, like you, it came later rather than at birth. I think that the spellbinding affected your magic and made it grow in ways it wouldn't normally. Spellbinding is designed to control the mind and open it to mesmerism; both of you have abilities that are strongly linked to the mind. Dessalines can make the body feel pain; you can slip into another's body and see through its eyes."

"And control it," she reminded him. "If I can do more like what I did today, then I can control bodies as well. Exactly like spellbinding."

"I think both of you will find you can do more than you think," Toussaint said. He paused. "The voice didn't speak in this battle, I suppose?"

The question startled her, not least because she'd been thinking of it herself. "No. Why?"

"It was a decisive conflict, and one we almost lost. I thought perhaps it might want to help us again."

"We didn't need any voice," she said.

"We may well, in the coming months. British ships have been sighted not far distant. It looks like only a handful of soldiers, but they want the island. And many of the planters here will support them in exchange for a return to slavery—especially now that the commissioners have turned so decidedly against them." He shrugged. "But perhaps the owner of the voice isn't here any longer."

"He's here," she said. She didn't need to stop and think about it.

"I hear him every night, in snatches. But he's talking to people a very long way away now. I don't know if he thinks about us at all."

"Perhaps he thinks it's our job to free ourselves now."

"I don't think that's the reason." She hesitated. "I'm not certain, these days, if his help is something we want."

"You came for his help in the first place, did you not? That was what drew you across the sea."

"At first. But I've heard more of him since—and seen him. It isn't like my other magic; I can't see through his eyes, even when I try. I see him in his own mind, or somewhere just outside it, talking to others. My mind can leave my body, too, and I think often, when he leaves his, I go with him. He's more powerful than me, so he draws me into his head without him even being aware of it. He's never addressed me, or anyone here, but... There's a man in France he talks to. I can hear them, but only in parts, like you'd overhear a conversation through a wind."

She had his full attention now. "Who does he talk to?"

"I never hear the name. He's a white man; when I see him, he looks very little and scared. He must be someone important in the Convention, though, from what the stranger asks of him. And he's what they call a necromancer."

"The whites kill what they call necromancers." Toussaint's face was troubled. "They fear them. Even in Africa, it's very rare for a person to be able to raise the dead. The houngans here consider it a particular gift from the loa—I don't believe there's been one on this island in living memory."

"Well, this little Frenchman is a necromancer. And the stranger is asking him to do something terrible."

"You don't know what it is?"

She shook her head. In the circle of light from the campfire, not twenty feet away, men laughed and drank from the casks of Spanish wine their allies had gifted them. Their song rose with the thread of smoke, joyous and angry.

"Freedom," Toussaint said, "sometimes requires terrible things."

Paris/London

September 1793

It was after midnight when Danton came to call on Robespierre. Robespierre had gone to bed less than twenty minutes before, but when Madame Duplay shook him gently awake to inform him of his visitor, he was on his feet at once. Danton had only recently returned from a mission to Belgium, where the French forces were being battered by the combined might of British, Dutch, and other Allied troops. He would have news that was desperately needed. But it was more than that. There had been a growing suspicion between the two of them lately, after Robespierre had supplanted Danton to become head of the Committee of Public Safety, and Robespierre longed to put it right.

He himself, when he had found that Danton had been thrown out of the Committee and he had suddenly been elected in, had felt the ever-present coil of fear in his stomach stir. It was not the first time he suspected that his benefactor was arranging things without any help from him. But in the last month or so, he had ceased to trouble himself about what lay behind his ascent to his greatest height yet. He was too busy; he needed every scrap of power he could muster just to get things done. He rose every day in the dark hours before dawn, writing until Éléonore knocked softly on the door to see if he wanted breakfast. All day he argued in the Convention; all evening he presided in the Committee; late into the night he spoke at the Jacobins. His speeches grew steadily more hysterical: by the time he collapsed into bed, he felt as though only a thin veneer of flesh and conviction was keeping him from flying apart. The revolt in the provinces had spread. Paris was under siege, and so was the Revolution, and so was France.

"I heard about your wife," Robespierre said after he had greeted Danton and ushered him into his room. "I'm so sorry. Truly."

"I was watching men die," Danton said. His usually powerful voice was dull. Perhaps he had found out the news himself only upon his arrival home, when he had stumbled into a cold, grief-stricken house. Certainly his gigantic form seemed shrunken, as if by sudden illness. "I saw our soldiers coming back from the fields broken and bloody. And as I watched, Gabrielle was dying as well, trying to bring our child into the world."

"I'm so sorry," Robespierre repeated.

Danton shook his head and sat down heavily. There was wine poured for him, but he did not drink; Robespierre, perching on the end of his bed, did not either. "Belgium is lost; there's no question of that. I watched it fall. The Allies have taken Valenciennes, or as good as. And now they tell me that Toulon handed itself over to the British without a fight."

The shift from the personal to the political did not surprise him; it seemed perfectly natural. But the news made his heart sink, and his chest constrict around it.

"I was hoping for better news," he said, as calmly as he could. "I knew about Toulon, of course. And—I don't know if you've heard, but the British navy has invaded Dunkirk. They landed last week. Obviously, we've sent men to reinforce it. But—"

"We need more soldiers," Danton said. "Our enemies are on our coast. There may still be a chance we can hold them there, or even push them off. But we won't win either war—the war with Europe, or the civil war in the provinces—without them."

"It was the conscription of more soldiers that caused a civil war in the first place. The people will never agree."

"Then they must be made to."

"I know it. Of course I know it. I've gone over it again and again in my mind. The question is how. How to educate the people, so we may use the constitution for their benefit. How to make them rally behind us. How to make them see that we are their only hope. That's the real trouble: they can't see that. There are too many conspiracists and royalists and Aristocrats and criminals, and they all sound very much like us. It's confused them."

Danton nodded. "And what answer did you come to?"

Robespierre took off his glasses and rubbed his eyes. "What makes you think I've come to any answer?"

"Because just at this minute, I have none myself. It's why I came. You must have wondered. I'm not in the habit of dropping in on you in the small hours of the morning."

"I assumed you wanted to bring me word from Belgium. Or perhaps that you didn't want to be at home. Not without—"

Danton waved this aside. "I didn't have to be alone at home; I didn't have to be here not to be at home. I came because—" He stopped and shook his head with a short laugh. "I don't know why I've come to you. Except that I've seen the war over the border, and we can't win it with the troops we have. I need to know how the Revolution can produce more. And for better or worse, this has become your revolution, Robespierre, not mine or Camille's or anyone else's. You're perhaps the only one left who understands it."

"When we first met, I had the impression you didn't think so very much of me." Robespierre wondered to hear himself say it. He had never spoken so candidly to Danton before; nor, he suspected, had Danton done so to him. They were always civil to each other, even affectionate; they were both close to Camille, which perhaps caused a degree of jealousy on Robespierre's part but also gave their political alliance a ready-made personal touch. Yet they did not entirely trust each other. Certainly Danton, ever since the morning Camille's child had been born, looked sideways at Robespierre. The night seemed to have burned inhibitions away.

"In some ways I still don't," Danton said with equal bluntness. It stung, but not as much as it would have at other times. "As a politician, you have passion, intellect, and conviction, but no objectivity. You believe everything you say. It will destroy you one day. But until that day comes, you understand the Revolution. You believe in it like nobody I've ever seen, not even Camille. You live and breathe for it. You won't let it die."

Soldiers dying. Citizens dying. Ideas dying. It all seemed one vast torrent of blood. As he'd lain in bed, exhausted yet fighting a return to the garden, he'd felt he was choking on it.

And so he said the words he had promised he would never say. "There is a way."

Danton looked at him, eyes hollow and red-rimmed. "What is it?"

"An army of the dead."

In the silence that followed, Robespierre had a brief flash of the two of them as if from the outside: two figures, haggard and worn in the light of a single candle, like ghosts haunting their own bodies in a world gone mad. *We are dead*, he thought with wonder. *We are already dead.*

"You're a necromancer," Danton said slowly. "Like your mother. I see. And I see why you would want to keep that hidden, even now. But...the magic to create an army of the dead no longer exists. Nobody knows it."

"It exists. I know it. I need only corpses, and shadows."

"Camille can call shadows," Danton said. "And I suspect he'd love to."

"I agree. It may be the corpses that prove the most difficult."

Danton laughed bitterly. "We have no shortages of corpses."

"It's not so simple. It's not ordinary necromancy. For them to be inhabited, they need to have died recently, and they need to have died in fear. We can't simply unearth a mass grave and walk them out of it in the dead of night."

"In fear?"

"It's dark magic," Robespierre said simply. "There's a reason why the Knights Templar tried to destroy all knowledge of it."

Danton hesitated. It was the moment when he might have turned back; Robespierre knew, and waited. The moment passed.

"Well," he said briskly. "My point still stands. These are days of blood. Corpses are not difficult to come by. Nor is fear."

Robespierre felt something inside him give way, and refused to look at what lay beneath. "We made a corpse of France's king," he said. "We can make corpses of her enemies."

"Tell me," Danton said.

"You know what I'm about to say."

"I suspect so. But I want to hear you say it. You don't mean the enemies outside our borders, do you?"

"I'm never afraid of the enemies outside our borders. The ones I fear are always the ones in our midst. The traitors, the conspiracists, the royalists, the Girondin sympathizers—the ones who want to see the French Republic of Magicians fail. That's who we need to punish if we want to end this civil war. And we need to punish them so badly that nobody will ever dare pick up their fallen banners."

"If they won't fight for us in life," Danton said slowly, "we make them fight for us in death." He was trying out the idea rather than agreeing, but he wasn't arguing. "We remove them from the streets, where they can do harm, and strengthen the army at the same time."

"More than that. We make an example of them. A terrible example of what happens to criminals who outrage liberty and spill the blood of patriots."

Danton was looking at him as if he'd never quite seen him before. "My God, Robespierre," he said. "What is it like inside your head?"

Dark, Robespierre could have said. *And I'm never alone in there.* Of course he didn't. Even in the heightened register the conversation had taken, it would have sounded alarming.

"If you don't agree—"

"No," Danton interrupted. "No, I'm not saying that. We're killing them already, at the guillotine. I see no harm in putting the bodies to use. But you do realize something, don't you? If this is to work at all, it needs to be open. You can't hide anymore."

Robespierre's thoughts had been racing too fast for feeling; at this, they slowed down enough to catch a trace of dread. "Not necessarily. We can carry out the executions at the Place de la Révolution. Then the bodies can be brought back to the Conciergerie. I—"

Danton was shaking his head. "No. No smuggling them away. As I said, I understand why you hid your magic: you've clearly been doing so your whole life. Your whole life depended on it. But it needs to stop. If we are to create an army of the dead, then we need to do it with strength, with conviction, and with the belief that we are right. We need to do it in the open."

"In the open? Before everyone?"

"On the scaffold itself. In the name of the Revolution."

Robespierre was silent.

"We are the Republic of Magicians," Danton said. "And you are a magician. If you can indeed create an army of the dead, you are one of the most powerful magicians we have. We need not be discreet."

One thing caught Robespierre's attention. "We?"

"I'll support you in this." The sense of security Danton could give an entire mob was in his voice. "And so will Camille, I'm sure. We will stand with you. We have nothing to fear."

They had so much to fear. Paradoxically, it made up Robespierre's mind. He was so tired of being afraid. "Then let us do it without fear. It is our enemies who need to fear. No more massacres. No more mob justice. No more innocent blood on the streets. We will take control and lead the people to a new age, at whatever cost."

"We'll address the Convention first thing tomorrow." Danton stood; when Robespierre did the same, Danton embraced him quickly. Robespierre, who hated being touched except by people very dear to him, managed not to flinch away. "This is it, Maximilien. I was beginning to despair before I came here."

Robespierre wasn't sure that he was not despairing now. He felt numb. Somewhere, inside his head, something other than him was laughing. Yet he was right. He really did believe he was right.

"This is not it," he said. "But it's a path to it. And yes. We'll both address the Convention tomorrow."

And they would agree. With the force of his benefactor burning behind his eyes, they would certainly agree.

Before he left, into a cloudy night shading into a pale dawn, Danton turned once again to Robespierre.

"My wife," he said. "Can you—?"

Robespierre shook his head quickly. "No. Don't even think it, my friend. It wouldn't be her. You'd see an echo, a shadow, and then you'd lose her all over again."

"That might almost be enough."

The hunger in his eyes was so achingly familiar that Robespierre felt tears come to his own. "It won't be. It would drive you mad. I won't do it."

"I loved her. I don't even know if she knew that: I was never faithful to her, and she knew it. But I loved her. You couldn't possibly understand—"

"I do understand! For once, I understand you perfectly, Danton. I feel what you're suffering. At this moment, I *am* you. And still I won't do it. Necromancy isn't an act of love. It's an act of grief. Grief is all that ever comes of it."

Danton didn't argue. Perhaps he had already known what Robespierre's answer would be. "And undead magic? What is that an act of?"

"Terror," Robespierre said. "But we believe in our cause. We do it for France, and for liberty. That must sanctify it."

"Are you satisfied now?" he asked his benefactor.

"Never," his benefactor said. "That much we have in common. But I'm pleased. I think you will be too, when it's done."

"You don't understand."

"Perhaps not. I have never attached much importance to death."

"Your magic is born of fear. My magic is born of grief. For this to work, I will need to grieve for each and every one of my victims. I need to feel their deaths like the death of my own family."

"Fear not, Robespierre," his benefactor said. It was one of those moments when his voice had an oddly archaic inflection. "I have no doubt in my mind that you will."

When Robespierre was a child, he had held a dead bird in his hands. His grief had filled his heart like salt water, drenched it, and drowned it.

I will never see it fly, he had thought, and it was too much to bear.

And then, inexplicably, he had felt his grief overflow his heart and spill through his fingers. He had felt it pool in the fragile body he held: through the bones, the organs, the blood vessels, the delicate wing feathers, and the glinting orb of its eyes. Without knowing what he was doing, he had pushed.

Its eyes had opened. Its wings had unfurled. It had taken off from his hands with the lightest tickle of pressure, and as he had watched it soar away for the last time, he had felt a joy so profound that it was almost pain.

Now he was hundreds of miles from that garden. He stood on a scaffold, high above a roaring crowd. Camille stood beside him: with his dark curls and fine-boned face, he looked something between a poet and a choirboy. Between Danton's powerful ugliness and his school friend's firefly charm, Robespierre sometimes felt painfully ordinary. Now he was glad of Camille's distracting presence. It was the first time he had appeared in public as a necromancer. There were eyes enough on him already.

It was a clear, beautiful autumn day. Behind him were the looming frame of the guillotine, and seven men waiting to die. He didn't turn, but the sun was at his back, and it projected the guillotine's thin shadow on the ground at his feet.

"Are you ready?" he asked Camille beneath the noise.

In answer, Camille closed his eyes and drew the shadows about him.

Commoner magic was not the spectacle nowadays that it had been even a year ago. By now, Robespierre had seen fellow magicians call shadows before, and so had most others. Still, Camille's magic had associations with the storming of the Bastille that moved hearts: it was one of the reasons the Committee of Public Safety had chosen him for this first display of power. The crowd cheered as the darkness crept from corners to form a ghostly figure. Robespierre let the applause go on for a few minutes before he nodded to the executioner.

The first prisoner to be brought forward was a stocky man, with ears that stuck out beneath his newly cropped hair. He struggled against the soldiers, shouting something that was lost in the tumult. It was a cry of fear, perhaps, but also of anger. Even in these circumstances, even knowing the man was a traitor, Robespierre recognized the anger as an echo of his own.

I'm sorry, he thought at the man, too secretly for it to reach his eyes. His face was still stone. *You're like me. You won't forgive me, any more than I've ever forgiven an enemy. But I'm sorry.*

It took three men to place him in the guillotine. The screams ceased only when the blade came down and his head dropped from his shoulders.

There was a corresponding roar from the onlookers, of course, but not of the strength executions usually provoked. Even when the executioner held the head above the crowd, scattering the closest with blood, the laughter was more polite than otherwise. They were waiting. And as the last heartbeat died in the man's chest, Robespierre's magic stirred.

This time, he did not push it out—not yet. He did as he had been instructed in a dark alley five years ago, by a voice in his dreams promising him a new France. Camille's shadow was standing beside them. Robespierre turned to it and, without words, let his hands fall to his sides and closed his eyes.

Come to me, he thought.

The shadow needed only that opening. At once, the faint, clammy smoke was on his skin, in his nose and in his throat, and then it was inside him. He shuddered and gagged as it rushed into his chest. It was like swallowing an acrid fog—worse, because mingled with the sensation were flashes of thoughts and images that were not his own. Some of them belonged to Camille, he thought—at least, he thought he recognized the bright joys and darknesses of his friend's mind. Others were darker yet, and set the hair rising on the back of his neck. Yet he held it as it mingled with his blood and curled around his heart. Only when he felt it was becoming part of him did he let it go.

The shadow passed through him with the tide of his necromancy. It poured from his fingers, magic and shadow and grief combined, and it poured into the corpse.

The corpse stood.

Robespierre had realized that it would have no head; he had almost preferred that, remembering the horrible glassy stare of the last one. He had not realized that the head of the shadow, without a skull to contain it, would be visible in its place. It looked at him, in the way shadows do, without eyes.

Robespierre had to swallow before he could speak. "Camille."

The crowd had gone so unnaturally quiet that his whisper carried. Camille was staring at the undead, his own face pale as death, but he shook himself at the sound of his own name. He raised his hand.

"I bind you to the service of France." Where his cuff pulled away from his wrist, Robespierre saw the puckered scar left by his old bracelet. "From now on, you will obey any order given to you by the government of the French Republic of Magicians."

The undead stood quiet. There was no sign that it had heard, or that it had not.

Camille nodded at Robespierre. Robespierre cleared his throat, steeled himself, and spoke.

"Step down." He could hear the strain in his own voice, but he was satisfied others would not. "Stand aside and await further orders."

There was one heart-stopping moment, between the words reaching the creature and its obedience, when Robespierre thought it was not going to obey at all. It seemed too ghastly to even hear the words of someone like him. Yet it did obey. It turned, stepped down from the scaffolding, and stood beside the guillotine. The crowds drew away, even those who were nowhere near it at all.

The next prisoner was brought forward. It was easier the second time.

Afterward, he collapsed back in his room. He felt desperately weak, not so much drained as gutted. Magic and energy had departed and left nothing inside him, not even his heart. The world around him was cold and dark and full of shadows.

Charlotte, for once, won the tussle over who would take care of him. She met him and Camille in the Duplays' courtyard and took Robespierre's arm protectively before Madame Duplay could.

"It's our bloodline," she said, and Madame Duplay nodded. Perhaps, Robespierre thought dully, she would no longer be so eager for his blood to marry into the family. That would hurt, when he had time to feel it, if it were true.

The Duplays hovered anxiously at the bottom of the stairs while Charlotte helped him to his bed. He lay shivering; across the room, he heard Camille's quick tread pace the floorboards.

"My God," his friend said. His stammer was stronger than Robespierre had heard it in a long time. "What did we just do?"

Robespierre forced himself upright. "What do you mean, what did we do? We destroyed France's enemies, and we made her stronger." He paused. "When your shadow mingled with my magic, did you feel anything?"

"Of course I did. Everything. I was inside your head for a moment. Just in glimpses. And then I was inside that corpse. Part of me still is, even though I've given control over to the Convention."

"You mean the shadow is. Your magic is."

"It's not that simple. You're a magician too; you know it isn't. Magic both is and isn't part of you—that shadow is both something pulled from the ether and a fragment of my soul. I can feel it like a ghost limb. That was dark magic."

"You knew that before you did it. I told you it was."

"I know. I didn't really believe in dark magic, I suppose—I thought it was something the Knights Templar made up, because they were fools. They *are* fools, but it wasn't. I'm not blaming you for it; I'm not even saying it's wrong. But I've summoned shadows before, Maximilien—I've never felt them *contort* like that."

There was nothing he could say to that. He understood too well what he meant. His own necromancy trembled inside him as though it were hurt. "Seven undead soldiers," he said instead. "It's a start. Soon it will number in the thousands."

"Can you manage that? I'm not sure I can. And you look half-dead."

The choice of phrase made him want to laugh. He conquered it, knowing that if he started, he would never stop. "You won't have to do every one. There are other shadowmancers, after all. And me—it will get easier all the time. With practice."

"Practice." Camille ran a hand through his curls. "I'm not squeamish about violence, Maxime. You know I'm not. I could have shot those traitors myself, and not lost a moment's sleep—unless I lost it out celebrating their deaths. But this—I've never seen anything like this."

"Of course you have. Under the old regime, you saw men hung from ropes, gutted alive, and torn apart by draft horses. You saw rape, murder, and corruption on a daily basis. You saw people thrown into prison without trial, never to see the light of day. You saw children dead in the street. You called for that violence to be revisited on our oppressors."

"I did," he said. "And I meant it. I suppose—I never saw anything like this from you."

He couldn't argue with that either. Every discussion he had ever had with Camille about the barbarity of capital punishment had already argued against him. He had quoted scores of philosophers and thinkers in those days. Now he could only quote himself. "Terror is nothing more than speedy, severe, and inflexible justice."

"Perhaps." Camille drew a deep breath and managed to laugh a little as he released it. "Look at me. I'm actually trembling. I must be getting old. Danton will be downstairs by now. Shall I go fetch him?"

Robespierre nodded. "Please. We all need to talk."

When Camille closed the door, Robespierre gritted his teeth and with a surge of effort pulled himself to his feet. He remembered the day the Girondins fell, when Camille had stretched out his hand and warmed him through with the flicker of his magic. His friend had no strength left to share this time.

Charlotte watched him. She must have noticed his condition, but she said nothing. "What did it feel like to you?" she asked instead. "To bring them to life?"

"It felt necessary." It was a nonanswer, and they both knew it. "We've come too far to go back now."

Robespierre ran a hand across his eyes. At the edges of his vision, shadows were dancing. He couldn't explain it. Perhaps he was imagining them; perhaps, as he suspected, a fragment of the shadow he had taken inside himself hadn't left. He felt more than empty. He felt haunted.

"Do *you* believe in what we're doing?" he asked Charlotte.

Charlotte had been short enough with him in the last few weeks. He knew she resented his distance from her since the Duplays had taken him in, and he, swept up in the tides of private and public wars, had not been able to make it up to her. But in that moment, he reached out to her, pleading, and as always, she could not resist.

"You're my brother," Charlotte said. "I've known you all my life. You frustrate the life out of me, but I've never seen you do a cruel deed. If you say this horror is needed, then it's needed."

He nodded. "Thank you."

She kissed his forehead, as she had not done since they were children, and smoothed back his hair. If it cost her anything to do it, after what she had seen, she gave no sign. "I'll get you another blanket. You're still cold."

It was only after she left that he let himself cry, and then not very much.

The skies hung cloudy above London that night. Back at Old Palace Yard for the opening of Parliament the following day, Wilberforce had for once managed to get to bed before midnight, but his sleep had not been kind. Slave ships and shadows had twisted through his dreams. When a servant came to rouse him to tell him that the prime minister was downstairs, he was more relieved to be woken than not.

"Do you just enjoy the prospect of waking me up if something occurs to you in the middle of the night?" he asked Pitt by way of greeting.

"Well, you enjoy the prospect of waking me up if something occurs to you in the middle of the morning," Pitt said. "It's all relative. I really am sorry to disturb you."

"It's really no matter." He yawned and rubbed his eyes. "Just please tell me there isn't another undead in Westminster Abbey. Or the Tower of London, or Kew Gardens, or any other major landmark."

Pitt laughed, but briefly, as if out of breath. "Not exactly. You might remember we managed to smuggle a daemon-stone into Paris?"

"I don't think I was supposed to know about it, but yes. I remember."

"We have two there now. The Downing Street daemon-stone just received a message from one of them. It was humming loudly enough that it woke me two doors away. This evening, Robespierre and Camille Desmoulins animated an undead in front of a crowd in the Place de la Révolution."

It took a few moments for this to penetrate his sleepiness. Then he was wide-awake. "An undead. Like the one from Westminster Abbey?"

"Exactly like."

Desmoulins summoned shadows—that was well known. "Robespierre is a necromancer."

"A necromancer who knows the method for raising the undead," Pitt said. "The one we've been trying to find since that night in Westminster Abbey. We've found him. And he happens to be the head of the French Republic of Magicians."

France

The Reign of Terror

France needed corpses. Many of them, strong ones, and quickly. The people were happy to oblige.

Marie Antoinette came first, though her tortured body was really too frail to be of any use. It was a ritual sacrifice, a way of cementing the new world order with the death of yet another royal. Her hair had turned to white, and her soft face had hollowed and aged during her long imprisonment. She ascended the steps to the scaffold with an air of buoyancy, even relief, and stepped on the foot of her executioner on the way.

"I'm sorry," she said to him, the last words she would ever speak. "I didn't mean to do it."

The twenty-two Girondins who had been detained and arrested since June were killed in October. The trial dragged on until Robespierre cut it short with the proposal that all subsequent trials would last no more than three days; after that, if the Committee felt they had enough to convict, they would do so without waiting for evidence. A trial of conscience, it was called, and it became the standard for the Republic. It made things quicker, and less dependent on fact.

"Anyone who trembles," Robespierre said, "is guilty."

Most of the so-called evidence given in the courtroom came from Camille's publications; in particular, the vicious satire of Brissot, who had once insulted Camille in public and been justly punished in print. The article had been a mixture of half-truths, clever allusions, and cruel lies, but it had been very funny. Brissot had been one of the witnesses at Camille's wedding.

Camille himself was in the courtroom as his words were read aloud and brought to life in front of him, like an author at opening night of a grotesque play. Those near him watched him turn paler and paler. When at last the sentence was read and the twenty-two Girondins sentenced to death, he covered his face with his hands.

"Oh my God," he whispered. "I killed them. I actually killed them."

"Are you all right?" asked a man sitting near him.

He shook his head, in one quick movement. He was swaying. "I need to get out. I can't breathe."

There was no way out. Too great a crush of people had come to see the last of the moderates fall; they were pushing, jostling to get closer, and Camille was too close to the barricades. He fell to the floor in a dead faint.

Not many noticed him. They were distracted by the greater drama in the dock. Charles Valazé, one of the convicted, had smuggled a knife into the court. Upon hearing the verdict, he had stabbed himself in the heart. He had no desire to be an undead.

There were too many magicians among those arrested. The Bastille was the only building with cells charmed to dampen magic, and it had been destroyed. And so bracelets were brought back, for those the Republic imprisoned. The spells on them burned hotter than they had even under the old regime: the first prisoner to test its boundaries, a young laborer suspected of giving shelter to Girondin sympathizers, fell into a fit from the pain and never woke up. They guillotined his limp body, and a shadow entered it.

⋆ ⋆ ⋆

Madame Roland was executed a few days after her friends. Her husband had escaped to the country, but after learning of her death would kill himself in a ditch outside Rouen. She met her death proudly, as so many did. Turning to face the statue of Liberty that presided over the executions, she declared "Liberty, what crimes are committed in your name!" before placing her head beneath the blade.

Dunkirk was a fortified seaport on the coast of France, and that autumn it was under siege. British troops had held the beach for weeks, under the command of the Duke of York and supported by Austrian, Hanoverian, and Hesse-Kassel troops. The coast was dotted with thirty-five thousand men, all ready to take possession of the town. When the British had first landed, the French had fled. It had seemed that their victory would be easy.

Magic had as yet done France little good in the heat of a battlefield, but they found many uses for it in causing discomfort to the Allies. Four days ago, water-mages had flooded the trenches across the dunes, leaving the Allied soldiers knee-high in water ever since. The weather-mages kept them stewing in a miserable localized fog of rain and heat that mingled sweat and water on the skin. Already, half the men were shivering with what they had termed Dunkirk fever. The rest were plagued with mosquitoes, lice, rashes, and boils; their food rotted, and so did their teeth. At least the protective charms they had placed along the lines stopped fire magic from ripping through the trenches and gutting them in one stroke. It was difficult to be too grateful to the English ministers for these charms, though. The ship that had brought them was supposed to bring heavy siege guns and reinforcements; it brought none of the former, and too few of the latter. Because of this, the troops struggled to hold their ground, and the town remained in French hands.

This, by the way, was Dundas's fault, and it was Pitt's. It was also Pitt's fault that the troops were on the beach at all, when he had been advised by other field officers that they would be better spent reinforcing the main invasion of France through Valenciennes. He was still inexperienced in war, and too used to achieving everything he wanted. In his defense, he was doing the best he knew how. In this case, his best was not enough, and that was his responsibility to bear.

In the early hours of a September morning, after an uneasy lull in the fighting, the British troops sighted movement on the horizon. Too small to be a battalion advancing, too many to be a single scout, too far in the distance as yet for rifles to pick off. Superior officers were woken quickly; the men were instructed in whispers to arm themselves and wait. Tense, poised, aching, cold, they waited.

A line of fourteen soldiers advanced over the dunes. They looked like men, from a distance: ordinary men, of different shapes and sizes, wearing French uniforms and carrying rifles. As they came closer, the gray light glinted on their chests, and those in front could see they were each wearing an iron breastplate, of the kind knights had worn on much older battlefields. The British soldiers with a strain of metalmancy felt the tug of their magic; the one or two who knew anything about their own Inheritances guessed that the breastplates had been fused shut by magic and charmed to repel all but the strongest assault. It would take a very powerful metalmancer to rip them apart. And yet the rest of their uniform was standard, open, vulnerable to attack. There was nothing to prevent a straight shot to the head, not even a hat.

As the soldiers drew nearer, the reason for this became apparent. They had no heads. Above their collars, black smoke swirled in an ever-shifting globe: the faces of shadows, which looked without eyes at the British troops. They wore the human corpse as a ghastly suit.

Word of France's army of the dead had not reached the British troops at Dunkirk. They had no idea what they were seeing. Some had read enough history to make the connection, or been told enough stories of the Vampire Wars; most had not. But every last one of them felt a rush of pure horror.

The order came to fire; many rifles were already cracking. The shots struck the advancing undead: legs, arms, insubstantial heads, armored breastplates. The undead twitched at the impact, over and over. They did not slow. Human hands gripped guns and swords, human feet marched on the sands, but they were animated by pure shadow. They could not feel pain, and they could not be stopped—except, of course, by a wound through the heart, and their hearts were locked away.

They entered the trenches a few minutes later. There was more rifle fire then, and swords flashing, and a good deal of screaming.

"Really, Robespierre," his benefactor said. "Is this so very terrible?"

Clapham

Autumn 1793

At Clapham Common, the sun was shining, albeit through a wall of iron-gray clouds. It gave the grounds a cool, watercolor tranquility that was completely at odds with its occupants. In the years since Wilberforce had come to live there, the area had grown from a quiet little patch of greenery not far from London to what resembled the world's friendliest, busiest, highest-achieving lunatic asylum. The rapidly growing collection of evangelicals and social reformers flitted in and out of each other's houses without bothering to knock, borrowing books, trying on ideas, and sharing knowledge. Wilberforce, he freely admitted, was the worst offender of all: he not only was in other people's houses with the best of them, but found it even harder than most to get out of them once he was there. Conversations tended to run away with him; or rather, he ran away with them, and took everyone else with him.

When Pitt came to call, he was instantly absorbed into the lively discussion taking place in the library of Thornton's house, Battersea Rise. Wilberforce tried to extricate him, knowing what he had really come to talk about, but was singularly ill suited to the task. He found what was being said too interesting.

"But, if I may ask, where are the magicians to come from if Britain *does* break the Concord?" Hannah More pressed him. "Only a relatively small portion of the army is braceleted. Would the government begin mass conscription of magicians, as France has?"

"We still don't intend to break the Concord," Pitt said. "But—"

"Even with this army of the dead from France?" Thornton asked. "Austria and Prussia are pushing for it. Help yourself to a drink, by the way."

"Thank you— No, not even with France's army of the dead. Most of the Alliance want to use magic since Dunkirk, you're right, but they won't as long as we don't. They don't want to lose Britain's support, financial and otherwise, and make an enemy of us in the process. And I have hopes that the army of the dead won't grow very much bigger—the dark practices needed to bring it about are too barbaric. Even the scale of the executions at the moment... The general population in France won't stand for them for long."

"But hypothetically?" Wilberforce prompted, drawn in despite himself. "If we *were* to break the Concord? It's good to see you, by the way."

"And you— Is this how you always greet your guests? I haven't even sat down yet."

"Oh, you love it. You'd be so bored if we greeted you with 'Good afternoon, how are you? Was your journey very smooth?'"

"I think I could stand to be a little bored."

"Good afternoon, Pitt. How are you? Was your journey very smooth?"

"God, how boring. Hypothetically: we already conscript in the navy—or press-gang, to be more precise. It's not pleasant, but we've done it for centuries. I don't think we'd need to resort to those methods for the army, though. People are flocking to sign up for the king's shilling as it is. If we increased the financial incentive for magicians, that along with the prospect of using their magic might entice them. We could afford it, at least as things stand now. But, as I said, I hope it won't come to that."

"It's a dark path we're on," Granville Sharp said. He shook his head. "Freedom of magic leading to revolution and dark magic on the battlefield. Repression of magic leading us to further prejudice against magical Commoners. It's difficult to know which way to turn."

The conversation turned after that, but didn't wane. Eliot's little daughter, now a year old, was visiting her father with a nurse; he brought her in for Pitt and everyone else to admire. (Fortunately, she was an unusually pretty child.) Thornton wanted to talk about the prison bill being raised in the House next session. Somebody, inevitably, brought up abolition. The sun moved across the sky outside.

"Pitt's my guest," Wilberforce said at last. "And this is his first time here in months. He's already seen this library; he designed the thing. I'm showing him the gardens. Pitt?"

"I'm very happy to see the gardens," he replied promptly. "But I object to my library being called a thing."

"Why is he *your* guest?" Eliot mock-protested, taking his daughter back from Pitt. "I'm the father of his niece. I should show him around the gardens."

"But you have a letter to write to Macaulay. He's written to us from the colony at Sierra Leone. I left it on your desk this morning."

"You could write back to him yourself."

"I could. But I'm showing Pitt the gardens. Besides, we have important secrets to discuss. It's why he came out here in the first place."

"Never mind, Eliot," Pitt said consolingly. "I'll see you again before I go. We can have tea here, in the thing."

The sound of laughter and conversation followed them down the path as they left Battersea Rise behind them; by mutual agreement, they held off talking about the real reason for Pitt's visit while there was still a probability of being overheard. In retrospect, Clapham probably wasn't the safest place for a private conversation, when every house, tree, and patch of grass was regarded as communal property by its inhabitants. But it was where Wilberforce had been when Pitt had contacted him with the promise of news, and it was infinitely better than anywhere Pitt could provide in London. Here, at least any eavesdropping would be accidental and friendly; in Downing Street, half the cabinet would be twitching about the door for news.

"Well," Wilberforce said. "What do you think of this place, now it's finished?"

"It's beautiful," Pitt said, in the faintly wistful tone with which people always appreciate real beauty. The path wound away from the house, meandering about the yellowing tulip trees and autumnal flowers. The breeze made the grass stir and brought with it the earthy smell of dried leaves. "I've been stuck in London entirely too much lately. I almost wish I could join you all here."

"You would hate it. We'd pester you all the time for your insights on everything from foreign policy to ancient Greek, steal your books, wake you at sunrise every morning, and make you go to church."

"I've changed my mind. Dear God, what realm of torments have you concocted?"

"The latter two would be very good for you. The former would only benefit us, alas, but we'd make it up to you with beautiful gardens, reasonable food, excellent company, and fireside conversation."

"That is indeed tempting, but I'm afraid I've now changed my mind once in the last few minutes. Changing it twice would look like indecision. The government would fall."

They waited until they were out of earshot before they spoke again.

"You probably saw the reports in the papers that the first battalion of the dead has been used in action," Pitt said. "Only fourteen of them were there, and yet they say they killed three hundred men apiece. Likely exaggeration—they were supported by an army of regular Commoner magicians who surely did their own share of killing—but many of our soldiers were certainly killed before they could be evacuated. Between the terror they inspire on our side, the hope they inspire on our enemy's, and the fact that they can't be killed, they form a formidable front."

"We lost Dunkirk, didn't we?" Wilberforce said, not sure why he made it a question. They had certainly lost Dunkirk. "They're calling it a disaster."

"I wouldn't call it that," Pitt said, to Wilberforce's complete lack of surprise. If Britain were to sink into the sea, Pitt would regard it as an unfortunate but not irretrievable situation. "It's certainly a severe check; I still hope it will be only a temporary one. If they send out many more undead, though, it's looking more and more likely that we'll have to break the Concord to have any hope of success. Spain will probably do so, if we don't first. There's a very good chance that this could bring widespread magic back to the battlefield for the first time since the fifteenth century."

"And we now know, or suspect," Wilberforce said, "that Robespierre sent an undead to Britain before the fall of the Bastille."

"I think we can suspect more than that," Pitt said. "I think we can safely say that he's working with the same vampire that tempted Clarkson all those years ago. Whatever its plan is, it goes well beyond abolition."

"It must," Wilberforce said. "Robespierre's always been a friend to abolition. There's no reason he'd want to kill me. But do we really know that he's in league with a vampire? I know armies of the dead are associated with the Vampire Wars; in that case, the vampire was usually the one to summon the shadows. But there's no vampire at the guillotine—from what I've heard, there's a series of shadowmancers, none suspected of being anything else. Could Robespierre not have found the knowledge on his own, somehow?"

"It would be extremely coincidental, given that we know there *is* a vampire in France with at least some of the traditional abilities, and the knowledge of how to create an undead has otherwise been lost for generations. Besides...someone summoned a shadow for him to create the undead that nearly killed you. He does indeed have a series of people working with him at the guillotine now: Camille Desmoulins and Antoine Saint-Just, usually. But 1788 was before Robespierre had moved to Paris; he was a poor lawyer in the provinces, living among nonmagical or braceleted Commoners. Desmoulins was miles away, and braceleted. Saint-Just was a child."

"You think the vampire was there?"

"The undead had been killed twice, according to the Templars. I told you this at the time, but you were very ill—you might not remember. The second time was your stake through the heart. The first time, it had been half decapitated, and—"

"—and drained of blood," Wilberforce finished. "I do remember, though I hadn't thought of it in years. Is that necessary to create an undead?"

"Not at all," Pitt said. "But if you happen to be a practicing blood magician trying not to attract attention in a provincial town, I imagine you take what you can."

The gentle autumn sun suddenly felt very cold.

"But why?" Wilberforce asked. "What does it want?"

"I don't know what it wanted with you, in '88. I'm not even entirely sure what it wanted with Clarkson and Saint-Domingue—unless it was to provoke war between France and Britain, and there are far easier ways of doing that. But the war, the breaking of the Concord, and the army of the dead—that, I suspect, is a vampire doing what vampires have traditionally done: take control, and expand their territories."

During the Vampire Wars, vampire families had been on the thrones of France and England. "He's removed the royal family from France. The throne is vacant."

"Exactly. Robespierre is the closest the Republic has to a leader at present. The vampire's working through him. He's using Robespierre to take power, and to create an army of the dead that can expand France's territory back to what it used to be hundreds of years ago."

"He'll want Britain as well, then. All the vampire kings wanted both Britain and France. King George's magic hasn't revolted this time, has it?"

"No. I saw him only yesterday. He's well—very disturbed over this, of course, but well. I suppose the vampire is less directly involved with these undead. Though it might be only a matter of time. Magic is unpredictable."

A thought struck Wilberforce. "Is this happening because of you? I mean... do you think this vampire is challenging you, in particular?"

"I don't know. Perhaps." He sounded tired. "It doesn't really matter, does it? Not from a practical point of view. Either way, we appear to be fighting the first vampire war in over three hundred years."

"Dear God." Wilberforce was quiet for a moment. "What can we do?"

Pitt caught himself firmly on the edge of despair. "As a matter of fact, I think we can do quite a lot. Far more than we had any hope of doing before. Robespierre's revealed his hand now—or rather the enemy's hand. If we're careful, and clever, and very fortunate, we might be able to put a stop to this right now. Because if we're correct, we finally have someone with a tangible connection to the enemy."

"Robespierre." Wilberforce began to get a vague inkling of where this was going. "In fact, if you're right, and the vampire physically helped Robespierre create an undead in Arras all those years ago, then that would mean he's actually *seen* the enemy vampire."

"Exactly. And that makes him our greatest opportunity. It's why I very much hope that we're right." He started to cough, suppressed it, and moved on. "Because if we are, he can help us find it."

"The trouble is," Wilberforce said, "he would never help us with anything, ever. Especially you. He thinks you're the devil incarnate."

" 'He never could abide carnation,' " Pitt quoted absently. It was a sure sign his mind was leaping ahead somewhere else entirely. " ''Twas a color he never liked.' "

It sounded familiar, and Shakespearean. "*Henry the Fourth*?"

"Fifth."

"Ah. The one where they conquer France."

"And just like that, the solution falls into place. We conquer France. That should resolve everything."

"And they say in the papers that you don't have a military mind."

It occurred to him too late that the joke might not be very tactful under the circumstances; if Pitt minded, though, he gave no sign. "They're quite right. So we'd better consider an alternative, just in case. The problem is, even if it could be brought off, I'm not convinced that talking to Robespierre would be the best course."

He broke off to cough again. This time, he didn't shake it off quite so easily; it sounded painful enough that Wilberforce frowned. "Are you quite well?"

"Not quite," he conceded, a little breathlessly. He cleared his throat. "But well enough, considering."

"Considering what?"

"Considering that I don't have time to be anything else." He shook his head. "It's nothing serious. As I said, I've been in London for far too long this summer, and I've been rather overworked—I wouldn't be doing my job very well if I wasn't. You're the one we all worry about. Eliot told me you haven't been very well yourself."

"Well, no. But I was stabbed by an undead on the eve of the French Revolution. I have an ongoing excuse." A thought came to him. "It isn't anything similar in your case, is it? I mean—the elixir still works?"

"It still works. I'm just taking slightly more of it than usual."

Wilberforce stopped to look at him. "Since when? Why didn't you say something?"

"I said it still works. Truly, there isn't anything more to be said."

"There certainly is. Why should you need more? You're not using your Inheritance, are you?"

"Not in the way you mean—of course not. But I'm using it to stay alive, unfortunately. Blood magic is how my heart pumps and my lungs draw breath. It takes a toll. Besides—I'm not sure I can explain this, but even legal magic doesn't work the way you might assume. It doesn't lie around and wait to be taken up, like a quill or a hairbrush. Magic *wants* to be used. In times like this—times when magic would be very useful—keeping it from manifesting is exhausting in itself." He sighed at Wilberforce's expression. "All of which is perfectly normal, and what every Commoner magician struggles with every day. Please don't be concerned. I'm not."

"I am. Of course I am. How much is slightly more? Half again? Double?"

"Something like that. It's not an exact science."

"It used to be, didn't it?"

"A great many things used to be. I think this path is going to take us back to the house before we're ready. Do you mind if we sit down?"

Wilberforce recognized the change in subject; he let it go, but it compounded his list of worrying things left unspoken. "Of course not."

There was a rough wooden bench under an oak tree, half-submerged in a mess of grass and dandelions. Once they'd sat, Battersea Rise fell behind the surrounding trees; as a result, the grounds seemed quieter, and more peaceful. The cloudy sky overhead felt like the curve of a glass jar, muffling the sounds of birdsong and voices in the distance.

"The difficulty about Robespierre," Pitt said, as though there had been no interruption, "is this: if we speak to him or show any sign of using him to find the enemy, the enemy will know. We'll never find it that way."

Wilberforce nodded. "I see. But we have supporters in Paris, don't we? If 'supporters' is the right word. Informers. Spies."

"*Des intrigants*?" Pitt said with a smile, and Wilberforce smiled too, remembering their brief imprisonment in a Rheims police station. "We have many—not as many as Robespierre thinks we have, unfortunately. I don't think there are as many spies in all of Europe as Robespierre thinks are in Paris. We still have two daemon-stones in Paris, though we don't expect to hear much more from one of them. At least for now their possessors are still at large. But there's very little they can do with this on their own. Neither of them is close to Robespierre. And if they denounce him, then they're likely to be executed themselves. At best, if they're believed, Robespierre will be executed in their place."

"That would at least end the necromancy."

"But it would lose us all trace of the enemy. We'd be back where we started."

"Far too familiar a location." The abolition movement, after all, seemed to spend the end of every parliamentary year back where they had started. "So there's nobody who will be able to help us."

"Well," Pitt said—so carefully, Wilberforce suspected he wasn't going to like what was about to be said. "There's Camille Desmoulins."

His suspicion had been correct. "Camille Desmoulins. The spark that ignited the Revolution. The writer of the most inflammatory material to come out of Paris. The shadowmancer who stood at the guillotine when the Terror took its first victims. The... Please interrupt if I leave something out."

"He was all those things. Because of that, we've had people watching him very closely since the Bastille. He's difficult to miss, it must be said. And recently, it seems, he's begun to show signs of remorse—or so our informers say. One of them sat beside him when the Girondins were put on trial."

"And is it a person whose information you trust? Because you do that too easily, you know."

"What do I do?"

"Trust information that you want to be true. Believe things are going to work out because they have to. Fail to consider the possibility that you are being misled."

"I do consider that possibility."

"But you tend to reject it. I don't mean to criticize; there are far worse faults than natural optimism."

"But possibly not less dangerous ones, in a time of war."

Wilberforce sighed. "Please don't be offended."

"I'm not offended," Pitt assured him, probably not truthfully. "I didn't mean to sound it. I take your point, and in fact, Dundas would agree with you. He doesn't think Desmoulins could be of any use to us: he's far too unpredictable, for one thing, and he's a true believer, not a pragmatist like Danton. He was calling for a republic long before anyone else dared. And yet, in this case, that could work to our advantage. There's a very good chance he could turn away from the Terror."

"But not toward us, surely? England and France are mortal enemies."

"No two countries are mortal enemies. We happen to be at war at this point in time, that's all. It isn't personal."

Wilberforce smiled. "Sometimes I think you just don't understand people very well."

"Sometimes I don't," Pitt conceded. "I certainly don't understand Camille Desmoulins. But no, I don't think he'd make an alliance with Britain, or help us in any way. He certainly wouldn't help me, any more than Robespierre would. He'd rather murder me in my sleep."

"I think you're important enough that it would be an assassination, rather than a murder."

"Comforting, still unhelpful. But I believe he would talk to you. You aren't part of the British government: you're an abolitionist and a reformer. You were declared an honorary citizen of the Republic of Magicians, back in the beginning."

"I know. It was kind of them, I'm sure, but it didn't help convince people that abolition was not synonymous with revolution."

"At the moment, that correlation might be exactly what we need. Desmoulins doesn't have to agree to help Britain. If France is falling under the influence of a vampire—if his revolution is being corrupted from within—then that's a far greater problem for the Republic than it is even for us. He only needs to listen to you."

"To the idea that the Incorruptible is being influenced by a vampire. I have to say, I can't imagine him believing it. And I can't imagine what he could do about it if he did."

"As to him believing it—who knows? The two of them have been close for years, Robespierre and Desmoulins. Who knows what he may have seen or suspected over those years? Whatever else he is, he's intelligent. I think he'll believe it. What he could do about it is the pointed question."

"Do you have a pointed answer?"

"At best, I think he could find out where the enemy is and get the information to us. That might allow us to actually capture the enemy, or at least end his control over France. But at worst—well, he'll have been told. He can take steps of his own, if he isn't willing to work with us. We'll know that someone close to Robespierre—a political ally, and a magician, and a friend—is trying to stop him. I know that's more of a blunt answer than a pointed one."

Oddly enough, it was the blunt answer that struck Wilberforce more forcefully than the pointed one. He wasn't convinced that Camille Desmoulins would help them—Desmoulins was no particular advocate of abolition, and he had no particular connection to Wilberforce or his friends. But he was Robespierre's friend—one of very few who could claim that, if reports were true. And if they were right, Robespierre was in the deepest, darkest trouble of anyone. In a similar case, Wilberforce would do anything he could to save his own friends. That, perhaps, was worth more than any political consideration.

He nodded slowly. "Very well. I agree it might be worth an attempt. But how can we talk to him?"

Pitt sat forward; this, clearly, had been what the conversation had been steered toward. "You might recall I mentioned that we had a daemon-stone in Paris from which we probably wouldn't hear a good deal more. It was the one that gave us the first news of Robespierre creating an army of the dead. At the moment, it's in the hands of a spy of ours in Paris. Unfortunately, it's no longer safe for him—for one thing, shadows talk to each other, and with so many being poured into life at the guillotine it's unlikely that the stone can stay hidden for much longer. I've just recently heard that, with any luck, we can get him across the border to Switzerland in the next few days, where Grenville's spymaster will be waiting for him. Before he leaves, I can ask him to transfer the allegiance of the stone to Desmoulins, so that only he can communicate through it. And then, if he's willing to listen, you can talk to him."

"I never did learn very much French," Wilberforce said.

"That doesn't matter when imparting a message to a daemon-stone. They use thought, not language. You hear words but understand meaning." Pitt frowned. "Have you never used a daemon-stone before?"

"Never."

"I knew I hadn't talked to you through one. But there's one in the York Guildhall that is supposed to be for emergencies. I'm sure we've received messages from it."

"Those were all from Wyvill. I told him only one of the MPs for York needed to use it. I never liked touching it."

Pitt started to laugh. "Dear God, Wilberforce."

"You know how I feel about shadows!"

"I do." He resumed a straight face, but his eyes were twinkling. "I'm sorry. I hope you don't mind making the sacrifice this once. I really think it should come from you."

"Of course. As you say, if it works..." He paused. "It isn't only superstition, you know. You and I have encountered high-level shadows—you must know it isn't. Even if you don't believe in evil in quite the same way I do, even shadowmancers say that shadows never forgive being imprisoned in daemon-stones. They do what they're required because they must, but they want to destroy the one they obey."

"I've heard it said, and I respect the people who say it—you included. But there are a lot of people and things that want to destroy us at the moment. I'm more concerned about them."

He sighed but didn't argue. "I hope you don't mind if I keep the message short."

"I was going to warn you not to let the message get too long. I've had letters from you—and conversations. You never know how to stop. And a person can lose consciousness if they hold a daemon-stone for too long—I speak out of consideration for Desmoulins in this, as well as you."

"I'm so glad you hold my welfare in the same concern as that of the spark that lit a revolution," Wilberforce said gravely. He said it mostly to make Pitt laugh again, at which he succeeded, though the laugh trailed into another spasm of coughing. Really, he didn't look well. Wilberforce wasn't sure how he'd missed it before, but he resolved to keep a closer eye on him in the future.

"Might it not put Desmoulins in danger?" he asked. "Especially, as you say, if the stone is detected."

"It will certainly put him in danger, which is another reason he may not agree to do it. What I'm more concerned about is the danger he'll be in if he does anything with the information we're about to give him other than what we suggest."

"Such as?"

"All of France is potentially under the influence of the enemy. I really do mean *anything*."

Jean Baptiste Henry, age eighteen, journeyman tailor, convicted of sawing down a tree of liberty, guillotined.

Henrietta Frances de Marboeuf, age fifty-five, convicted of hoping for the arrival in Paris of the Austrian and Prussian armies and of hoarding provisions for them, guillotined.

Jean-Paul Robert, convicted of using mesmerism to influence his neighbors against the Revolution, guillotined.

Francis Bertrand, age thirty-seven, convicted of producing "sour wine injurious to the health of citizens," guillotined.

Mary Angelica Plaisant, age seventy-seven, seamstress, convicted of exclaiming, "A fig for the nation!" Guillotined.

"Yes," Robespierre answered his benefactor. "Yes, this is so very terrible."

Paris

December 1793

Lucile Desmoulins usually greeted Robespierre with every appearance of delight. He had come to call on them often in the last few years, especially in the early days of their marriage; he tried to come when they had no other guests, so he would often find her there alone, playing the piano or working in her garden. If Camille was out or finishing up something in his office, the two of them would talk—about Camille, sometimes, or their other friends, but often about books. Lucile, like him, was a passionate devotee of the Enlightenment philosophers, in sharp contrast to her husband, who lived and breathed the air of ancient Rome. Camille, coming in to their conversations, would sigh and throw up his hands in exaggerated despair.

"Wonderful. My wife and my oldest friend are betraying me with Jean-Jacques Rousseau."

Upon greeting him this time, Lucile seemed subdued, even nervous. When Robespierre asked if Camille was at home, she hesitated before replying.

"I just got him to sleep an hour ago," she said, as though she were talking about little Horace. It was late in the afternoon; Robespierre had come straight from the Convention. "He's been awake all night—and the night before."

"Doing what?"

"Writing. Pacing. More writing. Sending sparks and shadows flying. I haven't seen him in a state like this since last August. I wish you wouldn't press him to the guillotine quite so often, Maximilien. There must be other shadowmancers you can use."

"There are, and I do use them. But to the Commoners, Camille is still the much-loved enfant terrible of the Revolution; that has power. Besides, the next strongest shadowmancer is Saint-Just, and he and Camille hate each other. Camille will step up willingly every time if it means forcing Saint-Just down." Besides, though he didn't say it, he had other, less public uses for Saint-Just's shadowmancy lately. His benefactor had spoken to him again. "Why? Has this something to do with him fainting at the October trials?"

"You heard."

"Everyone heard. They heard about his defense of General Dillon afterward, too, and his other indiscretions. It doesn't look good these days to show so much sympathy for our enemies. I've warned him of that, as his friend."

"As his friend, you know that Camille has no control over his sympathies."

"Then he needs to gain some control over himself."

"Is that what you came to tell him?"

"No. No, I didn't come to talk about that at all. Please, Lolotte, can you tell him I'm here? I'm due at the Committee soon, and then I won't be able to get away until the small hours of the morning. I was awake all last night myself."

She was clearly wavering, either at the "please" or the family nickname, but it turned out it was unnecessary. Camille chose that moment to enter. For once, his rumpled, just-out-of-bed disarray was probably quite genuine: his face had the soft, sleepy innocence of a young child in the morning. It was absurd—Robespierre knew that even as a young child, Camille had never been innocent, and now he was considered downright dangerous. Still, as it had in school, the look wrung the protective instincts of his heart. So did little Horace, curled against Camille's hip and watching Robespierre with inquiring eyes.

"I thought I heard your voice," Camille said. He sounded neither pleased nor displeased; he just said it.

"I need to talk to you," Robespierre replied.

"I need to talk to you too."

"Good," Lucile said, with a sigh of resignation. "You both need to talk to each other. I'll leave you alone, shall I? Camille, do you want me to take Horace?"

"It's fine," Camille said, still looking at Robespierre. "I'll look after him awhile. He was starting to make a fuss."

"He likes to be the center of attention. I wonder whose son he could be?" She stroked her son's fuzzy head; then, deliberately, she leaned forward and kissed her husband. It was not out of character; the Desmoulinses were not shy about displays of affection. But this time, from the sideways glance Lucile gave Robespierre as she drew away, he suspected the kiss was mixed with something a little more proprietary. "I'll be just outside."

"Don't listen at the door," Camille advised. "We might open it unexpectedly and trip over you. Use the chimney."

"Will do."

Robespierre smiled, but he nonetheless made a mental note to lower his voice, and he waited until he heard the door click shut before he turned back to Camille. The irony was, of course, that there would almost certainly be nothing spoken that Lucile couldn't hear, or that Camille wouldn't tell her. Paranoia was a habit these days, like biting his nails.

"It's going too far," Camille said, without prelude. "The Terror. The guillotine. The Committee. All of it. It wasn't supposed to be like this, with everybody turning on each other. I've been meaning to talk to you about it for some time, but—"

"I agree," Robespierre said.

Camille blinked, for once taken completely off guard. "You do? When did you decide that?"

"From the first—almost. From Marie Antoinette's trial, actually. The Committee bungled that—accusing her of child molestation and magical perversion and of all sorts, while she sat there a mother and a widow. It generated all the wrong kinds of sympathy. And again, at the Girondin trial. I know it's all gone wrong, again. I just needed the time to decide what to do about it."

"About the Terror?"

"About the extremists on the Committee." His words almost tumbled over each other; he forced himself to stop, and breathe. "I've gone over and over it in my head. Why is this going so wrong? We're rid of the Girondins now. The Convention belongs to the Mountain. That happened as we planned. What I didn't foresee was how much power their downfall would give the pamphleteers we used to bring about their end."

"I was one of those pamphleteers," Camille reminded him. "And I'd like to think, however incorrectly, that I wasn't *used* by anyone."

"I didn't mean you. I didn't mean Marat either—he might have been a problem, if he hadn't been murdered in his bath so soon after—"

"Convenient of him," Camille said, with a trace of his old humor.

Robespierre waved this aside. "I'm talking about Hébert and his supporters."

"Oh," Camille said flatly. "Him."

Hébert had undeniably risen in prominence since his writings had helped bring down the Girondins. Unlike Camille, he wasn't content to stay by the side of Danton or Robespierre—his writings were even more extreme, and they had an audience of their own who were far more brutal than even Camille's had once been.

"He's brought down our cause from the beginning," Robespierre said. "This is where the problem lies: not in the Terror itself, but in its instruments. At best, his people are enjoying it too much, and making a mockery of its virtue. It might even be worse than that. I very much fear they're doing it on purpose, trying to destroy the Revolution by excess. He's a clever man, you know. Just because he writes for men and women with almost no education doesn't mean that he has none himself—quite the reverse."

"You really do think that everyone is trying to plot against you, don't you? Danton told me that. I thought he was exaggerating."

Somehow, Robespierre didn't like the idea of Danton and Camille talking behind his back. It made him wonder what else they had said. "Then you don't agree that Hébert's the problem?"

"I didn't say that. He's certainly *a* problem—he's a monster. We all know that. He loves the killing. A lot of people do. But—"

"That's my point. This is meant to be a means of order, of justice. People like Hébert are turning it into a massacre, and they're inflaming the counterrevolutionaries. They need to be stopped."

"Then you *do* want to stop the Terror?" Camille asked. "I mean—you have no reason to want to keep it going?"

"Of course I want it to stop! It can't stop now, of course. We need it, if we want to keep order here, and of course for the army of the dead. We're at war. But I think if we can just take tighter control of it and get rid of those who are, well, *enjoying* it too much—I never wanted to kill people. You know that."

"Of course I know." He said it quickly enough that Robespierre wondered if it were true. "Of course. I should have talked to you about this sooner; I could have saved myself a lot of panic. You've just been so inaccessible lately, since you've been on the Committee..."

"I'm sorry for that. There are so many suspects to get through. It becomes all-consuming." The flicker of suspicion, so quick to stir these days, whispered to him that Camille sounded very much like a man making excuses when he shouldn't have needed to. What for? Why? (*Stop it*, he told himself. *This is Camille.*)

"Not your fault. We're all busy, I suppose. And everybody's turning on each other—it's so difficult to know who to trust."

Robespierre frowned. "Did someone tell you not to trust me?"

Camille shook his head. His curls fell across his face; with Horace in his arms, he had to toss his head to flick them away. "It doesn't matter. So you want to remove Hébert and his supporters?"

"The way we did the Girondins." He tried to shake off his own paranoia as easily. "The Girondins were too moderate; the Hébertists are too violent. They're just as dangerous, perhaps even more so. Only I want to avoid a riot this time, if at all possible. I was hoping you..."

"We're thinking on the same lines," Camille said. It wasn't until he moved his hand that Robespierre saw the sheaf of papers there. He held them out between his fingers, careful not to dislodge his son. "I wrote this last night. I couldn't sleep."

Robespierre took it, adjusting his glasses to peer at his friend's familiar scrawl. After a while, he looked up. He found himself looking at his friend as though he had never seen him before. "It's brilliant," he said simply.

"Brilliant?" Camille laughed. "And here I was thinking it was merely genius."

"No, I mean it, Camille. It's truly brilliant. This is exactly what we meant the Revolution to be, and what we've drifted away from."

Camille, uncharacteristically, blushed. "I meant it to critique the excesses of the Committee of Public Safety. I can tweak it to target Hébert more specifically, if that's what you need."

"It doesn't need to. Everyone will know who you mean. I think there are a few places where you could tone it down, make sure that everyone knows you mean to accuse only certain members and not the Committee itself—but yes. This is the start."

"Again." Camille managed a very pale smile. "We seem to make so many starts we'll never see an end."

"We'll see an end. How many issues do you intend to run?"

"As many as it takes. If we can turn the tide of public opinion again..."

"Yes. That's exactly what we need." Robespierre glanced down at the paper once more. "We waste you, putting you in all our committees and conventions and clubs. This is where you belong. On paper. In words."

"You make it sound as if I'm not quite real."

"Sometimes I think you're not. Those years when I was out in Arras, and all I saw of you was your handwriting, remember? I started to think you existed only in pen and ink."

"I know what you mean. Words frighten me sometimes. They're like magic. They're both me and not me at the same time. And yet this feels more like me than anything I've ever done."

He shifted Horace's weight in his arms; Robespierre, picking up on the hint, said, "May I take him for a moment?"

"Please. I keep forgetting how heavy he's getting."

Robespierre nestled his godson's solid bulk against his chest. Horace clung to him, unafraid, and raised one curious hand to touch the green-tinted spectacles. His parents' black eyes were startling in such a dimpled, cherubic face.

"What's the verdict on you now, little one?" Robespierre asked the child softly. He was remembering the morning after the attack on the Tuileries. "Politician or revolutionary?"

"Neither, if I can help it," Camille replied. He stretched and sighed. "I want him a long way away from verdicts of any kind. But he set the curtains on fire yesterday when we didn't feed him quickly enough, so perhaps revolution is in his blood."

"He looks very well. *You* look very tired." He didn't mention what Lucile had told him.

"One is not a direct result of the other, for once. This last month... But it's going to be all right now. I'm so glad you agree, about the Terror. I thought..." He rubbed his eyes. "Never mind what I thought."

Robespierre knew he should press, but he didn't. There were so many long hours of interrogation ahead of him already that night; besides, he didn't want to know. "Well. Get some rest, now you've calmed down; then come see me first thing tomorrow. We'll get the first issue finalized; then you can go away and write it up for the printer. Is seven o'clock in the morning too early for you?"

"No. I don't think any of us sleep much anymore, do we?"

Robespierre had to admit this was true.

"Oh, Camille?" he said, turning before he was at the door. It came to him, unwillingly, that this was the kind of theatrical nonsense Hébert might employ at the Committee of Public Safety to catch suspects off guard. He tried to modify his tone, and succeeded only in sounding too serious. "I need you at the guillotine tomorrow, if you could possibly manage it. It's a large batch: they found a royalist printing press. You're one of the few whose magic is up to the numbers."

Camille hesitated. "I think I'll be busy with this paper, actually."

"It's not until the afternoon. You'll be done with the manuscript by then, surely."

"I can't be sure."

"None of us enjoy it, Camille." He kept his voice as gentle as he could. It probably sounded threatening. "None of us with any imagination, at least; Hébert's problem is that he doesn't have any. It's a duty. It's for the Republic." He caught himself, remembering Lucile. "Still—never mind. Perhaps it's best you don't, if you feel you're not up to it."

"No," Camille said unexpectedly. "No, you're right. I'll be there."

Robespierre felt a wave of relief he couldn't quite name. "You're sure?"

"Very. As you say, it's a duty. And I'm not making a habit of fainting every time a royalist loses his or her head."

"Good. It would give entirely the wrong impression." He was joking, but only half. Perhaps not even that. "I'll see you tomorrow, with the manuscript."

"You're making a mistake," his benefactor said.

"I'm saving the Revolution," Robespierre said. "You'll still get your undead, don't worry. But they'll be true enemies from now on, not innocents and old Aristocrats. Once we clear the extreme elements out, as we did the moderates. Camille was right: Hébert and his people are monsters."

"Oh, that. No, I have no concerns about that. Choose your own victims, if it helps you, particularly if it tightens your grip on France. You're very good at targeting your political enemies, you know. I meant that you're making a mistake about Camille Desmoulins."

Something inside him chilled. Perhaps it was his heart. "What kind of mistake?"

"You trust him. Trust is dangerous. And Camille... I don't know. Something has changed in him lately."

"He doesn't like the undead. They've shaken him. It's my fault: I relied on him too heavily, especially in the first few weeks. But he's a true patriot. He'll recover."

"No, not that. It's something else." His benefactor paused, thinking. It occurred to Robespierre that he had never seen him uncertain before. "Proceed, if you like," he decided. "I agree, he's the best person for what you want. And Camille is the sort to hang himself, given enough rope, far more surely than anyone else can manage it. Let's see how this unfolds. But watch him carefully."

"If I thought I was putting him in danger, I would stop this now. He's my friend—my oldest and best friend."

"And that's why you need to be careful. It's the ones we love that know the most dangerous ways to hurt us."

He startled himself with the sound of his own voice. "I don't believe you love anyone at all."

"You're quite right," his benefactor said. "I was speaking rhetorically."

Camille's new journal, *The Old Cordelier*, flew off the shelves too quickly for printers to keep up. Robespierre and Camille had been worried, among other things, that the journal would be a lone voice crying out in the wilderness. In fact, it seemed that many were sick of living in blood day and night, as they had been for the past few years. They devoured his words against the Hébertists, as they had against the Girondins before them, and the royal family before that. Once again, four years after the Bastille, he was the spark that lit a revolution.

Robespierre was glad, of course. It was exactly what they had intended. People began to ignore the Hébertists at the Committee of Public Safety; in the streets, the Commoners jeered and hissed as they passed. Not all—Hébert's own pamphlets, with their filthy, street-language humor, still had followers. But the tide was turning against them, as it had against the Girondins, and Robespierre's power surged accordingly.

The trouble was, so did Danton's. And Robespierre had nothing against Danton; he really didn't. But if Hébert was becoming too extreme, Danton was becoming more moderate every day: the dark mood that had prompted him to support the army of the dead had passed, and he had found the subsequent purge of the Girondins difficult to accept. Perhaps he'd had a crisis of conscience—those took a great deal of will to forestall at times. Either way, he was no longer a friend to the Terror. And Camille thought so much of him. Really, now, he was far closer to Danton than to Robespierre. Sometimes Robespierre suspected that Danton was guiding Camille's pamphlets as much as Robespierre himself was, and guiding them into waters other than those originally intended. Dangerous waters. He started to glimpse Camille in a different, unfamiliar light, no matter how hard he tried not to.

Why, he thought one night as he lay awake staring at the ceiling, was nothing ever pure, simple, and easy?

The gnawing cold was no longer merely inside him, or at least he didn't think it was. The air had darkened around him. Shadows deepened as he passed, and at times he could hear a muttering of voices on the air as though he walked through ghosts. He didn't know if this was in his head, or if others saw and heard it too, but people had started to avert their eyes from him in the halls.

They had begun to do that anyway, of course. He was a necromancer. As far as he knew, he was the only necromancer in France, perhaps even Europe. They didn't trust him. Many hated him; many more wanted him dead. He started to see flashes of blades in crowds, concealed pistols in streets, poison in wine. Every whisper was a conspiracy against him. But they needed him. For now, at least, some of them needed him.

Saint-Domingue

January 1794

By the beginning of the New Year, Toussaint's army controlled the entire north. He had four thousand soldiers under his command. The Spanish no longer treated him with respect, but with reverence. He was, they knew, their greatest opportunity to wrestle Saint-Domingue from the French: more than that, though, he was difficult not to revere. Fina, at his side, found it more and more difficult to believe that he had ever been a slave.

It wasn't only the French against whom they had to contend now. Barely a month after Fort Dauphin, the first of the British troops had put to shore at Jérémie in the south and been greeted with open arms by the planters and white townspeople. They had come by way of Jamaica—the same journey that Fina had taken to get there. Something had hardened inside her when news of their approach filtered across the battle lines into the north. The old wounds in her heart that had opened the day she had saved Toussaint tore apart again, and her magic came pouring out.

From then on, she no longer only watched during the battles. As before, she sat at the camp as Toussaint's army rode into the fray, and moved among his enemies like a ghost. Now, though, any who came near him found themselves held rigid in her grip. It was difficult, and not just because her magic strained at each new use. More often than not, she found herself in their heads as Toussaint's own soldiers came to kill them. She felt their hearts pierced, their legs shattered, their skulls caved in, and each time woke shuddering in her tent. The superstitious among the camp began to give her a wide berth. Her magic was too strange, and too invasive.

"I promised you that I would never ask you to accompany me into battle," Toussaint said to her one night. "That, in some ways, is what you do now. You must let me know if you want to stop."

"I don't want to stop," Fina said. "I'm not afraid of their deaths, you know."

He said nothing, only sighed.

At Gonaïves they found the tattered remains of a British garrison, most of them half-dead or dying of yellow fever. Toussaint saw that they were given what medicine could be spared, instructed the healthy in caring for the sick, and arranged for their evacuation from the area. Fina, who spoke English, helped broker the deal. It was the first time she had heard the language in two years. Though they spoke to her far more politely than any overseer had, she saw the contempt in their eyes and about their mouths, and the foreign words rose in her throat to choke her. For the first time in months, she felt like a slave again.

"Why are you helping them?" she asked Toussaint when they had turned away.

"Because they're sick," he said. "And I know how to make them better."

"They knew how to make Molly better," Fina said. "They left her to die. She wasn't worth the time and money to save."

She had never told Toussaint about Molly's death; she didn't need to tell him now. He could guess exactly what she was talking about. "I'm sorry. But it wasn't these men. These men are soldiers."

"It doesn't matter! They trade in slaves when they can. They use slave labor when it suits them. They came here to enslave us again."

"You didn't protest when we let the townspeople go."

"Because I respect your vision; I understand that Saint-Domingue needs to be a flourishing colony. But these men aren't farmers or planters. They aren't part of your vision."

"They are. They are part of my vision of a Saint-Domingue that is enlightened, civilized, and free. This is a matter of pragmatism as much as morality: England needs to know that we're not savages or butchers, but people capable of dealing with them on equal terms."

She laughed. "If we dealt with them on *equal terms*—"

"Not the terms on which they deal with us—the terms on which they claim to deal with each other. They have to see us the way they see themselves."

"They won't." Something hard and ugly had been unlocked in her. "You don't understand, Toussaint. You think you do, because you were born a slave and you *saw* the worst of what could happen, but the worst never happened to you. You weren't snatched from your home and chained to the bottom of a ship. You didn't lie in darkness and filth as that ship stole you across the world. You weren't forced to swallow magic and watch your body turn against you. They never made you into their property."

She thought she had gone too far then, but he was unfazed. Only a twitch in his jaw betrayed him. "I know. And because of that, it's easier for me not to want to hurt them. But if I had—if I'd been captured, beaten, spellbound—then I would still have to try to do exactly what I'm doing now. Because it's the right way; I know it is. It would just be a lot harder. For God's sake, Fina. Do you think I'm not angry every day? Of course I am. But because I'm an intelligent man, not a murderer like Jeannot was, I hold it back. You held back your anger for years before you came here. When you were out in the fields, and the smallest twitch could betray you. That's all I ask of you now."

"I was a slave then."

"And now you're free. Don't be better as a slave in fear than you are as a free woman with all the power in the world."

She didn't reply. Her face settled into the familiar, impervious lines it had held for so many years. Inwardly, she seethed.

Toussaint looked at her and sighed. "I know this is difficult. These men are from the nation that enslaved you; I'm making you walk among them again. But we all do it. All of us who were enslaved by the French—we walk among them every day."

"It's different." She folded her arms tightly across her chest. "You're fighting them to free your people from the French. Mine—the men and women on Jamaica I grew up among—are still enslaved by the British. *Nothing's changed over there.* These men aren't here trying to take back what they've lost. They're here to take more. Even if we beat them back, it won't help my people at all."

From the flicker of understanding that crossed his face, she knew this hadn't occurred to him. "That's true. And if I could change anything about that, I would. But I can only fight the battles in front of me, and so can you. If you decide you can't fight by my side anymore, then I'll understand."

"I never said I didn't want to fight beside you."

"Then I'm afraid you need to obey my orders. And I've ordered that these men will go free." He turned away. Toussaint had an annoying habit of doing that: ending an argument when he had the upper hand, and moving on to something else. As if their disputes were tasks to be ticked off, or skirmishes in a long string of battles to be won. "If it makes you feel better, most of these men will die within a few days. They'll die like you saw many die in the Middle Passage: far from home, in their own filth, and in terrible pain."

Fina looked at the closest of the soldiers. He was a young man, a boy even. His ginger hair was plastered damply to his head; his skin was yellow under his sunburn. He shivered in the heat, eyes closed, and coughed in the back of his throat. Of course she didn't *want* him to die like that, not exactly. Nobody should die like that. He was her enemy, but he was still a person.

And yet no matter how much he suffered, how scared he would be to die, how much he screamed, it still wouldn't be like the Middle Passage. He wouldn't be spellbound. People around him would care that he had died and would honor him as a human being. It wasn't the same at all.

"That doesn't make me feel better," she said aloud. She didn't know which way she meant it.

Fina couldn't settle that night. It ought to have been easy. The mayor of Gonaïves had surrendered his house to them; for once, she wasn't curled up on the ground under canvas. She had a room to herself, with a soft bed; there had been enough food in the stores to quiet everybody's hunger; the streets outside were silent. There was no danger: she would know. Her magic was attuned enough to threats now that any evil intent in close proximity would stir it. Even without this, she had spent all her life keeping herself and her feelings quiet. Whatever was happening in her heart, she had always been able to lie still.

Not this time. Anger, guilt, and grief stormed in her chest; she crossed her arms tight to hold it in, and paced the tiny room in the hope of leaving it behind. It followed her like a cloud, and she couldn't breathe. Outside, the night was heavy with the threat of rain.

Before she had left the first camp at the Galliflet plantation, just after she had made her bargain with Toussaint, Celeste had taken her aside and given her a hug.

"Be careful of Toussaint," she had said as they drew apart.

"Why?" Fina had said, surprised. "You were the one who told me he was special."

"He is special. And, what's more rare, I'm pretty sure he's good. But he has his own vision, and nobody else can see it. Visions are dangerous when nobody else can see them."

She had been in Toussaint's head; she knew he was good. What's more, she had seen his vision, or a shadow of it. It was a beautiful vision: on her best days, when she was almost happy, it was what she wanted not only for Saint-Domingue but for Jamaica and the British colonies as well. But seeing it was different from believing in it, however much she tried to do both. And Toussaint's refusal to see that, to accept anything less than his own merciless forgiveness, was maddening. This rebellion wasn't a clean, fresh start. It was a fresh wound across a landscape where the scars already ran too deep, and Toussaint wouldn't hear the screams.

If only Molly were here, or Jacob. She always missed them; on that night, she longed for them with such force and intensity that it frightened her. Her heart was tearing itself from her in its desire to be with them. She hated her own homesickness; Jamaica wasn't her home. There had been nothing there but pain and fear and exhaustion. And yet that wasn't quite true. There had been people who loved her, and who didn't regard her as something powerful and uncanny. There had been the quiet hours between days when they could find some kind of freedom. She didn't know anymore what she was doing on Saint-Domingue.

At last, aching and tired, she threw herself down onto the bed. Her magic raged inside her.

She couldn't remember falling asleep, and yet she must have. The room with its slatted window had gone, and so had the clouds and the smell of the storm. She was standing, and there were wooden boards beneath her bare feet. Moonlight spilled through a tiny window, high in the rafters, and illuminated a large, ugly building, little more than a barn. It was empty of furniture, but the heavy door was bolted, and row upon row of sleeping forms lay upon the ground. Her heart tightened, and for the first time since her freedom, tears sprung to her eyes. She knew where she was. She had slept there every night for more than twenty years.

Jamaica. Somehow, impossibly, her magic had brought her home.

It was very quiet in the slave barracks. Perhaps it was early, and the spell had yet to wear away, or it was late, and their talk had dissolved into exhausted sleep. The men and women on the ground lay straight, stiff, and apparently unaware of her presence. Even in the dark, she saw Jacob almost at once. He looked older than she remembered, and there was a cut above his eye that was healing badly; as she rushed to his side, she wondered how she could ever have thought he was so indomitable. She had been away only two years among free men and women, fighting a war, but he seemed to her worn beyond endurance.

"Jacob?" she whispered. She put her hands on his shoulder and felt the bones beneath. "Can you hear me?"

He didn't stir; none of them did. It might have been the spell-binding keeping them locked in place; she suspected, though, that she wasn't really there. How could she be? Her body was hundreds of miles away, on another island.

"I'm so pleased to see you," she said anyway. She realized that she had lapsed back into Jamaican creole. The taste of the words on her tongue, after so long, released her tears. "I've missed you all so much."

And then, out of the corner of her eye, she saw someone else. A stranger, standing among the rows of sleeping people: even with his face shadowed, she recognized him. She froze.

Of course. What else could it be? She had reached for Jacob and Clemency, but she was here, not behind their eyes but awake and apparently capable of movement. Her magic didn't take her places. It saw through others' eyes, and inside heads. And there was only one person whose head worked in this way. Usually it was in a garden half a world away. Today, it had brought her to Jamaica.

Somehow, all of this was still inside the mind of the stranger: the owner of the voice that had called the revolution.

She got to her feet slowly. Now that she had seen him, she could hear his voice as well. It seemed more something in the air than from his lips: a low whisper, the words indistinguishable to her. They might not be in creole or English, but she knew her friends would understand them, as she had understood the words that must have been spoken in French. The ground beneath her feet quivered like a divining rod, and the air was growing hotter and hotter. She could barely breathe.

"Who are you?" she said out loud. "What do you want?"

The voice paused in its lilt. Perhaps the stranger's eyes rose to light on her for a second; perhaps they didn't.

"When I first heard you, I thought you wanted to free Saint-Domingue," she said. "But I know better than that now. Toussaint is trying to free Saint-Domingue. So is Biassou, and Dessalines. The rebellion came about because of Boukman and the voodoo priests.

Even Thomas Clarkson from England helped. But what you did that night wasn't about freedom. It wasn't even about revenge. I know more about battles now; I've been in the heads of a lot of different soldiers. And I've seen you, in the head of that little Frenchman. I've seen how scared he is. You wanted violence. You wanted to make the violence worse."

The stranger had turned back to Jacob. His voice was muffled now, and far away, like an echo. It chilled her.

"What are you doing?" she demanded. "Whatever it is, you need to stop. You have no right."

All at once, light flared, and she was sitting bolt upright in her unfamiliar bed, gasping and shivering as Saint-Domingue returned to her. Jamaica had fallen away, and with it Jacob and the voice. It came to her as she struggled to quiet her breathing that she hadn't seen Clemency.

"Who are you?" she said aloud, in the language she and Molly and Toussaint shared.

There was no answer.

On that same night, across the sea, the motion to abolish the slave trade was heard again in the House of Commoners. Already, nobody was bothering to pretend that anything was being put in place to do so gradually. The question was, yet again, whether it would happen at all.

This time, Wilberforce spoke for four hours, and was careful to stress not only the inhumanity of the trade but also how little the British economy in fact depended on it for survival. Pitt supported this with far more calculations than Wilberforce could have supplied or made easily understood, and Fox's rotund form sprung to their defense, all the masterful oration and eyebrow-bristling indignation usually directed at the government now being flung at the traders. Once again, nobody mentioned the possibility of emancipation from slavery or even from spellbinding, but the trade, they insisted, needed to stop.

The House was not responding. Wilberforce knew it wasn't, even as the walls resounded around them, and he knew what Clarkson meant when he said that brilliance and honesty weren't enough. Words needed somebody to listen to them.

"In all honesty, I don't care very much what this House decides," he said, and heard in his own defiance an admission of what that decision would be. "Whatever you might do, the people of Great Britain will abolish the slave trade, when, as will soon happen, its injustice and cruelty shall be fairly laid before them. It is a nest of serpents, which would never have endured so long but for the darkness in which they lay hid. Never, never will we desist until we have wiped away this scandal from the Christian name, released ourselves from the load of guilt under which we presently labor, and extinguished every trace of this bloody traffic, of which our posterity, looking back to the history of these enlightened times, will scarce believe has been suffered to exist so long as a disgrace and dishonor to this country."

The walls sang. When the votes were counted, eighty-eight members voted to put an end to the slave trade. One hundred and sixty-three voted against.

Paris

February 1794

In the New Year, a party of delegates arrived in Paris from Saint-Domingue. There were three men: one white, one mixed race, and one a free black man. They had come to report the French governors had ended slavery in the north of their colony, and the men, women, and children who had once been spellbound were now made French citizens. They had come to ask that the Republic of Magicians make their freedom legal and binding, and that they extend it to every enslaved soul on the island.

The Convention met to rule on the issue the following day. Robespierre took Danton briefly aside before the meeting began, much to the other man's surprise. They had not been on friendly terms lately. Danton, like Camille, thought the Terror had gone too far; unlike Camille, he was not inclined to blame everything on the Hébertists.

"Just for once," Robespierre said, "let's do this properly. Let's actually do what we always meant to do. If we do nothing else, we'll have done this."

Danton nodded slowly.

And so, in February 1794, slavery was abolished in the French Republic of Magicians. They were the first nation in the world to declare the people they had once enslaved free and legal citizens. The voice in Robespierre's head said nothing about this, neither in praise nor in condemnation. Perhaps, as usual, he had his own reasons for allowing freedom to be declared; perhaps the tide of public opinion had turned to the point where it would be more effort to stop abolition than bring it about. More likely, Robespierre suspected, his benefactor truly cared for nothing he did anymore, as long as he was still increasing the army of the dead. It was a terrible freedom, and he feared to test it too far, but it gave him hope.

The following day, Robespierre stood up in the Convention and shared his vision of France. It was the most important speech of his life, and he was almost too exhausted to give it. Apart from the work he had carried out with Saint-Just in the Conciergerie the night before, he had made undead forty-six men and women at the guillotine that day. His skin was ice, and it hurt to breathe. Yet the crowd listened, enraptured.

"We want to substitute morality for egoism, honesty for love of honor, principles for conventions, duties for decorum, the empire of reason for the tyranny of fashion, the fear of vice for the dread of unimportance." Pause for breath. "We want to replace good company with good character, intrigue with merit, wit with genius, brilliance with truth, dull debauchery with the charm of happiness. In the place of an easygoing, frivolous, and discontented people, we would create one that is happy, powerful, and stouthearted and replace the vices and follies of the monarchy with the virtue and astounding achievements of the Republic."

It was a shadow of the vision in his head: he had never, despite all his efforts, found the words with which to articulate that. It grew more insubstantial the more he tried to pin it down. But he tried to imbue the mesmerism pouring from him with the glow of that vision, and the applause was deafening. This, he argued, was why the Terror needed to go on; this was the end that sanctified all the means. This was why the Terror needed to be protected from those like Hébert, who took it too far, and those who would prevent it from going far enough. This was what it was all for.

The following morning he couldn't get out of bed. Éléonore found him when she came to get him for breakfast, shivering convulsively, barely conscious, struggling for breath.

"Maximilien!" She sank to her knees at his side, shaking him. He couldn't focus his eyes, but his pale lashes parted to reveal a sliver of green. "My God."

"It's all right," he managed. His voice was a whisper. "It's the magic. It was too much yesterday. I just need to rest this morning."

"You went out again last night, didn't you? You do that all the time lately. Where? What did you do?"

He said nothing.

"You never tell me things," she said. It was as if she had realized it for the first time. "We talk every day. And yet you never tell me anything."

"Please," he said. His eyes closed again.

The Duplays called a doctor, who recommended that he be confined to bed for at least a month and eat fewer oranges. He didn't attend the Convention or the Committee for some weeks, but he still went to the guillotine. He still went to the Conciergerie at night too. His benefactor insisted, and Robespierre, though he no longer trusted him, still needed him.

In his absence, Hébert attempted to rally an insurrection to expel Robespierre from the Convention, a pathetic copy of the one against the Girondins the summer before. It failed miserably. Hébert was no mesmer, and the crowds simply weren't inclined to stir. In March, Robespierre returned to work, and amid the ecstatic applause denounced Hébert and his supporters as traitors to liberty. They were arrested almost at once. The time for Robespierre needing two days of violent riots to have someone killed was long past.

There had been two main parties in the Convention once: the Girondins and the Mountain. The Girondins were gone.

There had been three loose factions of the Mountain: the Robespierrists, the Dantonists, and the Hébertists. Now the Hébertists were gone as well.

"This is all very well," Saint-Just said as they left the Committee. "But you have to do something about Camille."

"What about Camille?" Robespierre said, too impatiently. He knew very well what his friend was going to say.

Saint-Just wasn't fooled. "You know what I mean about Camille."

The week before, Camille had published an issue of *The Old Cordelier* that had certainly not been approved by Robespierre. It was really no more than a loose translation of Tacitus, outlining the tyrannical Law of Suspects that existed in the age of the Roman emperors, and which Camille claimed was an illustration of the evils of the monarchy. It was all too obvious, though, what the Roman Law of Suspects truly paralleled. Robespierre had felt his blood run ice-cold as he read it.

"Augustus was the first to extend the Law of Suspects," Camille wrote, "in which he comprised writings which he called counter-revolutionary. As soon as words had become state crimes, it was only a step to transform into offenses mere glances, sorrow, compassion, sighs, silence even..."

It was perfect: brilliant, sparkling, cutting, devastating. And in that moment, Robespierre knew that his benefactor had been right.

"Camille is being Camille," he told Saint-Just. "He doesn't mean any harm to us—to *you*, perhaps, but you don't exactly wish him well either."

Saint-Just didn't answer that; they both knew it was true. Camille had laughed at Saint-Just too many times, and his laughter had too much of real contempt. Saint-Just, Camille, and himself, Robespierre reflected—perhaps their only common attribute was that none of them could stand to be mocked.

"Whatever he means," Saint-Just said, "he's causing harm: he and Danton both. You know this. That last issue of *The Old Cordelier* was treason. You wouldn't hesitate to put a stop to it if it were anyone else."

"But it isn't anyone else." He had been feeling much better that evening, before he had stepped into the committee room. Now his head was pounding, and the twitch in his left eye was back. He resisted the urge to rub it away; even in front of Saint-Just, these days, it would look like weakness. "I asked Camille to start *The Old Cordelier*. I wanted him to rile up public opinion against the Hébertists. And it worked exactly as we planned. They'll be dead tomorrow, and their corpses will fight for the Republic."

"And that, as I said, is all very well," Saint-Just said. "But do you really think Camille will stop there? He's going too far, as always. He wants to bring the whole Committee down, not just the extremists among us."

"Camille wants an end to the Terror. So does Danton. So do I. The only difference is that I know it's too soon. We're not there yet."

"Exactly. And we never will be if views like his are allowed to go on. He has opposed the Terror."

"He hasn't quite done that."

"A technicality. You said it yourself: there are three sins against the Republic. One is to be sorry for state prisoners, another is to be opposed to the rule of virtue, and the third is to be opposed to the Terror."

"That was what *you* said."

"I was saying it on your behalf."

Robespierre said nothing.

Saint-Just, uncharacteristically, sighed. It might have been that, just this once, he was tired as well. "You have to do something about Camille," he repeated.

The following morning, the fourth edition of *The Old Cordelier* rolled off the press and was gobbled up by the waiting public. In it, Camille Desmoulins referenced the possibility Robespierre had once raised of a Committee of Justice. He called instead for the establishment of a Committee of Mercy, to bring about an end to the Terror.

"'O my dear Robespierre!'" Robespierre, reading it in newsprint, imagined his name in Camille's small, scratchy handwriting, amid crossed-out lines and perfectly sculpted sentences. "It is you whom I address here. O my old school friend, whose eloquent discourses posterity will read! Remind yourself of the lessons of history and philosophy: love is stronger, more lasting than fear; admiration and religion are born of generosity; acts of clemency are the ladder of pride by which members of the Committee of Public Safety can elevate themselves to the sky (the Romans tell us this). They will never reach it through paths of blood."

Robespierre didn't go to the Committee that evening. He pleaded illness, which was not entirely a lie: he was still very weak, and his magic at the guillotine that afternoon had pushed him back to the edge of exhaustion. To his siblings and the Duplays, all of whom were worried about him, he explained that he just needed a few hours to rest and collect his thoughts. He hadn't slept the night before. He knew what the voice in his dreams would say, and he didn't want to hear.

He was at his desk, trying to write, when a soft knock came at the door. He wasn't sure how late it was. The courtyard outside was velvety dim, and quiet but for the odd bubble of conversation drifting in from the street.

"Maxime?" It was Éléonore. "Am I disturbing you?"

"Come in," he said, and the door opened. Éléonore glanced around until her eyes found him at his desk. He wondered if the room looked as dark to her as it did to him.

"Camille's downstairs," she said. "I told him you were busy, but he insisted I come up and check if that meant busy to specific people, and if so, was one of those people him."

One of those people was indeed him, but he could hardly say so. "I'm not really in any state for company at the moment."

"I told him that too," she said. "Do you want me to tell him again?"

"Yes—no." He took off his glasses and pinched the bridge of his nose. "No, you may as well send him up. He'll only make a nuisance of himself otherwise. Thank you."

Éléonore looked around his room again, taking in the small bed, the desk, the shelves of neatly sorted books. Shadows lurked in the corner, and whispered. All she said, though, was "Don't let the fire go down, will you? It's cold in here, and you're not well." She closed the door behind her on the way out.

Earlier in their acquaintance, Éléonore had asked him about the pictures in his room. Even then, the walls had begun to fill with medals, prints, and engravings, all designed to commemorate moments of the Revolution and many depicting himself. Babette had teased him already, and so had Camille, but Éléonore had really been asking.

"They're gifts," he had said. "I can't hide them away. Besides, I like pictures and engravings."

"But pictures of yourself?"

"I suppose it reminds me who I am," he said, because it sounded well.

This didn't fool her for a second. "But those aren't who you are. *This* is who you are." She touched his chest lightly—too lightly to be flirtation, but it had made his heart jump anyway. He never felt that anymore. "Right here. Maximilien Robespierre, who is kind and hardworking and ambitious, and forgets to come to dinner on time. You only need a looking glass for that. Those pictures are who the people out there think you are."

He considered his answer properly this time. "Well," he said, "I suppose it might be to remind me of that."

"I think," Éléonore said, "you just like to remember that people think well of you."

He wondered now, as his own images in copper and paint frowned at him from the walls. They were images of a young radical, sharp-featured and proud. The face of a revolution. He didn't recognize himself anymore. Perhaps he had changed, or the revolution had.

Madame Duplay had shown no signs of minding his necromancy, after all. She still wanted him to marry Éléonore. He wondered if Éléonore still wanted to marry him. She had been just as companionable as ever, but he thought something had changed. The door that had been between them had been locked—perhaps just for now, perhaps forever. He might have cared more once.

Camille's thoughts were perhaps running on the same lines as his own; in any case, his eyebrows rose as he entered the room. "Éléonore wasn't exaggerating."

"About what?"

"You really do look dreadful."

"You thought that could ever be an exaggeration?"

It was a weak joke—humor had never been his forte—but it raised a chuckle that was probably more relief than amusement. "I honestly thought that there could only be improvement. In seriousness, Maximilien, what is this doing to you?"

"It doesn't matter." Around him, the shadows whispered. "I intend to let it keep doing it, as long as it takes. We're so close."

"So close to what?"

"France. Our France. The army is growing every day." He looked at him a few seconds longer before he spoke again, considering. Unusually, Camille shifted under his gaze. People were doing that now, more and more often, but not Camille. "I need you at the Place de la Révolution again tomorrow."

"I might have things to do," Camille said. His flippancy didn't quite reach his face.

"What things? Whatever it is, it can wait. You're still one of the best shadowmancers we have. And your magic entwines with mine better than anybody's."

"That sounds very romantic. But I do have a busy day tomorrow."

"It's going to be a busy day at the guillotine tomorrow as well."

Camille closed his eyes for a long moment. When he opened them again, their playful light had died, and Robespierre's heart sank. Here it was.

"I won't do this anymore," he said flatly.

Robespierre did his best to force calm into his voice. "What won't you do?"

"You know what. I won't call any more shadows. I won't give my voice to your Committee. I won't stand by and watch you do this to yourself, and to all of us."

"Saint-Just is telling me you mean to oppose us. That you and Danton have set yourself up as my enemies. Are you telling me he's right?"

"Oh, for God's sake. Forget Saint-Just for a moment. Listen to me. I don't know what this is doing to you either, but I've been reading all I can about armies of the dead. There's no magical theory still extant, of course, but there is history, even though you need to read all the way back to the Vampire Wars. No necromancer behind such an army ever lived past the age of thirty-five. Not one."

"It was the fifteenth century, Camille! Not many lived to eat solid food!"

"You know that's not what I mean."

"I know. And it wasn't what I asked."

Camille nodded. "I'm your friend. I would never oppose you. Nor am I opposing the Committee, particularly. I am opposing the Reign of Terror."

"I *am* the Reign of Terror!"

"That's not true—not yet. Maxime, I meant what I wrote; I don't think I ever meant anything more. This has to end."

"In the past, you wrote that the time had come for violence," Robespierre said. "Now you're saying that was wrong?"

"Perhaps. That doesn't bother me either way. I don't know whether we were wrong to call for violence in the past; perhaps the situation called for it; perhaps it didn't. I wanted it, so I called for it; everyone else wanted it, so they listened. Part of me thinks it was needed; the other part can't get the smell of burning bodies out of my dreams. I'm not like you: I never claimed to be incorruptible, and I certainly never claimed to be infallible. But here, now, we're wrong. The time for violence is over. It's time for mercy—for love, if you can remember what that is."

"I'm doing this from love," Robespierre said. "I love France. I love you too. But if you carry on in this way, I might not be able to save both of you."

Camille's face stilled. "What are you saying?"

"You know what I'm saying. Our country must come first. Right now, I've convinced the Committee that you're a spoiled child fallen into bad company."

"I am not a child. I know you all think I am, but I'm not."

Robespierre ignored him. "I've told them we need to condemn your words, not you. You don't know what you're doing. You need our compassion, not our censure—"

"Which is exactly what I said about the last victims of the guillotine."

"Camille!" He bit his words back; they tasted like ash and bile in his throat.

"Yes?"

Robespierre rubbed his brow, which throbbed under his fingers.

"You need to stop this," he said, slowly, deliberately. Mesmerism rolled from him in hot waves. It was the only time, these days, he felt any warmth at all. "For your own good, you need to stop this. And if Danton is to be saved, he needs to be persuaded to stop this too."

Camille faltered; his eyes clouded, and his mouth opened silently. Then, with what must have been a supreme effort of will, he shook himself. His dark curls tumbled into his eyes; he brushed them away, and his jaw set.

"Oh, don't you *dare*." There was true fury in his voice. Flames danced about his fingertips, and Robespierre knew he would not hesitate to send them in his direction. "Don't you bloody dare, Maximilien. Not to me."

Robespierre broke off the mesmerism at once. Somewhere he felt surprise, but it was a long way beneath the surface. "You know, then."

"That necromancy wasn't the only skill you were keeping hidden? Of course I know. I've known for years. It may be almost impossible to detect mesmerism in action, but I know you. I can recognize your magic when I see it. I don't care. You can do what you like to the Convention or the Committee or the crowds. Mesmerize all of France if you can. I would. But not me. Call it a personal preference.

I've been silenced and subdued against my will for years, under the old regime. I won't take it from you."

"I haven't been mesmerizing all of France," Robespierre said. It seemed important, somehow. "I've only used it for speeches. Only to get my point across. I've never used it on an individual before."

"I'm flattered." The flames about his hands flickered and died. "Also rather dizzy. If you're not going to take over my mind, do you mind if I sit down?"

"Since when have you asked if I mind?"

"You're quite right. I don't care." His voice had regained almost its customary lightness, but it was deceptive. He sat on the edge of the bed cautiously, poised to get to his feet in a heartbeat. In another time, he would already have thrown himself on it full-length if he had felt like it. Or he would pace the room, his hands in constant motion, his face alight as his tongue tripped and flew over his words. Times had changed. Robespierre's home was enemy territory now. "God. You really are used to whole crowds, aren't you? That was about as subtle as a hammer to the skull. Light touch, remember, if you're going to be a proper tyrant."

"Perhaps I shouldn't have done that," Robespierre said. It was the closest he had come to admitting he was wrong in a long time.

Camille did not seem to take the admission as the honor it was. "There are a lot of things that perhaps you shouldn't have done." He rubbed his eyes again and looked up. "I've had correspondence," he said abruptly, "that I really don't know whether or not to give credence to. At the end of last year, I came home one day to find a daemon-stone on my desk. A powerful one—the shadow anchored to it called to me the moment I entered the house. When I touched it, it had a message for me, and me alone. It said that you were in the grip of a dark magician, and had been since at least the year before the Bastille fell."

Robespierre's heart tightened in his chest; in his head, something stirred in alarm. "You need better reading material" was all he said, and he knew his face had shown nothing.

"I do, don't I? I'm out of the classics. Somebody should write more. What do you say to this one?"

"People say things like that about me all the time," he said. "It's called treason. They tend to meet the guillotine for it these days."

"People tend to meet the guillotine for saying they don't like your waistcoat, these days. It's a good thing I'm not people. I don't like your waistcoat, by the way. Stripes don't become you."

"You *are* people, Camille," Robespierre said. "Please don't think otherwise."

Camille nodded. "I don't."

But it wasn't true, not really. Camille did not believe he was truly in danger. Not from Robespierre.

"I'm a necromancer," Robespierre said carefully. "I raise the dead. I create undead. I don't need a dark magician for that. I *am* a dark magician, if you like, though I hope in name only. Those powers are entirely my own."

"I know. But there's something about your undead that worries me. I can't find out how to make them. As I told you, I've been reading about them a great deal; I read very quickly, and I'm very clever. And yet nowhere, in all the libraries in Paris, can I find anything that offers even a glimmer of the dark magic needed to raise an undead. That includes your own library, by the way. I had a good look through all your books one day, when you were out on business and I was waiting for you to get back. Plenty of books on law, on philosophy, that old copy of Rousseau you keep under your pillow as a talisman. Nothing on magic at all. Not only have you not found a spell to raise an undead; you apparently have never even looked for one."

"My mother was a necromancer. Perhaps it was passed down to me."

"Perhaps. But you were seven when she was taken, and she was taken unexpectedly. It's unlikely she taught you a spell to raise the dead with your alphabet. And it's not something somebody could stumble on by accident: there are very few acts of magic that work by combining the powers of two magicians. I think if anyone told you how to create an undead, it was someone with firsthand knowledge of it."

"Firsthand knowledge." His mouth tightened. "You're not talking about a dark magician. You're talking about an immortal."

"A vampire. Yes. If not one from the fifteenth century, then one who has close personal knowledge of that particular time. That is what the message alleged. And it made me remember something."

"What?"

"The first time we were at the guillotine together, I sent my shadow to you. You took it in. Our magic entwined, as you so romantically put it. I told you that I was inside your mind in glimpses."

"I know," Robespierre said. "You always are. It's one reason I prefer you and Saint-Just over anyone else—I trust you not to take advantage of the fact."

"What I didn't tell you was that there was something else in there as well. Something watching, and waiting."

Dear God. "It was your imagination. It must have been."

"That's what I thought, when there was no trace of it ever again. I spoke to other shadowmancers who worked with you afterward; none of them noticed anything. But now I think it simply hid itself better after that first time. It felt me notice it, and withdrew."

"It's possible," Robespierre said flatly. "It's far more likely that you really were just imagining it. That it's all in your head."

"It's interesting you should put it like that." There was no trace of play in Camille's voice now. "In my head. It reminds me of something else I read about vampires. They're very mesmeric, you know, just as you appear to be, though I could have sworn you weren't when we were at school together. They have mesmeric control over their entire territories. Not absolute control, not over everyone at once, like slaves in a field. But they can nudge and suggest; usually their touch is so light and subtle that the subject doesn't even distinguish the suggestion from their own thoughts. Most easily, they can stir up violence."

"Are you suggesting the Revolution is a product of a vampire trying to take what is theirs?"

"The Revolution? No. The Revolution has been almost the whole of my life. But it hasn't gone right, has it? We can't get it to work—at least, not the way *we* want it to work. And I just keep thinking..." He drew a deep breath. "I've written a lot of things over the last few years. Some of them I meant, some of them I half meant, some of them I thought it would be clever to pretend to mean...and how do I know, really, how much of it came from me, trying to stir a revolution, and how much came from someone else, trying to stir something darker? When those crowds stormed the Bastille, what if there was something already among them, directing their rage into channels we haven't seen the end of yet? Why do we have armies of the undead rampaging across Europe? Why has the Republic become Saturn devouring its own children?"

"You can't think like that," Robespierre said. The cold inside him had reached a new low. "Really, Camille, you can't."

"I can't," Camille agreed. "And that's what scares me the most of all. It's what tells me that all of this might be true. Because when I try to think this through, I find I can't, not without effort. It's like trying to fight through a stammer, but in my brain rather than my tongue. My ideas stick, and search for new tracks. I can barely get this out to you now. And why should that be? We both know that if there's one thing I've never been afraid of, it's ideas."

Robespierre was silent for a long time. "All this, based on a daemon-stone," he said at last. "Who did it come from, by the way? Where is it?"

Camille laughed. "So those who sent it can lose their heads? You really do need to master the art of subtlety. They're not in the country, I'm afraid. They're in England."

"So you're communicating with enemies of the state."

"No. I threw the stone away as soon as I'd held it once—I imagine it's at the bottom of the Seine. You must know this—your National Guard would have found it otherwise. I know they've searched my house, and Danton's. Enemies of the state have communicated with me. Can I help it?"

"Can you? What did they ask you to do?"

Camille shook his head impatiently. "It doesn't matter. I don't care about them. I came to *warn* you, can you get that in your head? Whatever you're doing, England knows about it. If they choose to expose you to your enemies in the Committee, that would probably be enough to end you. I'm not sure why they haven't, one way or another. Instead, they spoke to me, as one of the increasingly few people close to you. They told me what you're doing will destroy you. I didn't need them to tell me that. I can see it right now, looking at you."

"What are you asking me to do?"

"What I've been asking you to do for weeks! Stop this. If something is talking to you, stop listening to it. Make us all stop listening to it. Stop the Terror, and the dark magic, and the Committee of Public Safety. We don't need it anymore. We're winning the war; we don't need to keep growing the army of the dead. The country doesn't need an executioner's blade hanging over it. Or if it does, then the cost is too high."

"The cost of the French Republic of Magicians is too high?"

"Yes! Why can't you see that?" Camille shot to his feet. "How can you *be* like this? How can everyone be like this? I've given everything I have to this revolution. How can people now be talking about how close I am to the guillotine? They've denounced me at the Jacobins, you know."

"Of course. What did you expect?"

"I expected to save France! I skewered people on paper for years. I've caused the deaths of hundreds. I said terrible things, and I meant them with all my heart. I let you and Danton use me as you saw fit, because I believed in you both. I was the voice of your revolution. I told you to tear the world apart, and you all listened. And when I start to talk about mercy—about *not killing people*—all at once I'm a monster. I never thought that people could be so ferocious and unjust."

Suddenly, Robespierre saw the Camille who had, not five years ago, stood on a table and set a revolution on fire. It should perhaps have worried him; curiously, though, he felt more secure with this Camille than with the quick-witted, clever, worldly one he had been dealing with before. This one was indeed a child, buffeted by his emotions on strange and dangerous seas. Robespierre, cool and superior, could handle that. Something in him could even feel contempt for it.

"I won't talk to you about this anymore," Robespierre said, very carefully. "You're clearly upset. I'll see that you're not asked to serve at any further executions. I wanted to give you an opportunity to show your loyalty, but if you won't... We don't need you. There are thousands of magicians with your skills who will be honored to do what needs to be done."

Camille gave a quick, breathless laugh. His composure was back. "You mean Saint-Just."

Robespierre didn't answer. "As for the papers—perhaps I can persuade the Committee to let you renounce them publicly. Burn every issue."

"Burning is not answering," Camille shot back.

That, after everything else, was suddenly it. The line had been Rousseau's response when the old order had burned *Emile*. The book was written on Robespierre's heart, and Camille knew it. Twisting it against him now was worse than taking a knife to him. It might not have even occurred to Camille that this would be the case until after he had spoken—it was exactly the kind of quick-witted, lightning-fast allusion that came easily to him. It didn't matter.

Robespierre drew himself up. Anger was coursing through his blood, hot and stinging. The shadows around him grew darker, so dark his friend's face was almost hidden from him. Camille took a step backward.

"If you were anybody else," Robespierre said, and heard every word drip with venom, "you would already be awaiting the guillotine. Do you understand that? I've *protected* you. You and your family. Everyone told me that I was letting sentiment blind me. My enemies laughed at me behind my back. And still I protected you. Now you've publicly turned against me."

"You—you let me write that journal." He was fighting his stutter now. Robespierre looked at him coldly, knowing he was making it more difficult. "You *asked* me to—to write that journal in the first place. You practically dictated—"

"You didn't show me what you printed today. That wasn't me; that was treason."

"The Revolution was treason, remember? We didn't care. We had to save the country. That's all I've tried to do now. I know you wanted me to stop with denouncing the Hébertists, but it wasn't enough. Hébert wasn't the problem. The problem is that we're killing people, and it needs to stop."

"There's only so much I can protect you from. There's only so much I *want* to protect you from. Your activities are becoming too dangerous. *You* are becoming too dangerous."

"I don't—I don't want you to protect me. I—" He gritted his teeth and tried again, frustrated with himself. "I want you to listen to me. I— You need to—"

"Get out."

Camille opened his mouth, but his words jammed in his throat, and finally he had to close it again. He turned, and he left.

And that was how Robespierre would have remembered him: stammering and frightened, realizing for the first time in his life that he had gone too far. Except that he turned back once before he reached the door. "What about Lucile?" he said. "And Horace? He's your *godson*."

"And I'll do what I can to make it easy on them," he said. "But it's not up to me. I'm not a dictator. This is a Republic."

"This is a bloodbath," Camille said. "And you will drown us all."

Robespierre gritted his teeth. A pulse throbbed painfully in his temple. "If I were you," he said, as calmly as he could, "I'd get out of France as soon as possible, and I would take your wife and child with you. Go to your English friends."

"This is my country," Camille replied. He still knew he had gone too far, but he wasn't frightened anymore. "I'm not going anywhere."

★ ★ ★

They came for him at dawn.

Camille answered the door on the third round of knocking. He looked shockingly white and exhausted, as though the last of his youth had fallen from him over the long, sleepless night. There were streaks of gray in his hair that hadn't been there before. Yet he addressed them with his usual schoolboy charm.

"Good morning," he said. "We expected you hours ago. We waited up."

"I'm sorry, Citizen," the guard replied dryly. "We stopped to arrest Citizen Danton first. Are you ready to come with us now?"

Nothing was provided in prison. Lucile had to help him pack a bag, as though he were going away on business. She folded clothes as if in a dream. Would it be warm or cold in the cells, this time of year? Would his stay be long? How many clean shirts? Camille selected two books, both in English, and quantities of pen and ink.

Lucile cried out loud when they came with the bracelet open.

"Oh no," she said. "No, don't."

Camille squeezed her hand tightly. "It's all right," he said, but when the metal clasp clicked tight around his wrist, swallowing up the old scars, his bravado cracked. His eyes filled with tears.

"You bastards," Lucile said flatly. "You'd still be under the old regime if it weren't for him."

"It's not our fault," the same guard said. He looked uncomfortable. "Come on. Time to go."

Camille drew a deep breath and brushed his hair from his eyes. The familiar gesture was made clumsy by the metal encircling his arm. "May I say goodbye to my son?" he asked.

"If you're quick," the guard replied.

It was too quick, in the end. They tore him from Horace before he could finish saying goodbye; from Lucile before they could finish their last, desperate kiss; from his home before he could finish taking one last look. They tore him away before he could finish.

* * *

The Old Cordelier, seventh issue: "I believe that Liberty is humanity; thus I believe that Liberty would not prevent the relations of prisoners from seeing their fathers, their husbands, or their sons; I believe that Liberty would not condemn a mother to knock in vain for eight hours at the door of the Conciergerie, in the hope of speaking to her son, and when this unhappy woman had accomplished a hundred leagues in spite of her great age, to oblige her, to see him yet once again, to wait for him upon the road to the scaffold. I believe that Liberty is magnanimous: she would not insult a condemned criminal at the foot of the guillotine, and after his execution, because death wipes out the crime."

Paris

March 1794

Robespierre had not wanted to go to the executions of the Dantonists. He never wanted to go to the guillotine, he admitted to himself; in another world, he would hide in his room every time and not come out until it was over. This one might be finally too much. This, surely, would destroy him.

"They'll still be dead," he said out loud, in the gray dawn. He had been awake all night. "Can't they just be wheeled away and forgotten?"

Don't be ridiculous, a voice said in response. It might have been his benefactor, but he suspected it was just himself. Perhaps, somehow, it was Saint-Just. He couldn't tell anymore. *How would that look? If they alone don't become soldiers in the army of France. How would it look?*

And so, because of how it would look, Robespierre was standing on the scaffold as his friends were wheeled toward him. Saint-Just was at his side, steely and uncompromising, and perhaps just a little triumphant. Robespierre looked ahead, and his face showed nothing. It was a fine, cold day. He wasn't wearing his glasses, and without their green tint the colors seemed too bright to be real.

Camille was third in the line of eight. He had not come quietly. Small and light as he was, it had taken three strong men to get him to the tumbril; his shirt had been ripped from his back in the struggle, and on his wrist his new bracelet glinted silver. On the way, he had alternately pleaded and cursed the crowds as Danton tried in vain to soothe him.

Now, approaching the gigantic silhouette of the guillotine, his voice had finally failed him, but his face was drawn and frightened and his dark eyes were enormous. They had cut his mass of dark curls to avoid impeding the blade. His neck without them looked white and naked.

Many people had been to the guillotine before them. Many had faced their deaths bravely, with stoicism and dignity and resignation. Camille had never been one for any of those things. He was young, and distraught, and he did not want to die.

It was only steps from the guillotine itself that he stopped fighting the men whose job it was to wrestle him to the blade. Robespierre was trying not to look at him, but when he heard the noise of the scuffle quiet, he turned his head before he could help himself. For the rest of his life, he wished he had never moved. Suddenly, Camille was in front of him: not a blurred figure in a cart but real, familiar, as he might have been standing a thousand times in the past for a thousand more innocent reasons. There was a sheen of sweat on his bare skin; it mingled with dirt and dried tears and a tiny trail of blood where the shears had nicked his ear. A bruise was blossoming on his right cheekbone. His brilliant eyes were dark in the hollows of his face. Robespierre had thought somewhere in the back of his mind that Camille would forgive him, or at least pity him. It was nonsense. Camille didn't forgive, and this wasn't forgivable. He looked at Robespierre with utter hatred.

"You won't survive us by long," Camille said. Then, quite deliberately, he turned his back and looked at the executioner.

"There's a locket in my hands." He sounded almost calm. "It's from my wife. See that her mother gets it, won't you?"

The executioner took it, and they put Camille's head on the block.

Later Robespierre would find out, against his will, that Danton had rescued the locket for Camille before it could be cut from around his neck, and been allowed to slip it to him before the men had bound their hands. Camille had carried it, curled about his fingers, all the way down the interminable road to the scaffold. When he had learned that his wife had been arrested a week after him, they said, he had all but lost his mind. The touch of the metal that enclosed her hair, and the physical support of Danton beside him, were all that had kept his trembling, beaten body upright on the tumbril. Amid everything he was trying not to feel, Robespierre actually felt jealous of Danton. Camille had once been his to protect.

Robespierre had known Camille for twenty years. The guillotine cut him away in less than a second. His magic stirred within him, and as the blood flowed he took Saint-Just's shadow and pushed it into the frail corpse that was left behind. Soon, it was all over, and a new undead went to join the ranks. He didn't look at the head in the basket, but he never did anyway.

Danton was last. He stepped up to the guillotine, magnificent to the end. His murdered supporters, now animated with newly summoned shadows, stood in line awaiting further orders. He did not look at them, nor did he look at Robespierre beside them.

"Show my head to the crowds," he told the executioner. "It's worth the trouble."

The worst part was that it was not too much. It did not destroy him. As he had discovered in Arras the day he signed his first death warrant it was possible to do truly terrible things, and go home to bed afterward, and get up the next day.

"You're weakening," his benefactor said.

"I'm not." Robespierre wiped his eyes; they were as wet with tears here as in the real world. Perhaps he was crying within as well as without. "How can you say that? I used to kill my enemies. Now I kill my friends. If strength is measured by corpses, I grow stronger every day. One day I may even kill you."

He said it with bitter irony but was astonished to find how much he meant it.

His benefactor showed no sign of surprise. "Possible, but unlikely."

Robespierre drew a deep breath and let it out through gritted teeth. He *was* weakening—not in his will, perhaps, but in his body. His magic was not meant to be mingled with shadows. It felt poisoned.

"Was Camille right?" he asked. He could even say his name. "Could this magic kill me?"

"Yes," his benefactor said. "It could."

"Will it?"

"Would you stop if I said it will?"

"No. But I would like to know."

His benefactor smiled. "No," he said. "The magic will not kill you."

Ten days later, on the other side of the Channel, a shadow appeared in the garden at Battersea Rise. Henry Thornton was away in town on business, and the house was very quiet. Wilberforce was writing a letter at his desk, enjoying the crisp sunlight after a week of rain, when the butler came to fetch him.

"It's a real one, sir." His Cockney twang sounded apprehensive. "I mean, a powerful one. Human form. Sort of wispy, though—more gray than black. We thought we'd better fetch you."

"Yes," Wilberforce said, as calmly as he could. His heart was pounding. "Yes, of course. Thank you, Thomas. But—you're sure it's not rogue?"

"Not sure, sir. But it's not hurting anyone. It's just standing there. And..."

"And what?" Wilberforce prompted after a moment.

"And it's saying your name, sir. At least, we think it is. They don't really speak, you know. But... it's in the wind."

"The shadow?"

"Your name. Your name is in the wind." He paused. "One of the maids nearly fainted."

"I don't wonder," Wilberforce managed. He felt he could faint himself. "Poor thing. Was it Laura?"

Thomas was unsurprised by the question. "Yes, sir."

"She's very nervous. See that she's given the night off, will you? And I'll go down to see what this shadow wants."

"It's dangerous, sir," Thomas said. "And you're too important to lose. Best call the Knights Templar and let them deal with it."

"Come now," Wilberforce said lightly. Thomas's fear made him paradoxically braver, perhaps simply because the other man's regard for him made him feel that he had to be. "That's no way to talk. It might have something interesting to tell me. If the Knights Templar came, they'd cart it off or destroy it, and we'd never find out what it was."

"I'd live with the disappointment, sir. Anyway, shadows never tell anyone anything."

In the end, Thomas insisted on accompanying Wilberforce with a rifle, at a distance of a few feet. Wilberforce had his own stake too, just in case, but when he stepped out into the garden, he was glad of the added protection. The wind was indeed calling his name. It whispered through the leaves of the trees above his head, and swirled around the rosebushes that circled the house. It raised the hairs on the back of his neck.

The shadow stood in the center of it all, grotesque in the bright light of day. Thomas had been right: it was a peculiar shade. Usually they were solid black; this one was soft gray, darker in the middle and almost invisible at the edges. The feet seemed not to touch the ground. It was utterly still.

Wilberforce, the wind hissed.

"I'm here," Wilberforce said. He wasn't sure it would understand him, but its head turned in his direction. "What do you want of me?"

The shadow turned. Nestled in its chest, just below where the heart would be, a folded piece of paper lay shrouded in cloud. A letter. It had no seal, and the address could not be read.

A shadow bearing a letter. To Clapham. Such a thing had never been done, as far as Wilberforce knew. But it was here.

"Do you wish me to take it?" Wilberforce asked. "Is that it? Is it for me?"

It didn't move. Even if shadows could communicate, perhaps that was the only answer his question deserved.

He had been thinking of the phrase "to steel oneself" lately. He had watched Pitt do it countless times, before stepping into the House of Commoners or a cabinet meeting or a dinner party. There would be the faintest intake of breath; then he would draw himself up, ramrod straight, head high, face unreadable, every inch as though encased in inviolable armor. Wilberforce launched himself into things unarmored, with his mind and heart wide open, not a defense in the world. He had wondered, once or twice, which of them was the more vulnerable.

This time, he steeled himself. He drew a deep breath and held it, as though about to plunge into water. He imagined himself coated in metal, a barrier between his skin and the shadow in front of him, unable to be touched. Then, before his nerve could break, he plunged his hand into the shadow's chest and snatched out the folded paper. It wasn't as terrible as he had feared. Really there was no sensation at all. It was almost certainly his imagination that his hand felt tainted and the scar on his side ached.

"Thank you," he said to the shadow, belatedly.

It gave no sign of hearing him. It shivered in the breeze, like a ripple across a pond, just once. Then it was gone. It dispersed into the bright April afternoon, as another shadow had dispersed in France with a shot through the heart. Wilberforce had never heard of such a thing happening spontaneously before. He didn't know whether it had died or been set free.

He opened the letter. It was from Camille Desmoulins.

London/Saint-Domingue

April 1794

Citizen Wilberforce,

Forgive the Latin. I can read English, but I write it clumsily, and I'm not sure if you have enough French to appreciate my more delicate verbal flourishes. If this is to be my last surviving letter, I want it *appreciated*.

If you ever receive this, I did what you told me not to do, and it went badly, and I was executed. I doubt I make a very good undead. My head is generally conceded to be my best feature.

I haven't been executed. I refuse to believe I'm dead. You will never get this. But I write it anyway. A lot of things have happened over the past few years that I would never have believed. And I know too well that life is made up of evil and good in equal proportions. For some years evil has floated around me, so that it seems to me my turn to be submerged must come.

Even if I am indeed dead, you still may never get this. I realize the difficulty in trying to write and smuggle a letter to England at the best of times, much less under the nose of an enemy who is in the mind of every citizen of the Republic. I might have done better with the daemon-stone, of course, but I fear I threw that thing into the Seine as soon as it had delivered its message. Robespierre's men search for such things regularly; I had no wish to be arrested. But. Whatever this thing is, vampire or not, it can't watch everything at once. Right now, Robespierre is speaking at the Convention; I can hear him through the door of the private office he's set up just off the debate chamber, where I've ducked for a few minutes. Picture him, if you like: standing at the tribune, glasses pushed up on his forehead, surrounded by flickering candles. His speech low, hypnotic, punctuated by long pauses that bear no relation to grammar or sense. There's no air around him these days. When he speaks the room can't breathe. I suspect mesmerism is flooding his every sentence. My hope is that this thing cannot give such help to Robespierre, and be so present among his audience, and notice me scribbling at the same time. I'm finding this as easy to write as can be expected, so either I'm right, or it's playing games with me right now. I can play games too.

Information. Here it is. I am, as I've indicated, going to do what you told me not to, and confront Robespierre with what I know. My allegiance is to France—and, yes, to Robespierre—not to you. But I also did what you suggested. I took my place at the guillotine one last time, and this time, when my magic touched Robespierre's, I felt for the third presence lurking in our midst. I had felt it once before by accident; this time, I looked for it on purpose. It was hiding very deeply, but I found it. You were right. It's there. It's always been here: before the Revolution, before I was born, for hundreds of years. But—and here is the interesting part—it's not *here*.

I can't give you a geographical location, but I can guess. It's somewhere very hot, surrounded by water; I can hear distinct sounds of revolution in the background. (Believe me, I know what a revolution sounds like by now. It's very angry, and there are slogans.) The West Indies, probably. I would say Saint-Domingue, judging by the upheaval, but that is no longer a French colony, surely. Or is it? I suspect your friend Pitt would know better than me. My knowledge of intrigues is fairly domestic. That is all I have, and I'm giving it to you, an honorary citizen of the Republic and yet the friend of its greatest enemy. It goes against everything I am to do it, but then, if what you say is true, I no longer know who I am.

No. I know who I am. I am Camille Desmoulins, the spark that ignited a revolution, and if I speak to you now, I speak to you from the dead. I have married a wife celestial by her virtues; I have been a good husband, a good son; I would have been also a good father. I carry with me the esteem and the regrets of all true Republicans, of all lovers of virtue and of liberty. I may die at thirty-four years of age, but it is a miracle that I have passed unscathed during the last two years, over so many of the precipices of the Revolution, without falling, and that I still live. I rest my head calmly upon the pillow of my writings—too numerous, but which all breathe the same love of mankind, the same desire to render my fellow countrymen happy and free, and which the axe of tyrants cannot touch.

Sound of tumultuous applause now. Robespierre's finally finished. I need to get back.

Don't you dare let me down.

Camille Desmoulins

"Saint-Domingue," Pitt said. "I should have thought of it. I knew vampires like to stay within their territory; the French colonies are still its territory."

"We thought it was in France," Wilberforce pointed out. "It *was* in France, the last we knew of it being anywhere in particular. It was in Arras when Robespierre created his very first undead."

"And that's exactly how I should have known it was no longer there. When Robespierre and the enemy created that first undead, the king's magic went into revolt against it. It could feel that there was a vampire king—or at least an aspiring one—just across the Channel engaging in powerful magic. Then it settled again. It's still relatively settled even though Robespierre and his shadowmancers are sending armies of the undead across Europe. Something obviously changed—something more than just the enemy no longer being directly involved in the creation of the undead. The enemy must have left France around the time of the king's recovery. I should have thought of it."

Wilberforce sighed. "Well, I don't see what difference it would have made if you *had* thought of it. It would have been a guess until now. You would have told me, I would have told you it was a very interesting guess, and we could have done nothing about it. I'm not sure what we can do now."

The Downing Street library had one large window, and by Pitt's count Wilberforce had paced to it and back eight times over the course of the last few minutes. It was the first opportunity they had found to discuss the contents of the letter all night. Wilberforce had brought it in the early evening, just as a collection of generals and war ministers arrived for dinner; as they were there in part to discuss the army of the dead, they couldn't exactly be abandoned to their own devices, even if politeness had allowed it. Fortunately Wilberforce was more than capable of animating any discussion; by the second course, most of the table was enthusiastically outlining for him the difficulties in facing magical combatants, and he was listening with entirely unfeigned interest. Still, more than once he had caught Pitt's eye meaningfully, and Pitt had found himself longing more than usual for the duties of entertaining to be over.

It was near midnight by the time the two of them were left alone.

It was a cold night, and the London streets outside were like frosted glass in the lamplight.

"And you say a shadow brought this all the way from Paris?" Pitt asked, from where he sat by the fire with the letter. He felt the heat only distantly. Possibly it was the three daemon-stone messages he'd received, but his head had been aching all day, and he couldn't seem to get warm.

"I presume it must have," Wilberforce said. "It dispersed almost as soon as I had removed the paper from its center. Camille would have been braceleted as soon as they took him prisoner, and he would have had very little warning beforehand; I can only assume that he had the letter waiting, and when the knock came at the door, he called forth the shadow and sent it on its way to me. It must have taken days to cross France, and then the Channel, and then find its way to Clapham."

"Shadows can't usually carry things at all, much less for any distance," Pitt said. "They're too insubstantial. To summon one of that strength—I know he was a strong magician and a talented one, but it must have nearly killed him."

"He knew it would be the last act of magic of his life," Wilberforce said. "I doubt he cared what it cost him. He did it. Then they took his magic from him, and then they took everything else."

"Don't feel too much sympathy for him. He called for the deaths of countless men and women, many of them for no other cause than that they were born Aristocrats."

"His wife is dead now," Wilberforce said. "Did you read that in the papers? They claimed she was conspiring to start an uprising to free him. They cut off her head the day before yesterday."

"I know." Pitt sighed. "I feel too much sympathy too."

"We can't let them down. We simply can't. We need to end this."

Pitt did not trouble to answer this; Wilberforce would not expect him to. He returned his attention to the paper, trying to find some new meaning in it. It was eerie reading. In the last year, he had read many reports from men who had died in battle before their words had reached him, but they had been different: those men had not known they would die when they wrote. Camille Desmoulins wrote as one already speaking from beyond the grave. Except, of course, that he had no grave. His body was on its way to battle as they spoke.

"He says it's been here for hundreds of years," he said, almost without meaning to. It was what they had feared from the start, and never quite put into words.

"The list of names my Templar friend Holt gave me," Wilberforce said hesitantly. "The list of vampires killed after the war. I realized what was wrong with it. I meant to tell you—well, I suppose I am."

"Wrong with it?"

"It was my fault for dividing the list. If it had all been together, we might have realized it earlier. There are 650 names on that list, all recorded by family, rank, and age. It's meticulous, as the Templars always are, even back then. And none of them are under two years old."

It took a moment for the import of that to sink in. "Might they not have left the children's deaths unrecorded?"

"Perhaps that is indeed all it is. Or perhaps they left the infants to die of natural causes—though I can't imagine they would take that risk in order to avoid spilling blood they'd never shown any qualms about spilling. But the other possibility—"

"Is that they kept them alive for some purpose of their own," Pitt finished. "Dear God. What could they possibly have been doing?"

"If one survived, then as long as it was fed on lifeblood, it could still be alive today. Which would mean we were indeed dealing with a pure-blooded vampire."

Strangely, the cold fist around Pitt's stomach didn't tighten or loosen at that information. On some level, perhaps, he had always known.

"It would explain why its magic was powerful enough to reach from Saint-Domingue," he said, because he had to say something.

"But not what he was doing with Saint-Domingue in the first place," Wilberforce said. "That's still the part that puzzles me. I understand the war, and the army of the dead. But I can't understand why he would want to help enable a rebellion."

"Nor I. I don't understand why it sent an undead to delay abolition in 1788 either—although we can assume that it left for Saint-Domingue almost immediately afterward, given the king's recovery."

"If that was indeed why he sent it. It might have been aimed at you. You are the rival vampire, in this instance."

"We don't know that." He said it as firmly as he could. He wasn't even quite sure why. But if it were true, then they were fighting something far more terrible than he was ready to deal with. "We have no evidence it knows I exist at all."

Wilberforce seemed about to argue, then looked at him. Whatever he saw, he let the argument die and exhaled it as a sigh. "I don't know. There's something very big and very dangerous looming just out of sight, and I can't see it."

"No." He rubbed his temples absently. "Wilberforce, if you must pace, I wish you'd pace over to my desk, pick up that decanter, and pace it over here."

"Is that one of those wishes that is really an order?"

"I'm prime minister—all my wishes are orders. If you would be so kind."

"I'd be a better friend if I paced over and tipped it out the window," Wilberforce said, doing what he asked anyway. "You've already had a full bottle at dinner, and I don't believe you ate three bites. Are you still not feeling well?"

"All the best strategies are formed when things are slightly blurred around the edges. That's how my government has always been run."

"You've just lost my vote. Right there and then. I'm going over to Fox. You heard it here first."

"Oh, the fickle nature of the British people. Thank you." He took the decanter from Wilberforce and refilled his empty glass. "In any case, Fox drinks more than I do, and I'm fairly sure he's not thinking of the defense of the nation as he does so."

Wilberforce snorted; then a shadow passed over his face. "The defense of the nation." He fell into the chair opposite Pitt, with far more force than that chair had probably ever encountered before. "That's the pressing issue, isn't it? What *are* we going to do to defend the nation? Especially if we're correct, and our enemy is a pure vampire."

"In some ways it makes it easier," Pitt said. "We know its capabilities."

Wilberforce laughed. "We do. We know they're virtually without limit."

Pitt had to smile, wryly. "Well, not quite. If it was indeed an infant during the Vampire Wars, it means that it probably has little more knowledge of that time than we do—aside from the secret to creating an undead, which it must have discovered somewhere. Its natural abilities aren't so unlimited. And more to the point, if it's a true vampire, then its powers are tied far more closely to its territory than they might be otherwise."

"And how does that help? What can we do about it?"

"We can do the most simple of all things," Pitt said, after a moment's thought. He took a sip from his glass and tried to focus his mind. "We know where it is. We can trap it there. We have ships and men amassed in the West Indies, many of them already on the shores of Saint-Domingue. I can send others to reinforce them. If we can take Saint-Domingue once and for all, and prevent any ship from leaving it..."

"We can't comb every inch of Saint-Domingue looking for a vampire that has successfully hidden itself for hundreds of years."

"No. But if we take Saint-Domingue, it becomes a British colony. The enemy will, at one stroke, be trapped outside its territory. That's very dangerous for a true vampire—far more dangerous than it would be for me. It might not break its power over France, but it will certainly weaken it. And it will make it very, very vulnerable. That has to be worth something."

Wilberforce nodded slowly. "You mean 'he.'"

"I'm sorry?"

"You said 'it' would be vulnerable. You mean 'he.'"

"I do. Does it matter?"

"Not practically. I just want to remember that we're fighting a human being. Not a shadow, or a monster. Do you think our fleet capable of taking Saint-Domingue? Completely, I mean. We've barely held on to a few provinces in the south, from my understanding."

"If we concentrate all our efforts on it, then yes. I do." And he did, of course. He had to. They simply didn't have another plan.

"Then I suppose it must be attempted." Wilberforce didn't sound happy.

"What is it?" Pitt asked.

"Never mind. It's nothing."

"No, really. What is it?"

"If we take Saint-Domingue," Wilberforce said, "it means a re-instatement of slavery over the island."

"It depends on the terms." He saw where this was leading. "We might end up needing to negotiate with the insurrectionists, in which case—"

"But if we take the colony now, with the help of the planters. If all goes according to plan."

"It's the most likely outcome, yes. For now. And it's considered the most advisable, in order to stop the revolts from spreading to our colonies out there. The rebel armies are moving to liberate others, once they've secured their own freedom. They might spread across the sea to Jamaica, if they chose."

"Do *you* think it's the most advisable?"

"For now? While we're at war?" Of course he'd thought about the question, over and over. But when he spoke, he still wasn't certain if he had the answer. "Yes. It doesn't mean I don't want the end of slavery. I do; you know I do. I supported you against the trade again only last week. But I don't want it like this. I want it legal, binding, and honorable, not through bloodshed and dark magic and chaos."

"I understand. I want that too. But what if we can't have all those things? What if we can't have freedom without chaos?"

For one rare moment, Pitt could have wished he was a thousand miles away, and a different person, who had nothing more to worry about than his own household, who didn't have to wonder if you could have freedom without chaos, and who, if he was really still not feeling well, could just go to bed and sleep. But he hadn't been that person for more than a decade, if he had ever been at all. The moment didn't last very long, and he didn't wish it.

"And how would you answer that?" he asked.

"I don't know," Wilberforce said. "I wish I did. I'm not a revolutionary. Perhaps I should be, but I can't be. I don't have that kind of anger in me. But quelling a rebellion is an act of violence as well. It's quite a different thing from preventing one. And you said once that 'just this once' is the most dangerous phrase in the English language."

"I don't think I'm saying 'just this once.' I'm saying 'just for now.' Just for now, we need to maintain political stability. Just for now, we need to prevent magical uprisings. And just for now, yes, we may need to reinstate slavery on an island that's fought very hard to free itself, if that's what it takes. We can go back and set it right afterward, and we will, if we come through this. But first we need to come through this."

"I imagine that Robespierre is saying much the same things about the Reign of Terror."

"I know he is. That's because, repulsive as his methods may be, and as different as his personal vision may be to mine, we both want to keep our countries safe."

Wilberforce smiled very slightly. " 'If we cannot expect a magician to refrain from magic in the defense of their own lives, how can we possibly expect them to do so in the defense of those they love?' "

"That sounds familiar."

"It should. You said it, ten years ago. You argued that people were allowed to defend others as well as themselves, through magical means if necessary."

"I remember now. Dundas warned me when this started that it

could be read as an invitation to break the Concord. You weren't even in the House that day."

"I read it in the papers afterward. It's what you're talking about, isn't it? It's how you see the war. It's a fight to defend what you love."

"It sounds rather sentimental, put like that." He said it as lightly as he could, knowing that it wouldn't fool Wilberforce for a moment. He didn't even want it to.

"No," Wilberforce said. "No, it isn't sentimental at all. But how far are you willing to go to do it?"

"As far as is honorable and right. And before you ask, Wilberforce, I can't say how far that is. For one thing, I'm a part of a larger political process. It isn't my decision alone."

"It could be. Mesmerizing any opposition could be just for now too."

"No. It couldn't. I believe in the system of government we have, and the processes it goes through. It's far from perfect; our job is to continually refine it and make it better, but those refinements need to themselves come through the system. They reflect the will of the country, its Parliament, and its king. You and your friends at Clapham aren't the only ones who see yourselves as an instrument of something greater than any one individual, you know."

"I know," Wilberforce said. "And I know you hold that trust every bit as sacred as we hold ours. I do believe you have the purest of motives at heart. But—"

"You don't like the war. I know that. And I know you don't like the attempts to take Saint-Domingue."

"I don't. I never have. I accept that it might be our only chance against this vampire, and I won't oppose it. But—I know you believe in the system. But please remember that it *is* an imperfect system, and our job is not only to uphold it but to fight to change it. Don't stop fighting."

"I'll never do that. But I need to fight one battle at a time. We *are* at war."

"You say that all the time now."

"Well," Pitt said, "we happen to be at war all the time now."

Within the week, a fleet of two hundred ships had been dispatched from Britain. On board were thirty thousand redcoats. It was the largest single naval operation in British history. It was on its way to Saint-Domingue.

Not long afterward, a stranger walked into Toussaint's encampment.

Fina was cutting aloe leaves to make an ointment, as Toussaint had shown her. It was a hot day: flies settled on her fingers as she extracted the clear gel, and sweat dampened her brow. She didn't know what made her glance up, if anything did at all, but when she did, her heart went cold.

The stranger was very tall, clad in a blue coat and white breeches. He wore a wide-brimmed hat, and his face was in shadow. The fact that a white man was in the camp was nothing unusual: there were many among Toussaint's followers, and he always dealt generously with the white population of the island if they came to deal with him. But she knew this one. She had seen him before—only never clearly, and never when she was awake.

In the time it took her to rise, wiping her sticky hands on her skirt, Toussaint had greeted the stranger and invited him into his tent. It had closed behind them; from the look of it, they were there alone together. Toussaint's current scribe, a scrawny young mulatto named Jean-Philippe, sat outside idly poking the dirt with his saber.

"Who is that man?" Fina asked him, doing her best to keep urgency from her voice.

Jean-Philippe glanced up, squinting in the sun. "I don't know. He sent a message to the camp in the morning asking for an audience. No name. Toussaint seemed to be expecting him."

Her stomach twisted. "Can I see him?"

"He's not to be disturbed. And they might be in there awhile."

She had promised Toussaint she would never enter his head, and he would know if she broke the promise. Instead, she turned to the canvas wall and threw her magic at the stranger. She could feel his mind and body: tense, coiled, powerful. Yet when she tried to grasp it, her magic slipped and recoiled. She scrabbled for purchase as she would at a slippery metal. Clearly, his head was open to her only in the hinterland where he talked to others. She gritted her teeth and cursed quietly.

Jean-Philippe frowned up at her. "Fina?"

"I'll wait," she said.

She sat cross-legged on the ground outside, ignoring the curious glance of the scribe. Her nerves strained to catch any hint of what was transpiring on the other side of the canvas; she felt as though she were trying to hear not only with her ears but with her eyes, her nose, her skin. It might have been a wall as thick as a stone fort.

It wasn't long before the tent flap parted; perhaps a quarter hour, perhaps less. Toussaint emerged first. Then, as Fina scrambled to her feet, the stranger stepped past him. For the first time, Fina saw the owner of the voice in person and in the full light of day.

He paused beside her. She had time to take in his face: stark white, angular, confident. She saw the way his fair hair curled, a little darkened by sweat, under the brim of his hat; the way the tip of his nose was starting to peel in the sun; that his eyes were pale blue green, with long, fair eyelashes, and faint creases at the corners. He had time to take her in, too, but he didn't. His glance slid over her, disinterested, in the manner of any master surveying his territory. She knew then, once and for all, that he didn't care about their freedom.

At a nod from Toussaint, two of the nearby soldiers stepped forward to escort the stranger to the gates. He went quietly, inclining his head to Toussaint but not speaking. It didn't matter. Fina knew what his voice sounded like.

"That was him, wasn't it?" she said to Toussaint as soon as the stranger was out of earshot.

"Not now, Fina," Toussaint said. He looked older than he had when he entered the tent.

Once she would have been content to be brushed aside. Not anymore. Not about this. "That was the voice in the night. The one that told you all to rise up. He *was* on the island."

"Yes. You were right. He's been here all along. He spoke to me last night, while I was asleep, and this time I heard him."

"What did you promise him?"

"Safe passage back to France. He wants to return to his home. I've told him we can certainly attempt it, though Britain controls the seas."

"And what else?"

He didn't reply.

"That wouldn't be enough for him. He wouldn't come out of hiding after so long just for that. What deal did he make with you?"

"I told you, Fina. Not now."

"Don't tell me *not now*, Toussaint Louverture!" For once, she wasn't pretending to be Molly or Clemency or Jacob in order to be brave. Her frustration was her own. It shot clear through all the years of fear and hiding and despair, and blazed. "I came over here because of that man. I was the one who heard him in the dark. I was the one who told you what he did to you all. I told you what I saw in his head, in France and in Jamaica. Whatever his plans are, they involve my people as well as yours. I have a right to know what they are."

It was rare to see him angry, but his eyes flashed now. "You're a soldier in this army." He had a way of making his voice cut like a whip, and he used it. "You don't decide what rights you have."

"I'm a free woman." In that moment, she believed it. "I've spent far too long being told what to do. I won't take it from you."

He might easily have struck her then. His jaw tightened, and a muscle in his cheek twitched involuntarily. Then he turned and disappeared back into his tent, motioning with a jerk of his head for his scribe to follow him.

Fina stared after him. She had been angry before in her life, many times. She had never been so disappointed. Toussaint was not some arrogant white man, nor was he one of those rebels who led by force because they lacked the imagination to lead any other way. He knew better than that; he knew *her* better than that. She was not foolish enough to think that he couldn't have come so far without her, but he *hadn't* done it without her. He had given her self-respect. It was no longer his to take away.

The following day, another white man came to the camp. This one caused more of a stir: he was a member of the French army. And no minor member of the French army either: this was Laveaux, the commander of the French forces in the north. Fina had been inside his head at times, and she grudgingly liked him. Unlike the English commanders, who tended to bribe and deceive as often as they fought, Laveaux met Toussaint in battle as an equal—she had felt his respect, and it was unfeigned. He had offered Toussaint an alliance once or twice before; Toussaint had always turned him down, but she knew the respect was mutual. But for him to be here now, in the midst of their camp, he had to have been invited.

His meeting with Toussaint was short. This time, Fina had no difficulty in seeing inside the tent: Laveaux's gentle, courtly mind opened to her with ease. She felt his goodwill, and his delight; she saw Toussaint speaking to him, and she saw him smile. At the end, they clasped hands. Toussaint's felt rough and strong through Laveaux's gloves.

She was still standing outside the tent when the two of them came out. Laveaux's eyes met hers for the briefest of moments, and he inclined his head on reflex. She wondered who he thought she was. Unlike most of Toussaint's fighters, she had never been seen on the battlefield.

Toussaint didn't look at her, but he stopped beside her. They watched Laveaux ride away together. When he spoke, his voice was cooler than usual but not unfriendly. "Was he telling the truth?"

She didn't bother to deny her presence in the tent. "Yes. Whatever he said to you, he meant it."

Toussaint nodded.

By that evening, the news was out. Toussaint told his lieutenants, and it spread like wildfire. France, against all expectations, had upheld the commissioners' promise to end slavery. As of now, every man, woman, and child on Saint-Domingue was legally free. And, as of that very afternoon, Toussaint had broken with Spain and transferred his allegiance to the French forces against the Spanish and English.

The news was greeted with mixed joy and consternation by the camp. In one day, their enemies had become their allies; their freedom had been given to them months after they had taken it for themselves. Nobody quite knew what to think.

Fina said nothing. As night fell, she walked to the edge of the camp, where the tussocky ground gave way to steep crags and cacti. The ground was still warm from the day's heat, and a gentle wind tugged at her skirt. She knew the stranger wasn't far away.

If she and the stranger were indeed enemies, she thought, she now had one advantage. They had been face-to-face, and she had looked at him. He had not looked at her.

Saint-Domingue/London

July 1794

It began with a battle.

A few weeks after the stranger's visit, Fina was shaken roughly awake by Dessalines.

"We're taking the British fort," Dessalines said. "At Môle Saint-Nicolas. Toussaint told me to bring you."

She stared at him for a few moments, uncomprehending. He shifted uneasily. Toussaint's people were afraid of her stare, she'd discovered over time. Some were superstitious of her power; others were more practically afraid that she was slipping behind their eyes. She'd heard whispers that her gaze was eerily blank—and it was, she knew. That had nothing to do with her magic, except that its resistance to spellbinding had forced her into the long habit of letting nothing show on her face. Her stillness had been for survival then; now she found it gave her an unexpected power.

"Not all the way into battle," he said, as if she'd asked. "Just to the edges. He wants you to be able to watch from the cliffs, and stop men in their tracks if the occasion calls for it."

"I'll come," she said, more relieved than she would admit. It wasn't that she was afraid of battle anymore, but the implications of Toussaint breaking his promise to her without a word after their argument would have been frightening. For that one moment, she had wondered if he now wanted her dead. The fact that the thought could even cross her mind frightened her most of all.

Fort George, as it was now called, had once been a French fort, manned by the remnants of white colonists attempting to take back the island. When the British had landed, some nine months ago, the colonists had surrendered with relief, even with gratitude. The fort stood on the brink of a high cliff grown over with inhospitable trees, overlooking dazzling seas. A path led down to the bay of yellow-white sand, where some of the British ships remained docked, but there was no real track over the mountains. The rebel armies struggled through and around the undergrowth, Toussaint on his black horse at their head. At his side, two fire-mages walked. They clapped their hands, and a line of flame shot from their palms toward the closed door of the fort.

As the doors shattered, Fina closed her eyes and slipped into the head of the enemy. It was like ducking beneath the surface of the ocean: a silent frenzy of color and movement. All around her were heat and gunfire and swords.

"Stop," she said, over and over. "Stop now. Stop."

The battle did not last long. Perhaps half an hour, perhaps less. The British numbers were far greater, but so many of them were ill and unable to fight, and the attack had taken them by surprise. They surrendered the fort willingly. Toussaint granted them permission to leave in their ships and even ordered his own men to help carry the wounded and sick down to the bay.

Fina came down as the last of the British were leaving. She came stumblingly after so long out of her body, her vision barely feeling as though it belonged to her. She scratched her arm on a thorn and felt it as though it happened to somebody else. The sensation wasn't helped by the surreal sight of the British filing down onto the beach, prodded encouragingly by strong African men with swords.

Dessalines grinned at her, his unease melted in his exhilaration. "It's ours," he informed her. "We've taken it."

"We'll never hold it," Fina said. "He must know that."

"He knows. He says we don't need to hold it for long."

She wondered. "Do you know what he's planning?"

Dessalines laughed. "Nobody ever knows what Toussaint is planning."

More than four thousand miles across the ocean, the stars were out over London, and the streets were empty of all but the most determined drunkards and pickpockets. Westminster lay behind a curtain of fine summer rain; droplets rippled in the wind, catching the lamplight in cascading, ever-changing shapes. Rain soaked the battlements of the Tower of London, where Thomas Clarkson sat reading old ships' manifests by candlelight. It fell on Wilberforce's house at Old Palace Yard, and on the Houses of Parliament, both abandoned now for the long recess. Wilberforce was in the Lake District, sound asleep under broader and moodier skies.

It lashed against the windows of Number 10 Downing Street and startled Pitt awake. It usually took far more than a light sprinkling of water against glass to do that; he admitted it to himself, even as he was also forced to admit that his heart was beating unusually fast and the remnants of dreams twisted uncomfortably in his mind. He had been restless and uneasy all evening, with no cause that he could determine. The magic in his veins had burned distractingly, flashing bloodlines across his vision like fragments of glass. The hours before bed had been filled with conversation, work, letters, and arrangements for travel to Holwood the following day, so it had been relatively easy to push his feelings down and let his thoughts take over; now, in the dark of night, it was more difficult. The house was too large and empty, and his sleep not quite empty enough. He was sorely tempted to get up, light a candle, and read by the window until the sky grew bright enough to be considered morning and he could start his journey out of London. But he was tired and not given to indulging vague feelings of dread, so instead he told himself not to be ridiculous, settled down firmly, and closed his eyes.

He wasn't aware of falling asleep.

There was no garden, and no crooked street. The scene around him was as close to nothingness as his mind could conceive. Darkness. A faint susurration of wind and what could be splashing waves. The occasional hard glint on the horizon that could be a star behind clouds, or the reflected light of a star on water. The air had the salt tang of the sea.

"William Pitt," a voice said. It was a pleasant voice: light, educated, beautifully enunciated. The kind of voice that would carry weight in the House of Commoners. "The younger William Pitt, of course. I remember your father. Our territories had a sort of war when he was prime minister—nothing like this. You were conceived and born in the middle of it. I wonder if that's why the magic in your blood ignited the way it did, after so many generations."

It wasn't what it said. It was the fact that it was here, talking to him, and what that meant. There was no pretending anymore that the enemy had no idea what he was, or didn't care. Some terrible threshold had at last been crossed.

"How are we speaking?" Pitt asked, as calmly as he could. In the waking world, that was very calmly indeed. Here, in whatever hinterland of thoughts and dreams they inhabited, it was much harder. "I know what you are. Britain is outside your territory. Even if you are indeed a full-blooded vampire, you can only enter the minds of its subjects when they step onto your soil, or afterward with their express invitation. Clarkson gave it. I haven't."

"You're not a British subject, William Pitt," the enemy said. "You're a blood magician—of a sort. And I haven't entered your mind. Our minds are meeting halfway. This is a parley."

"I have no desire to parley with you."

"Nor I with you. I want to warn you not to break the rules."

In his sleep, Pitt frowned. "What are you talking about?"

"I've seen your ships on their way here. Somehow, you've found out where I am, and you mean to kill me. I can only assume that Robespierre was involved, or rather someone close to him. He has been my one weak link all these years. But it doesn't work like that. Perhaps you don't realize, going entirely from books as you are, but you must kill me in person or not at all. Otherwise, you confine yourself to the capture of my territory, please. Those are the rules."

"What rules? What do you want?"

"Do you really not know?" The darkness constricted around them. "I want my birthright. I want what was taken from me and my bloodline three hundred years ago."

"Wilberforce was right, wasn't he? You survived the Vampire Wars. You were one of the royal families."

"I was a *child.* A child who lived in a castle in Marseilles. My parents had a faint connection to the royal bloodline. The Templars broke through the shadows guarding the door and slaughtered them before my eyes. Did you know our blood looks the same as any other spilled onto wet stone? Perhaps you'll see it for yourself one day."

The venom in his voice was startling. It was laced with too much grief to be describing something he knew of only by record. "How old were you? You weren't under two like the others missing from the records. You wouldn't remember."

"So you know about that? No. Most of them were, the ones the Templars took. But not me. I was seven. They thought it might work better with an older child, and they underestimated me. They had no idea how young I was taught, and what I knew how to do. I imagine people made the same mistake with you at times, when you were younger."

"They thought what might work better?" A terrible suspicion was crystallizing in his mind. "What were they trying to do?"

"They thought they were being kind. They thought we would die anyway, without blood—why not see if they could save us and make us safe at the same time?" The irony bit painfully. "You know what they were trying to do. You wouldn't be alive without it."

He did know. "The elixir. It never worked on pure-blooded vampires."

"No, it didn't. Every one of those children starved to death.

Something else you may have the opportunity to experience, if you live long enough. I nearly died myself. But, as I said, they underestimated me. I hope you understand, though, why your way of staying alive is as repugnant to me as mine is to you."

The darkness was so thick about them it could have been a living thing. It was the air before a thunderstorm, heavy and rumbling and ready to crackle with energy.

"I'm sorry," Pitt said, and meant it.

"Don't be." The air around them caught like a breath; as if by force, the skies lightened. The enemy laughed a little. "I suppose I should thank the Templars in one regard. I would have been nobody of much importance had the vampire kings lived. A blood magician with power over a country estate, five hundred and first in line to the throne. Now the whole of France is my territory, and one day soon it will be acknowledged as such. And so will yours. You know what rules I refer to. The rules of the Vampire Wars."

"I have no intention of playing by the rules of vampiric territorial disputes." Inwardly, his heart was racing, and so were his thoughts. It was very important that he admit nothing, but he didn't think, in this state, it would be possible to lie. "I'm not one of you. This is a war between nations, and I am a British minister. Those are the rules by which this war is being fought. Your kind is extinct."

"So I thought too. Then you came into my territory, a decade ago. I should thank you, too, by the way. I'd been content to hide until then. I'd forgotten how much we need this."

"What do you need?"

"Not me. Us. We need power. We need intellectual stimulation. We need the knowledge that we're changing the shape of history. You must admit, in that you're a true vampire."

"I admit nothing of the kind."

"You can admit what you like." Scorn entered its voice. "A war between nations, indeed. Haven't you felt the magic stir in your blood? What did you think that was for? Budgetary considerations? We are at war. Not France and Great Britain—us. You and I. From now on, your magic will only get stronger. You'll have to try to rein it in, or give it its head. Either one will probably take more strength than you have."

He waited until he could trust himself to speak. "You've delivered your warning. Get out."

"Oh, that wasn't my warning. My warning is this: if you're going to try to find me, I'm going to have to disappear again. This will be our last contact. You can forget about Robespierre: it was clever, whatever you did, but you won't be able to use him again. And I have a surprise waiting for you on Saint-Domingue—or rather, for your fleet."

"For the fleet?"

"Yes. I'm sorry about your fleet. But you should have known better. This isn't a war you can end. This is a war you have to win."

The darkness around them lifted, all at once, as though the sun had risen within the space between heartbeats. In that flash of light, the sky above was dizzying blue, and beneath them was a dazzling sea.

The sky he'd never seen. The seas he'd never been able to imagine. The West Indies. The seas in which his brother had drowned.

The waves were filled with bodies. Not the handful of men who had died with James. Thousands of them: bloated, pale, their eyes wide and staring. Seawater darkened their red coats. Around them was the splintered wood of two hundred ships.

Pitt's eyes flew open. His bedroom was back around him. His heart was hammering so fast he couldn't breathe; his stomach heaved, and bile rose in his throat. His magic screamed the awareness of one million bloodlines.

The advantage to his elder brother being first lord of the admiralty was that Pitt, unlike the officers waiting downstairs, did not feel at all guilty for intruding on his sleep. It was barely dawn when he arrived at his brother's London town house, but it would have made little difference if he had waited: the Earl of Chatham was notorious for not rising until almost midday, preventing business from being done. His unpunctuality had, around the time of Dunkirk, earned him the nickname "the late Earl of Chatham"; this alone was enough to cause a breakdown in discipline, to say nothing of the mismanagement of naval affairs themselves. It was a problem for another time.

The late earl was hurriedly emerging from the covers as Pitt entered the room; the young footman sent to rouse him had just drawn back the curtain.

"Good God, William." His brother's handsome face registered more bewilderment than alarm. "It's six o'clock in the morning. What's wrong?"

Pitt barely waited for the footman to leave the room before he spoke. He didn't answer the question; there was no time. "John. Is there any way to recall the ships we sent to Saint-Domingue before they reach its shores?"

"Wha—?" Chatham blinked and rubbed his eyes. "The…No. Of course not."

"No, really. Don't just say that reflexively. Is there really no way?"

"We can't communicate directly with the West Indies. Daemonstones won't stretch that far across water, so it has to be done by ship. It takes weeks—months, if the tides are wrong. You know that. For all I know, the fleet is there already."

"It isn't."

"How do you—? No matter. Very well, it isn't. But it will be there soon, unless they've gone very far off course. You can't stop them. Why would you *want* to stop them?"

"I can't explain, I'm sorry. But I have reason to believe that if we don't do something to turn them away from Saint-Domingue, every man on those ships will soon be dead."

Chatham stared at him. His face was still puffy with sleep. "Then I'm afraid they're going to die," he said at last. "I'm sorry. There simply isn't anything to be done."

Pitt drew a deep breath and released it very slowly. In his head, he tried to consign thirty thousand men to the bottom of the ocean. Some people might have found the number impossible to visualize. His brain was used to numbers. He thought perhaps he might be sick after all.

"Really, William," Chatham added. "What is this about? You can't burst in here, tell me my men are going to die, and not tell me why. If it were anyone else, I'd think they'd gone mad."

"Perhaps I have."

Chatham snorted. "You're my younger brother. I've known you since you were an infant. You're not that interesting."

Pitt managed to smile but also took it as a firm warning to get himself under control. Their father's vampiric strain had wreaked havoc on his mind toward the end of his life, in ways that none of them had ever understood—and his father had been far stronger and more brilliant than Pitt. He couldn't afford to have people suspecting the same of him.

"I truly can't explain," he said, more calmly. It was an imitation of himself. He was getting very practiced at those. "I received information this morning. It might be wrong. If what you say is correct, we'll have to hope it is."

John nodded slowly, not quite convinced but placated for now. "If I think of anything, I'll send word to you at once. Are you staying for breakfast?"

"No, thank you. But please, John, do get out of bed and go and speak to the officer waiting downstairs. I know it's barely sunrise, but there *is* a war. It's damaging to your credibility as first lord if they have to wait for you, and I truly don't want to have to remove you from office."

"You wouldn't. I'm your brother."

"And that's precisely why I would, you know that. I'd have to. Besides, if I have to overcome my natural inclination to stay in bed until dinner, I don't see why you shouldn't."

"I was about to get up." Clearly, he knew this wasn't the time to argue. "Where are you going?"

"If we can't get a message to the fleet," he said, "then I need to know if we can at least get a message to France, and how quickly. Then I need to speak to the king. And after that, all going as I expect, I need to arrange for an emergency sitting of the House of Commoners as soon as possible."

Paris/London/Saint-Domingue

9 Thermidor, Year II of the French Republic of Magicians / 27 July 1794

The Paris guillotine was devouring larger batches than ever. A few weeks before, it had taken sixty-seven people on one day, an increase over sixty-one, the record set the week prior. Robespierre was there for each one. He was even more careful now to use only the weaker magicians, the ones who stood no chance of glimpsing his thoughts or anything else that might be in his head. This and the workload meant it sometimes took up to twenty different magicians to call forth the number of shadows required, yet Robespierre alone pushed them through to the corpses and awakened the dead. The batches were sent to Spain, where the British army would soon meet the French in combat. After that effort, Robespierre disappeared for a few hours, pale and shivering, but he was back at the Committee that night as usual.

He knew there was speculation that he was mad, and an unspoken belief that he was cursed. He was probably both. Shadows clustered around him constantly, whispering, so that he was always cold, and never at peace. Nobody else could see them, so perhaps he was indeed simply losing his mind. He didn't think so, though. He had sent a vast number of shadows through his blood now; he suspected that each time he did, even after he pushed them out into their new headless bodies, part of them remained with him. Each one played upon his vision, taunted him, reminded him of what he had become.

Nobody who summoned an army of the dead ever lived past thirty-five, Camille had said. Robespierre was two months past thirty-six, and the darkness was accumulating in his veins.

Yet the Revolution was not safe. The France in his head was being born, he still believed, but slowly, so slowly, and with so much pain. He could not stop.

Saint-Just agreed with him. Since Camille's downfall, he had emerged as by far the strongest shadowmancer at the guillotine—the only strong shadowmancer, in fact, that Robespierre would let near him. He could stay at Robespierre's side for up to thirty dead, sometimes more, and when at last his magic was spent, he would still remain at the scaffold. Few knew that he and Robespierre went to the Conciergerie every night, and none knew what they did there, but perhaps they noticed that Saint-Just's young face had grown harder and more remote, like a star on a frosty night. They called him the Angel of Death. If he had noticed the touch of anyone else in Robespierre's mind, as Camille had, he never said.

"We need to push through," he said to Robespierre. They were in Robespierre's room at the Duplays', before the start of the meeting of the Convention. The last of the daylight played gently over the familiar furnishings: his desk cluttered with papers, the plain bookshelf Maurice Duplay had made for his books, the old memorial engravings from the start of the Revolution. "But be careful tonight. The Convention are scared. Some of them are starting to say that Danton and Camille were right. They blame you for their execution."

"I know they do," Robespierre said, with bitterness. "The *cowards.* Not one of them would speak for the Dantonists when they were alive. Now they all piously regret their deaths, as if they could have done nothing to save them. Do they think I don't regret them? They were my friends. But it had to be done."

"It had to be done," Saint-Just agreed. "You know I don't regret them. But watch what you say at the Convention tonight. You do have a tendency lately to be—"

"Go on," he said as Saint-Just hesitated. "Hysterical? Half-mad?"

"Incautious. I mean it, Robespierre. The public mood is shifting. I really am concerned for your life."

"My life has been in danger for a very long time," Robespierre said. It didn't seem as important now as it once had. He was so tired. "But it won't end tonight. I'm still needed."

It had been five years since the fall of the Bastille.

Éléonore was standing in the kitchen at her easel as the two of them left. Her brush was in her hand, but the canvas was barely smudged with color.

"Are you going?" she asked—both of them, presumably, but her eyes were only on Robespierre.

"Yes," he said. His mouth managed a twitch that was not a smile. "I should return late, but I'll see you all in the morning."

She nodded, her face grave, and embraced him quickly. It was nothing unusual; the family all embraced him on occasion, as they would a brother or a son. It was only because he was so tired that he closed his eyes and breathed in the smell of turpentine and charcoal that hung about her like smoke. She was just a little taller than him, and the wispy bits of hair tucked behind her ear tickled his nose. Her grip tightened before she let him go.

"Good luck," she said.

The Convention felt different this time. Not so very different—wrapped in his own pain and fear, Robespierre didn't at first realize anything was amiss. It had certainly been hostile to him before; many on it had always wanted his death. Yet it felt, imperceptibly, as though a current had shifted, and darkness was stirring in its depths like silt from the bottom of a river.

Saint-Just felt it too. His frame was tense as he took his seat beside Robespierre.

"Be careful," he repeated.

For once, Robespierre felt a flash of irritation at his protégé.

"Saint-Just," he said. "You weren't here at the start of the Revolution; you're too young. We didn't begin it by being careful."

And yet he hadn't begun it, not really. He had been careful. Those who had not were far braver than him, and now they were dead.

Robespierre had been called on the day before to defend his stance on the Terror; this was nothing new, and he had required only short preparation the night before. Before he could stand to do so, however, another man shot to his feet. Robespierre's glasses were still on his head, awaiting the moment he would need them for his notes; he couldn't tell who it was until the figure spoke, and then he had only vague recollections of the owner. A new member. In the last five years, there had been a lot of changes in government.

"Citizen Robespierre," he said. He was a young man, with high cheekbones and ginger hair rough about his face in the manner of the Commoners outside. "I'd like to ask you a question before you start."

Robespierre gave him his coldest look and felt the room shiver.

The young man carried on regardless. "Not so long ago, in this room, you called for the Girondins to be removed from the Convention, and the people obeyed."

"As I recall," Robespierre said, still coldly, "the people spoke first."

"Citizen Roland spoke on that day. He said that you were a magician, and you had enchanted them all. His wife had made similar claims."

"They were traitors."

"But they were right about you being a magician. You turned out to be a necromancer. You had been hiding that for years. Were they right about anything else? Have you been practicing illegal magic upon the people of France?"

It was the question he had always feared, the question he had killed Madame Roland and her party to silence. Somehow, he had always known it would come back.

Are you there? he asked the voice in his head. *I need you again. Help me.*

Saint-Just spoke up over the rising excitement. "He can't answer that. There's no such thing as illegal magic anymore."

"There is such a thing as betraying the principles of the Revolution. The sentence for that is death. And coercing the National Convention would be a betrayal."

"You can't kill me!" Robespierre snapped, his cold silence melting abruptly. "I animate the dead. Without me they'd be only corpses."

A new voice. "So you admit you've committed crimes worthy of death?"

"No, I do *not*!" The Convention was stirring now, as were the crowds in the galley. He had to raise his voice, which hurt his throat these days. He recognized the sounds of a wakening mob too well. "How dare you even suggest it? Do you have any idea what I've given to this revolution?"

"It seems to have given you more." The first speaker again, but with a rumble of agreement behind him. "You're the most powerful man in France. Somehow, every step of this revolution has raised you higher and higher, while others die at your command."

"Do you think I *wanted* this?" It had been a long time since anyone had dared to question him. Anger was rising in his chest, but also fear. "Do you think I wanted to *be* this?"

"What *are* you?" someone called, and chaos ensued.

It wasn't one-sided chaos: many still spoke for him. Saint-Just; his brother, Augustin; Lebas, Babette's new husband. But he didn't like it.

"Stop it!" he ordered. It took all his strength to project over the mob, but they stopped. "I'll answer your questions. Just let me speak."

"Let him speak!" his brother echoed loyally, and many took up the cry—not, perhaps, all with friendly intentions. Robespierre drew a deep breath and made his way to the front of the room. All eyes were on him.

As he mounted the tribune, he stumbled. Everyone saw it; they noted it as a sign of his weakness. Nobody realized what they had actually seen. Robespierre did not realize himself what his sudden faintness portended, until he stood before the hostile eyes of the

French Republic of Magicians. He reached deep inside himself for the well of mesmerism that had propelled him through the last few years, knowing he would need it as he never had before.

It was not there.

Panic stabbed him; he fumbled for it in his mind as one searches a pocket for a missing coin. He knew it was no use. It was gone. In the moment between him sitting and standing, something had reached out and snatched his power away. Or rather, his benefactor's power. Robespierre recognized the feeling from the long months when he had refused to kill the king and his benefactor had withheld his mesmerism to punish him. But this was different, and infinitely more perilous. This wasn't the Jacobins, but a whole room out for his blood. And he had done nothing wrong this time. He was not being punished. He had been abandoned.

In a life full of corpses and shadows and blood, this was the worst moment of all.

His own gift was still there—as he'd learned three years ago, that could not be stolen or diminished now that it had been awakened. He tried to gather that, if it was all he had, and send it out into the room. But it was so small and pathetic in the mass of hatred and suspicion—like dashing the dregs of a cup of wine into the ocean.

"I was here from the beginning," he said. He had said such things, with variation, for years. He knew no other way to prove his revolutionary credentials. "I was there at the Estates General when the meeting pledged to free Commoner magicians from persecution and imprisonment. I was there when the crowds rose up and tore the Bastille to the ground. I was there when the king fled, and when we punished him for it. I was part of the first Convention of the French Republic of Magicians. When France was battered by its enemies, I gave it an army of the dead, at the expense of my own safety and my own strength. I have given this revolution everything I have, and I will continue to do so until my last breath."

"Of course you have," someone said. He couldn't see faces or distinguish voices now, in the darkness that shrouded him. "You've controlled it from the beginning. It's the product of your insatiable ambition."

"No. No, that's not..." He gathered his voice. "You don't understand. This revolution is the first to have been founded on the theory of the rights of humanity and the principles of justice. Other revolutions required nothing but ambition; ours imposes virtue."

"Then where is that virtue? Why has it led us to the foot of the guillotine?"

"Because this revolution has been persecuted constantly since its birth, as have the men of good faith who have fought for it! It has been persecuted by conspiracists, and liars, and traitors who seek their own gain. And all the deceivers have adopted, each more convincingly than the last, all the formulas and the rallying words of patriotism."

"Then what marks them from you? If the enemies of the Revolution can speak its language as well as you, then how do we know you are not such a one yourself?"

There was no real answer to this. He knew it only too well. It was what had plagued him from the beginning, what had haunted his fears all along, what he had seen happen to the faces of the Girondins and the Hébertists and Danton and finally even Camille. There was no way of telling. Words were only words. What lay behind them was an eternal mystery, and he had never learned how to penetrate it. Perhaps there was no way.

"You know," he said, "because I am Maximilien Robespierre, the Incorruptible, and I have never once lied to you. Those who accuse me are the ones you need to fear. I dare not expose them here. But believe me, when I do, you will know in your own hearts who is innocent and who is guilty."

The room hissed with a group intake of breath, and he realized, too late, that this had been a misstep. He had assumed they would wait to see whom he would accuse: in truth, he had not yet decided himself where the blame for all this lay. But the Convention had now also seen him throw his closest friend under the blade of the guillotine. Almost everybody in the room would fear that he meant to accuse them.

The same thing must have occurred to Saint-Just. He sat by Robespierre's empty seat in the Mountain. His face was its usual mix of impassivity and contempt, but just once he shot Robespierre a look of alarm.

He couldn't back down. It would be an admission of a mistake. All he could do was forge ahead.

And so he forged ahead, reaching for his mesmerism again and again without effect, trying to pour his conviction into the little magic he had left, trying to do without magic at all. It was like fencing with a man in armor when his blade was no larger than a pin.

"If you are so pure, so virtuous," the Convention said, "then why are so many dying every day?"

"It isn't my fault!" His green eyes blazed. "I'm not a dictator. I've never sent anyone to the guillotine. I sit on the Committee, which finds people guilty of treason; the Convention sentences them to death. And then you blame me. You all blame me. You blame me for Danton, and for Camille. You blame me for the Girondins. But all I ever did was speak; you all listened, and you all acted."

"Did you use magic to control us?"

"I used magic to give you a revolution!" It was the closest he would ever come to the truth. "We have that revolution now. It belongs to all of us. And it can still survive. *It has to still survive.*"

It was not his best performance; he knew that. He had nothing to say that he had not said before—a hundred times, a thousand. He had no powerful magic left; only words, and feeling, and the conviction that he had been right—he *had* to have been right. The room was against him. He could feel their hostility, and knew, without doubt, that it was being encouraged and stoked by an unseen force. They were tired of blood and terror. They were scared of what he had become.

And yet still, when the Convention ordered his arrest and the soldiers came forward and gripped him by the arms, he could feel nothing but complete and utter shock.

* * *

That night, a letter was brought to the Duplays' house, addressed to Robespierre. Duplay put it on Robespierre's desk with his other correspondence numbly, out of sheer habit, as his family wiped their tears and struggled to plan for a future rapidly dissolving. The letter was in French, but it had been dictated by Pitt the morning before to an English spy, over the very last daemon-stone left in Paris. It warned Robespierre that his silent partner meant to destroy him. Nobody would ever open it.

On the same day, an emergency sitting of Parliament took place in Westminster. The House of Commoners buzzed with disgruntled politicians, most called back posthaste from summer residences or luxurious retreats they insisted were for their health. The debate was to be on the breaking of the Concord, and many thought it was really about time.

The war had changed things in the House of Commoners. The symphonies that played about the walls were darker and full of foreboding; debates stretched out longer into the night and ended less often in laughter; the crowds that gathered in the gallery overhead were angrier. The conversations were no longer about taxes and treaties and magical reform alone, but troops and naval battles and sedition.

It had changed other things as well. Things that Wilberforce had never thought would change, things that he did not think he could bear.

"I can't do this," he said quietly as the House assembled. Over the noise, the only person to hear him was Thornton, taking his seat at his side.

"You don't have to do anything," Thornton said. "I intend to stay quiet myself."

"But you always stay quiet. Your silence won't be remarked upon, or taken as tacit agreement with government policy."

"Your silence or your support is a matter for your conscience and nothing else, Wilber," Thornton said. "It always is. It doesn't matter what people think."

And Thornton meant it. For him, perhaps, it truly felt that simple. Wilberforce, though, had been seeking that kind of simplicity all his life, and had never found it.

The House of Commoners was emptier that evening than usual: there hadn't been an emergency session during the summer for decades, and many had been too far away to come in time. Wilberforce himself had arrived only an hour before, hot and travel worn, from the north. It gave an air of unreality to the familiar room as Pitt stood and told them that, in light of the surge of executions in France following the death of the Dantonists, the government proposed the Concord be broken as soon as possible. The army of the dead was growing.

Wilberforce found he was barely following his friend's words. Instead, he watched him closely, as he hadn't in years. When Pitt had come to power, he could, unhelpfully, have passed for much younger than twenty-four. His features had still been too soft; his energy and confidence were too youthful; even his reserve was too much that of a teenager trying not to be laughed at. He looked older than his age now. The last year had thinned his face and whittled lines at the corners of his eyes; months of being continually tired and not quite well were wearing at him like fine grit at sandstone. Other than that, he was much the same as he ever had been. He presented the case for the breaking of the Concord as he had presented everything since before he had taken power: clearly, reasonably, cleverly. Whatever had prompted the decision, it was not written on his face for anyone to read, not even Wilberforce.

Fox, predictably, shot to his feet after Pitt had finished. Wilberforce barely heard him either, though judging from the walls, he and Pitt were well matched as ever. Some things, at least, were familiar.

"I should have gone to see him earlier," Wilberforce said quietly—to himself, but of course Thornton heard.

"Who? Fox?"

"Pitt. I don't know why he's doing this."

"When could you have seen him? In the hour before the House assembled? You'd never have pried him away from Dundas and Grenville, even if he'd wanted to be pried. Besides, why would it make any difference?"

"It wouldn't, of course," Wilberforce said, which was probably true. But he felt he was losing his mind, or something worse.

Another speaker. Then another. And then, as the night wore on, it was his turn, or could be—should be, if he were going to take a turn at all. Eyes were beginning to look in his direction, not expecting anything in particular, just for him to speak. He was the Nightingale of the House of Commoners. He was known for it.

I can't do this, Wilberforce thought, and then he got to his feet and did it.

"Mr. Speaker," he called, and all heads turned to him. "Might I address the House?"

The Speaker was a man their own age: Henry Addington, the son of the doctor who had saved Pitt's life. He and Pitt had been childhood friends, and Wilberforce had dined with them both at Downing Street a thousand times. It was strange, Wilberforce thought irrelevantly, how many of them caught up in all of this, on both sides of the Channel, seemed to have been born at the same time. Pitt, Robespierre, Camille, Danton, Clarkson, even himself—all of them within a year or two of each other, and none of them past thirty-six.

He drew a deep breath.

"I am afraid it falls upon me to perform a painful act of duty. I must express a difference with those with whom it has been the happiness of my political life so generally to agree."

Those who had talked to him recently must have been prepared for it: Eliot would have been, at least, and Thornton, sitting protectively at his side. But for most of the House, it was a bolt out of the blue—or a betrayal. Shock and excitement rippled the room. Even the walls resounded, for one brief note, like an exclamation.

Pitt should perhaps have been prepared as well: Wilberforce had certainly told him of his opinions about the war and the Concord, many times. And yet when Wilberforce dared glance in his direction, he knew he had not been prepared at all. His face had become utterly still, as it did on reflex when he wanted to hide his feelings. His eyes were not so easy to veil, and the surprised hurt in them went straight to Wilberforce's heart.

The Speaker was calling the House to order, but it was unnecessary. Wilberforce's voice, tiny as he was, had always been more than capable of speaking above the crowds. Against every natural impulse, he raised it now.

"I know that my honorable friend has the greatest interests of the country at heart," he said, "and of no man's political integrity do I think more highly. But I am sent here by my constituents not to gratify my private friendships, but to discharge a great political trust; and for the faithful administration of the power vested in me, I must answer to my country and my God. I therefore cannot agree to the breaking of the Concord. I cannot believe that it will save us; I believe instead that it will plunge us into black magic and misery of the acutest kind, at the very moment when we most need to come to terms of peace with France."

Pitt had mastered his shock now—at least, to the eyes of those who did not know him very well. He rose, quietly, with the utter confidence that transformed him in the House of Commoners. His voice betrayed barely a tremor. Even after all these years, Pitt still appeared at his most self-possessed when he had been badly shaken. "Mr. Speaker, might I question my honorable friend as to the nature of these terms he proposes? As far as I'm aware, France has offered us none that we might accept with honor or security."

"I propose that we ask them what terms they might accept from us," Wilberforce replied, over the renewed clamor Pitt's words prompted. "And then we in turn might suggest what we might accept from them.

I propose we *talk* to them, for God's sake, before we both fall headlong into something from which we can never extricate ourselves."

Wilberforce looked Pitt directly in the eye, willing him to understand. Pitt looked back. And suddenly, without warning, Wilberforce found himself unable to speak. Reluctance to harm the government—to harm his friend—rose in his throat to choke him. It was very like his own reluctance; he recognized the doubts rising in his own mind. But he had spent hours struggling with his own reluctance in the dark: he knew it too well, and more to the point, he knew Pitt. He recognized the touch of his magic in his brain, even though he'd never felt it before. His surprise was so great that he barely had a chance to feel angry or afraid.

This, it came to him, was what it felt like to be spellbound. This was what abuse of magic looked like.

Paralyzed, he met Pitt's gaze evenly. It seemed they were locked in silent struggle for long minutes. In fact, a matter of seconds passed before Pitt looked away, and Wilberforce felt the hold on him release. He caught his breath with relief.

"Please," he said, as though there had been no pause. He felt weak and dizzy, but his tongue was free. "I know this House is afraid; I know this entire country is afraid. But we need to be better than this."

He sat down amid a torrent of voices, too shaken to care who was shouting what and why.

Part of him was furious now that the shock had settled; it was difficult not to be when the memory of the magic was still so vivid that his limbs seemed barely his own. And yet that was wrong. He remembered the last time he had seen that mesmerism, the night at the Tower of London. He had understood then that it had come from grief, from exhaustion, and from desire to keep the country safe. It came from the same place now, only this time, Wilberforce had been at the center of it. He had not blamed Pitt for his magic when Clarkson had been the recipient; it would be hypocrisy to be outraged now, simply because the magic had been used on him.

He wasn't angry. But he was sick with guilt, and with worry and fear. Everything had gone horribly wrong, and he didn't know how to make it right.

"Are you well?" Thornton asked quietly as the next speaker stood. He was unaware of the mesmerism, of course, but he understood Wilberforce's internal struggle perfectly.

Wilberforce managed a tight nod. "Yes. Yes, I think so."

"You did the right thing," Thornton said. "Pitt won't blame you. He would never expect you to go against your conscience."

"In his eyes, I've betrayed his trust and endangered the country," Wilberforce said miserably. "He'll blame me."

He thought he had indeed done the right thing, morally speaking. He believed that—he could never have done it otherwise. And yet morality was a harsh, cold thing, as uncompromising as a blade, and Wilberforce was only a human being who never wanted to hurt anybody. He sighed deeply, and felt that he was trying to expel something that could never be expelled.

They had taken Robespierre to prison. It was nothing like the grim torture chamber of the Bastille: the Luxembourg had until recently been a palace, and was still an impossibly graceful building of pale stone. The gardens around the palace were dry in the summer heat. It was the same prison to which Danton and Camille had first been brought upon their arrest. Lucile had stood in those gardens, hoping that Camille could see her from the dark, secured rooms inside. Robespierre's room had no window, only a bed, and a desk in the corner.

"Please," he asked the men who delivered him to it, "may I have pen and paper, and a candle?"

"We'll see," one of the men said awkwardly, and Robespierre knew that they had been told not to give him a thing.

For the first time in his life, Robespierre had a bracelet clamped around his wrist. It was not as heavy as he had expected, and it did not burn. If anything, it felt cool against his skin, and only a little too tight. As an experiment, he rallied the magic in his blood, and at once the metal stung as if drawn close to a naked flame.

Camille must have hated it, he thought before he could stop himself, and knew it was an understatement. Imprisoned again, braceleted again, he must have almost lost his mind. No wonder news of his wife's impending execution had pushed him over the edge. He would have been standing on the brink for two weeks.

The shadows had been waiting for him to be alone in the dark. They converged on him the moment the door closed behind the guards. He no longer had the will to force them back.

The dark and cold were like drowning in winter nights, and yet the worst part was the screams. The shadows called out to him, mocking him with the cries of his victims, and he couldn't close his ears to them, because they spoke inside his head. He lay on the bed, curled in on himself, shuddering. He couldn't breathe.

Perhaps he slept, or a dream came to him without sleep, because at one point he recognized the garden. His benefactor who was now his enemy stood by the dying rosebushes. Behind him, the Knights Templar were coming for his mother.

"Camille was right, wasn't he?" Robespierre said. His tongue felt thick in his mouth. "I felt you in the Convention back there. You didn't just abandon me. You stirred them to attack me."

"Yes," his enemy said. "I did."

The ability to nudge and influence, Camille had said of vampires. It would have been so simple. He'd been using mesmerism in public for years. Mesmerism was very difficult to detect, but it was not impossible. All it would take was a whisper in an ear, a tweak of the eye. *Look at him. The Incorruptible. Don't his eyes seem a little too aflame? Don't people seem to die at his word a little too easily?* He had told them all to be suspicious, after all. He had urged them to share his fear.

"I felt your influence over the crowds, just as Camille described. I felt it for the first time at the Bastille, against the guards. You kept me away from the riots after that, but I wouldn't be surprised if you were doing it all across France."

"No," his enemy said. "You shouldn't be surprised."

"You tried to stop Camille from working it out, didn't you? He was right about that too. You were inside his head."

"And you, Maximilien François Marie Isidore de Robespierre," his enemy said, "you cut off his head, reanimated his corpse, and sent it to fight in the fields of Spain. I think neither of us can claim an unblemished conduct with regard to that gentleman, don't you agree?"

"Why?" he asked, but the garden was gone, and then there was simply shadow after shadow, and all of them screaming. Robespierre curled up in a ball, but he couldn't hide. They were inside him: they could haunt his dreams and follow him to the waking world. All he could do was endure, and perhaps he couldn't even do that.

"Camille," he said once, out loud. "Oh God, Camille, I am so sorry."

He didn't know what he was apologizing for. Even now, he could think of nothing else he could have done. But he was still sorry.

By the time his brother came to let him out, Robespierre was scarcely aware of time or place. It had, he thought, been only hours, but they had been hours spent somewhere he didn't understand, somewhere far darker and colder than a mere prison cell.

"Maximilien," Augustin was saying, low and urgent. Through the fog of shadows, he felt his brother's hands on his shoulders. Two other men held the door, talking in low whispers. "It's me. Us. Are you well? We need to go."

It took a good deal to stir himself out of that place in his head and into the real world. He never quite made it all the way. "Go?"

"You surely couldn't imagine any prison would agree to hold us for long?" His brother bent down and took up his wrist. Robespierre felt the bracelet loosen its grip, and then his brother slipped it off and threw it aside. "The National Convention may have turned on us, but this is the middle of Paris. You're Robespierre. The Paris Commune forbade any prison to take us at all."

So the government of Paris was defying the Republic of France—or, more accurately, the Republic was splintering yet again. It might almost be possible for Paris to seize control of the Republic: all the strongest magicians were in the city, and always had been. But it would depend on all of Paris being with them, and he had walked in suspicion too long to believe that was true.

"Maximilien..."

"Yes." He blinked hard, willing the shadows to clear. "Who do you mean by 'us'? Who else was arrested?"

"Don't you remember? I was, for a start—I asked to go with you, but they separated us all. Saint-Just was taken, of course. Couthon, too, and Lebas. Hanriot tried to stop them, and so they took him too." The names were coming too fast to fit to sense. Couthon had lost the use of his legs some time ago; he would make a pathetic figure at the guillotine. Lebas, of course, was Babette's husband.

"Is Babette safe? And the rest of the Duplays?"

"I think they're safe. Their house is boarded up. Now there's an uprising out there. The—"

Augustin stopped as Robespierre laughed once, shortly and hysterically.

"I'm sorry," he said as he caught himself. "But you have to admit those are in the air these days."

Augustin smiled, perhaps in relief that his brother seemed to be coming back. If so, he misjudged. "This one is for us—for you, really. The Paris Commune are rising against the Convention in support of you. I've just been there, talking to them. The city gates are closed. Listen. Can you hear the tocsin ringing from the Hôtel de Ville? It's a call to battle."

Robespierre didn't bother to tell his brother that he could hear little at that moment above the whisper of ghosts. He shook himself, his brief hilarity gone. "It can't be. Not again. Let me talk to the Convention. Surely—"

"You have talked to them. That's what started this," Augustin said bluntly. He tightened his grip on his shoulder at once, comforting.

"No, no, not really. It would have happened anyway. It was inevitable. But it can't be undone. We need to leave, and get to safety."

His limbs were like water; his brother needed to haul him physically to his feet, and still his head swam.

"The Commune don't have control of all the districts of Paris," he said when he was capable. "And they can't stop the people from rioting. If the Convention finds enough support within the city, closing the gates won't be enough."

"I know," Augustin said. "That's why we need to leave quickly."

They were hunted men in a city that could at any moment turn on them. In a similar position, the Girondins had scattered and fled, melting into the stones of Paris and the surrounding country. It was madness for them to return to the Hôtel de Ville. Yet Robespierre raised no protest as the carriage bumped and jolted its way across the Seine. The Girondins had not escaped death either—perhaps one or two had survived, but not in any way that mattered.

It was night, yet the streets were blazing with lamps and candles. Once, as he leaned against the window to fight a wave of faintness, he saw a cannon being rolled past. The rumble of its wheels on the cobbles shook the carriage.

"Everything that hasn't already been sent to the front is being brought to the Hôtel de Ville," Augustin said when he caught his glance. "I told you, this is war. The call has gone out to the city to rally in your defense."

The Hôtel de Ville looked glorious at night. Every room was lit up from within, and the great bell sounded like a chime from the stars.

Robespierre and his brother were shepherded upstairs, to a room with only one small window and a fire blazing. There seemed to be people everywhere, coming and going and whispering. Three of the other members of the Convention were waiting for them in the same room: Lebas, Couthon, Hanriot. He managed to acknowledge them; they barely managed to return it. All were pale and determined. Saint-Just was still missing.

Augustin helped Robespierre sit down and handed him a glass. He drained it without tasting; the rim clinked against his chattering teeth. He couldn't stop shaking.

"It's all right," Augustin said, over and over. Perhaps, even in the circumstances, he could find some comfort in the novelty of looking after his elder brother. "It's all right now. Rest here. We're safe."

They weren't safe. He knew this too well. If his own intellect and experience were not enough to tell him so, he could still feel the presence in his head, and it was not at all concerned about his escape.

"Where's Charlotte?" he managed to ask. "Did she get out?"

"She's gone into hiding for now. A friend is helping—even I don't know who. She'll be safe."

That was something, at least, if it were true. He tried to feel that. But the shadows were thick about him, and he was so cold.

"They don't understand," he heard himself say. "It wasn't me. It was France. It was the Revolution."

"You *are* the Revolution to them," Augustin said. "You made yourself the Revolution. They can't see where you end and it begins."

He wasn't sure if this was what he had meant to do. It didn't matter.

Saint-Just came in only minutes later. He alone of them looked much as he ever had: proud, contemptuous, ice-cold and marble white. The Angel of Death. Their own death was coming very close, and he didn't seem to notice or care. He didn't acknowledge the others or talk to them, not even to Robespierre. Perhaps he was right. They had been friends before, even close friends; now they were strangers in a waiting room, and the gulf between them could have spanned a thousand miles.

They didn't have long to wait. A man, one of the mayor's staff, put his head in the door as the clock was striking one in the morning. Augustin rose to speak to him; their voices were low, but not so low that Robespierre couldn't hear through the shadows.

"They're coming," the man said. "Soldiers are marching on

the building. Some of them are being stopped. Many are being let through."

Augustin closed his eyes briefly. "How many men do we have?"

"Only thirteen sections have sent men to fight for us. The rest are either neutral or with the Convention." He glanced sideways at Robespierre. "What's wrong with him?"

Augustin followed his glance. "He's—"

"Nothing," Robespierre said suddenly. His pride flared inside him, enough to pull together the shattered fragments of his identity and his sanity. The shadows were blown back. He got to his feet and stayed there. "Why do you ask that? How many are with the Convention, for certain?"

The man flushed, and his voice was more respectful when he replied. "We don't know yet. But they'll be here soon enough."

"Then we need to be ready for them."

Augustin spoke up tentatively. "I hate to ask. But—if circumstances allow it—if we manage to kill any of them before they kill us—could you give us an army of the dead? We have the two of you. The Incorruptible and the Angel of Death. You and Saint-Just, between you—?"

He hadn't thought his heart could sink any further. He hadn't even been certain he still had a heart. But he did.

He glanced at Saint-Just. His friend met his eyes for the first time since he'd entered the room, and nodded slowly.

"We don't have the corpses yet, of course," Augustin said. "But if we do— I mean, I know you're unwell—"

"Of course I can," Robespierre said. "If circumstances allow it. Of course."

He knew he couldn't. But perhaps he was wrong. Perhaps he could. That power was his own; it didn't come from his benefactor. Perhaps, even if it killed him, he could. For France, or at least the France in his head, which still was not quite dead.

He had to sit down again after the man disappeared, and the shadows flocked back the thicker in payment for his brief moment of clarity. His brother put his hand on his shoulder, and recoiled.

"My God," he whispered. For the first time, he sounded frightened. "You're freezing. Is there— Can I do anything? What can I do?"

"Nothing." Robespierre rubbed his brow, which was aching. "There's nothing. Just—"

He didn't finish his sentence. His pride wouldn't allow him to ask his brother to stay near and drown out the voices, and besides, they were his voices. He had agreed to hear them when he had agreed to raise the dead. He had no regrets about what he had done, but he deserved to hear them all the same.

Very soon, the voices were mingled with the sound of soldiers at the door.

Five thousand miles away, Fina heard no voices. But she was watching. Her body sat, knees drawn to her chin, on the ground of a storehouse within the British fort. Her mind looked through Robespierre's eyes. Her magic had strengthened lately with use, like a muscle; now she could feel not only his cold but his fear, humming like a vibrating string pulled too tight.

"What's happening?" she whispered. "What did it make you give?"

The French room shook, as if from a cannon blast; even without sound, her eyes flew open with a start.

In the Caribbean, night had not yet fallen, and she opened her eyes to a storeroom bathed in gold. Toussaint was standing in front of her. He might have been there for an hour, or for a few moments: she had lost track of time. It was the first time she had seen him close since the stranger had come to their camp.

"I was looking for you." His voice was softer than she had heard it in weeks. "Where were you?"

She had been right here, in body, but she knew he didn't mean that.

"The stranger betrayed him." Her words came clumsily as her mind came back to her body. "The other man, the little French necromancer. Right now, half a world away, he's killing him. I still don't understand why, or what it has to do with Saint-Domingue. But whatever else the little Frenchman was, he started out by wanting to help us."

Toussaint sat down on the crate opposite her. He was dusty from the road, and his hair seemed more grizzled without him seeming particularly older. "You saw the stranger with him?"

"I tried to look through the stranger's eyes," Fina said. "I wanted to see him when he was awake. I couldn't—I couldn't even when he was in the tent with you. But part of him is still in the head of the Frenchman, half a world away, and so I saw through the Frenchman's eyes instead. I saw the shadows around him. And just once, I heard the stranger laugh. You have no reason to believe me—"

"I believe you," Toussaint interrupted. "I owe you an apology for speaking to you the way I did the day the stranger came to the camp."

"I don't care about that," she said, which wasn't true. It had hurt deeply—and, what was worse, disappointed her. She felt the rift between them begin to knit together now, like skin healing over. But it wasn't the most important thing. "It doesn't matter how you *spoke* to me. I wanted you to *listen* to me. I still do."

"I should have," he said. "I didn't want to hear. I know you tried to warn me about the stranger; I know you have doubts about his intentions. I share them. Whatever he meant by helping us to freedom, I don't think he did it to be kind."

That put into perfect words exactly what she had felt from his head. It surprised her—not that Toussaint had understood, but that until now she hadn't.

"No," she said slowly. "He isn't kind. Perhaps that doesn't matter, in itself. After all, Dessalines isn't kind either, in battle." Toussaint's mouth twitched, and she smiled faintly at the understatement. "But it's different. Dessalines is angry. The stranger turns people's own anger against them. He uses it, and them, and then he throws them away. And whatever his plans are, they aren't for us."

"And you think we shouldn't be a part of them."

She might have said so, even a few minutes ago. But the horror of being inside the French necromancer's head was fading; so, too, was some of her fear, now she knew she was being trusted and believed. It was easy to concede that she knew nothing about the man the stranger was killing as they spoke; nothing but that he had believed in their freedom, and that he had killed thousands of people. It was hard to forget that she had come here, after all, because a cry for revenge had gone out across the ocean and she had wanted to answer. Perhaps she still did. Revenge and justice were still very confused in her head.

"I'm sorry for speaking when I shouldn't have, before," she said, and knew she was delaying.

"When you shouldn't have? You mean when I didn't want to hear it? They're not necessarily the same thing." He didn't take his eyes from her. "I'm asking you to speak now."

She knew it. It became so much more difficult to speak when someone would actually listen.

"I don't know," she said at last. "I don't know what he promised you, or what you promised him—beyond his safe passage, and your allegiance to France. That *is* why we've allied ourselves with the French, isn't it?"

"It's part of it," he agreed. "Though I wouldn't have done it without a guarantee that France had already outlawed slavery."

"The necromancer wanted to outlaw slavery a long time ago. The stranger stopped him. I think he let him do so now only to secure your allegiance."

"That would be no difference to most of France," Toussaint said. He wasn't arguing, just listening. "Most of the Convention don't want us to be free. They want us to help them keep the island from Spain and England, and our freedom is the price they're finally willing to pay."

"But we know that," Fina said. "We know the worst that could happen from them when we're no longer useful. We don't know what the stranger plans for us."

"True. Yet we have plans of our own, and we might need him to accomplish them."

"That's what I need to understand," she said. "Before I answer your question. Even when I wanted his help, when I first came here, you didn't trust him. You still don't. And you would never be guided by anger or fear. So what has he promised you?"

"That's why I came to fetch you. I wanted to show you. I told you, didn't I, that I had weather magic in my blood? Barely awakened, but there."

"I know. It's useless." She was half joking, and he smiled.

"The stranger offered to awaken it. To make it less useless—to set it free, perhaps, as we were set free." He stood. "I promised you that I would never ask you to stand by my side in battle. I still won't order you; as you so rightly said, you're free to do as you want. But I'm afraid I've come to break my promise, nonetheless. I have a battle before me now, this very moment. Will you stand with me?"

Fina got at once to her feet.

She expected to be led up to the battlements of Fort George, perhaps through soldiers arming themselves for war. Instead, she found herself following Toussaint down the winding cliff track that led to the sea. It was rough going, even with a clear path: twice she stumbled, and the thorn bushes that jutted out from the cliffs snagged on her skirt. The beach was deserted; now that the British troops had been pushed south, there were only fishing boats in the harbor, and none of them were crewed. The sea was silent and glittering in the dazzle of the sun.

Toussaint caught her arm as she descended the last few steps. He pointed out to sea.

"Do you see them?" he asked. "There, on the horizon."

She looked, squinting against the glare. It took a while for the haze of waves and light to resolve into shapes, and when it did, her heart jolted.

"Yes," she said. "I see them—who do they belong to?"

"Britain," Toussaint said. "What we can see is only the first of the fleet. There are two hundred of them, the stranger told me."

The shapes were white sails on the edge of the sea—sail after sail after sail. They seemed never ending. They caught the breeze, straight and tall and proud. She remembered the first time she had ever seen a ship, when she was five, and had thought it was a hollow monster come to devour her. She hadn't been wrong.

"Is that enough to take Saint-Domingue?" she heard herself ask.

"We'll never find out," he said. "They'll never reach us."

"Why not?"

In answer, he closed his eyes.

The wind began to stir in the trees; Fina felt it in her hair and against the cooling sweat on her skin. Overhead, the clear blue sky darkened with clouds: no small, fluffy wisps, but mountainous, rolling, the sort that heralded a hurricane. Rain prickled her upturned face. The sea, so calm and still, began to rise.

Weather magic. They had a few among them who could perform it. A woman who could raise winds strong enough to force back soldiers; a man whose rain could break the banks of a river. She had seen it once in Jamaica, from a magician called to the big house after an unusually long dry spell threatened the sugarcane fields. But he had drawn clouds only in patches. It had almost been comical, watching the small tufts delivering their light showers like water wrung from a washcloth. This stretched as far out to sea as her eyes could reach. Toussaint's face, eyes closed, was furrowed in concentration.

The waves were rising now, higher and higher, it seemed almost to the fort itself. The ships were battered, spun around in circles. On the closest, her eyes were good enough to see the mast crack in two like a twig. The rain lashed about her body, whipping at her hair and clothes; on the horizon, the sea surged and crashed. It was triumphant: a celebration of violence and chaos, of a magic that was wild and cruel. She felt her heart respond, and she cried out. She couldn't tell if the cry was joy or terror. Her own voice was lost in the roar.

Paris, the Hôtel de Ville

"My God," Augustin said quietly.

Robespierre was signing his name to a document Hanriot had given him: a message to rally the loyal districts to their cause and to reassure them that liberty survived. It was very difficult to do, with the trembling of his hand and the darkness before his eyes, and it was only with great concentration that he had managed the first three neat letters. He was determined to achieve the others, if for no other reason than to show his enemies he was still alive. Yet at the sound of his brother's voice, he broke off, almost with relief.

"What is it?"

"Nothing," Augustin said, in the tone that, when he was a small boy, would have meant that he had broken something. Robespierre joined him at the window to see what had been broken this time.

The courtyard of the Hôtel de Ville was thick with people, all bearing torches and pikes and the red caps of magicians. The cannon that had been firing throughout the evening had been swarmed and overturned; mob magic crackled in the air. The riot stretched back as far as they could see, clogging crooked streets and carpeting the ground in front of them. It was as though Paris had cracked open, and a dark, silty current spewed forth.

Robespierre watched without speaking. It didn't feel quite real to him, or perhaps it felt too real, and too familiar. Another burst of violence, another uprising that he was watching out a window. There had certainly been enough of those. The only difference was that this time, it was coming in to find him. Behind him, he heard Hanriot swear.

"We won't get out of here, will we?" Augustin said. "Not alive. The tide's turned too far."

"I don't think we were ever meant to," Robespierre said.

There were noises in the corridor; there had been for a long time, but they had ignored them. They had hoped it meant their aggressors were being held back. Looking at the scale of the aggression outside, they knew now it did not.

"What if I were to die?" Lebas said suddenly. They turned to look at him. "I mean it. Robespierre and Saint-Just...If I were to blow my own brains out, here—could you make me one of those things? Would that save you?"

"It might," Saint-Just said. It was the first time he had spoken. He looked at Robespierre, a flicker of something in his cold eyes. "If there were few enough soldiers—an undead could hold them long enough for us to get away."

"And go where?" Robespierre asked. His stomach churned. "There's nowhere left to go."

"Still. If there's a chance—"

"It wouldn't work. The victim needs to die unwillingly. Lebas would be sacrificing himself willingly."

"You said the victim needs to die *afraid*. It may work. I'm sure Lebas is afraid."

"We're all afraid." Augustin spoke up. His chin was set firmly. In that moment, he looked very much like their mother. "I know I am. And we have two pistols. There could be two undead."

"No!" Robespierre snapped. "That death was meant for enemies of France. That's what they're saying we are, out there. They'll kill us on the guillotine if they take us, as enemies of France. But they can't do *that* to us, not without me. And I'll die a thousand times before I'll do it to you myself."

"I don't mind," Lebas said. "I truly don't. You're my friends. And you—you're *Robespierre*."

"And you're Babette's husband. You're the father of her child. Augustin's my brother. I won't do it. I've done so many things for this revolution, and I've done them without hesitation, and I've paid for them over and over and not regretted it. I've taken the ghosts, and the nightmares, and the cold. Not that. It's too much."

Perhaps he should have said it earlier. But he was saying it now.

The fighting in the corridor was getting louder. It was almost time.

A shadow formed in the air, a strong one, cold and clear. Saint-Just's eyes closed as it took shape. It wouldn't be enough to save them; the soldiers would take it almost at once. But it was the last pure use of magic Saint-Just would ever be likely to perform. It was an act of defiance and, in a very Saint-Just way, an act of faith. The revolution that was coming to kill them was still their revolution. Magic was still free. He would celebrate the Republic of Magicians even as he used it against them.

Robespierre wished he could do the same. He longed for one last, perfect act of magic—not the kind he had performed at the guillotine every day for the past year, but the kind he had performed once a long time ago, when a bird had taken flight in a childhood garden. But that magic had been tainted now, and so had the garden. He had mixed it with something evil, over and over, and now the dregs of it swirled inside him like the sediment at the bottom of a beer glass. They couldn't be purged.

Lebas handed him the second pistol. It felt cold and unfamiliar in his hand.

"We're with you, Maximilien," his brother said quietly, and the others nodded, even Saint-Just. They were. But Camille no longer was, nor Danton. They had gone to their deaths on the scaffold, and their corpses were fighting in foreign fields. And his benefactor was with him too. It was sitting there in his head, a bloated spider in a web of its own making. He would never be free.

The door was buckling.

I regret that it has to end this way, Maximilien Robespierre. It was the third time he had ever heard the voice in his waking thoughts. Five thousand miles away, Fina heard it too. *It has been an interesting acquaintance.*

"Get out," he hissed, too quiet for anyone to hear. He had told Camille to do the same, the last night they ever spoke. The memory broke what was left of his heart. He cocked his pistol. "*Get out.*"

The door burst open.

They said afterward that he tried to blow his head off—that he placed the mouth of a pistol under his chin and pulled the trigger. One of the arresting officers was a metalmancer and managed to spin the shot before it penetrated his brain. It smashed through his jaw in a shatter of blood, leaving the Incorruptible alive and gasping as they came to wrench him away. Robespierre's friends, the ones who survived, always maintained that the soldiers were lying. In fact, they spoke as truthfully as they knew how. He did raise a pistol to his chin, and he did fire. They never knew what he had really been trying to blow away, and he could never tell them.

The storm might have lasted hours, or minutes. Gradually Fina became aware of the wind about her quieting, settling; at the same time, she became aware that she had been pushed to her knees by the force of the rain, and her fingers clutched the cliff walls in a death grip. She forced herself to relinquish it. Her hands were bleeding, and she was soaked and shivering. People died in storms like that.

"It's over," Toussaint's voice came, ragged with exhaustion. He had fallen to his knees as well. "You can stand now."

She drew herself to her feet, carefully. The sky was once more harsh, unforgiving blue; her clothes and hair were already beginning to dry. The horizon was clear.

"Did the ships sink?" Her own voice sounded husky to her ears.

"I hope not," he said. "I hope the storm pushed them back to British waters; perhaps some may have shipwrecked near your old island, on Jamaica. I hope the damage done to their ships could be patched enough to let them limp to safety. I had no wish to harm them. But the effects of a storm cannot be so easily controlled. Above all, I wanted them to go away."

Two hundred British ships. An invasion fleet.

"They might come back," she said. "If they're still alive."

"If they do," he said, "we will be waiting for them."

"The stranger told you the British fleet was coming."

"He did. That's what he intended the magic for—he didn't want them to take the island before he was away, and if possible not even after that. But I want it for more than that. If this magic is used correctly in battle, we can hold our ground against anybody. Not just the English or the Spanish. We can make our own terms with the French. And, what is more important, we can bring this island to life again. Everything that was burned and destroyed we can replant and make grow. We can be a nation."

He drew himself upright. His face had a grayish tone, and his legs trembled underneath him. Yet he met her eyes steadily.

"The stranger will betray you," Fina said. "Once he has what he wants from you."

"Yes, he will. Or he'll try. But think what we can do before that. Imagine what this place can be."

Once again, he was asking her to see through his eyes—not with her magic this time, but with her mind. But he was asking for more than understanding this time. He was asking a question. If she told him that it wasn't worth the danger, then he would listen. He might even act on her word. In this, at least, he trusted her completely.

Fina looked back at the sea. It was still now, and empty, but she remembered the moment it had been full of crashing magic, wild and cruel and free.

She was free. She realized it as if for the first time. It meant nothing to her yet: it was too strange and too fragile. It was a quirk of circumstances rather than something innate. She felt, if anything, that she belonged to Toussaint. He was bound himself now, to the French, and to the stranger. But it was a bondage he had accepted willingly, for his people, and if he paid for it, he would do so by his own choice. Perhaps that was part of what freedom meant too.

Saint-Domingue could be free. That, more than her own freedom, meant something; she felt it all around her, in the promise of the storm and the surrounding sea. A nation built by men and women who had once been slaves—even, though she could not be as forgiving as Toussaint, by some of those who had once enslaved them. A new world.

"Yes," she said. "Yes, I can see it."

Seventy-three MPs voted with Wilberforce against the breaking of the Concord, including Charles Fox. Two hundred forty-six voted for.

Fox stopped by Wilberforce on the way out and thumped him on the shoulder—not unsympathetically. "You'll find you must join with us completely, before this is over," he said.

Saint-Just's shadow killed two men with a touch before it was shot through the heart. Saint-Just himself sat watching, quiet and calm. He was the only one who was led away clean from that fight. Augustin and Hanriot escaped through the windows and tumbled to the street. Augustin fell on a saber and a bayonet wielded by two citizens below. Hanriot lay broken in an open sewer, screaming in pain and begging to die. They were collected and manhandled into carts like sheaves of wheat. Couthon tumbled down the stairs and cut his head open. Lebas died by his own hand as the soldiers poured in.

Robespierre, for a few hours, seemed about to do the same. Half his jaw had been blown away by the pistol shot; by the time they had carried him to a small room in the Conciergerie, he had slipped into unconsciousness. He hovered there as the clock ticked on, flat on a table, on the edge between life and death. It would have been the most natural thing in the world for him to slip just a little further, and the Incorruptible would have never faced the mobs outside baying for his blood. Instead, he pulled himself the other way. His eyelashes flickered, then parted. His glasses had been lost somewhere in the scuffle. Without them, his eyes were the palest green, and their gaze was curiously soft.

As dawn broke, a healer came to bind his broken jaw—bandages only, he was told, no healing magic or medicine. He had been lying bleeding on the table for five hours. They marveled that he made no sound or sign of pain, when he must have been in agony.

When the healer had finished, Robespierre sat up. He swung his legs off the table, shying away from the hands that reached to support him, and crossed the five paces to an armchair by the corner window. It was the time of the morning when he usually rose, answered his letters, and made notes, waiting for the barber to shave him and dress his wig. Nobody would come for that today, but the tumbril would be there soon. His sky-blue coat was dark with dried blood and sweat, but he did his best to straighten it, and smooth the silk stockings that had bunched about his ankles. He could manage no more than that. He sat—exhausted, pain racked—to wait.

It was still with him. Perhaps it would be with him until the end. And it was not going to see him afraid.

London

28 July 1794

It was almost dawn when Pitt returned to Downing Street, coming in as quietly as he could to avoid talking to those he knew were lingering downstairs. He had a handful of colleagues somewhere on the premises, but right now he felt he needed quiet more than he needed any of them—and, he hoped, more than they needed him. He'd listened to enough consolation and righteous indignation and barely concealed gloating from his supporters for one evening. A number of them had walked with him right to his carriage outside the House of Commoners and had barely been put off from following him inside.

"I always said he was a wicked, fanatical little imp," one of them maintained, despite the fact that he wouldn't have dared say anything of the kind a scant few hours ago.

"Well, he isn't," Pitt replied. It was all he could muster at that moment. "Good night."

In his office, surrounded by the comfortingly solid wood paneling and the less comfortingly solid mounds of unanswered correspondence, the Downing Street daemon-stone was humming. It might have been doing so for hours, or mere minutes; everyone had been too preoccupied to notice it. It had a sinister note, a note almost of satisfaction. The very last thing Pitt wanted to do at that moment was touch it, but he forced himself to take up a quill in one hand, poise it over the paper, and take up the stone in the other. He shivered as the cold crept down the back of his neck and the shadows swirled in his head, and then wrote its message down.

He read it back without a flicker of surprise. There was a headache building steadily behind his eyes, and he rubbed his temples briefly to ward it off. At least the votes had gone their way, he tried to tell himself, and dismissed the thought as useless. Of course they had. They had expected them to. It was scarcely the point.

There was a knock at the door.

"Come in," he called automatically, and suddenly William Wilberforce was there.

It was far from an unusual circumstance: over the last few years, Wilberforce had remained almost a daily visitor to Downing Street, and they'd spent hours talking over war and slavery and thoughts until deep into the night. This was the first time, however, that Pitt had wished he hadn't come.

"I told them not to announce me," Wilberforce said awkwardly. His eyes met Pitt's with an unspoken question. Pitt refused to answer it. "I thought perhaps you'd turn me away."

"Of course I wouldn't," Pitt said, but without warmth. He had drawn himself up without meaning to, and his face had settled into reserve. "I never turn anyone away with business to discuss."

"And if I said I'd come only as a friend?"

Pitt stifled a sigh. "It's been a very long night, Wilberforce. If you've come to tell me anything, I'd be grateful if you would come to the point. And if part of that point would involve warning me to what extent you intend to lead the opposition against me in future."

"I have no intention of leading, or indeed joining, any kind of organized opposition against you," Wilberforce said firmly. "I truly do not."

"Excuse me, but one could be forgiven for thinking so. You do realize you just stood up in the House of Commoners and told them all that the government of this country was leading it into black magic and misery?"

"I told them that we can't break the Concord. We simply can't."

"We can. We have no alternative, if we're to carry on this war."

"The war needs to end. Now, tomorrow, as soon as possible. We can't keep on like this."

"So you said. Dundas is certain you mean to set up your own party and turn on us."

"Dundas!" Wilberforce snorted. "He turned on *us* when we needed him five years ago. And he wants this war extended as long as possible expressly for the purpose of colonial expansion—everybody knows it, except perhaps you."

"For God's sake, Wilberforce, I wish you'd give up the idea that I'm utterly naive to people's ulterior motives. I know that Dundas wants to use the war to expand the British Empire. So do most people, if they're honest. That's what wars have always been for. I don't think there's any chance it will happen that way, not anymore. Either way, I can promise you it wasn't why we entered this war, and it certainly isn't the reason we need to keep fighting."

"Do you believe Dundas? About me?"

"No. I told him he didn't understand you at all, and then I told him he was being ridiculous. I told all of your detractors they were being ridiculous, in some shape or form."

"Thank you. Do *you* understand why I did it?"

"Because you believed it was right, of course. That's why you do anything."

Wilberforce was clearly still uneasy; he knew Pitt's moods too well. "I always told you that I was an independent," he said. "And that my beliefs might one day cause me to differ from you publicly. I hoped that day would never come; until recently I would have sworn it couldn't."

"So would I," Pitt said.

"You said that even if it did, it would never shake the sentiments of friendship you felt toward me."

"I did. I just never expected you to capitalize on those sentiments at a time of war."

"Does this really still need to be a time of war? We entered into this conflict with the aim of restoring the French monarchy; I don't think any effort on our part will bring that about now. Breaking the Concord will just plunge us deeper and deeper into a war of magic. Lives are being lost. All of Europe is under siege. Can we really not accept the authority of the French Republic of Magicians and come to some reasonable terms of peace?"

"No," Pitt said flatly. "We can't. You know what's happening over there."

"It's different now. The tide has turned against Robespierre; for all we know, he's been supplanted already."

"He has," Pitt said. "Tonight; this very hour. I just heard it over the daemon-stone. I was about to send word to the king and the cabinet when you came in."

Wilberforce caught his breath. "Then surely... that makes breaking the Concord unnecessary now, if it wasn't before. Robespierre's death will almost certainly mean an end to the Terror. Surely that means that the enemy's hold has weakened."

"Do you know why Robespierre has been supplanted, Wilberforce? Because the enemy saw through our attempts to use him. Because he'd become more of a liability than a strength, and he had no further use for him. Because we are about to move on to a greater and more terrible stage of the war."

"How could you possibly know that?"

"Because it told me." He hadn't meant to break the news quite so bluntly, in a burst of frustration, but perhaps it was for the best. "It came to me a few nights ago, as it came to Clarkson. It knew our plans; somehow, and I still haven't received word of how, it destroyed every last one of our ships without very much effort at all. It warned me that this was only going to get worse."

Wilberforce was, for once, silent. "And you believed it?" he said at last.

"It wasn't lying. I doubt you can lie in a nightwalk, any more than you can through a daemon-stone. I would have told you this, by the way, if you'd come to see me before standing up and opposing me in the middle of the House of Commoners."

"I'm sorry I didn't. I barely arrived back in time for the emergency session as it was, and then it happened so suddenly—and, I confess, I was afraid you'd talk me into backing down again. It was cowardly of me. But what the enemy told you—I wish I'd been able to talk it over with you first, but it wouldn't have changed my mind. If the enemy intends to lead us into more terrible conflict yet, that is all the more reason to make peace before it can."

"France is in chaos. There are no terms of peace we can make with them that will ensure the security of this country. But you heard that argument in the House, and clearly you were unconvinced then. I see no benefit to repeating a disagreement in private that we've already had in public."

Wilberforce sighed. He looked exhausted, and the shadows under his eyes spoke of the long, sleepless nights to which he was prone. "I was afraid you would be like this. It was stupid of me to call on you so soon; I'm trying to force your forgiveness before you're ready to give it, if indeed you'll ever be ready for that. I would understand if you find my opposition unforgivable. But I had to do what was right."

"Of course," Pitt said, and heard the coldness in his own voice. It wasn't the tone he usually heard when he was talking to his closest friends. But the insinuation, which he knew Wilberforce hadn't intended, stung. "I myself don't usually feel I have to do what is wrong."

"I didn't mean that!" Wilberforce protested, with perhaps as much exasperation as alarm. "I mean that in this case I honestly feel you to be, with all the best intentions, making a mistake. Perhaps the enemy can't lie outright, but it can certainly deceive in other ways, and it can certainly manipulate. I think it scared you, and I think it meant to do it. And as a result, you've reacted to France's aggression in kind, without considering the alternatives."

"And when have they offered us any alternatives?" Pitt demanded, drawn in despite himself. Wilberforce was the only person in England who had heard about his meeting with the enemy—the only person who knew about the enemy at all. He had told Wilberforce because he had trusted him, as he had told him other things. He hadn't told him any of those things so that they could be used against him.

"They never will if you give them no indication that you would be amenable to them!" Wilberforce answered. "All they hear is what the House is saying in public, and that is nothing but clamor for war. I don't think you hear yourselves sometimes. It's sickening. It needs to stop. Have you seen the wounded and the dead coming out of the ships at Portsmouth?"

"No, I haven't. But I'm very aware of them. And of course it makes me sick. I want to end this war as much as you do—but not now, and not like this. You know what we're fighting."

"*I* know. I'm not quite sure you do."

"For God's sake. What is *that* supposed to mean?"

"You told me you wanted to stop France without breaking the Concord."

"I did want that, more than anything. That was what everything we've done this year has been designed to bring about. And we failed. Do you understand that? We *failed*." It was the first time he'd said it, even to himself. The word tasted bitter on his tongue. "Camille Desmoulins died without being able to help us. We don't hold Saint-Domingue; if we ever do take it, the enemy will be long gone from there. It abandoned Robespierre before we could use him to track it."

"It lost a necromancer in the process."

"Not before building a substantial army of the dead. I'm still waiting to hear how large it may be, based on the number of executions in Paris. If that army is more than a few thousand, then even breaking the Concord might not be enough to stop them. And in the meantime, with Robespierre gone, we've lost all sight of our enemy. It could be anywhere, and behind anyone."

"It wants you to break the Concord. You know it does. It wants a war of dark magic and mesmerism and blood. It thinks it can win."

"Yes. I can only hope that it's underestimating us."

"I think that *you're* underestimating the French Republic of Magicians. You don't understand what's happening in France; I'm not sure any of us can. But Clarkson told us something about being over there when it started, and I've talked to the French nobles arriving to town in droves. And they all say the same thing: England can't turn back the tide of revolution in France. When people have a cause like that, they don't stop."

"And that is precisely why we can't yet come to any terms with them. They have no intention of coming to terms with us, and at this stage, there would be real danger in accepting any terms they did put forward."

"There's danger in continuing a war!"

"Of course there is. There's danger on both sides. But on the one side there's danger accompanied with honor, and on the other side danger accompanied by indelible shame and disgrace; I know which one I would prefer for us."

"This isn't a question of honor. People are killing each other."

"Which is exactly when questions of honor are the most important!" He caught himself before his anger flared, and forced himself to hold still until it cooled. It was rare for him to lose his temper; he didn't think anybody had seen him do so since he had taken power eleven years ago. But it was times like this when he found himself, unjustly, resenting Wilberforce's absolute faith in his own moral judgment. He knew Wilberforce frequently struggled over the right thing to do; Wilberforce had burst into Downing Street to talk his doubts through with him often enough, usually at unsociable hours of the morning when Pitt was still asleep. But when it came time to act, he always seemed so deeply, profoundly *certain*. Pitt never had time to be certain anymore. He was too busy trying to be decisive.

"I never wanted this country to be at war while in my care," he said, more calmly. "I never wanted to spend half my time trying to suppress rebellion in England and the other half trying to hold back the tides of revolution in Europe. I wanted to change things for the better, not devote myself to keeping them the same or taking them backward. I certainly never wanted to see the Concord broken in my lifetime. But this is where we are. We're at war. This is where we stand right now, and the tide is coming in. I need to protect this country, both in terms of its physical safety and in terms of its integrity. France has challenged us, and we've responded. There is no way that we can withdraw from that conflict at the moment without compromising the principles that drove us to war in the first place, and there would be no guarantee of security in doing so. All we would do is open ourselves to further hostilities from the Republic of Magicians—and from worse."

Wilberforce shook his head. "I can't accept that. There has to be a different way."

"The House of Commoners disagreed with you. Now a great many of them are very angry with you, and a number of the wrong ones are very happy."

"I'm sorry," Wilberforce said with a wince. "But I can't let my behavior on serious matters like this be governed by the opinions of anyone. Not even you."

"I'm very aware of that," Pitt said. It was layered with more sarcasm than he intended to show, but probably not than he meant. "And if you came here to explain that to me, you've done so. Is that all?"

Wilberforce still looked unhappy, but he steeled himself.

"I felt you looking at me when I stood up to give my speech," he said hesitantly. "It was very hard for me to speak against you, but I did it. And then you kept looking at me. And it suddenly became nearly impossible."

"It could only have been for a few seconds." Inwardly, his heart sank; Wilberforce had kept going so strongly, he had hoped that his mistake had gone unnoticed. "It was a momentary lapse, and I corrected it. Despite the political cost."

"You were mesmerizing me, weren't you?" It was phrased as a question, but it wasn't one.

"I was willing you," he corrected. "And my will broke through into something else. I apologize for it. It wasn't intended."

"But it happened. Just as it happened with Clarkson, in the Tower of London."

"I know. I didn't intend that either."

"I'm not for a moment suggesting you did. That doesn't reassure me."

"There are many younger sons of Aristocrats in the House of Commoners. Abilities *do* break out during debates sometimes."

"Not yours," Wilberforce said flatly. "You told me that yourself. You keep them under perfect control. What's happening to you?"

"To me? Wilberforce, France has risen against the Aristocracy, freed their unregistered magicians, and killed their royal family. Now they're threatening our country and all of Europe. Control is not something that is coming easily to anybody." He shook his head irritably. "If it reassures you, I've doubled the alchemy again as of yesterday. It should start to work very soon."

Wilberforce frowned. "Is that safe?"

"You've existed on laudanum since you were stabbed."

"Yes, I have," Wilberforce said frankly. "And I'd be very wary of doubling the dose. Particularly over and over again."

Pitt nodded, trying to concede the point. He wasn't feeling very fair. "In answer to your question, then, I should imagine so. Safer than letting its effects wear off."

"If I understand it correctly, that effect is simply to keep you alive. It doesn't negate anything you might feel or desire."

"Are you asking me if I feel any desire to kill people?"

"Aren't you fighting a war?"

Pitt looked at him. It was a long moment before he trusted himself to speak. "Get out," he said flatly.

Wilberforce blinked. "I'm sorry?"

"Get out of my house. Immediately." The shock, hurt, and betrayal that had been simmering inside since Wilberforce had got to his feet in the House of Commoners had suddenly flamed to the surface. He felt his eyes light with what he knew was mesmeric fire, and just for once he didn't care.

Wilberforce flinched and took a single faltering step backward against his will. Then he set his jaw and raised his head with the obstinacy that was so familiar to those on the other side of the slave debate.

"Of course I'll leave if you want me to," he said, a little thickly through the effort of resistance. "You don't have to force me. Please do consider something, though. We know that there is a vampire in France. I know you think it must be fought with everything we have. Please do consider that this, too, might be exactly what it wants."

Pitt didn't reply. The throbbing in his temples had been replaced with the singing of blood in his ears, and he knew in that moment that if he chose to, he could snap the tiny figure in front of him like a twig underfoot.

Wilberforce inclined his head stiffly, turned, and left the room.

As the door closed behind him, Pitt drew a deep breath and released it slowly, willing himself back into calm with all the force he had just directed at his friend. It was difficult; magic was rampaging through his blood, and he was too tired and too troubled to rein it in as he usually did. He breathed in again, and out, and realized his hands were clenched into fists. He relaxed them.

He was already starting to feel ashamed of his own behavior, but the hurt was too recent for it not to be foremost in his mind. He had been accused of almost everything under the sun in the time he had been prime minister, from warmongering to drunkenness to dishonesty. It was the fate of senior politicians, even generally popular ones. But Wilberforce had always known what he was, and had believed in him. That had just changed. What had already been an unexpected public criticism of his methods had deepened, seamlessly and terribly, into a private question of his motives. And at the moment, he could only think, *How dare he?*

The window was speckled with falling raindrops as Pitt walked over to it and looked out. Out on the street below, he could see Wilberforce climbing into his carriage. He would probably be going back to Clapham, despite the lateness of the hour: he would want the comforts of his home and friends at a time like this. Pitt would have been very grateful to disappear into the country himself, but he had half his cabinet waiting for him downstairs. He had news to impart to them, and to the king. And then everything would begin. On his desk, the smooth black stone sat silent and ready.

Daemon-stones would serve you but never forgive you. Pitt didn't really believe that—it was too close to superstition. Even Wilberforce believed it more as a parable about evil than a practical reality. But it came to him, unwillingly, that their plans had twice been dependent on the shadow in that stone: first to alert Desmoulins, and then to warn Robespierre. Now both Desmoulins and Robespierre were dead.

Without warning, pain lanced through his stomach, accompanied by a wave of nausea that made him gasp involuntarily. He leaned heavily against the window ledge, trying not to breathe. His heart shuddered in his chest.

Hold still, he ordered himself. *It's just a reaction to the mesmerism. It will get better in a moment.*

It did get better, but slowly, over several agonizing moments. Around him, upstairs and downstairs and in the streets, bloodlines flashed into sharp relief: bright shards of divination, warm strands of empathy, cool gleams of water magic. The daemon-stone on his desk was a burning cloud of ice. He remembered being fourteen, newly arrived in Cambridge, far too excited and nervous to care about the occasional flash of pain or nausea or the flicker of other people's bloodlines at the edge of his awareness. This was how it started. This was what it felt like when blood magic awakened.

What's happening to you? he heard again.

It was nothing, he told himself firmly. It couldn't be. He wouldn't let it be.

He heard a knock on the door and collected himself hurriedly before it opened and Eliot came in. His friend's sensitive face was furrowed in concern, laced with just a trace of awkwardness. Eliot hated people to be at odds, and certainly was not used to seeing his two greatest friends so.

"Are you all right?" he asked. "I met Wilberforce on the stairs; he was worried about you."

"What did he say?"

Eliot looked faintly surprised, indicating that perhaps that question hadn't come out quite as neutrally as he had intended. "Nothing unusual. He said that you were very much hurt, and it was his fault."

Of course he had. The characteristic simplicity and concern made Pitt want to laugh and cry at the same time, but he summoned a faint smile instead. It was neither sincere nor convincing.

"It's not his fault," he said. "Except in that public difference with someone whose support I value is always going to be hurtful."

"He was very distressed himself," Eliot said tentatively. "More than I've ever seen him."

"Did he warn you he was going to speak tonight?"

"No—not in so many words. He said he was going to have to follow his conscience on this vote, whatever the cost. He didn't ask me to support him. He knew that would be impossible—given my position on your cabinet."

He caught the addendum. "And what would you have done if you *weren't* on my cabinet? Do you agree the war should end?"

"I truly don't know what I think," Eliot sighed. He looked more troubled than Pitt had seen him since the early days after Harriot's death. "I value both your judgments too much to choose between you. I do know that Wilber would never have opposed you had he not thought it absolutely necessary."

"I wasn't doubting his feelings or his motivations. Others are, though. And it does make my job a good deal more difficult." He shook his head, trying to find his usual wellspring of optimism somewhere inside. This was not the time for self-doubt. The country was at war, and it needed him to be better than that, or at least to seem to be. But Wilberforce's words were still echoing in his ears, and he did not seem to be able to hear anything else.

"I'm afraid Grenville's asking for you downstairs," Eliot said.

"News has just come from France. I could tell them to send it up to you."

"No, don't do that. I have news to convey as well, probably more recent. Could you tell him and anyone else down there to meet me in the cabinet room?"

"If you're sure." Eliot frowned doubtfully. "You look rather white, actually. Have you eaten at all today?"

"Yes," he said, which he thought was true. He couldn't quite remember. His body now had settled to a quiet throb; his magic had settled to the same degree. "It's been a long night, that's all."

Eliot nodded. "Poor France." He said it lightly, but there was a definite thread of wistfulness in his voice. "It seems a long time since we were there, doesn't it?"

It did. Pitt thought of the French court, with all its glamor and opulence, and then, suddenly, of the tiny hotel room in Rheims where the three of them had drunk cheap wine as the stars had come out, and not cared that they had nowhere else to go and nothing else to do.

"I imagine it will look very different there now," he said.

And he knew, with pain that had nothing to do with magic, that he and Wilberforce would not be returning to the way they had been then. They were in a different world now. It had changed around them, almost without their noticing, and now they were standing in the middle of it, and somehow they were no longer standing quite together.

Paris/London/Saint-Domingue

10 Thermidor, Year II of the French Republic of Magicians / 28 July 1794

They carried Robespierre down to the tumbril in the morning, in the chair in which he still sat. He had wanted to walk, but his strength had failed him. The bright light outside after the long, dark night staring up at the ceiling was too much for his eyes. He opened them sparingly, with effort, taking in as much of his surroundings as he could before he had to let his eyelids drop.

Every inch of the road was crammed with people. Mile after mile, an endless stream of them, all crowding to see him and clamoring for his death. He couldn't believe Paris still held so many people, after all who had died. The press of them was overwhelming. They called to him and spat in his face.

"Monster!" he heard a woman say distinctly. He didn't know why that should stand out, in the midst of so much else.

Once the cart stopped. He forced his eyes open, expecting to see the guillotine. The ride had felt long enough. But they were at his lodgings, where he had lived with the Duplays. The windows were boarded and the door shut tight. The cart stopped long enough to dash the contents of a bucket against the wall, and Robespierre watched without feeling as the pale stone walls turned the color of blood. Then the cart jolted on its way.

He was aware of the city and the jeering crowds. It was thin and translucent over his vision, like one of Éléonore's watercolors.

He was also in the garden. It didn't surprise him to see that it was on fire.

"Why?" he asked. "Why are you doing this to me? What did I do wrong?"

He didn't know whom he was asking, the mob or the vampire. But only the vampire could answer, for Robespierre's jaw was shattered, and he could speak only in his head.

"Nothing," the vampire said. He said it almost kindly. "You did nothing wrong—well, nothing that couldn't be easily amended. Everything happened exactly as it was meant to happen."

"You mean I was always going to die."

"You were always going to die. This is perhaps sooner rather than later. Your power is too distinctive—people across the oceans are already using it to lead them to me. And I have my army of the dead. That was always your purpose."

Those on the cart with Robespierre saw him close his eyes. They didn't see that, in the world in his head, the trees were turning black and the sky was red as blood.

"I thought— You said you were making a place for a leader of France."

"I am. But that leader was never you. There's no need to be jealous of him, though. He, too, has his purpose to serve, but not forever. Sooner or later, you all fall, and you all die."

"But the Republic will survive, won't it? If not for me, for others? My death will help the Republic live."

"This is the end of the French Republic of Magicians," the vampire said. "That mob out there don't know it yet, but they have already signed its death warrant. I will have my leader at the head of an army of the dead, but he won't lead a republic. He will lead an empire."

When Robespierre next opened his eyes, the Tuileries Gardens swam into view. The guillotine stood at the Place de la Révolution, just for the occasion. The trees were green in the summer wind. The voice in his head had gone.

* * *

He had believed he was right. Truly, deeply, and completely. That was his only defense. Perhaps it was enough. Perhaps too many had died for that to make the slightest bit of difference.

Downing Street cabinet room

"Two thousand guillotined in Paris," Grenville said. He held the dispatch open in his hand. "That's the final count. And every last one of those a soldier of the dead now."

Pitt nodded and kept his face perfectly still. "Well. That's worse than we hoped, but not than we feared. If we can keep those forces spread thinly across Europe, we can manage."

"That was in Paris," Grenville said. "It seems that—it wasn't public knowledge, which is why we didn't have this information sooner. But those being executed elsewhere in France were being shipped into Paris after their deaths. They were brought to the Conciergerie after dark. It looks as though Robespierre and Saint-Just would, at least in the last year, visit them at night and..."

"Animate them," Pitt supplied when Grenville's voice failed.

"Yes. Animate."

"I see. How many?"

"I assume it was done in secret precisely so we wouldn't know—and so that we wouldn't move sooner to stop it. Not even the National Convention knew. We still can't know for certain how many executed were made undead. Surely not all of them."

"But how many were executed?"

"Since the start of the Reign of Terror—a little over sixteen thousand."

For the first time since Pitt had become prime minister, his cabinet saw him completely speechless. "Dear God," he said at last.

Approaching the guillotine now. Death was very close.

They wrenched him to his feet before the tumbril had even stopped. He stumbled, but somehow, miraculously, managed to stay upright. He could walk himself to the guillotine, at least. He had walked those steps before, a thousand times, to stand by the blade and animate the broken bodies of its victims. He knew the look of the grained wood, scrubbed every day but still stained with dark shadows of blood. Camille had walked this path, and Danton. Saint-Just would walk it after him, and his brother. It was only a short walk, the last any of them would ever take.

A few steps up, and he was standing above the crowd. The sky was blue above him. The sun glinted on the statue of Liberty that Madame Roland had addressed before she died. He saw his France, the French Republic of Magicians. He held it in his head, shining and pure, free and equal and united. It was not difficult to do so. His vision was dim. The shadows were thick about him, and whispering. Through the darkness and the roaring in his ears, the crowds and the buildings and the sky were no different from the ones in his dreams, and the noise could be the voice of the people cheering him to speak.

Liberté. Égalité. Fraternité. Surely they would still have cheered at that.

Saint-Domingue

Fina sat, feet tucked under her, on the wall of the fort. Above her, the sky was still and cloudless; below her, Toussaint's army was yawning and stretching awake, or coming off night patrol, or sitting eating and talking on the stone bones of the enemy fort. The day was barely breaking. She knew it was there, but she saw none of it. She was behind the weakening eyes of the little Frenchman, whose name she still didn't know.

She saw the crowd of white faces, blurred and ugly. She saw their lips move in shouts she couldn't hear. She saw the strange contraption stretching into the air, and though she had never seen anything like it before, she knew an instrument of death when she saw one. The little man was pushed toward it. His lungs expanded and contracted with their last taste of sunbaked air.

They forced him roughly to his knees and forced his head onto the block. His broken jaw crunched against the wood. Still he endured in silence. He drew his vision tighter about him, and it was there with him as the executioner lowered the stocks and positioned his neck. It was there right until the executioner studied the bandages that bound his jaw together and without ceremony ripped them off.

He had thought he was in the worst pain he could be in; he had borne it, silently, throughout the dark night and the long morning. Now new agony shot through him like a second bullet—excruciating, piercing, all-consuming. With it came sudden, sickening clarity. The crowds burst into relief. Their voices crowded into his ears. The breeze was sharp and cruel.

The French Republic of Magicians shattered. There was no revolution anymore. He was not its embodiment. He was just a frail, broken body, with nothing in his head, not even his enemy.

He screamed.

The blade came down and silenced him.

"I'm sorry," Fina said. "I know you tried to help. But this is our war now."

The story continues in...

A RADICAL ACT OF FREE MAGIC

Book TWO of The Shadow Histories

Keep reading for a sneak peek!

Acknowledgments

Stories are big, wild, ridiculous, impossible things. It takes a lot of people to tame them into anything resembling a book. I still can't quite believe this one made it, and I have many people to thank for it.

To my agent, Hannah Bowman: thank you so very much for rescuing the early version of this book from your queries, for pushing me to take it apart and make it better, for not giving up on it when I did, and for seeing it through to what it finally became. I hope we get to tell many more stories together.

To my editor, Sarah Guan: thank you for believing in this book, for seeing what it could be, for asking perceptive questions, and for making the story so much deeper and richer. It's an honor to be one of your authors.

Thank you so much to everyone at Orbit/Redhook for everything you've done to bring this book into the world: to Alex Lencicki, Ellen Wright, Laura Fitzgerald, Paola Crespo, and Stephanie Hess for your tireless work in publicizing and marketing; to Lauren Panepinto and Lisa Marie Pompilio for the beautiful cover; to Bryn A. McDonald, managing editor; to Tim Holman, publisher; and to Emily Byron, my UK editor. I'm so lucky to work with you all.

This book is a mythologization of the real history of Britain, France, and Haiti in the eighteenth century, which is more interesting and dramatic and downright weird than anything I could make up. Thank you to the many, many brilliant historians whose work helped illuminate that time period for me. Everything I know comes from their research. Any errors, simplifications, inaccuracies, vampires, and acts of stray magic are my own.

As always, thank you, Mum and Dad, for your continual belief and support, and to my sister Sarah, not only for your patience and insight, but for letting me drag you across Hull in the rain to see Wilberforce's birthplace, for hours of rambling conversations about the eighteenth century, and for telling me to write this in the first place. This book wouldn't exist without the three of you.

Thank you to my beloved rabbits, O'Connell and Fleischman, and to the guinea pigs, Jonathan Strange, Mr. Norrell, and Thistledown. None of you were any help with this book at all. Thank you also to our cat-lodger, Angel, who at least sits beside me and purrs encouragingly sometimes.

Finally, if you've read this book, if you've read my last book, if you think you might like to read my next book: thank you. That means more to me than I'll ever be able to say.

Meet the Author

Photo Credit: Fairlie Atkinson

H. G. Parry lives in a book-infested flat on the Kāpiti Coast of New Zealand, which she shares with her sister, a cat, three guinea pigs, and two overactive rabbits. She holds a PhD in English Literature from Victoria University of Wellington, and has taught English, film, and media studies.

if you enjoyed

A DECLARATION OF THE RIGHTS OF MAGICIANS

look out for

A RADICAL ACT OF FREE MAGIC

The Shadow Histories: Book Two

by

H. G. Parry

The Concord has been broken, and a war of magic engulfs the world.

In France, the brilliant young battle-mage Napoleon Bonaparte has summoned a kraken from the depths, and under his command the Army of the Dead have all but conquered Europe. Britain fights back, protected by the gulf of the channel and powerful fire magic, but Wilberforce's own battle to bring about free magic and abolition has met a dead end in the face of an increasingly fearful and repressive government. In Saint-Domingue, Fina watches as Toussaint Louverture navigates these opposing forces to liberate the country.

But there is another, even darker war being fought beneath the surface: the first vampire war in hundreds of years. The enemy blood magician who orchestrated Robespierre's downfall is using the Revolutionary Wars to bring about a return to dark magic to claim all of Europe. Across the world, only a few know of his existence. And the choices they make will shape the new age of magic.

Somerset

1773

William Pitt the Younger was fourteen years and seven months old, and he was dying. He had been sent home from his first year at Cambridge in order to do so. He was doing his best to die well.

It had been two months since he had woken shivering with fever and racked with nausea. He had barely retained any food or water since, and he knew he was desperately weak. He could see the thinness of his own wrists, and feel how hard it was to sit up, to talk, to hold a book or, increasingly, to breathe. During the day, he mostly kept as still as he could and pretended he didn't even have a body; during the night, he felt stronger, but so did the throb of bloodlines in his mind, until it became difficult to think over them. He wished he could say he barely cared anymore, but he cared bitterly.

He didn't want to die. Even now, feeling worse than he had ever felt before, he didn't for a moment want to die. He had only just begun. It was a crisp, bright winter's morning outside, and there were books on his desk. He wanted to live. It wasn't *fair.*

The voices outside his room drifted in and out of his hearing as he dozed, so that when Dr. Addington entered quietly, he seemed to do so all at once.

"We need to talk, William," he said.

William's mind made the adjustment from rest to engagement immediately, but it took a beat and a surge of effort to communicate it to his limbs.

"Of course." He straightened on his pillows and blinked hard to clear his haziness. His head swam. "I— Do my parents know you're here?"

"They allowed it." The wording was strange, as was the tone. It sounded as though they had been *persuaded* to allow it. And yet what was there about their family doctor's visit to allow? Unless, of course...

Dr. Addington sat down at the bedside, and looked William in the eye. "You know what's happened to you, don't you?" he said, without further preamble.

William nodded, and tried to look as though his heart wasn't pounding rapidly. "Yes. I've come into an Inheritance late. An illegal Inheritance."

"Blood magic. Vampirism. I know that you won't like to say it aloud, but I'm afraid that if we're going to talk about this, I must insist that we give it its correct term."

Technically, only the first term was correct. "Blood magic" was the official classification; "vampirism" was an insult. William didn't dispute the point. It would look too much like weakness. Instead, he nodded again, and this time tried not to look as though he had been flayed alive and something private and grotesque inside him wrenched into the light. "Of course."

Perhaps Dr. Addington had expected a protest after all. He looked at him hard before he continued. "The abilities have settled now; that's not the problem. The problem is that your body, in its altered state, can no longer sustain itself. It requires magic of a very particular kind. With it, you can live forever. Without it, very soon, you will starve to death."

It was nothing he didn't already know. He told himself this, firmly and fiercely, and so he was able to raise his head and look Dr. Addington in the eye. "Yes."

"The question is," Dr. Addington said, "do you want to live?"

"Of course I want to live," William said. "But—"

"On what terms?"

The question made him pause. "Any that are reasonable and honorable."

"And which do not include murder?"

"Surely you don't need to ask me that." He felt a chill. Dr. Addington's voice was no longer kind, and he had never known it not to be kind.

"And legal?"

"They couldn't be, could they?" William said evenly. "I'm not legal."

"No," Dr. Addington said. "You're not, legally, human. You're a blood magician. A vampire."

"Please don't," William said, before he could stop himself.

"You agreed to use the word."

"Yes, I know, but . . . please don't use it like that." He didn't quite know how to explain that, however much "vampirism" hurt, "vampire"—an identity, a noun that described him and not the magic inside him—hurt more deeply yet. He would have been stronger about it usually, he hoped, but in that moment, everything hurt, and so words hurt too.

"It's what you are," Dr. Addington said. There was certainly no kindness in his voice now. "You're illegal, William, because your survival now depends upon the death of others. The mesmerism in your blood has awakened now, hasn't it?"

"I haven't touched it."

"But it's there."

He didn't answer, but he didn't have to. Of course it was. It burned in his veins, silent and secret, screaming to be used.

"And you know why, don't you? It isn't like other mesmerism. You know what blood magic requires."

"Yes," he said.

"It's awakened to kill me," Dr. Addington said. "Your mesmerism will hold me in place, so that I can only obey your voice telling me to hold still. Your mesmerism will hold me still while you cut my throat, or I cut it for you. And when the blood spills and the light dies from my eyes, your mesmerism is what takes my magic and my life and feeds it to you. That's what blood magic is. It's holding another's will in your own while they die at your hand."

"I know," he said, or tried to. His head throbbed.

"And do you know because you've read it in a book, or because you feel it?"

"Both. Please—you don't need to tell me this. I know."

Dr. Addington continued, relentless. "Then you know that it doesn't stop there, with one death."

"Stop it," William said. "Please."

"Vampiric mesmerism can hold entire countries in its grip, and it does. They can't stop, or at least they never do. Because it isn't only lifeblood they crave; that's only what they need to survive. They crave power. They always have."

"I said, *stop it*." The words burst out of him, and at once, for the first time in his life, a flare of pure mesmerism burst from the place he'd been keeping it hidden and flamed in his eyes. Dr. Addington faltered, and his mouth closed. William saw it, and he didn't stop. Blood was singing in his ears and heat was scorching his veins, and after two months of weariness and agony, he felt strong and clear and powerful. It was intoxicating.

This is it, the magic told him. *This is the way you do not die.*

And then, with a surge of effort, he forced it back. It was like swallowing back a flame; he choked and closed his eyes tightly as the heat drained from his limbs. All at once, he was cold and aching, and shivering with the horror of what he had done.

"I'm sorry," he heard himself saying, and his voice seemed to have become a child's again. He was so tired. "Please forgive me, I didn't mean to—"

"No, *I'm* sorry," Dr. Addington said unexpectedly, and William looked up in surprise. The doctor's voice was once more the gentle voice he remembered. "I knew I was hurting you. I was trying to do so. I had to know that you understood what your Inheritance meant."

He was determined not to cry now, after so many long weeks, but his eyes were stinging, and when he blinked, he felt a hot tear escape his eyelashes.

"I'm not stupid," William said. He had never had to tell anybody that before.

"You certainly are not. But you've been so calm about it, every time I've seen you—I was concerned—"

"That I wasn't human?"

Dr. Addington laughed shortly, which told William that the thought had crossed his mind. "Perhaps that you weren't allowing yourself to truly think about what was happening. Or to feel."

"I have," he said, as firmly as he could. "Both thought and felt. I know what I have to do."

"I know," the doctor said. "Perhaps your mother was right. She told me I was punishing you for being fourteen years old and trying to be brave."

That, of course, was more likely to make him cry than anything, but instead he drew a very deep breath and didn't let it out again until he could trust his voice to be steady.

"Are you going to kill me?"

"I'm not a Templar. I'm a doctor."

"Doctors have killed sons and daughters with illegal Inheritances in the past, to keep the family bloodlines clean on paper. It isn't legal, but it's perfectly acceptable. The Knights Templar make sure they're never prosecuted."

"I didn't realize you knew that. If I had—" He shook his head. "When that happens—and I concede that it does—it happens at the request of the parents, while the child is an infant. Do you really think your parents would allow me to harm you?"

I am not an infant, was what he knew he should have said. *And we wouldn't have to tell them*. But he couldn't say it. He hoped he could do it, if it came to it, but he couldn't say it.

"No," he said instead. "But...do you intend to tell the Temple Church what I am?"

"What would you say if I did?"

"I doubt they'll give me the opportunity to say very much at all," he said, on reflex, and Dr. Addington's mouth quirked. "It's your duty as a medical practitioner to report me. I wouldn't blame you."

Dr. Addington regarded him for a very long time. "Your father is an Aristocrat now," he said at last. "So are you. It's not illegal for you to possess a magical Inheritance. Your particular kind, of course, would always be illegal, and I would certainly have to report it if it ran true. But you see, I don't believe it does, not quite. Your abilities didn't manifest until the onset of adulthood, which isn't usually the case with blood magic. You lived for fourteen years with no more magic than a pure Commoner. I believe there are a few things we can try, before we need to call the Knights Templar to take you away."

His breath caught in his throat. Hope had been smothered by resolve such a long time ago and so repeatedly since, it hurt to have it burst out again.

"I said 'try,'" Dr. Addington warned quickly. "I speak of a piece of alchemy that exists only in old textbooks, one designed to take the place of lifeblood. I warn you, though, that before I hit upon the right formula you're likely to become a good deal more ill than you are now. It may kill you outright; it may never work at all. And if it doesn't—"

"But if it does work, I'll be no different to anybody else?"

"Ideally, yes," Dr. Addington said. "But, William, your abilities will still be there. If you live, then as long as that life lasts you will need to be very, very careful that the darkness inside you never gets out. And if the alchemy should cease to work, for whatever reason..."

"I understand," William said quickly. His heart was racing again, this time joyfully; his body was too weak to sustain it, and it was making him light-headed. "Please—"

"It's all right," Dr. Addington said soothingly. He was rummaging in his bag, a small glass already held between two fingers. "I'm going to try my utmost." For the first time he smiled. "Good God, William, I've been looking after you since the day you were born. Did you really think that I could stop now?"

"Did *you*?" William replied, with a very small smile.

"Sharp as ever," Dr. Addington said, which wasn't really an answer. "Here, drink. I've overexcited you, and if I don't put it right your heart is going to give out before you get anywhere near the elixir."

William swallowed what was in the tiny glass obediently, making an involuntary face at the bitterness, and then accepted the much larger glass of wine that Dr. Addington held out for him in turn.

"There. Rest now. You have a very unpleasant fight ahead of you. I meant what I said earlier. If I can get the elixir to work, it won't make you pure ungifted Commoner—or Aristocrat, I should say, now your father's titled. You will have to make yourself that. For the rest of your life, you'll battle not to do again what you just did to me—when someone threatens you, or hurts you, or when something important is at stake. You'll be hiding a part of yourself until the day you die, and on that day, you'll decide to die rather than betray the promise that you're about to make. Do you promise to do that?"

"I promise," William said clearly.

Dr. Addington nodded. "Anybody would make that promise," he said. "But I'm going to trust you to keep it."

Brienne-le-Château

1783

It was after midnight in the boys' dormitory, and Napoleone di Buonaparte was supposed to be sleeping.

The room was frostbitten and sparse, little more than a monastic cell, and the single thin blanket on each bed seemed designed only to taunt the boys with the promise of warmth. When Napoleone had arrived at the military academy four years ago, the harshness had startled him despite his best attempts to pretend otherwise: not just the bitter cold, but the hard beds, the constant hunger, the rigid discipline, the deliberate isolation from family or home or anything soft and familiar. He was used to it now. The mattress bit into his back, and he shifted only out of habit; there was never any chance of being comfortable. At fourteen, he was a dark-eyed, smoldering contradiction of temper and discipline, arrogance and ambition, intellect and athleticism, and he had never been comfortable since he had left Corsica. While his classmates snored and snuffled in their own beds, he stared at the ceiling and combed through the day's events in his head, interrogating them like prisoners for ways they could have been improved upon. The day's events, it was true, comprised a snowball fight, his lessons, and a few stinging conversations with his classmates, but he brooded over them nonetheless. The nights were very long in winter, the dawn was far away, and he needed very little rest.

And yet, after a time, perhaps he did sleep after all.

The dormitory around him grew light, as though the sun had

come out; he stepped forward, wondering, and only then realized he was standing. The air was lazy with warmth and the scent of the sea and voices drifting through an open window. The room wasn't the dormitory anymore, but a wide, spacious room, a sitting room with pale wallpaper and soft carpet and curtains that stirred in the faintest breeze. The furniture was graceful, elegant: a sofa of gentle blue, a clock adorned with gold, a table on which a tea set rested. He knew, without being able to say how, that his family were nearby, separated from him only by thin walls and not by a vast ocean. Napoleone's breath caught, and his throat tightened. He knew where he was. But he had not seen it for four years. He had tried not to see it even in his dreams.

"Your home, I take it," a voice came.

Napoleone turned sharply. Only then did he see the man standing beside the door. A tall man, slim, his face half in shadow. His light, clear voice must have spoken in Corsican, for Napoleone had no need to translate it in his head, but there was something odd about it. The sounds altered before they reached Napoleone's ears, or perhaps they never touched his ears at all.

"It's very pleasant," the man added. His eyes flickered over the room. "I had a home like this once. From my room I could always hear the sea."

Napoleone gathered every ounce of his fourteen-year-old self-possession. "Where are we?" he demanded. "I'm not at home, I know. And who are you?"

"You're quite right, you're not at home," the man said. "You're still in France, safe in your bed. This is just the inside of your head, with a little of mine thrown in for makeweight. As to who I am—well. Let's just say I'm a friend of yours. Perhaps."

"I don't have friends in France."

"No." It might have been a question, or a statement. "Why not?"

He shrugged his thin shoulders and squared his chin. His eyes were suspiciously hot, as they never were in daylight. His childhood home was too close about him; it tugged on the homesickness buried like a shard of glass deep in his heart. "I'm Corsican. I'm smaller than some of them. I don't speak French well enough. My parents aren't wealthy and they opposed French control. I'm barely an Aristocrat. One of those, or all of them, I don't know. I don't care. I'm not afraid of them."

"Do you want them to be afraid of you?"

"I don't care what they think of me." It wasn't quite true, and he suspected the man knew that. He wanted them to respect him. "I'm in France to learn."

"To learn what?"

"Anything I can to become a soldier. History. Mathematics. Tactics. Magic."

"You're good at tactics," the man said. "I've watched you at your games in the schoolyard. Your fellow students respect you then, if that comforts you. You're not terribly strong in magic, though. I can feel mesmerism flickering in your blood, but only weakly. There's very little you can do with it."

"I don't need to do anything with it. The theory is interesting enough. And besides, other people's magic is stronger. I want to learn about it before I command men in battle. There are ways it can be used, even with the Concord."

"Wouldn't you like to use your own?"

"For what?" He considered his own question without giving the stranger a chance to answer. His eyes were already dry. "It's a good pitch for animals. I suppose I could calm a frightened horse, or summon a dog with a message across a field. Tiny things like that can turn a battle at times."

"What about on your men?"

He laughed. "I won't need mesmerism to command my men. That's what being a commander means."

The stranger smiled too. For just an instant, his face came out of the shadows.

"How would you like to command more than men?" he asked. "Not today, of course. But someday."

"It would depend." Napoleone knew better than to put any faith in words, either spoken or on paper. People said all kinds of things, all the time. Talk achieved nothing. Besides, he wasn't convinced this wasn't all a dream. But somehow, perhaps because the dream was so strange, he felt a cautious thrill. "It would depend on whom I would command, and at what cost."

"It's early days yet," the stranger said. "It might come to nothing. But there's a threat brewing over the ocean, and I might need someone to become the leader of France."

"I'm a Corsican," Napoleone said. "I hate France."

His new friend nodded. "Excellent. I think you might do very nicely."

When Maximilien Robespierre was guillotined twelve years later, Napoleone di Buonaparte was serving with the Revolutionary Army on a fact-finding mission to Genoa. He returned to Nice, only to be immediately seized as a Robespierrist sympathizer. It was his younger brother Lucien who had the strongest connections to the Robespierres, in fact—and not to Maximilien, but to his brother Augustin. His captors didn't care. France had been a nest of informers and mutual suspicion for years; the events of 9 Thermidor had churned it once again, and anyone could be devoured. Napoleone was imprisoned in Fort Carré, in a room that was cold despite the sunshine outside and bare. They clamped a bracelet around his wrist that burned white hot at the slightest flicker of magic. His mesmerism, indeed, was capable of no more than a slight flicker, and could never have been used for escape. They didn't care about that either.

Napoleone understood the Revolution's machinations clearly, and he knew that he would certainly die. It should have frightened him, but between the royalists and his fellow revolutionaries he had been living on the point of death for a long time. He was only filled with frustrated rage that he was to die in a such a stupid, passive way, before he had even had a chance to shine in the world. He paced the cell, his boots impacting the hard floor with a satisfying yet impotent stamp.

The cold reminded him of the dormitory at Brienne-le-Château, something that he had not thought about for many years, and that annoyed him too. At last he fell into a thin, discontented sleep, sitting on the camp bed with his back against the wall.

He was standing in his childhood home. The sun was high in the sky, and the light spilled across the floor. It hit the back of the man standing in the doorway, and threw his face into silhouette.

"Napoleone di Buonaparte," the man said. "Do you remember me?"

"Yes," Napoleone said. He kept his voice controlled, but his face was alight with curiosity and wonder. "Yes, I do. You visited me once as a child. You told me you were my friend. I thought you were a dream."

"I *am* a dream," his friend conceded. "So are you, at the moment. But we're not only that."

"I never thought you'd come back."

"I wondered myself. I've visited others like you, you know. Many others, over the centuries, but the time has never quite been right. It seems this is the time, and you are the one." He straightened, and the shadows altered on his face. "Come then. We have great work to do, and great destinies to unfold."

"I've been arrested as a Robespierrist," Napoleone said. "The order's been given for my execution."

"Never mind that," his friend said. "It's time."